BLOOD NIGHT

JONATHAN DANIEL

AUTHOR'S NOTE

Hi! Jonathan here. I wanted to take a quick second to thank you for buying Blood Night. Seriously, I know you have a lot of choices when it comes to horror fiction, and the fact that you made the decision to spend your money on my book means the world to me.

I had a lot of fun writing this. I genuinely hope you have a lot of fun reading it.

If you find yourself liking it (and even if you don't) I would love it (and I'm using 'love' in the strongest way possible...like bordering on creepy) if you took a moment to leave a review on whatever platform you purchased Blood Night. As an indie author, I live and die by reviews. Seriously, it's that important.

Now, on to Blood Night.

THURSDAY, JUNE 4, 1987

CHAPTER 1

Death descended upon Elden Mills, but not with the thundering hooves of a pale horse or the invisible horror of a rampant plague. For the unfortunate souls in that small town, it slithered in under the cover of night, driving a blue Ford stained with slowly drying blood.

The car idled at the intersection of State Road 74 and County Road 6, its headlights spearing the dark tangles of grass and small flowering weeds that lined the pitted roads. A pole with a fat green sign jutted up to the right of the intersection, its lettering of flecked white paint broken by over a dozen bullet holes.

The pole leaned toward the street as if tired of its existence and longing for a swift end under the tires of one of the many oil trucks that barreled past.

For long minutes, the driver – a shadow against the surrounding night – remained perfectly still, hands resting lightly on the steering wheel. The driver's head turned slowly, lazily, to regard the choices.

← Elden Mills 5 mi
Holly Pond 9 mi →

. . .

Just as languidly, a hand peeled away from the steering wheel and drifted to the dirty passenger seat. From a cold but tacky pool of blood littered with crumbs from various fast food meals, the driver's fingers pulled a quarter. He rubbed the surface of the coin, feeling the small particles and the syrupy stickiness of the blood. Neither the sensations nor the memories they stirred elicited any reaction. They simply were.

The driver gazed out at the sign again and flipped the coin, catching it without looking. When the fingers uncurled from around it like the legs of a dead spider, the man studied the result. He turned his wrist and let the quarter fall with a soft thump. It bounced list-lessly before settling back into the congealing blood. With the deci-sion made, the hands turned the steering wheel to the left, guiding the car onto the lane.

As the Ford continued on, the man maintained a steady but light grip on the wheel. He ignored the few homes he passed – isolated houses surrounded by long patches of thick, choking woods – just as the mask and killing weapon that lay exposed on the back seat were ignored.

There would be time for them soon.

They would sing their discordant notes of pain.

And the screams would follow.

The car continued toward the soft glow of Elden Mills, now visible over the black silhouettes of trees in the distance. As the glow grew closer, more and more signs of civilization began to appear. The Ford passed a Phillips 76 gas station. All of the lights in the small store were off, the only illumination coming from the orange ball atop a large post and one weak light shining down on the pump island. A few moments later, glimpses of lights came through the trees on either side of the roughly paved road; small winks of illumi-nation like fireflies.

Homes, the driver thought, and the feeling of readiness twisted in his guts like some diseased reptile turning around in its den, stirring for the night's hunt. The sodium lights of the town still hadn't shown themselves, but the driver didn't care. Instead, he crossed a lane and pulled onto a side street. As the car made the turn, its headlights swept over a yellow and black sign proclaiming that the road was a dead-end.

The driver parked just beyond the sign, shut off the engine, and sat for a moment in the dark allowing his eyes to adjust. Before him, sad, older houses lined either side of the short street, a single weak streetlight shining at the far end. A few battered metal trash cans gathered at its base like pitiful acolytes worshiping a dying god. The cone of the electric light touched the edges of yards and hinted at thick woods behind its pole.

In the pale light of the moon, he could make out peeling siding on one home, a broken second floor window on another. Very few had maintained yards, their grass mostly left to grow thick and choked with dandelions, clover, and other weeds that found early summer to be their time of dominance.

He reached into the back seat and let his fingers drift over the soft rubber of the mask for a moment before gripping it. Holding the mask before his chest, he smelled the muted sourness of the latex. The driver took in a large, cleansing breath, slipped the mask over his head, and fitted it into place before returning his attention to the quiet houses.

After almost a half-hour of remaining motionless behind the wheel, his arm drifted once more to the back seat, this time returning with the weapon. Through the dark holes of the mask's eyes, he looked at it and could feel the energy within it. The hunger.

The masked man stepped out of the car, softly closed the door, and regarded the houses once more. His eyes played over each one, moving from left to right and then back again, observing every dwelling on either side of the rough and potholed street. Most were dark, the Things inside having gone to bed. But, in a few, windows glowed orange or strobed electric blue light from televisions.

As he watched, his fingers turned the weapon around in his hand, relishing the weight of it. He gripped it tightly, feeling its power. It didn't feel like an extension of himself; rather, it felt like what it was, an instrument of pain, blood, and death.

One house, the third one on the right from where he stood, drew his focus. There were some lights on in the upper rooms, but the lower half of the home was dark. He crossed the street, the soles of his boots making soft thunks and scrapes as he passed over the loose gravel that littered the pavement. The sound changed to wicking whispers as he stepped up onto the grass, the thick Bermuda grass and weeds offering gentle resistance against his feet.

A single wooden door in the side of the house, around the corner from the roll-up garage door, proved to be unlocked. It pushed in thickly, the wood warped and dragging against the cement garage floor, but he only needed a few inches to slip inside.

The garage smelled of oil and gasoline, of mildewed cardboard, and dryer sheets. The bulky angular shape of a station wagon filled most of the space. He stood still once more, letting the silence stretch. Faint voices drifted from overhead. He flexed his fingers around the handle of his weapon and started around the car. Another door, also unlocked, opened to a small hallway, off of which yawned dark doorways.

The masked man went to the closest, a small half-bathroom that stunk of cat piss and old litter, and melted into the shadows.

To wait.

CHAPTER 2

When she was eight, Morgan Bell stopped believing in monsters. At that age, whenever her father would read her a bedtime story, pitching his voice to give the witches or ogres life in the mind of his young daughter, Morgan would roll her eyes and laugh. She would laugh and tell him to read something else, that monsters aren't real.

But when she was nineteen, she'd met a monster in the dark and dirty corner of the maintenance room of the Avondale Fabric Works. A *real* monster, wearing grimy coveralls over a stained and frayed t-shirt. In that cramped space, she'd stared in stunned horror as cracked lips framed by stubble-covered, sallow cheeks peeled back. The mask of a man's face sliding away to reveal the gap-toothed, malicious smile of a diseased soul. She understood his real nature when he punched her – lights exploding in her brain and sending the room into a spin like some horrible carnival ride gone haywire. The terror true monsters could inflict had smashed into reality when he had knocked her to the ground and pawed her jeans down. His dirty fingers shoved her panties aside roughly before he plunged into her while he pushed her face into the floor.

Morgan had lain there, too stunned to even react. Her own whimpers of pain came to her as if from far away with each thrust of the man on top of her. His tongue, thick and greasy, had slithered over her shoulders and neck like an eel. The rest of the attack was a dull, watery blur of motion until he had finished in a hot, wet explosion. Leaving her whimpering on the floor, he climbed off and staggered back out onto the factory floor.

The memory broke apart as Cole's muffled curses filtered through the bathroom door, bringing Morgan back to the present. She opened her eyes, her vision gauzy from tears and glanced over at the partially opened bathroom door. Its surface was warped faux wood. A shadowy movement beyond flickered across the gap as Cole shifted in front of the stained toilet.

The mattress she lay on was an overly firm slab in the middle of the small, cramped bedroom in an equally small and cramped single wide trailer. Blinking the room into focus, Morgan rolled over and exhaled heavily in an attempt to exorcize the memories of the maintenance room and the sour breath of her rapist. They faded into her subconscious like trash sinking into the darkness of a lake.

Confusion tinted with an alcoholic haze clouded her thoughts as she propped herself up on her elbows and looked around the trailer's dirty bedroom. Silver moonlight filtered in through a window illuminating the clothes, some hers, that littered the floor and the scarred dresser. More were piled on a chair shoved into one corner. The air stunk of cigarettes, booze, and the soft tang of sex. On one side of the bed, a nightstand made of milk crates held a digital alarm clock, its red lights telling her it was twenty after one in the morning. She'd been with Cole for only a few hours. Morgan's skin buzzed from the things he'd done to her. Bruises and scratches littered her skin. Done in the height of ecstasy, and at her urging. It hadn't taken much for her to convince him to abuse her; this wasn't even the first time she'd let him do anything he could think of to her.

It's what you deserve.

The voice came again from the bathroom as Cole mumbled curses at his unresponsive bladder. Then came the soft tinkling as his weak stream hit the toilet water. Moments later, the tinny scraping of the shower curtain against its rod preceded the squeal of knobs turning and the responding blast of water from the showerhead. Morgan fell back to the pillow and stared up at a water stain on the ceiling. She let her eyes play over it, her mind working to fashion it into different shapes and patterns. Here a cow, there a steaming pile of mashed potatoes.

Something hit the blanket next to her ribs with a soft impact that was just enough to pull her attention from the mottled brown and orange stain. The apricot-colored pill bottle lay upside down at an angle, its white cap against the mattress. A cold calm seeped into Morgan at the sight of it.

"Take them," Cole said. He leaned in the doorway, his shirt off as steam billowed behind him. "Robby and the guys are coming over in a bit, like you wanted. Those will help you be...agreeable." He pursed his lips in a mock kiss and then pushed back into the steam-filled bathroom.

"And you'll need to take a shower," he called as he stepped into the tub and pulled the curtain closed. "I'm not serving my friends sloppy seconds."

Morgan picked the bottle up, the small pills inside rattling with a cold, clicking malice. Valium. She hated when he made her take these and hated how she felt on them, with her mind and body disconnected and numb. She also hated what usually happened to her when she took them. Cole's friends were only marginally more gentle than he was.

What are you doing?

The question was stark, bright in her mind, and she blinked at it in surprise. What *was* she doing? It wasn't the first time she'd slept with Cole or his friends. Each time left her feeling no better than she'd felt at the start of the night. When it was over, she felt worse, both physically - after the first couple of times, Cole and the others had really opened up to indulging in their darkest fantasies with her - and emotionally. No matter how many times she felt another man sliding into her, no matter how many times she came, nothing seemed to make the pieces in her mind fit together the way she knew they should. She ended every encounter feeling less in control than she'd been at the start.

So, why are you still here? she wondered, not for the first time. And just like all the previous times, she couldn't conjure a real answer. *Do you really want to stay here and see what Robby and the others will do? You know what happened the last time. Remember the bottle they used? What do you think they'll bring this time?*

One of her feet slid across the mattress and dangled over the edge, the air in the room cool on her bare skin. Her mind brought up an image of Garrett's smiling face, his dark brown eyes lighting up as he looked at her. The vision sent a painful wrench through her chest. Garrett had been nothing but loving and kind to her in the nine months they'd been seeing each other. When Morgan had agreed to move in with him three months ago, his previous stream of affection had turned into a heavy, steady flow. He never questioned her when she stayed out all night, accepting her excuses of long shifts at the bowling alley with a "Well, of course, you're the best employee they have" attitude.

Her foot pulled back under the sheet as the sour taste of guilt flooded her mouth and twisted her guts. Garrett deserved better. He was genuinely a nice guy and she was a broken thing, dead inside. She deserved to stay where she was and just let Cole and his buddies use her however they pleased. Maybe, this time, she'd die and not have to worry about it anymore.

That thought raised new fantasies. Garrett, eyes bloodshot and cheeks streaming with tears. She pictured her parents and her brother Scott holding onto each other as they screamed out their grief, inconsolable in their misery. Then a real memory overwrote the fantasy. She saw the hurt looks in her parents' eyes as she'd told them she was leaving. The things she'd said to them, the black hate that had spewed out of her in those moments as she'd told them she didn't want to spend another minute stuck in that shitty town, working the rest of her life - *wasting* the rest of her life - in that goddamn mill like they had. Anything but the truth about what had happened to her in the maintenance room. *They'd never have believed me anyway. Probably would have asked what I did to provoke it.*

A soft tickling on Morgan's cheek broke the memory apart, and her heart jackhammered in her chest for a second. Had she wasted so much time that Cole was finished with his shower? Had her moment to actually get out before things got worse passed? The sound of the water rhythmically splashing in the tub along with the man humming along with the radio - Ann Wilson was asking who you were going to run to - made Morgan realize a wet tear had brought her back to reality.

She threw the sheets back and got out of bed. With the phantom images of her mourning family still dominating her thoughts, she bent and picked up her sweats and her long-sleeved purple and white Coca-Cola shirt. She pulled them on, dropped to her knees, and searched under the bed until she found her ratty Reeboks.

Heart gave way to Whitney Houston crooning about wanting to dance with someone. Cole's irritated grunt drifted from the shower, and the song cut off. Morgan's throat closed as she stood as frozen as a weed in January. There were a few soft clatters, and the growling of a guitar filled the bathroom and spilled out into the bedroom as Motley Crüe crashed into the opening of "Wild Side." Cole had put in a cassette from the pile he kept on the back of the toilet.

"No more," she said as she hurried out of the bedroom and through the small living room. She snatched her keys and purse from a coffee table made from a wooden construction spool, which sat less than a foot from the secondhand couch sporting wood accents and a burgundy flower pattern. The table's surface was scarred with gouges and burns, the rest of it covered with a copy of *TV Guide*, an amber glass ashtray overflowing with yellow cigarette butts, and seven empty cans of Budweiser.

At the aluminum door to the trailer, she hesitated once more. Cole was usually fairly even-tempered, but if he found her in the middle of slipping out when the guys were coming over, he'd turn mean pretty quickly. Over the sounds of the Crüe listing various strip clubs they'd been to, she couldn't be certain if the water was still running.

Morgan shoved the door open and rushed to her car, her legs light and weak, as if they were made of helium and at risk of deflating. She yanked open the Chevy Celebrity's door and tossed her purse onto the passenger seat. The engine coughed to life, she threw the gear shift into reverse, and stomped the gas pedal, never taking her eyes off the door to the trailer.

The Chevy rocketed backward, tires hissing angrily on the dirt that served as a front yard. Rocks tinked off the various items strewn around the lot, junk that Cole had somehow managed to acquire over the years. Her taillights flared, illuminating the trees that marked the heavy woods which surrounded the trailer. Her eyes locked on the trailer door, Morgan's hand dropped the gear lever down two notches while her other hand reached out and flicked on the headlights.

The tires spun in the dirt and fringes of grass at the edge of the yard, and for a heart-dropping moment, Morgan thought she was bogged down. Her body jerked as the tires caught and the old car kicked forward, shooting toward the paved road.

The drive back to the small house she shared with Garrett passed in a blur. She hurried inside leaving the lights off, despite her being the only one in the house. As she passed the small dining nook, she glanced over at the shadowy form of flowers on the table. Another painful wrenching passed through her chest. Garrett had told her he'd been planning something special for the two of them. The knowledge of it had driven an iron spike of panic into her, and another lie had emerged. She'd said that she'd been called into picking up another all-night shift at the bowling alley. Garrett had accepted the excuse placidly, nodding his understanding. He'd showed her the flowers he'd gotten, placed them on the table, and then kissed her cheek. He'd told her not to worry, that he'd go catch a late-night double-feature, and they could reschedule for the next night.

What was wrong with her? Morgan clamped her lips together, forcing back sobs as she threw clothes into a bag. She gathered her toiletries, then went back to the living room. For a moment she considered leaving a note. That would be the right thing to do, Garrett deserved an explanation.

He deserved a lot of things, and all of them were better than Morgan Bell.

"I'm sorry," she said weakly to the empty house before she walked out.

CHAPTER 3

"Hot dog!" Jerry Weaver cried out, and then immediately began coughing on the sip of beer that decided at that moment to find an alternate route down his throat. Jerry sputtered, beer spraying out as he sat up, his legs pushing the rest of the recliner down and locking it. He leaned forward, chest burning and throat closing, and hacked. All while watching Dale Murphy round second base through his watering eyes.

"You alright?" Christine called from down the hall.

Jerry coughed twice more before his throat relaxed. "Yeah," he managed. "Forgot how to swallow for a sec. Murphy just hit a run. Had a guy on base, so we're up two nothing in the first."

"That's nice." Her disinterested tone made it clear that Christine couldn't care less if Dale Murphy hit a home run or took a shit on home plate. "Just be careful."

Before he could reply, the throaty whirring of her sewing machine started back up.

Jerry took another sip of beer, got nothing but foam, and set the can down. He glanced over his shoulder along the dark hallway, and saw the closed bedroom doors - his and Christine's on the right, their daughter Stephanie's on the left - thin seams of light pouring from the cracks along the bottoms and tops. He considered getting up and asking Steph to come watch the game with him. She used to love watching the Braves with him, but he knew that those times were most likely long in the past. Stephanie was fourteen going on twenty-three and had more important things to fill her nights. Things that were most decidedly not watching taped baseball games from earlier in the day.

The game went to commercial, an ad for *As The World Turns*, and Jerry cursed the fact that Christine wouldn't let him spring for the VCR with a remote control so he could speed past all the ads. He considered getting up and fast-forwarding the tape, but decided against it. Instead, his bladder reminded him that he'd only rented the three beers he'd already had since getting home from the mill. With a soft groan of effort, he heaved his bulk - *Need to do something about that, Jer. Drop a few pounds, or you could end up striking out of the big game a bit earlier than you'd like* - out of the recliner and waddled to the bathroom just off the kitchen.

The game had resumed when he returned, and he settled back down, picked up his beer, and was happy to find that it had settled as well. He sighed contentedly. He hated to have missed the game in real time, but day games were impossible to catch when they fell on a workdays. All day long, he'd purposefully avoided the second floor break room, where a small black and white television had been set up for the sole purpose of showing daytime ball games. He'd also had to stay clear of the dyeing department, where one of the supervisors, Damon, had kept his radio blaring the play-by-play. Christine had rolled her eyes when he'd told her he was setting the VCR up to record the game and that she couldn't change the channel for the three hours it would be on. She'd said not to worry – that she'd be out doing some shopping anyway.

He drained his beer and dropped the crushed can into the small wastebasket to the left of his chair. It fell atop a small pile of tissues and magazine subscription cards that Christine had plucked from her copy of *Cosmo*. Without looking away from the screen, he reached to his own side table and snagged another can from the six-pack.

The game continued, the Braves holding the Pirates to only a couple of runs in the second and third innings. By the time the fourth began, the small wastebasket held four more cans and was threatening to overflow. Twice, Stephanie had exited her room and drifted into the kitchen. Each time, Jerry heard the fridge door open and his daughter rummaging for a few moments before giving an exasperated sigh – oh, the pitfalls and horrors of having nothing to eat but leftover tuna salad surprise - and slamming the door closed.

As she exited the kitchen the second time, Jerry looked over his shoulder. "Wanna sit with your old man and watch?"

She glanced at the screen, its glow painting her freckled cheeks a silvery blue, and then chuffed a laugh. There was a sense of pity in that laugh, Jerry thought. "No. Baseball's boring. Besides, I'm supposed to call Laney."

Jerry twisted his wrist, consulting his watch. "It's pretty late, hon. You sure you don't need to get to bed?"

"Whatever," she whispered, and slunk back to her room. The door closed quietly. *At least she's not quite to the slamming of doors yet,* he thought with a grunt, and sipped his beer. That would be coming, probably sooner than later, and would be a hard adjustment for her mother. The war for independence was always hard on the parents, but Jerry thought it was worse for mothers. Mothers seemed to have a deeper bond with their children, and when the connection of that bond had to be adjusted as a kid grew up, mothers tended to get the worst of it.

Maybe we'll get down to Birmingham this weekend, he thought, and nodded at the genius of his idea. *Go to the zoo. Create some good family memories before Steph is too mortified to be seen in public with her folks.*

A sudden movement just above his line of sight interrupted his thoughts a split second before a deep explosion of pain detonated in his chest. Jerry's body jerked in the chair, the recliner's back ratcheting another notch farther out so that he was closer to being prone. His chest struggled to expand, his lungs fighting to bring in even the tiniest stream of air. It was as if an elephant had sat on him. A thick wetness filled his throat, and he wondered if he was choking on beer again. The wetness oozed past his tongue and over his lips in a line of drool.

Jerry fought once more to draw breath, and a little did come, but the relief it brought was overshadowed by the stabbing pain in his chest. It felt as if there were shards of glass in his lungs.

His eyes ticked down to the fat head of a hammer resting against his chest. A long spike jutted up from the opposite side of the head – an alien tentacle reaching into the air. Jerry's mind scrambled to make sense of what he was seeing, to understand where the hammer had come from. Something else drifted into his view...something pale hovering over him. Was that a light?

Jesus, did I have a heart attack, and now I'm in an operating room? That can't be. They wouldn't play a commercial for Lowenbrau in an operating room. And do they use hammers like that in hospitals?

Jerry's eyes swam, floating on a lake of pain, but after a moment, they stilled and focused. It wasn't a light at all, but a mask. A plain white mask, shadows from the cheeks and the nose shifting as the images on the television moved. The eyes that stared down at him were black pits that looked as if you could fall into them and tumble, screaming, forever. The mouth was a ragged slash – ever so slightly upturned at one end, as if the wearer were mildly amused. But it was all wrong, he dimly thought. The eyes were in the wrong place.

No, it's upside down. Whoever it is is leaning over me looking down.

As if to prove this theory correct, the face retreated. The hammer lifted from his chest, and Jerry heard the soft scrape of footsteps on the carpet as the person walked around to the front of the chair. Jerry stared, eyes wide from panic and his dwindling efforts to breathe, as a black form stopped next to his extended legs. The mask was like a beacon atop a dark tower as it looked at him expressionlessly.

"Wha..." Jerry slurred. Instead of answering, the masked figure raised its arm and brought it down quickly. Jerry tried to get his head out of the way, but found that he couldn't move it very well. Fiery pain filled his left shoulder as the bones shattered. The impact drove a weak squeak of pain from his mouth.

"You alright?" Christine called. She paused, and then through the closed door said, "Don't drink too much. You know you have to work in the morning." Her sewing machine whirred back to life.

The sound of his wife's voice galvanized Jerry, and he blinked hard in an effort to force the world back into focus. With his good hand, he grasped the arm of the recliner. He had to sit up. He had to fight back.

He had to defend his family.

His attacker watched Jerry's thick fingers twitch and clutch at the puffed maroon fabric of the chair. Jerry tried to speak; tried to call out to his wife, to Stephanie, to anyone. His lips pursed, bloody spittle flying as he worked to form a single word.

He never saw the next attack. The hammer swiped from left to right, and Jerry lost all pretext of speaking as his entire lower jaw broke away. Blood flooded Jerry's ruined mouth and poured over his destroyed lips. He could feel rivulets of it running along his cheeks, freed by cuts in their flesh. His tongue and what remained of his jaw hung heavy, shifting back and forth like a swing dangling from the limb of a tree. Every movement sent brilliant pulses of torment through him.

Another immense knot of pain burst in the top of his head as the masked figure brought the hammer down squarely onto his skull. Jerry's scalp crawled as blood streamed through his thinning hair. The living room tilted and then spun crazily like water whirlpooling around a drain, down into the blackness of the pipes.

Jerry's body began to shake, spasming uncontrollably as, in his mind, he followed the room, his house, the entire world around and around and finally down into the black mouth of the drain.

CHAPTER 4

The Things inside the house were dead.

They lay where they'd been slaughtered, ruined pieces of meat and splintered bone. He surveyed each one, moving from the bedroom decorated with posters of other smiling, pretty Things, mylar balloons, and the smells of a cloying miasma of strawberries and blood. On to the bedroom that was more modestly decorated with a few framed photographs - most whose subjects were hidden beneath thick runnels of blood – and then to the living room, where the television continued to broadcast its show through splatters of blood.

He turned and left, moving slowly and comfortably down the stairs to a small landing next to the front door. The stairs continued lower, to the basement through which he'd entered. He looked through the small porthole window in the front door and saw nothing unusual outside. Only the quiet street blanketed in moonlit darkness.

He left through the same door he'd entered, not bothering to pull it shut, and stood in the shadow thrown by the house. From the darkness, he studied the street.

The flicker of something drew his attention toward the dead-end of the road, and he shifted to see it better. A light in an upper window of the last house in the row of homes, the one closest to the street-light, had just gone out.

Stepping slowly, he walked toward the house, a pitiful thing with a tattered American flag hanging at an angle from the sagging wooden porch. Two bicycles lay on their sides near the front steps, and he angled around them, moving once more to the side of the house closest to the garage door.

Inside, he began again.

And the wet screams followed.

CHAPTER 5

Morgan hesitated, her knuckles inches away from the apartment's door. He'd be asleep. Why bother him? She could just call him in the morning from a pay phone. That felt better. She clung to that plan and tried to ignore the sting of guilt coloring the edges of her mind.

She reached into her back pocket and pulled out the two separate piles of folded paper, the edges frayed from where she'd torn them out of the spiral notebook. Morgan's fingers plucked the pieces, letting them fall to the walkway like confetti. She looked at the black veins of her handwriting visible through the outer page of each letter. She'd written Garrett's name on one, Ryan's on the other. Morgan hated that she didn't have any envelopes to seal the letters into - Ryan would most certainly read both letters, the nosy little shit - or even a stapler to fasten the pages together, but it was what it was.

Morgan knelt and pulled back a corner of the rough brown doormat. She placed the letters beneath it, leaving about two inches visible, and then turned to leave. Just as her hand touched the thin metal railing of the apartment's balcony walkway, the door opened.

"What the fuck are you doing?" a sleepy voice drawled. Ryan stood in the doorway with a blanket draped over his shoulders, his head resting on the edge of the open door. He glanced down at the papers. "Are you in third grade? Leaving notes under the mat?"

"I didn't want to bother you."

Ryan rolled his eyes and stepped back, pulling the door open. "I was about to go to sleep. Come on." He angled his head, indicating for her to enter the apartment. "And bring your notes, Strawberry Shortcake."

Morgan retrieved the letters and forced herself to walk into Ryan's home. Her body hummed with the need to leave, to avoid a difficult conversation. But then she was inside, and Ryan shut the door before brushing past her. "Give me a second," he mumbled as he drifted away, picking his way around the furniture in the living room and turning down a hallway. "Make yourself at home," he called, his voice echoing slightly in the small space.

Morgan hesitated, standing on a small patch of linoleum, the toes of her Reeboks an inch from the start of the dirty beige carpet that filled the rest of the living space. The apartment was small, with a single bedroom and bathroom down the hallway off of the living room, and a kitchen around the corner to the right, beyond the black leather sofa. A crumpled pillow on the sofa and a sweating glass of what looked like watered-down Coke on the glass coffee table told her the story of Ryan's night. The air smelled like apples and cinnamon.

Ryan returned wearing light blue sweatpants and a white sweatshirt featuring the rainbow-colored Benetton logo. He ran a finger through his blonde hair and looked at her. "You look like shit. You didn't work tonight, did you?"

Morgan shook her head. "No."

"Lucky bitch. How'd you manage to get a league night off? Oh, wait..." his eyes widened. "Didn't Garrett have some special thing planned?"

At the mention of it, Morgan's heart leapt. "How'd you know?"

"He called me the other day. Said he was planning some shit and asked if I'd work for you if you were scheduled. So. Spill. What did he do? Did he bring out the edible underwear? Did he pick you up something frilly from Frederick's of Hollywood?"

Morgan's mouth was dry, her tongue a fat desert worm against her teeth. "I'm interrupting you. I'm sorry. I'll just go. I-"

"Greg isn't here. He's at his pool league and won't be home till at least two. Now, sit down."

Morgan asked, "He's still doing that?"

Ryan rolled his eyes. "Lord, yes. And don't think that the fact he's been doing it for five years now prevents him from making the same tired-as-fuck joke about long sticks and balls."

Morgan breathed out a smile. She suddenly found herself unable to look at her friend, and decided to focus instead on how dirty her fingernails were. The polish, a deep red that Garrett had always liked, was chipped and peeling away. Without thinking, she began to scratch at it.

"What's going on?" Ryan asked after a moment. Morgan just shrugged, realizing even as she did it how it made her look like a sullen teenager. Ryan didn't say anything – just sat quietly waiting. When Morgan said nothing, he sighed and leaned back. "You did it again, didn't you?" Morgan gave a small nod. "For fuck's sake, girl. I mean, I know you're dealing with some shit. You may not have told me exactly what, but I have a good idea." Morgan looked up sharply. Ryan just regarded her coolly. "We all have shit we're dealing with. But if you keep doing what you're doing, you're going to lose that man. And believe it or not, he's one of the good ones."

The words amplified her guilt, and for a horrible moment Morgan was certain she was going to vomit. She swallowed thickly and said, "I know."

"And that's why you decided it was a good idea to run away in the middle of the fucking night? Oh, don't look at me like that. You think I'm dumb? Just because I pour beer at that shit-trap of a bowling alley doesn't mean I'm stupid. I have eyes." He nodded at the folded papers. "Those are your 'Dear Garrett' and 'Dear Ryan' letters, aren't they? Give them here." He held out his hand, and Morgan hesitantly passed them over. Ryan considered them. "You want coffee? Or tea?"

"Tea's good."

He plucked the letters from her hand. "Sit back. I'll get us something while I read."

Slowly, Morgan shifted back and resumed picking at her nails. She removed the polish from two of the fingers and picked up the *TV Guide* while she flipped through the pages. Her brain registered none of the information. Instead, she listened to the soft rustling of notebook paper and Ryan's breathy curses as he read the letters. A shrill whistle began, and died almost as instantly, as he pulled the pot away from the stove. Morgan tensed, knowing she was about to face questions about the contents of the letters.

Ryan returned with two mugs from which steam wafted. The white strings of teabags dangled from each like clock pendulums. He set the mugs on the glass table, and then leaned close and pulled Morgan into a tight hug. She stiffened against the contact, but only briefly. They stayed that way for several moments, Ryan holding her firmly, his breath a gentle and rhythmic tickling across her hair.

Finally, he said, "So, you thought the best idea was to leave these at my doorstep and assume I would clean up the mess?"

Morgan grimaced at the icy tone of the question. This had been a mistake. She should have just kept driving. Mailed the letters later. "I'm sorry," she said, sliding one leg off the couch. "I shouldn't have bothered you." As she made to stand, keeping her eyes off of Ryan, she felt his hand on her knee.

"Bitch, I'm fucking with you. Take a chill pill. Where were you planning on going?"

Morgan chewed her lip. She'd not given it any thought before leaving, and once she'd gotten into the car, she'd just been driving. "I have no idea. Just...away. Somewhere I could start over – start fresh and maybe, I don't know, put things behind me." She gave a half-hearted smile. "Seattle, maybe?"

"And you think that if you ended up there, or L.A., or Buttcrust, Arkansas, that things would be different?" He waved the letters, the paper rattling like dead leaves. "You can't outrun trauma. Trust me."

Morgan didn't know everything about Ryan. She'd only known

him through work for the last two years, their conversations mostly revolving around people in the bowling alley or movies, music, and fashion - of which she'd quickly learned that she knew next to nothing. But she did know that, despite the fact that he worked almost exclusively at the bar pouring drinks and pitchers of Michelob and Bud, he was a recovering alcoholic.

Ryan went on. "I know what you're looking for. You're trying to find a way to get a handle on everything. It's like someone knocked your suitcase out of your hand and you're trying to grab everything and shove it back in. All the while, people keep trampling over your stuff and kicking it out of the way."

Morgan nodded.

"You're not going to find it in Seattle. And you absolutely won't find it in Buttcrust, Arkansas."

"It sure as hell isn't here," Morgan said. The words came out acidic, and she hated herself for sounding like a petulant teenager.

"It's closer to here than you think," Ryan said as he sipped his tea. "No, there's no magic pill or anything you can take to make it all better. Nothing's ever going to make it all better. You were wounded pretty fucking badly, and that's not going away. It'll scar, but it'll heal. You're always going to know that scar is there. But you can learn to live with it. You can learn how to get all the shit back into your suitcase – underwear, socks, and dildos included."

Keeping her focus on picking the polish from her left middle finger, Morgan asked, "How?"

"How do you think I'm able to pour beer after beer, shot after shot, every night and not just go apeshit and start chugging them all myself?" By way of answer, Morgan shrugged. "After I went through AA and decided all that holy roller shit wasn't for me, I found another path. Greg helped me find it, and put me in touch with William."

"Sponsor?" Morgan asked.

"Sort of, yeah. Not officially, but he's been through the program a couple of times and been sober for twenty years now, so he knows what he's talking about. He told me the best way to harden myself against the temptation was to confront what put me there in the first place. He made me get down to the 'why' of it all. It went deeper than just 'Oh, I drank because that's what we all did in high school.' It went down to me being the only gay kid in town. It went down to me being pushed away by my dad, who knew I was different before I even realized who I was. You see? I had to get all the way down to that level and confront it; face that trauma and understand it before I could put my own shit back into the suitcase."

"My parents were great," Morgan said. *Even when I was a complete bitch to them.*

"I'm sure they were. But let's focus on me for a minute, shall we?" He gave a flash of a smile. "Once I had the shit in my suitcase, it was just a matter of finding my rhythm through life to keep the latches closed on it. I got the job at the bowling alley because that's what was available to me. But working the bar forces me to see alcohol, to smell it, and to make the conscious decision every single time not to pick it up. The more I'm around it, the more I get used to it and the easier the choice becomes not to drink."

"You read the letters," Morgan said slowly. "You know what happened to me. I'm not going to put myself in that kind of position again."

Ryan shook his head. "That's not what I'm saying. What you need to do is go back to..." He paused, his face screwing up. "What was the name of that town you're from?"

"Elden Mills."

Ryan laughed. "Elden Mills. Sounds so quaint. So *Mayberry*. You need to go back there and, at the very least, have a real conversation with your family."

Morgan leaned back and began chewing on the nail of one of her fingers. The idea Ryan proposed caused her skin to tingle with nervous energy. "I don't think I could go back. I was so horrible to them after...you know. I said some awful things."

"Which is why you need to make amends with them. You need to at least ask forgiveness from them and anyone else you were a complete shit to. Just doing that will go a long, long way to getting a handle on that suitcase. If you really want to get good, then you need to confront that scumbag who attacked you, or," he said quickly, seeing her reaction, "at the very least, file a report. But you need to look your family in the eye, apologize, and ask forgiveness. Whether or not they give it is up to them. You can't control that. But you'll know where things stand, and you *will* be able to move forward from there. Because right now, all you have is a mess of confusion, unknowns, and panties all over the floor."

Tears welled in Morgan's eyes and her throat constricted at the thought of her family. She took in a ragged breath, and felt the dam inside her starting to break. Immediately, Ryan's body was next to hers, his arms enveloping her. She buried her head in his shoulder and cried, the sobs coming all at once and with shocking force. She let it all out – the fear, the pain, and the shame. All mixed together to form a poisonous frosting on top of a toxic cake.

Ryan held her until the moment passed and she sat back, sniffling. He passed her a tissue, then three more, and waited as she wiped her eyes and blew her nose. When she was done, he said, "It's late. You can stay here, crash on the couch, and get a fresh start in the morning. I'll make waffles. When Garrett shows up, which we both know he will, I'll give him the letter. And when he asks, which we both know he will, I'll tell him you went back home to visit family. Unless you want me to lie to him?"

Sniffling and dabbing at her nose with the wadded tissue, Morgan shook her head. "No, don't lie to him. Thanks for the offer to crash, but if I'm going to do this, I don't want to put it off any longer. It's a five-hour drive. If I stay on your couch, there's a chance I'll talk myself into either staying or driving to Buttcrust, Arkansas."

Ryan laughed, and Morgan found herself smiling along with him.

FRIDAY, JUNE 5, 1987

CHAPTER 6

At 6:30 a.m. James Turner sat at a red light, tapping a staccato beat on his steering wheel as Robert Palmer decried his addiction to love. His movements were purely subconscious; the majority of his thoughts centered on the previous afternoon and the look on that rat-fink Vandermark's face when he'd called Turner into his office.

Turner had almost reached the stairwell, already thinking about the box of Tuna Helper he was going to prepare for dinner - a sixer of Stroh's from Martin's would pair perfectly with that, he'd decided - when the door to Alex Vandermark's office had swung open, and the balding head of the plant manager had emerged.

"James," Vandermark had said – neither a question nor a greeting, just a simple declaration.

Turner's entire body had stiffened at the sound. Even after all these years, the sight of him and the sound of Vandermark's voice set James' teeth on edge. Turner glanced over at the man. He didn't answer, only raised his eyebrows questioningly.

Alex Vandermark was the same age as Turner, fifty-seven, but wore it better. Where Turner's hair had begun thinning up top, right around when he'd hit the mid-century mark, Vandermark's was holding strong and thick, if not with a few degrees more silver. The plant manager wasn't classically handsome in that old Rock Hudson way, but had no problems with the ladies. Bitterness, that constant companion, rose in Turner in an expanding bubble.

Turner took a cleansing breath, scattering the image of Anna's face that came whenever he saw Vandermark.

Vandermark's eyes flicked over Turner's shoulder, scanned the loud winding machines and then returned to the mill supervisor. "Need you in early tomorrow."

"Why?"

Vandermark's gaze settled on the shift supervisor, his expression softening as he understood the tone Turner's question held. "I don't want to fight with you. We're making an announcement to the crew, and I need you here early for a briefing and to help get things ready. Do me a favor and tell Wade and Harold on your way out. We need you all here at seven."

For the briefest moment, Turner thought about telling the boss to relay the message his own damned self. "You authorizing the over-time?" Before the supervisor could answer, Turner added, "Wade's on afternoons starting tomorrow. He's going to want to know why he's got to come in that early."

Vandermark scanned the floor again, and said in a voice that was barely audible over the clatter of the equipment, "Just let them know, okay? I'll brief you in the morning." He gave a nod by way of dismissal and stepped back into the low light of his office, closing the door behind him.

On the drive home, Turner had considered the directive. Vandermark was making an announcement and wanted two extra security guards? It didn't make sense. Well, he thought, one option did, but it was too far-fetched to be real. There was no way they were conducting mass layoffs. That would be something they'd do individually, not through an announcement. Vandermark was a piece of shit, but even he wasn't that cold-hearted.

Or was he?

The worry over the coming announcement had stayed with Turner all the way home and through the night, like a tooth that had suddenly become sore and painful to the touch. And just like a pained tooth, Turner had continued to poke at it, hyper-focusing. As a result, he'd burned the Helper, finished all but one of the Stroh's, and passed out on the sofa.

Now, he steered his Dodge along the tree-lined streets toward the mill, the tight bands of apprehension ratcheting ever tighter with each passing block. The truck's AC struggled to keep up with the warm morning, and Turner's gray work shirt already showed dark, wet stains at the armpits.

As he passed the Rollin' In the Dough Bakery, he caught the top of Julie Peterson's head as she worked on something behind the counter. Then, he was moving past, and Robert Palmer gave way to Huey Lewis and the News. Ten minutes later, he parked in the lot of Avondale Fabric Works.

The mill was a three-story monstrosity that spanned a full block. A single, massive smokestack jutted from the roof near the backside of the building, sending a steady stream of dishwater-gray smoke into the morning sky. Halfway along the front of the building, a tall, square tower rose up and over the roof of the rest of the factory, the top of it ending in a series of windows and ornamental battlements. Turner had worked at the factory for all of his adult life, and every time he looked at the top of that tower, he imagined archers firing down on invading hordes. *The yarn-hungry Hun,* he thought. The tower gave the factory a bit more of a stately air and served as the primary entrance for visitors. Not that a lot of people visited the factory - other than the annual fifth graders' field trip - but he supposed it was nice to at least give the illusion.

In the lot, the usual cars for those working third shift sat waiting for their owners to return. However, what wasn't so usual, and what caused his foot to hover over the gas pedal and allow the Dodge to coast to a lazy stop, was the crowd of people milling around between the cars and along the tall chain-link fence that surrounded the mill. Several people turned at the sound of his truck entering the lot. A few pointed toward him as he recovered from his shock and drove to his assigned spot near the access gate.

He got out and gathered his thermos and lunchbox even as a few of the people drifted closer. Now that he was among them, he realized they were all the third shift crew. His eyes drifted over the lot. *Christ. They emptied the whole building.*

"What's going on?" he asked a group of workers whose clothes and exposed skin still had the white furring of cotton dust.

"They said there was a gas leak," said the closest, a large Black man whose name Turner didn't know. The man's tone made it clear he didn't believe it. "But they better hurry up. And they ain't docking our pay for this shit." A chorus of agreement rose from the others.

Turner moved on and nodded a greeting at the third shift security guard, Harold Watkins. The young man stood behind the closed gate, his own face a mask of surprise and worry. "Let me in," Turner told him.

"I don't know if I'm supposed to," Harold said. "Mr. Vandermark told me-"

"Open the fucking gate, you halfwit!" Turner snapped. He normally made it a rule to be nice to everyone except Vandermark, but there was something seriously wrong about this whole situation, and he was on edge. Harold flinched at the command and stepped forward, removed the lock, and allowed Turner to pass through. As soon as he was clear, the security guard snapped the lock closed again and stepped back quickly, as if he were afraid the fence would bite him.

"How long have they all been out here?" Turner asked.

"Vandermark and his guys had everyone shut down and evacuate about thirty minutes ago."

"*His guys?*"

Harold shrugged.

"You the only security?"

Harold shook his head and jabbed a quick finger toward the security office that sat attached to the main building. "Wade and Brad are in there."

Inside the security office, he found the other two guards talking in low voices. Brad leaned back in a chair while Wade perched on the corner of a desk. A lit cigarette bobbed in his lips as he talked, the smoke spreading in thick, wavy lines over his head. Turner was about to ask them if they had any idea what was going on when the door to the factory floor opened and Vandermark stepped in, followed by three men Turner had never seen. The plant manager wore his normal attire, Dickies and a light blue work shirt, but the other three were in suits. Even after being promoted to Plant Manager, the asshole had continued to wear a working man's uniform in an attempt to look like 'one of the guys.' Though he had worked his way up to the position, Vandermark had tried to remove any trappings of the office.

"James. Wade," Vandermark said, setting a Styrofoam coffee cup down on the desk. "Thanks for coming in so early."

Like it's just a favor, one buddy to another. Turner stood just inside the door, thermos and lunchbox clutched in his hands, the tension in the air pressing into him. Something heavy loomed around the men in the office. "What's going on?" he asked, the question coming out more clipped than he'd intended.

Vandermark glanced at the other men. "We're going to wait for the first shift guys to arrive before we make the announcement. Shouldn't be too long. We'll need your help when they do."

"Okay," Turner said slowly. "What's with the third shift guys? One said something about a gas leak. Are they going to finish their shift?" None of the suited toadies would meet his gaze. Even Vandermark would only hold it for a brief second before looking away. Alarm bells started to go off in Turner's mind.

Vandermark sighed. "The mill is closing. Effective immediately. We'll make the announcement in the parking lot."

The reality of what had been said slammed into Turner like a sucker punch to the gut. "Wait," he said, shaking his head. "You're closing the mill? For how long?" Soft curses floated from the two security guards. Turner looked past Vandermark to the guys in suits. They didn't answer – only watched him. "Oh, Jesus Christ. Are you fucking serious? Do you...do you have any idea what that's going to do to this town? For fuck's sake, some of these guys have worked here since high school. Hell, I've given thirty-seven years to this place! What about me?"

Vandermark's face was a stone mask lacking any expression of remorse. "What about you? I've been here the same time, remember? I'm losing my job, too. But it's not my call. Avondale is closing a lot of locations. Operations are going overseas. You know how it is."

"No, I don't! That makes no sense. We hit our numbers every goddamn quarter. That's what I know. What I also know is that you're going to be putting most of this town's population out of work. What are they supposed to do? You're basically killing this town."

Vandermark turned to the security guards. "I need you to secure the building and help Harold set up barricades along the fence. When the first shift guys show up, have them gather in the parking lot. I'll be out at eight to make the announcement." He threw Turner another hard look, and then went back out to the factory floor, his suited entourage close behind him. Turner fought the urge to follow. The vibrating anger over the decision had been reinforced with a newer, darker thought. This new idea had just appeared, dredged from the swamp of Turner's subconscious, and it added a poisonous tint to his fury. Turner knew, at that moment, that if he followed Vandermark into the plant, he'd end up beating the man with the closest piece of metal he could find.

Forty-five minutes later, Turner stood behind a set of sawhorses which Harold and the others had dragged from the maintenance building and positioned in a line at the edge of the gate. In the parking lot, the third shift workers and several of the first shift crew shouted questions at the guards, who could only stand there and do their best to ignore the inquiries.

"This is fucked up," Harold said in between wet smacks of his lips as he nervously chewed the life out of a stick of Juicy Fruit. He shook his head, watching as more cars rolled into the lot and slowed as the drivers took in the scene. "Totally fucked."

Turner squinted in the sunlight, and could only nod as the workers drifted slowly across the lot, exchanging confused looks with one another as the people near the back of the gathering passed along gossip.

"How are we supposed to keep them out?" Harold asked.

Turner cut his eyes to the young guard, but said nothing. His mind played a short fantasy of unlocking the gate and watching as the enraged crowd tore the plant manager apart.

"Oh Jesus, that's Frank Gallagher," Harold whined as a large bull of a man pushed and twisted his way through the crowd to the fence.

"You gonna piss yourself?" Wade growled at the guard from where he stood on the other side of Harold. "If so, go into the fucking mill and do it." Harold glanced back at the building as if he were seriously considering the offer, but to his credit, he remained where he was. He did reach out and touch the wooden sawhorse, as if for reassurance.

"Wade," Frank Gallagher said when he reached the barrier. His eyes ticked to Turner and then back. Frank was a big guy with a square jaw, and a nose that had been broken more than once - usually down at the Lantern Lounge - but the man had started to go soft in places. He spoke with the sharp, clipped tone of a guy who was used to getting his way.

"Frank," the security guard countered, having to raise his voice over the shouted questions from others in the lot. "Y'all gotta stop and wait here. Can't let anyone in just yet."

"The fuck not?" asked Geordie Dupont. Next to Frank, clearly having followed the larger man like a car following an ambulance through traffic, stood the toothpick of a man. A toothpick, *if* said implement had swallowed a grape. Geordie's thin, sunken chest gave way to a bulging belly that strained the buttons of his work shirt. Turner could see the faded tattoo of a grim reaper peeking above the man's collar. Geordie looked, as usual, like he'd neither bathed nor shaved in at least a week. His light brown hair was matted in some areas and plastered flat against his head in others. Turner thought if he put the guy's scalp into a press, he'd be able to grease the engine of his weed eater with some to spare.

Wade shrugged, putting on a lazy air of not really giving a shit about reasons. "Don't know. I was told to hold everyone here. That's all I got for you."

Frank shifted his attention to Turner. "What do you know about this?"

Turner almost hadn't heard the question. His mind was shrouded in that poisoned angry cloud, thoughts becoming certainties that drove spikes of fear through his soul. He blinked the fog away and processed the question. For a split second, James had the urge to tell the truth. "I don't know any more than Wade or any of you do." He twisted to see if Vandermark or any of the suits had emerged. "I think they're going to make an announcement."

Geordie sneered, his buck teeth making him look more like a rat. "What if we just go on in anyways? You can't keep us off the clock."

Frank held up a hand to the smaller man. His attention back on Wade, he asked, "What's really going on?"

The guard gave his lazy shrug again, just as the employee entrance door opened. The crowd of workers all shifted from foot to foot as they watched Vandermark approach, the three suits suspiciously absent. Turner scanned the windows of the plant to see if he could catch them spying from the safety of a high window. The sun was at a bad angle, however, and he couldn't find any evidence of them.

The plant manager approached the security gate and stopped next to Turner, who took a half-step away. Vandermark seemed not to notice as he looked out over the sea of faces and lifted a red and white bullhorn. Turner noticed that someone had plastered part of the bell with a sticker depicting an angry elephant, the mascot of the University of Alabama.

The bullhorn squelched, whined with a painful shriek, and then cleared. The plant manager's voice came through tinny and robotic. "Ladies and gentlemen, I'm sorry for the confusion this morning."

"The fuck is going on?" someone shouted from the rear of the crowd.

The outburst didn't faze Vandermark, who continued, "I have an important announcement to deliver this morning, and wanted all of you together to hear it. Effectively immediately, operations at the Avondale Fabric Works are to be ceased. The folks at corporate have decided that this location is no longer needed, and that all assets within are to be evaluated and sold or redistributed."

Frank glared at Turner. "What the fuck is he saying?"

What does it sound like, you dumb shit? Turner almost answered. Instead, he shook his head and watched the rest of the crowd. He grimaced. Standing here like this made him feel dirty, like he'd crossed a picket line.

Vandermark lowered the bullhorn, looked out at the sea of faces, and sighed. He brought the tool back up. "Look, guys, I'm sorry, but the mill is closed, as of right now."

"So, when can we get back to work?" another voice shouted.

"The mill will not be reopening. Everyone will be given severance, and a delegation of a chosen few will be offered a brief extension to help with the inspection and cataloging of equipment and supplies. That transition team will begin work on Monday. If you are chosen for that assignment, you'll be contacted by phone over the weekend. Otherwise, your final paychecks will be mailed to you. The pay will include today, as a courtesy."

The last of that news was lost in the immediate uproar. Shouts, angry curses, and even a few threats to 'open the gates or I'll shove my foot so far up your ass' rose like morning birds taking to the skies. Harold let out a yelp when the chain-link fence rattled as a coffee mug was hurled from somewhere within the crowd. More trash followed, mostly half-eaten breakfast biscuits or the wrappers they came in, but Turner spied a couple of rocks arcing over the heads of the factory workers. Most of those cleared the fence to land harmlessly behind Turner and the guards, but their appearance was enough to cause Vandermark to flinch and beat a hasty retreat for the safety of the mill.

"You're keeping your jobs, aren't you?" Frank growled, pointing his finger at the guards.

"For today!" Bradley yelled back over the din of the crowd. More than a few had approached the gate and hooked their fingers in to begin shaking it violently. "But not for long, I'm sure. I'm sorry."

"*Sorry* won't feed my fucking kids," said another worker, a woman with jet black hair streaked through with white. "How am I supposed to feed my goddamn kids? Am I supposed to get fucking food stamps now?"

More questions were thrown. Most were laced with insults and accusations, as if Turner or the guards were responsible for the sudden turn of bad luck. As if, for some reason, the fact that security guards were still employed was a primary reason for the sudden loss of a paycheck. Several people climbed into their cars and sped out of the lot, tires screeching. For his part, Turner watched the heavy metal door close behind Vandermark.

He's stealing another part of you. Just like with Anna, he's taking what he wants, and he expects you to roll over.

Turner found the plant manager inside, standing near one of the shipping and receiving lanes.

"That could have gone better," Vandermark said bitterly.

Turner clenched his fists by his side. "What was that shit about an extension?"

"Well," Vandermark said, taking in a deep breath, "like I said out there, we'll offer about twenty people the opportunity to stay on and help. We've already identified them and will call them this weekend to start on Monday. The rest will get a sizable severance, and there'll be programs set up at City Hall to help them find new work."

"Oh, come on. You know there's not going to be any new work in this town," Turner said. "Everything exists to support the people in the mill or is supported by the paychecks earned from the mill."

Vandermark didn't answer. He only studied the empty shipping and receiving section of the floor, his cheek flexing as he worked his jaw. After a moment, he said, "You're going to stay on through the transition. So, you at least will have a job for a little while longer."

"Is that supposed to make me feel better?" Turner snapped. His fear and anger had settled into a hot layer just beneath his skin. "Am I supposed to thank you for that? Be grateful for two more weeks? Is that supposed to make up for everything? For you taking over the mill when we both know I was the more qualified? For Anna?" Vandermark's head snapped up at her name. Turner nodded, a smile playing on his lips at the knowledge that he'd landed a blow. "That's it, isn't it? You're throwing me a bone to make up for stealing her? For ruining my life? And now that you've fucked me, fucked all of us, you think an extra two weeks is going to make everything better?" He spat the hot, bitter words at the other man like poisoned darts. His fingernails dug into his palms as he fought the urge to pummel the plant manager.

Vandermark laughed, a short series of barking cough-like sounds. "You think I put you on the transition team out of some sense of guilt? *Please*. If I had anyone else qualified, I would have cut you loose this morning instead. And don't give me any of that bullshit about you not making Plant Manager. We both know that after she left, you let your life fall apart. You stopped trying and started drinking." He jabbed a thumb at his own chest. "It's only because of me, because we've known each other our entire lives, that you didn't get canned years ago. I watched out for you! I put you in the shift supervisor role even though you didn't deserve it. I'd have thrown your ass out years ago for being such a prick-pain in my ass if I had anyone with even half a fucking brain to replace you. No, this isn't about guilt over Anna - who, in case you don't remember, left me high and dry, too - or me extending an olive branch. This is me needing someone to supervise those people to make sure they don't steal anything. I have other things to deal with. So, take the extension and do something you've probably never done before. Be grateful." Vandermark marched across the floor, angling toward a stairwell door.

"Fuck you!" Turner shouted at the man's back. "Thirty-seven years! And that's supposed to make me feel better? An extra couple weeks of tearing apart this place I've worked for most of my life? I won't do it! Keep your goddamned charity." Turner tried to muster a wad of spit like Frank had outside, but found he couldn't. Instead, he gave a short, strangled cry of frustration and stormed out, slamming the heavy metal door behind him with a thunderous boom.

CHAPTER 7

Morgan's heart did a flip high in her chest as she passed over a rise in the road. The town of Elden Mills lay before her like an aging truck-stop whore crammed into a sleeper cab. The town sat in a natural depression, surrounded by low hills furred with thick stretches of hardwoods and evergreens. The silver ribbon of Mill Creek wound like a snake in the distance, and Morgan winced at the sunlight flashing off its surface.

He's down there somewhere. Your family, too. What are you doing? They're just going to tell you to leave. Why would they want to see you again?

She thought about Ryan's advice to confront the trauma or, at the very least, her actions in the wake of it. The prospect of seeing her family, of having to tell them what had happened to her in that grimy room of the mill, and of actually saying the words and hoping that they believed her...it was almost too much. The urge to turn around and speed away pulled at her insistently.

Her foot eased off the gas, her chest constricting in a tight, painful flare as she caught sight of the mill. It wasn't much that she saw right now – just a portion of the third floor and the ugly smokestack. The rest of the structure was sitting low along the banks of the river and obscured by trees. Then it was gone as she descended the hill.

Straight ahead lay the town's center, where the roofs of stores along Main Street sat next to one another in uneven rows of varying shades of gray, broken only by the occasional red brick or white wooden facade. Beyond the stores, there were small, boxy houses peering through the thick canopy of tree-lined avenues.

Is he in there now? Laughing with his buddies? Going about his day like nothing in the world is wrong?

Morgan concentrated on the road in front of her. She checked her speed - Sheriff Hollister and his guys loved catching people driving over the posted limit and gave no wriggle room on miles-per-hour over - and drove slowly back into her hometown, trying to remind herself to breathe. The courage and resolution she'd been buoyed with after leaving Ryan's had waned quickly and, more than once, she'd found herself staring hard at random exits or interstate junctions.

There were more people than she'd expected walking along Main Street on a Friday morning. Several kids on bikes or skateboards wove between pedestrians or cars like death-defying flies maneuvering to avoid irritated picnickers. Morgan rolled her eyes. Ever since *Back to the Future* had come out, every kid who could walk fancied himself to be the next Marty McFly, zipping along sidewalks on skateboards and trying to catch onto the bumpers of cars. As if to prove the point, before she reached the end of the first block, two boys who couldn't have been older than eleven skated across the street, left feet on their boards and right legs pumping. The two daredevils had no traffic in the oncoming lane, but Morgan had to slam on her brakes to avoid turning them into smears on the pavement. The lead kid - a ginger-haired boy wearing a shirt that screamed that Pepsi was the choice of a new generation - never even looked her way. His friend, however, a pudgy brunette with an upturned nose and a He-Man t-shirt, stumbled off his board and stared at her as if she'd appeared out of thin air.

Morgan pushed her hair back out of her face and glared at the boy. After his initial shock wore off, the kid gave her the finger and ran after his friend, skateboard tucked under one thick arm. "Fucking stain," Morgan grumbled at his back as she continued driving.

Her car slid past stores she knew were the same as they'd been two years ago. Yet, as she glanced from side to side, there was something unfamiliar about them. Seeing them was at once comforting and like putting on an old pair of sneakers found in the back of the closet; the soles conformed to the curves of your foot like you remembered, but at the same time felt hard, cold and unyielding.

Ahead, the light at Columbia and Main switched to yellow, and her foot automatically pressed the accelerator. At the same time, she saw the nose of a police cruiser slide up to the cross street intersection, so she quickly switched to pressing the brake. She leaned back hard against her seat, eyes watching the black-and-white as she hoped the officer behind the wheel didn't recognize her. The cruiser slid past, with the cop - Stephen Lafferty, who'd graduated a year ahead of her - not even glancing in her direction.

Morgan let out a long breath and glanced to her right. Dennis Campbell stood in the doorway of Campbell's Auto Parts. He held a broom, and was toeing a welcome mat into place with one foot. The man looked at her, stared for a long moment, and then returned to his task. Morgan's heart jackhammered in her chest.

What if Geordie knows I'm back? What if he can sense me and comes looking for me?

Two blocks later, Morgan passed the green space of the town square. A weathered gazebo that had once been white stood in the center of the lawn, and a comically small cannon with overly large wheels stood in front of it. She shook her head and rolled her eyes at the sight. There had never been a battle fought in the town of Elden Mills – not during the Civil War, not even during the Revolutionary War. Before the town's founder Elden Prescott had stumbled across it, the land had just been a random smear of rocks and trees that the Cherokee had once inhabited. In 1969, the mayor of the town, Dennis Hughes, had ordered the installation of the cannon in hopes of drawing in tourists who might allow themselves to be convinced that some significant event had occurred there.

Her next turn lay two blocks beyond the patch of green. Once she made that turn, it would only be another few streets to Bishop, where her parents lived. That reality forced her heart into a somersault. A nervous tingle rippled through her arms.

To procrastinate, she slowed and executed a U-turn, sliding the Chevy into an empty slot in front of the small library. She walked past the library and pushed into Mills Drugs – the glass door already plastered with notices depicting a cartoon dog dressed as Uncle Sam, inviting everyone to the upcoming Fourth of July celebration – and stepped into the cool air of the store.

Her momentum carried her several feet down the first aisle, the rows of hair care products passing unnoticed. She was immediately overtaken by the memories of coming into the store with her mother. Stopping in for a bottled drink after school. Morgan ran a hand through her hair, shaking both the locks and the memories loose. She drifted through the aisles, plucking things randomly from shelves: toothbrush, deodorant, a box of pads. Her mother would have some of these things - Morgan would be surprised if her old toothbrush wasn't still in the purple plastic cup next to the sink - but it wouldn't hurt to bring newer versions. Morgan grabbed a Coke from the cooler and a copy of *People Weekly* as she drifted past the pharmacy counter at the rear of the store.

"Holy shit!" The woman's voice brought Morgan to a stop and sent a flare of panic through her chest. "Morgan Bell, what the hell are you doing here?"

Morgan stood frozen, clutching her items like a talisman. Her heart couldn't even muster a pallid thump, the blood in her veins having instantly turned to a cold sludge. Jennifer Reynolds leaned forward, hands flat on the counter with her blonde hair hanging across one shoulder, pink hair clip on the opposite side. A gold necklace dangled free of her pink-and-white-striped shirt.

"Hey," Morgan croaked. Her voice was thick and guttural, so she cleared her throat. "You work here?"

Jennifer gave a slightly embarrassed smile. "Yeah. Almost two years now. Started here after you left for the big city. I couldn't stand the thought of being in the mill, so..." She held her hands out as if to say, *Here I am.* "Had to get a big girl job, you know?"

"Yeah," Morgan managed. "How's your grandmother?"

Jennifer's face softened. "She passed. Eight months ago."

Jennifer's dad had left before she'd been born, and her mother had been killed by an abusive boyfriend when Jennifer had been only three, leaving the girl to be raised by her grandparents. Morgan desperately wanted to crawl into the nearest hole. "I'm so sorry. I didn't know."

Of course, you didn't know. You were too wrapped up in your own shit to care about everyone you left behind.

"It's alright. They said it was a stroke. She didn't do great after Grandpa passed. You remember? Anyway, I wanted to tell you, but we hadn't talked for so long and I just figured you were busy. Life gets in the way sometimes, you know?" Jennifer gave a small shrug. "I get it. I wish you could have said goodbye. She really liked you." Jennifer's eyes glistened, and she gave her head a small shake to brush away the moment. "I got her house." That last came out with just a slightly forced upbeat tone. "And the car. But I sold that." A moment of awkward silence settled between them.

Morgan's mind reeled like a rodent trapped in a snare, seeking a way to remove herself from this moment while also struggling to come up with anything that would make up for her failure as a friend.

Jennifer's smile returned. "So, things are good for you? You left so fast, I didn't get to say goodbye."

Morgan winced, shifting uncomfortably. "I'm sorry about that, too. It's just that-"

"That you couldn't tell your best friend you were leaving town forever?" Morgan's cheeks warmed as the urge to run gripped her. Her throat tightened, a lump forming. This was it. This was how it would start. She'd come into the store as a way to delay this kind of thing, but here it was already. Jennifer laughed and flapped a hand in the air. "I'm messing with you. I mean, I'm not happy you didn't tell me or the others you were leaving, but your parents explained it to us."

Morgan nodded absently until what Jennifer had said registered. "They did?"

"Oh yeah, for sure. Your dad said that you'd gotten a job offer that was way better than working in the mill, and they needed you to start, like, right away. So…" She shrugged as if to say, *Makes perfect sense.*

Morgan's mind reeled at the lie her parents had told. Better to say she had a job than the truth; that she'd stormed out throwing curses and insults like a bitter smokescreen.

Jennifer went on. "I'm so jealous, though. You have to tell me all about it! Well, not right now!" She threw a look over her shoulder to where the pharmacist, Mr. Tillman, stood counting pills in a tray. His eyes, small dark pits beneath two oversized eyebrows, flicked toward the two women and back down to his task. "But soon. Oh! We need to get the gang back together! You're going to be around for a while, right?"

Morgan managed a jerky nod.

"Me and Heather were going to hang out at my place tomorrow night. She's rented a couple of movies. I'll call Jason. He and Todd work at the mill, ya know, but I'm sure they'd love to see you. Of course, Todd will insist on bringing Stephanie. She's okay, but can be a bit of a stick in the mud. I honestly don't know what Todd sees in her unless she's really great with—" Jennifer pressed her tongue against one cheek rhythmically.

"What about Chris?" The question was out of Morgan's mouth before she'd even realized she'd conjured it from her subconscious.

Jennifer's eyes danced with excitement. "You still think about Chris? Oh, that's funny. I mean, not really, now that I think about it. Considering you guys *were* kind of a thing. We can invite him. He hangs around Jason and Todd. But he's been seeing Amanda Turner this last year or so."

Morgan's mouth soured. "You don't say."

Jennifer popped a piece of bright pink gum in her mouth and chewed loudly as she talked. "Uh huh. Started dating last March, I think. They got together at Walter Bowman's bonfire party. You remember those? Man, those were a lot of fun. He didn't do one this year. Said something about getting too old for them. I think he got tired of not getting laid at his own parties. Well, that and the fact that Cynthia – you remember his little sister? She was like, three or four years behind us? – anyway, she got completely wasted at that same one where Chris and Amanda hooked up and almost-"

"Jennifer, does that customer need help?" Mr. Tillman asked as he twisted the cap on a small, burnt orange bottle.

Take them. They'll make you agreeable.

"No, sir," Jennifer said, raising her face to the ceiling. "She's an old friend I haven't seen in a couple years. Just saying hi."

"You can socialize on your own time, then. You have work to do."

Jennifer rolled her eyes comically, and Morgan smiled, a laugh bubbling softly from between her lips. It surprised her, but felt good at the same time. She'd missed her friend. She'd missed *all of them*, to be honest. It had been hard leaving them, knowing most of them would remain in town, succumbing to the steady tide of life that was Elden Mills.

"I better go," Morgan said, giving the items in her hands a little heft.

"Yeah, sure, totally. Listen, will you be at your parents' house? I guess you will, right? Okay. I get off at five tomorrow, so I'll give you a call when I get home." Jennifer's eyes widened as a new thought occurred to her. "But I have lunch at noon. Why don't you come eat with me?"

Inwardly, Morgan winced. "Sure. Sounds great."

Jennifer beamed. "It's so good to see you. I'm so happy that you got out of here and made a life for yourself!" She gave a flash of a wave and turned back to her work, her blonde hair flicking behind her.

The interior of the car was thick with summer heat, and despite the beads of sweat that sprung on her forehead and cheeks, Morgan sat behind the wheel with the keys pinched in her fingers. A tornado of thoughts swirled in her mind.

It had been great to see Jennifer. Until that moment, Morgan had forgotten how much she missed her friend. But the bitter taste of guilt soured her mouth at the reality that Jennifer, and everyone else, thought Morgan had moved and established a new, fantastic life. A lie her own father had issued. Why had he done that? Why not tell them the truth, that he had no real idea why Morgan had left; had no idea why, in the weeks leading up to it, she'd become moody and argumentative, withdrawn and sullen. Why not tell them the awful things she'd said to her parents?

The scene from the night she'd left resurfaced. Her parents, sitting in their usual spots on the couch, mouths slightly open as Morgan yelled at them while clutching her bags in each hand. The deep looks of shock that melted into even deeper hurt when she snarled that she didn't want to be stuck in this shithole town, another pathetic loser working in the mill and never actually doing anything with her life.

Morgan withered against the fierceness of the memory. Her shoulders pulled in, her head drooped, and she brought her hands in close to her stomach, her fingers clenched in tight fists. The last thing she wanted was to have to see them, and have them look at her with that same hurt. How could she ever ask them to forgive her? How could she ever *expect* them to?

Before the dark thoughts could press the matter farther, she jammed the key into the ignition and twisted. The Chevy coughed to life, and she backed out into the main avenue without properly looking. A horn blared, but no impact came, so Morgan threw the car into drive and slammed the gas. She sped away, throwing an apologetic wave up between the two front seats.

Her parents' house sat in a long row of similar houses along Bishop Street, just beyond Oakland Avenue. A block before theirs, Morgan passed the Elden Mills First Baptist Church. From behind the hedges that lined the front doors to the church peeked the balding head of Brother Camden. A pair of sheers came up and flashed in the morning light as he brought them to bear on the hedgerow.

Passing by, she slowed and parked along the curb in front of the split-level house. The street was quiet, and she took a moment to take in the solitude. Trees lined the avenue, with sidewalks bulging here and there from encroaching, underground roots. Most yards were starting to go thick, the spidery angles of bicycles carelessly left on their sides in a couple. She imagined that the next day all of them would be filled with men, pale legs jutting from shorts - a few would be in jeans or gray sweats, but not many - as they sweated through t-shirts and pushed their mowers back and forth, back and forth.

Bishop Street had been a good place to grow up. Several of her classmates had lived along the block or a quick bike ride away. Two blocks farther north lay Warren Park. When she'd been small, before Scott was born, her mother used to take her there to swing and play on the monkey bars – when her mother didn't have a shift at the mill, and before her accident, that was. Then, when Scott was big enough, the three of them would go. Sometimes her father would come, if he didn't have yard work to do, or if a ball game wasn't on.

She considered the house, her eyes moving over its siding and faux rock facade, finally finding her old bedroom window over the garage. It had always been a safe place. Always warm and inviting; her mother had seen to that. Her parents had worked hard to provide for the family and had always done their best to laugh, even through the rough times. Even when money was short, they always went to the beach every summer. Those trips were some of the best memories Morgan had with her family. Long days in the sand, eating fried shrimp at night before going back out to the beach with a flashlight and bucket to hunt sand crabs.

Her eyes settled on the graying, weathered wood that sloped at a gentle angle from the driveway to the front porch. The rough times had been few, but when they'd come, they'd come with a vengeance. Three years before Morgan graduated high school and left Elden Mills, she'd been called out of social studies class. The somber-faced principal's assistant wouldn't tell Morgan why she'd been summoned from a riveting lecture on the branches of government. They'd arrived at the closed door of Mr. Harris, and Morgan's escort had knocked once before opening the door and ushering her in.

In as calming and sorrowful a tone as he could manage, Principal Harris had informed Morgan that there'd been an accident at the mill. Her mother had been hit and pinned beneath a barrel of dye when a forklift had shifted the rack upon which the barrel had been placed. Her mother was alive, but had been rushed to Saint Mark's Hospital. Morgan remembered the feeling of sinking into the plastic chair across from the principal's huge desk, and the dull roaring that had filled her ears, drowning out everything else.

Her father had collected her, with Scott in the back seat - he'd been home sick that day and their father had stayed home with him. They'd waited in small, uncomfortable chairs in a waiting room painted a pastel green with pictures of deer and people Morgan assumed were saints doing all sorts of saintly things. Finally, a doctor – a thin man who projected an air of *I'm too busy for any of this* – came out and told them that Bonnie Bell would live, but would never walk again.

Morgan's father had built the ramp the next day, with the help of a few other guys from the mill.

Morgan blinked the memories away, swallowing hard against one last one that tried to push its way to the front: her mother, sitting on the couch next to Morgan's dad, stick-thin legs close together as she watched her only daughter, her oldest child, storm out of the house.

And now she was back.

"Fuck it," Morgan said, and she grabbed the bag from the drugstore. She got out and crossed the lawn, climbed the four steps to the porch, and opened the screen door. Her hand went automatically for the handle of the main door before she hesitated. This was home, but she'd not lived here for a while now. It felt wrong, just walking in. She redirected her hand, bringing her finger up to touch the dull, plastic strip of the doorbell. From inside came the muted chime, and she could imagine her mother looking up, confused.

Probably thinks a salesman is here to convince her to buy a set of carpet cleaning solutions.

The heavy wooden door swung in. Her brother stood in the doorway, blinking in the sunshine. His hair was a rat's nest, and he wore purple sweats and an AC/DC t-shirt. Scott stared at her for a long moment, and Morgan's resolve began to drain away. One of her feet even shifted back, preparing to turn the rest of her body and guide her back to the car.

But as she stood in the doorway of her childhood home, the smell of the interior drifted out and tickled Morgan's nose. It was the light, velvety smell of lavender and chamomile. It was a smell she'd never noticed before, having grown up in the house and long since gone nose-blind to it. Now her brain registered it, immediately associating with it the feeling of being home, of being safe.

The feeling slammed into her like a train.

Morgan caught the flicker of movement deeper in the house and watched as her mother wheeled around the corner from the kitchen, where another smell - this one of banana bread minutes out of the oven - wafted.

"Who is it?" her mom asked. Morgan stared at her mother, dressed in jeans and a white cotton blouse, her hair held back with a black barrette. One hand gripped a wheel of her chair, the other resting on the molding of the kitchen doorway. That sight, coupled with the smells of the home, consumed Morgan like a drowning wave. Deep within her, a massive bubble, a black balloon of sorrow and guilt, careened up from her guts. It popped, birthing into the world as a strangled gasp.

Tears spilled down Morgan's cheeks. Her knees began to buckle, and then Scott was laughing and pulling her into a tight embrace.

CHAPTER 8

Geordie Dupont pushed through the door and stepped out of the Mill Grill into the warm morning sun. He snorted and spat a large wad of phlegm onto the sidewalk. The door swung slowly shut behind him, and the dull roar of conversation dimmed further until it was cut off completely. Despite it being almost ten in the morning on a Friday, the grill's dining room was packed. Most of the current patrons were men and women who'd stood together in the mill's parking lot not two hours ago, and the topic of conversation was nothing but the mill's closure. Geordie had sat with Bill Reynolds and Linda Cooper, their trio sucking down coffee as they commiserated. The air over their heads - the left front corner of the dining room being the designated smoking area – had been a thick haze of white, and they'd taken turns dropping their used butts into a ceramic mug as the morning wore on.

Geordie had kept hoping that Frank Gallagher would stop by, but the man had never shown up. Finally, Geordie had gotten tired of waiting, so he'd thrown down a dollar and made his exit. The conversation had gone stale, as Bill had started rehashing the speech Vandermark had given, as if he were going to find some kind of fucking hidden meaning or something. Now, blinking in the sunshine, he considered what to do with the rest of his day. It'd been so long since he'd taken a day off work that he didn't know where to begin.

You're taking more than a day off work, bucko.

Geordie scowled and crossed the street to Martin's Liquors, pushing through the door as the bell overhead jangled. "We're not open for another hour," Martin Pope said as he fiddled with something behind the register.

Geordie ignored him, pulled a bottle of Jim Beam off the shelf, tossed a ten onto the counter, and kept walking. "Keep the change," he said as he went back outside. Standing on the corner, bottle dangling from his fingers, he was tempted to twist the cap off and start drinking right there. Another idea came to him, though – one that felt better than chugging half a bottle of whiskey and then staggering through the tiny downtown area of Elden Mills. It'd been a while since he'd gone fishing, and if the day was going to be as sunny and warm as it seemed intent on being, then the idea of laying on the banks of the Mill River, a pole in one hand and the bottle of Beam in the other, felt right.

"They can't take that away from me," he mumbled. He strolled toward his car and paused at another corner, waiting for traffic to ease up. With the mill closed, more people were out and about, and the increase in traffic – both foot and vehicle – made the small downtown area feel claustrophobic. Geordie hummed a tuneless song as he stood there, letting his eyes pass over the cars that drifted in front of him. A break in the flow of cars came, and he jogged across the street, gaining the opposite sidewalk with a short hop before he continued along the pavement toward Main Street, the bottle swinging next to him.

Geordie was considering the different lures he'd need when a maroon Chevy appeared, just around the corner from the hardware store. Absentmindedly, he watched it, picking out the dark figure behind the wheel.

All of the breath rushed out of his body, and a wave of nervous discomfort rolled into his guts.

Morgan Bell drove by, oblivious to him standing not ten yards away, a dumbstruck expression on his grizzled face. Geordie only got a brief look at her, most of her features being hidden behind rippling shadows and the watery reflection of sunlight on the windshield, but there was no mistaking that face. She looked just as perfect today - what had it been, two or three years? - as she had when he'd last seen her.

That memory floated in the inky blackness of his mind; the panting, the grunting, the way her skin had felt, and the way it had tasted. In those few minutes, she'd been so perfectly his. A previously unattainable prize that by some miracle he'd gotten to hold, to relish.

She'd belonged to him, then.

His body reacted to the thoughts, the phantom sounds of her breath...her cries of passion, of longing, of *need*. Drool slid over his lower lip, the tickle of it bringing him back to the moment, and he sucked the excess spit up and ran the back of a hand across his lips. Morgan was past him now, the Chevy having continued down the block, to where her brake lights had flared, the nose of the car angling into a spot by the drugstore.

She got out, her soft curves shifting perfectly beneath her shirt. Her dark hair hung in gentle waves around her shoulders, and Geordie grinned at the thought of how it had smelled of whatever fruity shampoo she'd used at the time when he'd last been with her. Morgan walked into the drugstore and, for a long second, Geordie considered following her. But the weight of the bottle of whiskey in his hand reminded him that his day held other options. Besides, if Morgan was back in town for longer than today, then maybe he'd get another chance at the brass ring.

That thought ringing in his mind, Geordie turned to continue toward his car. Something slammed into his shoulder, however, knocking him a couple of steps toward the gutter, and for a sickening moment, he was afraid the bottle was going to slip out of his grasp. He managed to gain his balance and saw what he'd collided with. An older woman, her hair a salt-and-pepper mix, glared at him with a mixture of surprise and disgust.

"Watch where you're going," she said as she slid her purse higher onto her shoulder.

"Watch yourself, you dumb, blind cunt!" Geordie snarled. The woman's eyes went wide at the vulgarity, and Geordie smiled. He strolled away, humming his nonsensical tune again, louder this time. *Maybe today isn't going to be so bad after all.*

CHAPTER 9

Regina Eriksson had been the dayshift dispatcher for the Elden Mills Police Department for going on thirty years. Before that, she'd done three years on the night shift and that was more than enough, thank you very much. In all those years, Regina could only remember a small handful of times when any calls had come in on the little red phone designated for 911 calls. The majority of all calls to the station came in on one of the main lines, the numbers to which almost everyone in town knew. As a result, the emergency line phone sat forgotten, often covered with folders or paperwork.

Her hands shuffled the papers on the desk which was normally a study in tidiness. 'Everything has a place, and everything in its place' was not only a motto she lived by, but a deeply held belief that sat snuggled up next to 'The Lord thy God' in her heart. But today there were a lot of forms, and to organize them so she could attack them in a precise, logical manner, Regina had to spread them across the entire wooden surface of her desk. As such, she couldn't currently see her calendar, neither the tan colored main phone nor the red emergency one, or her wire In/Out basket. Most were standard forms, regular reports filled in by the officers on calls they'd been sent to. There were copies of permits that had been filed regarding noise ordinances, and requests for street closures during the Fourth of July parade. The celebration was a month away, but it never hurt to get the requests in early. Regina hated people who filed requests at the last minute, and had been known to fail to get Sheriff Hollister's signature on even the simplest application if she felt it had been submitted too close to an event's date.

The glass doors at the front of the station squealed on hinges that badly needed oiling - she'd have to complain to Toby again when he came in that afternoon for his summer job as the department custodian - and Regina watched as Bill Adams crossed the lobby, his gun belt draped over one shoulder and a white, grease-stained bag clutched in one hand.

"Getting here when you feel like it?" she asked, gazing at him over her reading glasses.

Bill grinned a wide smile and held the bag out. "I brought biscuits," he said as an excuse. "Fresh from the Grill. Buck made 'em just for us."

Regina humphed as she glanced into the bag, seeing all the softball-sized lumps wrapped in white wax paper. "And how is Misty?" She picked one marked 'Smoked Sausage' and moved a call form aside to place the biscuit on the desk.

"Who?" Bill asked, feigning ignorance, but the smile fighting with the corners of his mouth told her the truth.

"Mmm hmm," she muttered disapprovingly. She shook a finger at him. "You know that girl is too good for you."

"Why do you think I like her so much?" Bill laughed and pushed through the swinging wooden half-door that separated the lobby from the rear of the station. The greasy smell of biscuits, lard, and sausages trailed in his wake.

Regina continued organizing. The station filled with voices of officers praising Bill for the gift of food, a mumbled response that included a curse word – though the boys were generally good about not cursing in front of her - and a round of laughter.

Footsteps on the linoleum announced the arrival of Sheriff Hollister. Regina knew the sounds of every officer in the squad house.

The dispatcher swiveled her chair as he approached. She'd been on the desk since he'd come to the department as a rookie and worked his way, quickly, up the ladder. She'd never failed to be taken in by his dashing good looks. Men like him should only exist in movies and the types of paperback novels they sold on the rotating wire rack at the rear of Mills Drugs.

"Sheriff," she said. "You get one of those biscuits?"

"Nah," he said with a slight smile. "Things have enough cholesterol in them to kill a bull. Leigh made breakfast before I left the house." He glanced over one shoulder and then leaned close, putting his elbows on the small wall that enclosed most of her desk. "Listen, I need you to call Walter and Deke, and have them shift over to the mill."

Regina's hand automatically began reaching for the dispatch microphone. "Something going on?" she asked. She hated sending any of the guys to an area without giving them a heads-up of the reason; that was asking for trouble, and keeping the officers out of trouble was of paramount importance to her.

Hollister winced and shook his head. "Don't know. Vandermark, the boss out there, called me this morning. Said that he's going to be talking to a lot of the guys and that he'd appreciate it if a couple of our boys were in the area just in case."

Regina's hand stopped, fingers lightly touching the dull, gunmetal gray microphone. "That doesn't sound good. You don't think he was laying off a bunch of them, do you?"

"I have no idea. He didn't say. And don't you say anything to Walt or Deke, either. Just have them reposition and hold. Tell them to post up off of Holly and monitor the situation, okay?"

Regina nodded, and the sheriff rapped his knuckles twice on the wooden divider, pushed off and walked back to his office. Regina made the call, telling the officers only what she'd been instructed to say, and answering their questions with, "Monitor what's happening. Information to come." Walter and Deke acknowledged, and Regina returned the microphone to its metal clip.

"Oh, Regina!" Hollister called as he emerged from his office.

"Forgot to tell you-" But what he said next was lost as a phone began ringing. Regina held one finger up to the sheriff, who once more leaned on the wooden partition as she began pushing papers away to uncover the tan phone. She plucked the receiver from the cradle and held her finger over the row of milky plastic buttons that lined the bottom of the dial, looking for the glowing one corresponding to the extension through which the call was coming. All were dull. Lifeless.

Regina realized what was happening at the same time Hollister said it, his voice pitched higher with surprise. "It's the 911 phone."

Regina's hands slapped papers away, sending some of them curling up off the desk to drift lazily down to the floor. Her heart gave wild, flapping leaps in her chest. The dull red plastic of the emergency line phone became visible, and Regina hesitated for just long enough to take a steadying breath before picking it up.

"Nine-one-one, what's the emergency?" she asked with what she hoped was a calm voice, but which felt like water breaking on a rocky shore.

"Oh, Christ," the voice came through, breathless in its own right. But it was more than that...it was strained, as tight as a piano wire. "Y'all gotta get over here. They're all dead. It's a fucking nightmare."

CHAPTER 10

Morgan flexed her fingers, wrapping them tighter against the warm ceramic of the mug. The coffee smelled heavenly and, as her mother had joked while fixing it the way Morgan liked, stopped being primarily coffee after almost half a pint of milk and four heaping spoons of sugar had been added. Morgan sipped the drink, its warmth spreading through her like she was slipping on an old sweater, and she plucked a chunk of banana bread from her slice.

"I still can't believe you're here," her mother said. Her own piece of bread sat untouched atop a plate that featured images of roosters around the outer edge. For some reason that Morgan had never understood, it was her mother's favorite plate. "I mean; why didn't you call us? Let us know you were coming? I would have had your room made up! There are no sheets on that bed."

"It's okay," Morgan said. "I can put the sheets on if me staying isn't a problem." *Here it comes. Here's where she'll remind me of what I said when I left.* The words came back to her, ringing fresh as if they'd been said only moments before. *'I hate it here. I can't stand any of it, any of the people. This place is a pit and I'm not going to be stuck here, wasting my life.'* Across the table, Scott watched as if sitting in the stands of a tennis match. He chewed his bread slowly, almost mechanically, as he focused on the interaction.

Her mother made a sound somewhere between dismissiveness and disgust. "Of course, it's not a problem. I'm just saying, I would have loved to have known." Then, seeming to remember she had food in front of her, she cut a piece, stabbed it with her fork, and slipped it into her mouth. An uneasy silence fell across the room, broken only by occasional sips of coffee and light scrapings of forks across plates. Morgan picked at her banana bread, disinterested despite the grumbling in her stomach. She could practically see the elephant in the room, the massive shape of unasked questions.

"Are you seeing anyone?" her mom asked.

A tear grew in one eye, gathering at the edge of her eyelid. Morgan blinked it free, and it crawled slowly down her cheek. "No. I mean, I was, but we split up."

Her mother's hand slid across the table and patted Morgan's. "I'm sorry to hear that. Don't worry. You'll find someone." She gave a reassuring smile before settling back in her wheelchair and picking up her coffee. Before it reached her lips, her eyes went wide. "Oh, I didn't tell you about your cousin Sheila, did I? You remember her, right? Your Uncle Sammy's oldest? Well..."

Morgan let her mother's voice drone on, fading into a kind of white noise in the background. She finished her coffee, forced down the last bite of bread she'd taken, and put her plate in the sink. As she refilled her mug, she let her eyes drift across the rest of the kitchen. There wasn't a thing in the room – not the clock, not the phone mounted next to the doorway with its curled cord knotted and kinked and stretched five times its initial length, nothing in the space – that didn't bring back memories of her life in the house.

She was home. She was back where she belonged, at least for now. A measure of relief settled over her as she accepted that she wasn't going to have to face her past behavior just yet. There was still a lot to do - her father hadn't gotten home yet, and then there was the matter of her friends and Geordie - but for now, she was okay. She was standing in her parents' kitchen listening to her mother prattle on about family gossip, as if this were any other day and the last two years hadn't happened. A small ember of relief blossomed in her chest, growing and spreading its warmth through her extremities.

You're going to be alright.

The rumble of an engine, deep and throaty, drifted from the front of the house. It cut off abruptly, followed by the sound of a door slamming shut. The screen door to the house whined open. Heavy footsteps thumped on the linoleum of the foyer.

"Pete?" her mom asked.

"They're closing the goddamned thing!" her father said. Morgan replaced the coffee pot and leaned against the counter, overwhelmed by the feeling of intruding on a private moment. "Just like that! Closing it!" Two heavy thuds indicated the removal of his work boots. He stomped heavily around the corner and tossed his keys onto the counter. Morgan's mother's eyes ticked to the key holder, a wooden cutout of a smiling raccoon with its paws held out expectantly.

"Did you hear me? It's closed!" her father said again, his voice an explosion in the kitchen. His cheeks were red with anger, and he was so focused on his wife that he didn't notice Morgan in the corner, just to the right of the doorway. He pulled out a chair and sat heavily down into it, letting one hand slap against the table in frustration.

"What...?" her mom started, but he cut her off.

"The mill! Vandermark had the security gates locked, and had a blockade set up. Even had Wade and Harold standing there - like they could have done anything - and told everyone that operations were shifting elsewhere, and that Avondale had decided to close the mill."

A cold electricity filled the room, and Morgan's mother gasped, one hand drifting up to her chest.

If she had pearls on, she'd be clutching at them, Morgan thought.

Her father shook his head in frustration, running a hand through the tangle of his dark hair. His gaze fell on Morgan. For a split second his eyes went hard. In the next moment, everything about him softened. He looked from Morgan to his wife, then back again.

With effort, Morgan took a step toward the table. "Hey, Dad."

Her father stood up, his chair scraping against the floor as he pushed up. He walked around the table until he was directly in front of her. Morgan had always known her dad was a bigger guy, but - like the smells of the house – she'd long since forgotten what a presence he was. But as he stood there staring at her in disbelief, she felt as small as a field mouse staring up at a semi-truck.

"When did you...?" he stammered, and she heard a soft cracking in his voice. Before she could even answer, he grabbed one of her shoulders and wrapped her in a fierce embrace. He smelled of Dial soap, Aqua Velva aftershave, and coffee. She gripped him as tightly as she could. She knew she was crying, her tears soaking into his dark blue work shirt, but she didn't care. All she cared about in the moment was the fact that her father was holding her. His voice, soft and reassuring, repeating, "It doesn't matter. It's okay."

After a few minutes, she let her father guide her back to the table. They all sat, and Morgan wiped her face with a napkin. She noticed her mother swiping away tears with her fingertips. Scott, who had so far been quiet, had his jaw clenched so tightly that Morgan could see the muscles in his neck working as *he* fought to keep from crying.

Her mother broke the spell. "They're closing the mill?"

Her father let out a long sigh. "Yeah."

"But why? How could they just decide to close? Don't they know what that would mean to the town? To all the people?" She lurched forward and gripped her husband's arm. "Do you still have a job?"

"If the mill is closing, then he doesn't have a job," Scott said, looking at his father. "Right?"

Peter sat back, the chair creaking with the movement. "I honestly don't know. The short answer is, probably not. But they did say that some people would be asked to work through the 'transition' as they called it, helping prepare equipment for removal. I think they're selling most everything."

"Will you be one of those people?" Morgan's mom asked, and Morgan heard the desperate hopefulness in her voice. Since her accident, the family had survived on her father's paycheck and the small disability check the mill provided each month.

"I don't know," her father answered. "I'm going to see. Some of the guys are meeting at the Lantern later tonight. I'm going to go down there and see if anyone has any ideas on what we can do."

"But-" her mother began.

Her father waved the protest off. "We can talk about all that later. Let's do something. Let's get out of here. Go enjoy the sun," he said, turning his smile toward Morgan. "We have something to celebrate today."

CHAPTER 11

The smell hit Jared like an angry wind as soon as he entered the house. He stopped inside the small foyer, his hand flying to his nose. "Christ Almighty," he managed through a throat that was fighting back the remains of his breakfast.

From where he stood, he could see the wide expanse of the living room. A sofa, loveseat, recliner, and wooden rocking chair with a flower-patterned cushion on the seat sat arranged on the light blue carpet, positioned so that anyone sitting could see the television. Pictures of family members adorned the walls, with the whole group in front of a woodland backdrop - Jared had seen that same one in dozens of pictures, as it was a specialty of the JCPenney's photo department - and of kids forcing smiles on school picture days. He caught a glimpse of a shelf between the living room and the kitchen that held several collector plates, each one adorned with a different NASCAR driver's image, number, and signature.

A dark doorway looked to offer admittance to the lower half of the house while an open staircase immediately next to that invited people to visit the upper floor. One of his officers, Mark Grayson, stood at the base of the upstairs entrance, his face a pale gray. He looked across the room at the sheriff and shook his head.

"It's awful," he said, and the strained tone of his voice told Jared that everything he'd imagined on the drive over would pale in comparison to what he was about to face. Jared took another breath, lowered his hand, and forced himself to step into the living room. Behind him, another of his officers, Blake "BB" Bradley entered with light steps.

"What's that noise?" Bradley asked through his own raised hand. Jared cocked his head and realized that, yes, he could hear it, too – a low, soft buzzing like voices talking all at once, but muffled through thick layers of cotton.

Grayson jerked his head toward the stairs leading upward. "It's the flies. There's gotta be a million of them up there. Fucking summer. You can't get rid of them."

At the top of the blue carpet-covered stairs, more family pictures lined the walls in cheap black and gold frames. The thought of having to climb those few steps and see the mess that lay around the corner at the top was overwhelming. It was the last thing he wanted to do. The majority of corpses he'd seen in his time as a police officer had died of natural causes. There had been one suicide - a hanging - and one accidental death where a woman had dropped a bag of groceries as she'd carried them up from her garage. In her haste to collect them, she'd lost her balance and fallen back down the stairs, breaking her neck in the process.

Bloodless deaths, all of them. But the smell that permeated the house now, the coppery stench that seemed to invade every orifice and left an oil slick on his tongue, along with the flies having an early Christmas feast, made it clear that his streak of clean bodies was at an end. To distract himself and put off the inevitable for a bit longer, he peeked around into the kitchen. There was nothing out of the ordinary there. Just a few dishes in the sink, and a loaf of bread open on the counter with a closed jar of Hellmann's next to it. A couple of flies buzzed lazily in the air, and Jared turned back to the living room, looking closely at the faux woods backdrop picture.

"Are they all up there?" he asked.

"I think so," Grayson said. Jared frowned.

"What do you mean, you *think so*?"

The officer swallowed hard, his throat shifting with the action. "It's, uh…hard to tell."

Jared waited for more information – some explanation, something rational – but nothing came. Grayson just swallowed again, his Adam's apple bobbing in his thin neck. *He's trying not to vomit*, Jared thought.

"You want me to go up, boss?" Bradley asked.

"No," Jared said with a sharp exhalation. "I'll go. You stay here, keep an eye on the front, and make sure none of the neighbors show up to see what's going on. The guy I saw out front sitting in the back of Lafferty's car – that's who called it in?"

Bradley nodded. "Charlie Harris. Friend of the father's. They work at the mill together, and when this guy didn't show up, Harris came around." His eyes drifted to the stairs. "Found 'em up there."

Jared ran his hand through his blonde hair and mounted the steps on legs that quivered. He moved slowly, trying to keep an eye out for anything that could be considered evidence even while knowing that he was risking trampling hairs or blood. He pulled his flashlight from his belt and aimed its powerful beam at the floor, picking out a path he felt would be least disruptive to any evidence. At the top of the stairs he found himself in a hallway that stretched to his right, open doors lining either side.

Flies buzzed lazily along the passage, resting on the walls and passing in and out of the various open doorways. However, it was clear which room Jared needed to investigate. The door to the bedroom at the far end was choked with flies. The lights were on in that room, and based on what little he could see from his current position, Jared assumed it was the master suite.

More pictures lined the hall, most knocked askew. His flashlight picked up smears of blood on the walls and on the glass of the picture frames. A hole was punched into the wall next to the open door to the bathroom. Jared flicked his light into each room, finding bedrooms. Each one held its own miniature crime scene. Bedsheets were tossed violently aside, mattresses soaked in blood. Blood marbled every wall and covered parts of the ceilings. More flies danced around the pools as if they had found the fountain of youth.

Hardly a single surface within the bathroom was without blood. It puddled thickly in the sink, coated the shattered mirror, and streaked the shower curtain. A chaotic pattern of bloody footprints covered the blue carpet, showing wet, red patches where the fibers had been matted down. Some looked like drag marks; others were clear footprints.

Jared continued to the bedroom at the end of the hall, and when he reached the doorway, his flashlight fell from his numb fingers. It landed with a heavy thud on the carpet and rolled a few inches, the beam washing across the scene and sending shadows twisting across the walls and ceiling. He stared, his mind reeling, at the scene.

It's like a slaughterhouse floor.

"Boss, you good?" Grayson called up.

For a brief moment, Jared couldn't answer. He was afraid that, if he tried, everything in his stomach would come rushing up in a hot gush. He placed a hand on the doorframe, steadied himself, and waited until the house around him stopped see-sawing. He took in and let out a solid breath before he replied, "Yeah. Good. You called the county boys yet?"

"Not yet. I wanted to see how you wanted to handle this."

Jared picked his flashlight up. "It's not like we have the resources. You know that. Go ahead and call them in. Crime scene, coroner, couple of units for backup security." He reached a hand down and twisted the volume on his radio down as Grayson made the call to Regina. Then, Jared stepped fully into the bedroom.

What remained of the Butler family was piled on the blood-soaked queen bed in the center of the room. The bed was positioned at the midpoint of the right-hand wall, nightstands on either side, a dresser opposite the foot of the bed, and another immediately to the right of the doorway. A single window in the wall opposite the door gave a glimpse of the woods on the far side of the house. A smaller door in the corner by the window led to a bathroom, the sink counter littered with deodorant, toothpaste tubes, and hairbrushes. *Every-*

thing they would have needed if they hadn't ended up like they are, he thought grimly.

The carpet throughout the room squelched beneath his shoes, blood seeping up as it was displaced with each step he took. Jared positioned himself at the foot of the bed, his legs only a couple of inches away from the thin metal railings of the footboard. He directed his flashlight beam onto the tangle of limbs, ruined flesh, and blood-saturated clothing. Clumps of hair, matted by blood, plastered across cheeks that had gone fishbelly pale. An eyeball hung loose, veins and other connective tissues preventing it from rolling along the face of one of the boys. Jared's stunned mind searched for the kid's name, but couldn't come up with it. The light reflected brightly off of terrible, broken, white pieces amidst the mangled skin, and he understood that he was looking at bone fragments.

Whatever had done this had pulverized bones, driving the shattered ends up and through the skin.

Jared closed his eyes and took four slow breaths. *You need to look at them. You need to try to understand.*

But when he looked again, he knew there would be no understanding. There would be no making sense out of this. The bodies were broken and bent, thrown carelessly atop one another on the bed. The entire family had been slaughtered and piled up like garbage.

A rush of nausea crashed into him, and he knew he wouldn't be able to keep his stomach in check this time. He staggered out of the room and down the stairs. He pushed past Grayson, who held a hand up as if to offer assistance, and thudded into the kitchen and let everything come up into the sink.

When the moment had passed, he pulled a few paper towels from the rack mounted beneath the cabinets and wiped his mouth. Back in the living room, he exchanged a look with Grayson.

"Have you ever..." Grayson began, but Jared held a halting hand up.

"You know I haven't." He looked up the stairs and shook his head. "Whoever did that...." He shook his head again. Voices from the front of the house pulled his attention, and Jared moved in that direction, happy for the distraction. He found BB standing on the front walk at the base of the porch steps, talking with an elderly man holding the leash of a border collie. The dog was sniffing interestedly at a bush to one side of the porch. When Jared came out of the house, the old man lit up.

"Something going on, Sheriff?"

"Nothing for you to be concerned about."

The old man nodded, clearly not believing that, and gave the dog's leash a weak tug. "Get out of there, girl. Ain't nothing in there you need." To Jared, he said, "They get robbed or something?"

Instead of answering, Jared asked, "What's your name?"

"Elmer Collins. I live—" he twisted and pointed down the street toward the entrance of the small neighborhood, "in the first house on the left over there. This here—" he gave the leash another tug that the collie summarily ignored, "is Hedy."

"Thanks for stopping by," Jared said. "But we're a little busy here. If I need anything, I or one of my officers will knock." Elmer gave a soft grunt and nodded to himself. He gave Hedy's leash another pull, and guided the dog back along the street. Jared noticed how the older man stared at Charlie Harris sitting in the back seat of the cruiser, his feet resting on the pavement.

"Nosy dude," BB said when the man was out of earshot.

"What can you expect?" Jared answered. "Nothing happens on this street, I bet. Now, there's three cop cars? I'd be curious, too." He surveyed the street, following it to the dead-end and the old basketball goal and the woods beyond. "How did he get here?"

"The old guy? He walked from-"

"No. You know who I'm talking about."

BB jerked his chin toward the woods. "Reckon he came through there."

Jared considered the trees. "Maybe. But there's nothing beyond that tree line but more trees. Well, eventually you'd get to 52, but that's probably eight, ten miles? That's a hell of a hike to make in the dark. No." He looked at the entrance to the dead-end and saw Elmer

Collins leading his dog into the house. "My guess is that he came from there. Whether he walked or drove is the question."

"The guys from the county are on their way," Grayson said from behind them.

Jared nodded and took the steps down to the yard. "I'm going to take a quick walk along the street; see if there's anything interesting. Any more neighbors show up, you guys know what to do."

Jared moved slowly along the rough edge of the asphalt. The street here lacked sidewalks, the thick grass of each home growing sparse as it met with the dark gravel of the shoulder of the road. He walked with his hands in his pockets, eyes sweeping left to right, right to left, looking for anything. There was plenty of litter, including cigarette butts - many having long since lost their shape and now blossoming into a loose collection of white threads - beer bottle caps, and the sun-faded label of a soda.

At the junction where the street met the main road, he paused, poking around in the thicker grass. There were a few tire tracks, but it was impossible to tell if any were fresh or unusual.

Best let the county boys determine that.

He started back, reminding himself to have BB run down and string a line of yellow tape across the entrance to the street. That would put the neighbors on high alert, he knew, but once the county guys showed up, everyone would know something serious was up anyway.

His trip back along the opposite side of the street was shorter, his pace quicker. He reasoned that whoever had done the killing had probably stayed on the other side of the road, but he himself continued to scan back and forth as he walked.

Halfway down the road, he stopped, his breath caught in his throat. About three feet into a yard was a smear of wet red on the grass. Jared's eyes bored into it. Then, they slowly tracked across the yard. Between the street and the house were three more red smears. But it was the house itself that put a sour pit in his stomach.

The side door to the garage was open.

A small streak of blood on the casing was visible in the mid-morning sun.

Jared pulled his radio from his belt and thumbed the button. "BB?"

He heard the response through the radio, but heard the faint voice from down the street, as well. "Yeah, boss?"

Jared swallowed hard, the act difficult. "Call everyone. And I mean everyone. Get 'em here now." He clipped the radio back on his belt and started across the grass.

CHAPTER 12

Patricia Davis flicked the butt of her cigarette out of her car window and watched as it kicked up sparks. It skittered across the parking lot, coming to rest a few feet from the gutter. She rolled the window back up. It was only 10 a.m., but June was already in full effect, the digital thermometer outside First National Bank showing eighty-four degrees.

She let out a long breath, leaned her head against the seat's headrest, and looked across the empty parking lot to the long, single-story elementary school. The school year had ended only yesterday, and several of the windows still had papers taped to them, the roughly scrawled pictures made by students fluttering in the breeze of the air conditioning. Thank Christ the AC would be working in the school. If she had to be there, at least there was that.

Patricia's car was the only one in the faculty lot. Unlike the other teachers, Patricia had forgone the tradition of taking at least a day or two off before cleaning or starting summer school classes. She, Jason, and the girls were going to Gulf Shores in the morning, and the thought of leaving the classroom a mess for when she returned made Patricia twitch. She'd never be able to relax on the beach knowing that there were papers to throw away, glue stains to chisel off of desktops, and crayon graffiti to clean off of chairs.

Giving another glance around the parking lot to ensure she was alone, Patricia reached over and flipped open the glove box. She pulled out a pint bottle of Wild Turkey and added a long, generous splash to her thermos of coffee. No sense in not at least enjoying the day a little bit, she reasoned. She checked herself in the mirror, brushed some of her auburn hair back from her forehead, and got out of the car and crossed to the school. She used her master key to enter, hurried down the hall to the office, and crossed to the security panel that was slowly beeping its warning countdown. She fingered the disarm code so that the panel gave a satisfied chirp. She let out a long, relieved sigh. Despite having worked at the school for over a decade and interacted with the panel countless times, she always found herself nervous that she'd do something wrong and find herself on the business end of a police pistol after triggering the alarm.

"At least you worked this time," she muttered. The panel had a history of not always cooperating and sometimes ignoring doors or even windows left open. Principal Harris - after all this time, she still refused to call him Randall - swore he was going to get the system serviced, and that the real problem was the sensors on the doors and windows being, as he put it, "cheap Chinese crap." Patricia didn't know about that, as some of the better things she owned claimed Chinese origins, but to each his own.

Remembering Principal Harris' rules about non-school days, Patricia returned to the front doors and locked them. She gave the doors a gentle tug to ensure the mechanism had caught before returning to the mail cubbies in the office. She shuffled through papers, saw nothing of interest or directed to her, and proceeded along the long western hallway of the school toward her classroom. Hers was the second from the end on the parking lot side – though her windows were devoid of drawings, as she'd seen to that yesterday - and near the restrooms. The location had been both a blessing and a curse. Second graders tended to need to go to the bathroom a lot, but it was part of her job to train them to hold it until designated break times. As a result of her room's location, she'd only had a small number of accidents to deal with, for which she was thankful. She loved her kids - well, that might be a little strong...she *liked* most of them, anyway - but as a parent herself, she'd put in her time cleaning up pee. And she'd not enjoyed it then, either.

The classroom held twenty-four desks, all in four neat rows facing the chalkboard. Her desk sat in the corner near the windows, opposite the door. Posters featuring cartoon characters boasting about math and reading adorned the walls, and several colorful streamers of crepe paper hung from the ceiling tiles – remnants of the end-of-year pizza party. Stepping into the room, Patricia could almost hear the echoes of her children talking, laughing, and shouting over one another.

She placed her purse, keys, and thermos on her desk and surveyed the classroom, deciding where to start. The door to the small supply closet at the rear of the room hung open a crack, and she looked at it for a moment, not remembering having left it open. Not that it mattered, yesterday had been so chaotic; one of her students could have done it. She was going to have to go in there anyway at some point, so she may as well leave it open.

Her first task was to take down the streamers, and she stuffed them into the metal garbage can she kept under her desk. Then, she moved around collecting other small pieces of trash from the students' desks. That done, she gathered up an armload of textbooks and walked to the closet, toeing the door the rest of the way open.

The light from her classroom windows was just enough for her to see a couple of feet into the closet. Shelves ran waist-high around the three walls and were filled with books, extra packs of loose-leaf paper, a few boxes of pencils and chalk, and other things she'd long ago learned were key to success in the classroom.

But as she reached out to place the books in their rightful place, Patricia's heart leapt high in her chest and her arms retracted, the stack of textbooks crashing to the floor. She jerked back, a startled cry filling her mouth and immediately withering on her tongue.

A figure stood in the left corner of the closet. The big man wore dark clothes. That was all the description Patricia's mind could handle, as her attention was forced to the bone-white mask he wore. Stringy black hair hung in long clumps around his shoulders. His bottomless black eyes bored holes into her, the rough edges of his mouth leering demonically.

He lunged toward her, one powerful hand thrust out, fingers grasping. Patricia stumbled backward, arms flailing as her shoes scraped across the tile floor. Her shoulder crashed against the door frame as, deep within the recesses of her mind, a voice screamed for her to run.

Pawing her way free of the doorway, Patricia continued backpedaling through the classroom, chairs and desks scraping loudly as she shoved past them. The mask materialized out of the closet, a hideous moon floating in the night sky of the doorway. As the man stepped out into the classroom, his boots thumping like an executioner's blade against a blood-soaked tree stump, Patricia managed to turn and run for the doorway and the hall beyond it.

Her footsteps slapped against the tile, echoing through the wide, empty hallway as she raced toward the office and the main entrance. She reached the intersection and darted to the front doors. The double doors rattled in her grasp as she pulled on them, leaning back with all of her weight. But her eyes fell to the lock, and her mind flashed the image of her keys lying atop her desk.

Patricia spun around to face the school and considered her options. Like a slow-ticking clock, the masked man's footsteps drifted from the hallway, throwing her mind into a state of confused panic. Her entire body trembled as she tried to focus. The footsteps grew closer, and Patricia sprinted away, angling to the right and the hallway that led to the upper level classrooms.

After several feet, she changed direction and raced down a new corridor, this one leading to the cafeteria and more classrooms. Posters held up by only a single thumbtack to corkboards or small strips of clear tape to the painted cinder block walls flapped noisily as she passed. Patricia thought about the cafeteria. There weren't many places to hide there, as all of the tables would be folded up and moved to the outer walls, but maybe she could squeeze in somewhere in the kitchen. Also, there would be knives.

The cafeteria was as silent as the rest of the school. The air smelled faintly of grease and bread as she pulled open the door and started across the floor. Halfway to the serving counter, her foot slid out from beneath her, and Patricia slammed into the floor. She lay sprawled on the cold, hard tile, stunned and gasping for breath. Wetness soaked into her back, and for a heart-stopping moment, she thought she'd cracked her skull. *Oh, Jesus, I'm bleeding.* A dark shape leaned over her, filling her vision, and Patricia screamed, her arms and legs spasming as she fought for traction on the slippery floor.

"Shit, are you alright?" the shape asked as it bent forward and grabbed at one of her arms. Patricia slapped at it feebly, but strong hands gripped her forearm and pulled her up. "I'm so sorry, I didn't... Hey, it's okay. Patty, it's me."

At her name, Patricia's struggles faltered, and she allowed herself a moment to focus on the roadmap of acne scars and freckles that dominated the face of Eddie Waller.

The janitor gave her an apologetic smile. "I didn't mean to scare you. Are you alright? That was a hell of a spill you took. I didn't have signs out; I didn't think anyone else was here."

Patricia looked down at the glistening tiles where Eddie had been mopping. Eddie stepped back, giving her space. A set of orange headphones dangled around his neck, tinny music drifting out. His red hair, fashioned into a long mullet, fell behind his shoulders, and he ran a hand through it nervously. Patricia threw a look over her shoulder at the doors and the shadowy hallway beyond, but saw no movement. No masked man.

"You about gave me a heart attack," Eddie went on. "I was mopping up and never heard you come in. Hell, I didn't even hear you fall. I turned around and there you were, all laid out. You sure you're okay?"

Her back ached, and she could tell the pain would make the drive to the beach in the morning hell on earth, but she managed a nod. "Yeah. Sorry. You're sure you're the only one here?"

Eddie's smile faltered. "Pretty sure. Why?"

"There was a man in a mask. He chased me out of my classroom."

Eddie watched her, his face screwed up in confusion. "You think it was maybe one of the kids? Maybe snuck in here to play a prank on you?"

"No," she said, shaking her head. "He was huge. He was following me." She pointed toward the doors.

Eddie crossed the room, mop in hand, and peered through the thin vertical window of one of the doors.

"Don't see anyone," he said as he transferred the mop to his left hand and pulled open the door with his right. Patricia took an instinctive step toward him, her lips forming a warning for him not to go out there. Eddie shoved his head through the crack and stared for a long moment. "Nope. Nobody out there." He thought for a moment, and then said, "Say, you wouldn't happen to have any of your special coffee in your classroom, would you?" He gave her a knowing grin.

"I'm not drunk and hallucinating if that's what you're implying."

"Not at all," he said. "Just thought a sip or two would calm both our nerves. Plus, it'd give me the energy for that." He pointed to the ceiling. Three small light brown squares were stuck to the tile overhead. Two had small crescents cut into their sides. Before she could ask, Eddie said, "Grilled cheese sandwiches. I don't know how the hell they got them up there, much less to stick. Little shits even took a bite out of them first."

She started to ask another question, but a wet thump followed by a soft gurgle interrupted her. One of Eddie's eyes bulged wide open while the other fluttered like a trapped butterfly. Something was sticking out of his mouth – a long spike that looked like a perverted tongue. Patricia stared as the tongue vanished with a noise that made her think of a shoe being pulled out of mud. As soon as it was gone, blood poured out of Eddie's mouth. Covering his chin, soaking into his gray coveralls, and pattering down on the tiles of the floor.

Eddie started to collapse, but then something reached in and shoved him, hard. He practically flew into the room, landing on the floor with a painful crunch. Through the roaring of blood pounding in her ears, Patricia was certain she heard something in his face crunch and break when he landed. She watched his body settle, the blood spreading out from beneath him like an invading army conquering new lands. Then, her gaze was pulled back up to the masked horror filling the doorway.

"What...?" Patricia croaked. The masked man stepped slowly into the room, his heavy footfalls loud in the dead air of the cafeteria. He took one long step, clearing Eddie's body, and continued toward her. In one powerful hand, he clutched the handle of a wicked hammer. Patricia saw a gore-covered spike on the back side of the hammer's head, and then she was running across the cafeteria for the emergency exit doors beyond the rows of folded tables.

Her hands pounded on the crash bar of the doors, the metallic clattering filling her ears and drowning out her own desperate cries. The doors remained locked. Patricia slapped at them, screaming for help as she stared through the wire-reinforced glass. Thirty yards away, her car sat alone in the empty lot. Further on stood the brick sign for the school, and the flagpole. Past that was Old Bradford Road and First National Bank with its electronic sign showing the temperature and the time.

I'm going to die at 10:17, she thought numbly. She stared at a man getting out of his car in the parking lot of the bank. He closed the door behind him and walked to the lobby doors. *He's making a deposit, and I'm about to die.* The knowledge slammed into her with such horrifying force, she almost collapsed. In the moment before she did, the masked man's reflection shifted in the glass.

The first impact of the hammer hit her in the crook of her shoulder, just at the base of her neck. Agonizing pain sent fiery jolts down her arm. Her vision flared white as the blow sent shockwaves through the nerves in her spine. Patricia slammed against the door, blood coughing out of her mouth and spraying the glass. One of her hands flailed, landed in the middle of the blood spray, and slid, her fingers carving grooves in the red smear as she fell.

The hammer hit her again. Her ribs crunched under the force of the attack. Spines of pain slashed through her abdomen and into her chest. Patricia drew her legs in and wrapped her arms around her torso as she struggled to draw a breath. Her throat had closed to the size of a straw, and there seemed to be a constricting belt across her chest.

Again, the jolt of the hammer came, fast and savage. Patricia felt her arm break, the pain from the injury already lost in the clouds of agony that surrounded her.

She was dead long before the masked man stopped hitting her.

CHAPTER 13

Jared removed his ball cap and ran a forearm across his brow. It came away soaked, and his forehead felt dry for a second... before more sweat beaded on it and he replaced the hat. *No point in even trying,* he thought. *This humidity, you'll never get dry.* He plucked at his uniform shirt, the sweat-soaked material peeling away and then slapping back. He'd been out here most of the day. The county guys and the coroner hadn't shown up until after lunch, and now it was closing in on four. At some point, neighbors would be coming home from work and he'd have to figure out how to deal with that.

Cross one bridge at a time, he told himself, and reached into the cooler, fished around in the half-melted ice and frigid water, and pulled out a bottle of orange Gatorade. With a quick flick of his wrist, he snapped off the cap and tilted the drink into his mouth. He didn't know which of the county boys had thought to bring the cooler, but if he'd been a different type of guy, he'd have considered kissing the man in thanks.

When he'd drained half the drink, he twisted the cap back on and set the bottle on the truck's hood. The vehicle was positioned across the street as a makeshift roadblock. Not that anyone would be getting into the small neighborhood. He had two patrol cars nose to nose over the main entrance and had pulled Wade and Deke in from their monitoring station by the mill to guard the entrance. He watched the activity at the second house he'd discovered. *The Weavers*, he thought sadly. *Good people.* County forensics guys dressed in white coveralls stood on the porch, one holding the storm door open while the other waved forward someone inside. Seconds later, two men steered a gurney out. Jared sipped more of his drink as he watched them struggle to get the rolling bed and its sizable cargo - enclosed neatly in a black rubber body bag - down the stairs.

That'd be Jerry, he thought, looking at the hulk within the bag. For a moment, Jared thought he'd feel a wave of nausea at the sight, but none came. *Guess I've gotten numb to it.* It felt odd to already be somewhat numb to such things. But, he supposed, the mind could only take so much before it started to compartmentalize and protect itself.

Still. What had been done to those people, both families, had been beyond anything he could have imagined. Sure, he'd seen crime scene pictures and studied various cases in the county academy. But those pictures had been grainy, taken in bad lighting, and had involved - mostly - gunshot wounds or stabbings. That fact didn't take away from the gruesomeness of them, but compared to his walking into those rooms in both houses, they were pictures in a child's book.

The coroner's guys managed to get Jerry down the stairs and loaded into their van. They took a few seconds' break and then trudged back into the house. *Gotta get Christine and that poor girl.* A shudder came to him when he thought about the damage those women had taken. The torn skin, the shattered bones, the exposed organs. He shook his head and tilted the bottle again, surprised to find it empty.

He walked toward the coroner's van, its rear doors open and giving a glimpse at the stacked body bags. He resisted the urge to count them. One was too many, and there'd been several already taken out of the Butlers' house. Based on what he'd seen in that bedroom, he couldn't imagine how those guys had managed to separate the bodies and get the right parts together in the same bags. *Maybe they didn't. Maybe they just piled them all together.*

He nodded a greeting to the county officer who stood nearby keeping an eye on things. The man returned the gesture with a curt nod before shifting his gaze to the surrounding homes. Jared continued to the front of the van and found William Parker sitting in the driver's seat, door open and legs dangling out. He held a thick metal clipboard in his lap and was scribbling furiously on a piece of paper. He grunted a greeting before returning his attention to the form.

Jared waited patiently until the coroner stabbed at the paper, putting a final period somewhere, and then set his pen down. The man ran a hand over his salt and pepper hair.

"What do you think?" Jared asked.

The coroner pushed his thin, gold-framed glasses up on his nose and shook his head. "That's the nastiest business I've ever seen. And I've been doing this for forty years."

"Any thoughts on the weapon?"

Parker considered the question, waggling his head side to side. "If I had to guess – and this is off the record until I can examine the bodies better, mind you – I'd guess some kind of heavy, blunt instrument."

"You mean like a sledgehammer?"

"Possible."

"Fuck."

"Yeah."

Jared thought about that for a moment. His mind tried to recreate the moments of the attack, a sledgehammer rising over the victims. If that were the case, the killer had to be massive. He would've had to swung that thing dozens of times, and quickly, too. Once the screaming had started, he would have needed to have worked fast.

"Boss!" Mark Grayson gave him a half-wave and trotted over from the Butlers' yard. Jared thanked the coroner and told him to get something to drink, pointing to the cooler in the truck before he left to meet his officer.

"What is it?"

Grayson shook the radio. "Regina asked if we need more county boys. I guess their commander was wondering."

"I don't think so. We'll hold onto the guys he's sent over as long as he can spare them, but I don't think we'll need anyone else."

Grayson's eyebrows raised. "You sure? This is a pretty bad thing. Don't you think this guy will attack more people?"

Jared shook his head as he watched William Parker fish for a drink in the cooler. Men and women came and went along the street, trudging across the yards as they went about their individual tasks. It was the single largest scene Jared had ever presided over, and as a result he felt as if he were teetering on the edge of control. *But you have to be in control,* he thought. *They're all expecting you to know all the answers.*

"I don't know what to think yet," he said. "What I do know is that we only have two crime scenes and they're very close together. This could have been a robbery that went badly; it could have been drug related. Whatever it was, we can manage the scenes ourselves."

"I'm not trying to second-guess you here," Grayson said, "but we may need more people."

Jared held up a hand, irritation at the pushback sending heat into his cheeks. "I just told you-"

"Not for this," Grayson said quickly. "Although this is going to be bad when word gets out. Don't think for a second any of these neighbors will keep quiet about this. I'm talking about the mill."

"Shit," Jared muttered. In all the confusion around the murders, he'd forgotten about the mill. When he'd called everyone in, Bill Adams had told him the news.

"That's what they wanted officers close by for," Adams had said. "In case there was a riot or something." Hearing that, Jared had felt bad about pulling Wade and Deke in, but reminded himself that a levee of two officers against the raging river of several hundred pissed-off mill workers wouldn't be worth a squirt of piss on a bonfire. Luckily, there hadn't been a riot. Yet.

"We'll deal with that if it comes to it," he told Grayson. Tell Regina we're good for now, but if that changes, I'll have her reach out and get more guys."

The slamming of doors drew their attention, and both men watched as the coroner's van - Parker now in the passenger seat - executed a careful three-point turn. The coroner gave the two men a flip of the fingers, and the cops returned the gesture. The van drove carefully around the county truck, having to pop the curb to do so, and then braked while Wade and Deke backed their cars up to let it pass.

"You already interview the people home?" Jared asked.

"Yeah. Well, just the ones on the Butlers' side. Of the eight houses, three occupants were home, but one, Mrs. Edginton, was a talker. A bit hard of hearing, too, so it took me a while to ascertain the old biddy didn't hear shit. I was about to start on the other side of the street now."

"Come on, we'll do it together."

The two angled toward the first house across the street from the Butlers' house, and had just stepped onto the lawn when Jared's radio crackled.

"Sheriff?" Regina asked.

"What is it?" he asked. There were a few seconds of silence, and he was about to press the talk button again when his radio crackled and the dispatcher's voice came out, thin and electronic.

"Gonna need you to get over to the elementary school. Quick as you can."

Jared's teeth ground together. If he was being asked to leave a major crime scene because some kid had flushed a goddamn cherry bomb down the toilet, he was going to string some people up. "I have my hands full over here."

"They're about to get a lot more full. Just got a call from Susan Wicky. She says there's two bodies in the cafeteria. Adults. Not kids."

Jared and Grayson looked at each other. Then, at the same time, said, "Shit." They ran for Jared's patrol car.

CHAPTER 14

"Don't you burn those goddamn chops!" Jackie Gallagher yelled through the screen of the kitchen window. Frank took another long pull off of his beer and shoved one of the pork chops with the meat fork, sliding it across the grates of the grill. The movement caused fat to drip onto the coals, and they responded with a flash of fire and a hungry hiss. "Goddammit, Frank, I'm warning you!"

Frank belched his response and grinned. *Just stay in the kitchen, you cow,* he thought, and used the fork to shift and turn the other chops. The sun was doing its nightly Irish exit, slipping behind the trees and leaving the rest of the world in a thinning light. The sky was what his mother used to call a 'cotton candy sky' – all bright pinks and purples, hues of blue fading to dark at the edges. He took another sip from the beer and watched the slow, lazy winking of lightning bugs. They moved along the rear of the yard, where the chain-link fence was covered in honeysuckle, but every once in a while, he'd see them come a little closer. As the night deepened, the lightning bugs found their courage and ventured farther into the open spaces.

The yard was small, the grass holding tenaciously in sparse, knobby patches. An ancient hickory tree stood in one corner, its gnarled branches twisting out and covering half the yard in shade. It killed Frank that he couldn't grow grass there; the damned tree blocked enough sun that the grass refused to do anything. But the other half of the yard did have grass, and that was fine. Of course, every year brought a battle against dandelions and clover, but what could you do?

The screen door squealed open on its rusty spring and slammed back like a gunshot. Frank scowled. He'd told Jackie ten thousand times not to let that fucking door slam shut, but the woman had a head full of concrete. He heard the slap-thwack of her flip flops beating an irregular rhythm along with her labored breathing as she came down the deck stairs.

She put the tray she'd been carrying, laden with onions and tomatoes, on the small table he kept next to the grill, and leaned over the grates to peer at the pork chops. Her eyes squinted in the dim light from the sunset - the back porch light wasn't strong enough to reach all the way down here.

"You ain't burning them, are you?" she huffed. Frank looked calmly at his wife. She wore old denim shorts made from jeans that had been cut off mid-thigh. Long white strings dangled from the legs and swayed against her thick, pale legs. Her shirt was a pink tank top that strained under the heft of her belly and large chest. Frank's gaze lingered on the mounds of her breasts. She was annoying as shit most days, but goddamn if those weren't glorious tits when they were unleashed. Jackie remained bent over, but turned her head to glare at him. "Quit staring at my tits and answer me."

Frank jabbed at the chops with his fork. "Do they look burnt to you?"

She regarded the meat again, then stood straight. "Not yet. But you keep watching me and not what you're doing, and they will be. And I ain't eating burnt pork chops. There's not enough ketchup in the world that can fix that."

Frank smiled. "What will you give me if I cook them to perfection?"

Jackie pulled a can of beer from the remains of the six-pack on the table, popped the tab, and held the can, dripping with condensation, in front of her mouth. "I won't jam that meat fork up your ass. How about that?"

"How're the beans coming?" he asked.

"Beans are fine. You worry about the meat. I-"

Beyond the fence, headlights swept across the bushes at the end of their driveway. The crunch of tires on gravel came next, drowned quickly by the grumble of an engine and the soft knocking of something under the hood that needed repair. Frank averted his eyes until the headlights cut out, and then exchanged a look with Jackie.

"Fucking Geordie?" she asked.

"Yes. He and a few others are coming over. We have things to talk about." He gave her a knowing look. She was just as mad about the announcement of the mill closing as he'd been - more, possibly, since she was only bringing in what money she could earn on the weekends by selling her homemade dream catchers and other weird crafty shit at the farmer's market in Birmingham. She watched the figures climbing out of the car before looking back to Frank.

"They ain't eating supper."

"Just beers. Why don't you go fetch some? There's a couple of six-packs in the garage fridge." Jackie stomped off, her flip-flops providing the soundtrack of her departure as the gate hinges squeaked - he really did need to oil some things around here - and Geordie Dupont entered, followed by four others. Frank tossed the onions and tomatoes on the grates, arranging the chops to make room.

"Hey," Geordie said. He held up a six-pack of Coors by way of a wave. The other people – dark shapes at first, but becoming clearer as they approached – fanned out and threw up their own hands and personal beer offerings. Frank waved his meat fork at them and prodded the chops again, causing another flare-up. The group huddled around the grill, all watching it as intently as if it were the Super Bowl.

Frank looked at those who Geordie had brought. "Jimmy," he said, "almost didn't see you there till you smiled."

The Black man grinned wide. "Fuck you, Frank." Everyone chuckled, and Jimmy cracked open a beer. The others, Frank knew fairly well; Billy Reynolds worked the dye room, Chuck Bennett worked in the blow room, and Linda Cooper was a weaver. All of them had been in the group yesterday morning for the announcement, and none expected to be invited to stay on through the transition.

Jackie returned and slapped two sixers of Budweiser on the ground next to the table. She grumbled a greeting to the new arrivals, and then looked at Linda. "You want to help me in the kitchen?" she asked the other woman.

Linda, a stick of a woman with a thicket of curly hair, shook her head. "Nope. If it's all the same to you, I'm going to stay out here and chat with the boys for a bit." Jackie blinked in surprise at the answer, but nodded.

"Suit yourself." To Frank, she asked, "How much longer?"

"They'll be ready in ten minutes. Maybe less." Jackie retreated to the house, mumbling about the meat being burnt. Frank finished his beer, crushed the can, and tossed it into the yard. He pulled a fresh one from one of the packs Jackie had delivered and opened it. Looking at those gathered, he asked, "How are all y'all holding up?" There was a chorus of mumbled responses.

"Let's dispense with the touchy-feely shit," Linda said as she bent her head to a plastic lighter. The small flame turned her face into a garish clown mask, which disappeared and left the cherry of her Virginia Slim glowing bright. "What are we going to do about it?" There were a few mumbles of agreement.

"What do you suggest?" Frank asked.

"Personally," Linda said as she thumbed the ashes from her cigarette, "I want to go over to Vandermark's house and drag him out by his short-and-curlies. Beat his ass black and blue with an ax handle." That got more mumbles of support, but Frank noticed that Chuck was quiet.

Frank raised the hand with his beer and pointed his index finger at Chuck. "You're pretty quiet. Do you not think doing a tune-up on Vandermark in his front yard is a good idea?"

Chuck seemed to chew on it for a long minute, the short stubble on his cheeks and chin shifting as his jaw moved. Despite the warmth, he shoved his hands deep in the pockets of his jeans. After a moment, he shook his head. "No, I don't. Don't get me wrong, I'd like to put my fist in that man's face, but mostly because he fucked me out of some overtime pay a couple months back. I don't reckon he had anything to do with this decision, other than having to be the poor son of a bitch to tell all of us. I mean, he's going to be just as much out of a job as the rest of us. Only, he gets to hold on to his for a few weeks longer."

"It's going to kill this town," Jimmy said. "I mean, it's really going to be the end of the town. What are any of us supposed to do? My wife works part-time in the craft store. It's not like we can live on her paycheck. She told me that this afternoon there were at least ten people from the mill who came in and asked for work. I'm talking people like David Cooley and Jasper Townbridge. Can you imagine those guys working in a damned craft store?"

There were a few soft chuckles at the thought. Geordie said, "Something has to be done. They're fucking with our lives here. Jimmy's right. The whole town's gonna die now that the mill's closed. It's a question of how long, you know?"

Frank stared at the pork chops. They were on the cusp of burning, and a small part of him wanted to let them slip over that edge; just stand here and watch them turn to hockey pucks. See how Jackie liked that. Instead, he transferred them and the vegetables to a paper plate he had waiting for just that purpose. Holding the plate, he said to the others, "Y'all come on in. We can talk while I eat." He took the plate through the sliding glass door and into the kitchen, thick with the smell of green beans simmering in onions and pork fat. Jackie sat at the glass octagonal kitchen table, a glass of sweet tea on the wicker placemat in front of her. When he entered with the others in tow, she looked up from the pages of *Omni*.

"If you ask me if I burnt them," Frank said before she could open her mouth, "I'll throw them in the trash."

Jackie scowled at him before turning the dark look on the others. "Are they eating too?"

Frank dropped the plate onto the counter to the right of the stove. "I told you, they're just here for a couple of beers and to talk. You want beans?" He fixed the plates, set one in front of his wife, and then took a seat, his back to the bay window that overlooked the deck. Linda and Jimmy took the other two chairs while Chuck and Geordie leaned against the counter. Frank cut a piece, chewed, and looked at the others. "Well, I agree that we can't just sit on our asses and let this happen."

"Damn right," Jackie chirped. "I told you, you should go down there-" She stopped talking when Frank swung his heavy gaze toward her.

He stared for a long second. "And I also agree that putting an ax handle to Alex Vandermark isn't the way to do it. Chuck's right. He's no better off than the rest of us. He just got his execution stayed for a few more weeks, is all."

"Then, what?" Geordie asked. He leaned against the edge of the counter, his feet crossed at his ankles and his arms folded over his scrawny chest.

Frank took his time, eating more of his meal and savoring the moment. Finally, he said, "How much do you think they'll be able to sell that equipment for? All the dryers, the bleachers, the dye vats? All that stuff."

The others were quiet as they thought. Finally, Bill said, "A shit-load, I guess. I ain't no math teacher, but I figure there's several hundred thousand dollars' worth of machinery in there. And if they're selling it overseas to the Chinese or something, they'll probably jack the asking price up."

Frank leaned back in his chair. "I'm thinking you're right. Could be as much as a few million, truth be told. Hell, some of those sewing machines are brand new, bought just within the last year. Now, let me ask you this: How much of a kick in the balls would it be if that equipment was ruined?" He smiled as he felt the shift in the air within the kitchen as the others took in what he was saying. Three of the others visibly stiffened. Linda breathed a disbelieving laugh. "What's so funny?" he asked her.

"What are you proposing? We go in there with hammers and beat all the equipment to shit? You know how long that would take? How much noise it would make? Hell, they have security there."

Geordie sniffed. "Wade and that shitbag Harold aren't worth a squirt of piss, but Brad could be a problem. Still, they spend all their time in the office. How often do you think they actually walk the floor?"

"Before today, never," Jimmy said. "There was always a shift running so they couldn't, or had no need to. But now that the mill is closed?" He put his face into a *who knows* expression. "Once the fellas doing inventory cut out for the day, maybe once or twice at night? I can't imagine they'd do any more than that. They'd patrol the perimeter first; make sure nobody was trying to sneak in. Kids and shit, you know?"

Geordie's thin fingers snapped, and he pointed at Jimmy. "Exactly. If we slip in on the other side of the building, we can get in, fuck up some equipment on two or three, and be gone before either of those assholes figures out what's going on." There were a few nods of agreement, and Frank could see that the others were warming to the idea. Even Jackie had an expression of agreement.

"But what good does that do?" Frank asked, and couldn't help but smile when all four – five, including Jackie – looked at him like he were a simpleton.

"The fuck you mean?" Geordie asked.

"Let's say you do that. Let's say you slip in, take some hammers, and bust up a few of the looms, some of the winders, and hell, maybe even the pickers. You bust them to hell and get out of there. What good will you have done?"

Geordie puffed out his chest. "We'd be sending a message to them that they can't fuck us over and expect to get away with it."

Frank nodded sagely. "Sure, and they'd miss out on probably fifty, sixty grand on the resale of those machines. But they'd still make money on all the rest." There were no contradictions or challenges to that last point, and he pressed forward. "But we want to hurt them like they've hurt us. We'll get our last checks in a week or two in the mail. But those pricks will get a payout a thousand times more than ours when they sell off all that equipment. And they'll keep making money off the other mills they have around the country, assuming they're keeping some open, which I'm betting they are."

"What are you saying?" Jackie asked, fully invested in the conversation. Her plate was pushed aside, the meal forgotten.

"I'm saying we take it *all* from them. Make sure they don't earn a penny more on the place we put our lives into...that our families put their lives into going back generations. They're killing our town, so we'll hit back just as hard."

"How?" Linda asked.

"We burn the whole fucking thing down."

"Come on, you dweeb," Alicia said. "I know you're faking."

One of the boy's eyes peeled open, his mouth splitting into a wide grin. "How'd you know?"

Alicia stood up with her hands on her hips. "I've been your babysitter for three years. You think I don't know when you're faking being asleep and really watching tv through your eyelashes?" Russell laughed, and Alicia flapped her hand in a *come here* gesture. "Come on. We need to get you home." A burst of laughter erupted from the dining room, and both kids looked in that direction. The sound made Alicia smile. For most of the afternoon and early part of the evening, the mood in the house among the adults had oscillated between somber and a fearful buzzing of energy. All but two of the adults worked in the mill. *Worked*, as in past tense. The news of the closure had swept through Elden Mills like a brush fire, and even a teenager like Alicia knew that it meant only one thing: trouble.

Since the gathering had started, the men and women had grumbled and cursed – clearly trying to keep their voices low for the sake of the kids, but as more and more beer had been consumed, failing at even that. But, a couple of hours ago, something had shifted. She'd heard her dad start making jokes, the curse-laden worrying by the others breaking apart occasionally and falling into uneasy chuckles.

He'd persisted and, within a few minutes, had gotten everyone laughing, the demon of the mill closure banished at least temporarily.

From where Alicia stood, only half of her mother's back was visible around the open doorway. She looked past her mother to Roderick Shance, Russell's dad. The man was big, sporting a thick mustache that curled down around the edges of his mouth. He wore tinted glasses under his mop of black hair and was saying something to her father - Alicia assumed it was her dad he spoke to anyway, though she couldn't see - about horny goats and priests. Roderick took a long pull off his Michelob and delivered a punchline that was drowned out by the adults' laughter.

"Why do we have to go?" Russell asked, not moving from the large brown sofa.

Alicia looked back down at the seven-year-old. "Because your parents asked me to get you home. Come on." Russell groaned, but he got to his feet. She helped him find his shoes and his soccer ball. Then, he had to watch to see what Bo and Luke Duke would do before the commercial break. Finally, he insisted on telling his parents goodnight. Alicia stood in the living room and rolled her eyes with every delay tactic the boy employed. The longer it took her to get the little weasel back to his own house and into bed, the longer it was going to be before she could call Crystal. There was a rumor going around that a party was happening tomorrow night, and she needed to know where. It was supposed to be for seniors only, but Alicia didn't care. And if she undid a couple of buttons on her shirt, neither would the seniors. Crystal's older brother was going to be a senior, so he'd know the location.

The adults' tones changed as Russell shuffled into the room and slipped his arms around his mother. She laughed at some other comment, one of her arms automatically encircling her son. Then she spoke to him, and he smiled before kissing her on the cheek and peeling away to hug his father. Alicia's view of Roderick was blocked by her mother, who leaned around the corner.

"You okay with getting him home?" she asked. Alicia nodded. "Good. Tuck him in and come straight back. No-" she pointed a finger quickly to cut off what Alicia had opened her mouth to say, "detours! I know how long it takes to walk there and get back. You can see your friends tomorrow."

Alicia groaned, but mostly for show. "Fine." She wouldn't be able to get Crystal out of the house anyway, so spending the night on her bed with the phone in her hand was preferable. Her mom smiled again and withdrew. Russell emerged from the kitchen and, for a brief moment from the corner of her eye, Alicia saw his father looking at her. She raised her gaze to meet his, but he was already distracted by the new cards he'd been dealt.

"Okay," Russell said. "Let's go."

Despite the night having cooled slightly, a light blanket of heat and humidity pressed against them as they started along the sidewalk. From Alicia's to the Shances' house was a twenty-minute walk. The first blocks passed quietly, neither Alicia or Russell having anything to say. After a few minutes, Russell let his soccer ball drop to the ground and began batting it about from foot to foot. He would kick it ahead several feet, trot after it, tap it back and forth, and then repeat the move.

Alicia smiled despite herself. The kid was getting better. The hours he'd spent in his driveway kicking the ball against the garage door were paying off. As she thought that, however, the ball ricocheted off his foot and spun in tight spirals out into the street. Russell ran out after it, scooped it up, and turned to her, smiling.

"I meant to do that," he said with a grin.

"Sure, you did. You were showing off and stopped paying attention."

Russell frowned. "Showing off? To who?"

Alicia raised her eyebrows knowingly, and Russell winced and stuck his tongue out. "You? Grody."

"Grody? Really? Don't lie, squirt. We all know you have a crush on me."

"I'd rather kiss Jabba the Hutt."

Wow, Alice thought. He was just a kid, and could be hella annoying, but that stung a little. "That's a shitty thing to say." She sped up her pace and left him behind, ball tucked under one of his arms, watching her from the street. "You can just stay in the street and get run over, for all I care," she said over her shoulder. A second later, she heard the slapping of his shoes as he ran to catch up.

He shuffled next to her for half a block before finally saying in a soft voice, "Sorry."

"You shouldn't say things like that to girls," she told him. "You'll never get one to like you if you do."

"Girls are gross," he said, and she could hear the smile in his voice.

"You won't always feel that way. Trust me." They continued on, walking into the wide cones of light thrown by the streetlamps, and then enduring the longer stretches of darkness. Houses around them sat quiet, most with porch lights on, and many with the interior lights or the shifting blues and whites of television screens strobing the front windows. Occasionally, a dog would start barking its territorial warnings from behind a chain-link fence, and Russell would call out to the dog, taunting the animal until they were past.

When they turned the corner onto Briarwood Circle, Russell began dribbling the ball again. The houses on Briarwood were largely on the left side of the street. The other side held the patch of woods that people in town - for reasons lost to her - called the Veil. Alicia looked into the inky expanse beyond the front row of pine trees and wondered if that was where the party tomorrow night would be. That would make sense since high schoolers often used it as a place to drink and toke up. There was a natural rock field about a quarter-mile in, with large, bone-white boulders jutting out of the dirt like the exposed skeletons of some long dead behemoth, where most of those gatherings took place. She and Crystal had been there once during the day, and despite the litter from the most recent party and occasional spray-painted words or images - usually dicks and pentagrams - both had found themselves genuinely creeped out. She was sure it was different in the middle of the night with a bonfire raging, music blaring, and people dancing or making out, but during the day, it had been eerily quiet, and she was certain-

A face stared at her from between two trees.

Alicia took a few more steps before her body caught up to the shock that her brain had registered. The face was ghostly pale and almost invisible, but as she squinted, it was most definitely there. She blinked. Or was it? There was a bit of a moon overhead, but Briarwood had fewer streetlights on it, being on the extreme northern end of town, and she was still a few dozen yards from the closest lamp. As such, the face was no more than a faint smudge against the gloom.

"You okay?" Russell asked. He was several yards ahead, his soccer ball ignored on the sidewalk. Alicia nodded, her attention fixed on where she'd seen the face.

"What the fuck?" she whispered. She blinked again, and gave her head a light shake. There was nothing in the space now – only the quiet, sentinel trees. *Jesus, you have got to get a grip.*

"Alicia?"

"Yeah, sorry. Thought I saw a raccoon." Russell shrugged and ran to kick his ball. Alicia gave the patch of woods another glance before following him. They passed through the next puddle of ice-blue light, and she glanced back at the trees across the street.

The face was back, and clearly visible. It was a pale mask, with deep, uneven holes for eyes that hovered above a ghastly, jagged black slash of a mouth. A cold spike of fear lanced through Alicia's chest, and she jerked to a stop. *Who the fuck is that?* She started to call out, hoping that it was someone she knew – possibly Michael, Crystal's brother, or one of the other seniors. The sound of Russell kicking his ball and humming the *Thundercats* theme song froze her voice. The last thing she wanted to do was scare him.

She forced herself to turn and continue along the sidewalk, hurrying to catch up. As she walked, her Keds making soft whispers on the cracked sidewalk, it took everything she had not to constantly look across the street. Whoever was wearing that mask was only trying to get a rise out of her, and she'd be damned if she was going to let him.

The trees of the Veil began to thin after another block, giving way to an open field of knee-high grass. The meadow shifted and undulated as a light wind swirled across it. Alicia allowed herself to look back at the woods, but the pale mask was gone. She let out a long breath of relief.

They reached the next street, which boasted houses on both sides - although many of these homes were older and much worse for wear. Many featured peeling paint and a large amount of trash in the thick, weed-choked yards. The old, rotting oval of a tire swing hung listlessly from the branches of a pecan tree in front of one house that had what looked like tarps mounted on the insides of windows that had lost their glass some time ago. Cars sat in cracked driveways covered in acorns or pinecones. Some of the vehicles were mounted on blocks. One old pickup truck had its hood up, with hoses and other parts of the engine dangling over its fenders like dark entrails.

At the far end of the street the yellow porch light of Russell's house glowed. His parents had installed the special lights on the exterior because they'd read somewhere that yellow bulbs wouldn't attract moths. Alicia didn't know about that, but she did know that they looked ridiculous compared to the other houses around them. With their destination now in sight, she increased her pace. Russell danced in front of her, kicking his ball into the street and ahead. She could hear him narrating his actions, pretending he was cutting through defenders and closing in on the goal. He darted left, cut back to his right, and gave the ball a kick that, on the field, would have been really impressive. But in the darkness of Briarwood Circle, the ball rocketed forward, hit the metal post of a mailbox, and ricocheted across a yard. The ball spun and bounced off of the concrete driveway, and vanished into the darkness between houses. Russell stood in the middle of the street, hands by his sides, and stared after it.

"Looks like the goalie blocked your shot," Alicia teased him.

Russell just stared at the patch of shadows between houses.

"Hey, Pelé, you wanna go get your ball?" she asked. "We're almost home."

Russell shook his head. "That's Mr. Dupont's house. He doesn't like people in his yard."

Alicia frowned. "So, what, you're not going to get your ball?"

Russell shrugged. "Geordie Dupont isn't going to shoot you for going up there and getting it. Look, the lights are out in the house. I bet he's not even home. He's probably at the Lantern Lounge getting drunk and playing darts." She gave his shoulder a gentle shove. "Go on."

The boy didn't move. He said, in a very small voice that suddenly reminded Alicia that he was only seven, "I'm scared. Will you get it?"

Alicia thought briefly of the face she'd seen in the woods, but dismissed it. That had most likely been some loser from school and his buddies, just playing in the woods and deciding to prank her. They wouldn't carry that shit to where houses were, where people could see them. She glanced at her watch. If she wanted to get back before her mother started to worry, they needed to hurry up. She groaned and said, "Fine. I'll get it. But you owe me, you little dweeb."

Her feet crunched over acorn shells as she crossed the driveway. Pinecones skittered away like cockroaches as her shoes kicked them. She stuffed her hands in her pockets and tried to ignore the dilapidated house. She didn't like being in someone else's yard like this – it felt like an invasion, and her skin prickled in response. *Just get the ball and get out.* She reached the edge of the driveway, the cement ending where mangy grass started, leading all the way to the backyard. There was no fence, and she cursed at that. A fence would have stopped the ball from rolling.

The backyard was a pitch-black expanse, lit only by feeble moonlight that filtered down through the branches of a couple of large pines. But it was enough for her to make out the small, pale lump of Russell's ball sitting near the base of one of the trees. Alicia gave the house another wary glance and hurried across the yard, where she bent and retrieved the ball. She spun on her toes and took a single step before a loud crunch froze her. She stood with the ball clutched to her chest, heart hammering in her throat as she waited for the sound again. Had it been behind her? Or had it been in front of her? Had Russell finally gotten over his fear and come to help look for the ball?

Or was it the jerk with the mask?

The sound came again, this time slower – softer – as if the person making it had realized their first step had been too loud and was now taking care to proceed more cautiously. The noise wasn't behind her or ahead of her. It was, in fact, just on the other side of the massive pine tree next to her.

"Fuck this," she said and pushed off her back foot, starting to sprint.

The moonlight reflected off the thing that swung toward her. In the heartbeat before impact, Alicia could see that it was a long spike on the rear of what looked like a hammer. Then, it slammed into her eye, and her world exploded into brilliant white pain as her head jolted back. Her feet left the ground and she felt herself falling, enveloped by pain. She never felt herself land.

CHAPTER 16

Alicia had been gone for a long time, and Russell was starting to get worried. It was bad enough that she'd gone to get the ball and not come back yet - that could mean the ball was lost, or down in a ditch or something - but he'd been left all alone on the dark street in front of Mr. Dupont's house. What if Mr. Dupont had seen Alicia in his backyard and done something to her? He wasn't a big man, but - as Russell's dad said - what he lacked in size, he made up for in *crazy assholery*. His father's description brought a soft laugh bubbling up, and for a split second, Russell forgot where he was. It felt good to think those words. He'd never say them, though. Not out loud. Unless maybe he was hanging out in the Veil with Tommy, his best friend.

He opened his mouth to call out to Alicia, but stopped, his eyes drifting over and locking onto the dark edifice of Dupont's house. If the crazy asshole was in there, the last thing Russell wanted was to wake him up. But Alicia had said he was probably down at the bar drinking beers and playing darts. Despite her not really knowing a lot about *Star Wars*, Alicia was pretty smart.

But she'd still not come back.

Along the street, the houses loomed dark and silent, like toads watching his every move. From far away came the hooting of a train on the tracks outside of town. A block and a half away, the sight of his front porch pulled at him, promising safety. He really wanted to go home – to be inside his own house, to get into his own bed. If Alicia would hurry up, Russell wouldn't even stay up to watch scary movies on television. And that was a promise.

You're going to have to go help her.

He cringed at the thought, but knew that it was true. Alicia was older and bigger, but she was still a girl. The fact that she hadn't come back with his ball after all this time meant she probably needed his help. Without thinking, Russell crossed the street and walked along the acorn-littered driveway. His shoes scuffed on the cement, the acorn shells popped like firecrackers under his soles, and he looked at the dark mass of the house after every one.

When he reached the end of the driveway, feeling the uneven edge of the pavement beneath his shoes, he stopped and whispered, "Alicia?"

He squinted into the darkness, leaning left and then right as he tried to find her in the night-shrouded yard. A few feet away loomed a massive tree, its branches spread out like the arms of a horrible monster.

"Alicia? Are you back there? Did you find it?"

The only response was the final, fading blat of the train horn.

Something moved. A gentle scrape somewhere ahead, near the closer tree. Russell tensed. It could be Alicia trying to scare him, but it could also be Mr. Dupont sneaking across the grass, coming to deal with the annoying kid who'd dared come onto his property.

There was a soft, airy thump, and his soccer ball came rolling out of the darkness. It bounced gently over the uneven ground and came to a stop about two feet away. He stared at it, the simple black and white pattern, and then out into the yard. "Very funny," he whispered, "but that didn't scare me. Come on, I want to get home." He waited several seconds longer, and then he shrugged. He had his ball back, and if Alicia wanted to play games, he wasn't going to participate. He was tired and scared, and he would go home alone if he had to. "Fine. If that's how you want to be. I'm going home." He stepped forward, picked up his ball, and turned to leave. "Bye," he said, a little louder this time, hoping to force his babysitter to stop playing and come out of hiding. When she didn't, he continued walking toward the street.

His hands rotated the ball over and over again, a subconscious movement that he did a lot when carrying a ball. But the movements stopped when his left hand touched something wet and sticky. *Oh, grody, is that poop?* A dark smear covered his fingers. *Oh gag, it is poop!* He bent and wiped his hand across the grass.

In the moonlight, the smear on the ball didn't look like dog poop. And Mr. Dupont didn't have a dog. The only dog on the whole street was Dottie, the annoying Lhasa Apso that belonged to Mrs. Kleinman. And she never let that stupid thing out of the yard. He held the ball closer, sniffed the smear, and recoiled. It wasn't poop. It reminded him of the time he and Tommy had found a dead possum, its body torn open under some pine needles in the Veil.

This was blood.

Russell spun around and stared into the backyard. His entire chest hummed with the force of his heartbeat. Was Alicia hurt? He rushed forward several steps before stopping. *Wait. This could just be a big prank.* She could have found a dead squirrel or something, rubbed his ball in its guts, and tossed it back out to him. And now she was watching, waiting for him to come back into the yard so that she could throw the dead animal on him.

Well, she wasn't going to get the chance. He walked up the driveway and, when it ended, he crouched low and angled to the left. He was going to sneak up on her and scare her first. He could picture her hiding behind the big tree, a dead squirrel held by the tail in one hand, waiting for him. But when he popped up behind her, she'd scream and drop the animal all over herself. Then she'd have to walk home smelling like a dead squirrel!

The image made him grin. This was going to be great.

His path took him into the neighbor's yard, where he picked his way carefully through some flower bushes, their scents a heavy perfume in the summer air. He broke free of them and saw he was only about ten feet from the tree. From where he stood, he couldn't see Alicia, but felt certain she was on the other side of the trunk. He tiptoed quickly across the space and placed one hand on the tree. He took a breath, fighting down giggles, and jumped around the back side of the tree.

"Gotcha!" he started to yell, but then his feet tangled on a root and he went down hard and fast, his ball flying from his hands. Russell rolled over, grimacing at the pain in his knee and ribs. He put his hands on the root to steady himself as he gathered himself to stand. The root shifted beneath his grip, and instead of hard wood, his fingers closed around softness and denim.

The yard brightened slowly as the moon emerged from behind a cloud, and Russell's scream died in his throat. Alicia sat at the base of the tree, her back to the trunk. Half of her face was covered in blood, the other side a mass of bent and pulpy meat. One of her eyes was nothing but a huge, black hole. The other eye stared at him, as if pleading for him to help. Russell scrambled back, crawling through the dirt to put distance between him and the dead girl, his breath coming in short, vocal grunts.

Something stopped his backward progress, and he looked up into a nightmare. A man stood over him. But his face was wrong. It was pale white with a horribly ragged mouth and two deep, black eyes. Russell found his voice then, fully, and let out a scream. He didn't care if he woke the neighbors anymore. The masked man just stared at him while Russell scrambled to his feet. As soon as his shoes were firmly planted on the ground, Russell began running. He'd never been the fastest in his class, but he wasn't the slowest, either. He sprinted for the driveway and the street.

Something heavy and hard slammed into his back, and he went sprawling forward. Pain seared across his palms and cheek as he hit the driveway and slid. Suddenly, it was hard to breathe. He could pull in air, but only a little, as if he were trying to breathe through a very small straw. Russell lay face down on the cement, acorns and pinecones digging into him, and fought to breathe while his heart pounded.

Footsteps approached from behind. Russell's fingers clutched at the ground, his mind screaming for him to get up, to get up and run! *Get home!* But he found his body unwilling to move. The footsteps stopped, and he could feel the presence of the masked man standing over him again. He heard soft, rhythmic breathing that seemed to go on forever. Russell squeezed his eyes shut and begged the man to go away, to leave him alone. He wanted to go home and get in bed.

A heavy boot slid under his ribs and lifted. Russell rolled over. The masked face stared at him, head cocked slightly to one side. Then, the man bent and picked something up. It made a harsh, metallic grating as it was lifted.

That's what he threw at me, Russell thought.

He watched the man raise the large hammer with a wicked spike on the back side. Then, with no sound of effort at all, the man brought the hammer down on the side of Russell Shance's head.

SATURDAY, JUNE 6, 1987

CHAPTER 17

The instant Jared stepped out of his patrol car, the humidity of the morning slammed into him and pulled a gasp from his throat. *Feels like I'm walking through soup.* He swiped a hand over his face, closed the door, and started toward the steps of the station. He pressed his lips together in an attempt to stifle the yawn that tried to claw its way out. *Should have just slept in my office,* he thought. The day before had been one of, if not *the* busiest, in his career.

The majority of the day had been spent traveling back and forth between the houses on North Wind Drive and the elementary school. Between handling initial paperwork, taking a call from a distraught Brother Camden - the man being so close to tears that his offer of help and prayers had barely made it through the phone - and a visit from an equally distraught Mayor Simmons, Jared hadn't made it home until well after midnight.

In the kitchen, Leigh had left the light over the stove on for him. He'd found a plate of leftovers - fried chicken, turnip greens, and mashed potatoes - sitting under plastic wrap in the fridge. A hand-written note on the small dining table had told him, in his wife's flowery script, that she'd waited up as long as she could, but had to go to bed eventually. She loved him, hoped he enjoyed the meal, and would see him in the morning. Jared had read the note twice as he sat down and began picking at the cold food, opting not to risk waking Leigh by using the microwave. To further avoid disturbing her, he'd slept on the couch in his uniform after digging the small travel alarm clock out of a basket in the hall closet.

This morning, he'd left her a note of his own, written in his slanted, thin lettering. He'd thanked her for the food and told her that he had to go in early. Now, as he reached for the handle of the station doors, his stomach growled, and he wished once more that he'd had time for at least coffee before leaving. He'd have to make do with the oily sludge that presented itself as station coffee.

Through the glass and across the small lobby, he could see Regina looking at him from over her desktop. She offered a weary smile and wave. Jared returned the gesture, but a voice stopped him.

"Sheriff Hollister?" Three men and a woman stood in a loose cluster on the sidewalk next to the bottom step. Two of the men wore jeans and t-shirts with the University of Alabama logo on them, and the third sported dark blue sweats and a shirt with an image of a sailboat across the chest. The woman wore light jeans and a pastel pink top. Jared's coffee- and sleep-deprived brain struggled to identify them. He knew he'd seen them before, and had probably even spoken to them on a few occasions, but their names were blank spaces in his mind.

"Yes?"

The man with the sailboat shirt took a step forward. "We're wondering what's going on. We've heard about the deaths at the school, and then Eric here—" he inclined his head toward one of the other men, whose own head bobbed in acknowledgement, "said that some people were killed out on North Wind Drive."

Jared looked at all of them in turn. Finally, he nodded. "We've had some incidents that we're investigating."

"Incidents?" the woman asked. The question had come out as a disbelieving bark. "One of our teachers was killed in the school. I'd call that more than an incident."

I don't have time for this shit. He forced himself to temper his response, though. He was the sheriff and they were clearly nervous. It was understandable, considering the peaceful history of their town. "Don't misunderstand me," he said. "We're taking these matters seriously. I have officers from the county assisting."

"When do you expect to have an arrest made?" Sailboat asked.

"We're working all avenues of investigation. Now, if you'll excuse me-"

"No, we fucking won't!" one of the Alabama shirt men said as he took a step closer. "People have been killed. The mill is closed down. You giving us that bureaucratic bullshit line of 'all avenues' isn't going to cut it. We pay our taxes, and we expect you to keep us all safe." There were slightly less than enthusiastic mumbles of agreement from his compatriots.

"As I said, we have extra officers in town and should have a few more arriving later today. You'll see an increase in patrol cars on the streets as we conduct our investigation and work to make sure that everyone else is safe. We'll find who did this. I promise you that."

As he spoke, Jared noticed a handful of people down the street take notice of the gathering and begin to drift closer. *Christ*, he thought, *this is going to turn into a press conference.* The newcomers arrived just as the original four began demanding to know exactly what was being done, what these 'avenues of investigation' were, and how they could know for a fact that their families were safe. It didn't take long for the new additions to begin lobbing their own concerns at him. Theories of the culprits being satanists were among the more common comments Jared heard, followed by someone angered by the closing of the mill, which was actually a theory Jared had been considering. He even caught one person positing that it was those 'goddamn Libyans come over here to kill us hardworking Americans in retaliation.'

Behind him, the station doors squeaked open, and he heard BB ask, "You good, boss?"

"Yeah," Jared shot over his shoulder. He then spread his arms as if he were a preacher holding revival in a canvas tent thrown up in a cow pasture outside of town. "Look!" he shouted – by now, the crowd had grown to close to twenty people, all of whom were talking to and over each other, several shouting questions or theories at him. "I assure you we're doing everything we can. You don't need to panic. You don't need to worry about the safety of your families. We expect to-"

The screeching of tires on pavement cut into his words, and Jared caught movement down the street to the left. A white car fishtailed as it took the corner, wheels squealing as it fought to gain traction. The engine screamed as the driver hit the gas and the car rocketed forward. Someone in the group on the sidewalk made a comment that garnered a few nervous laughs. Everyone turned to watch the car, eager to see what the driver would do.

"Jesus, he's going to kill someone if he's not careful," BB said. Jared watched the car speed along the avenue, getting closer. The driver wasn't clear behind the sun-dappled windshield. The vehicle rocked back and forth as whoever steered it worked the wheel. For a moment, Jared thought maybe it was a kid – some youngster who'd stolen the car for a joyride.

The car's tires wailed again as the operator spun the wheel, angling it toward the police station. Screams exploded out of the crowd at the base of the stairs as people pulled back and tried to scatter clear of what looked like someone intent on ramming into the building. Instinctively, Jared started down the stairs, reaching to pull people out of the way. The car hit the curb at an angle and stopped with a loud thump, one tire on the sidewalk. Jared thumbed off the strap to his holster, his hand firmly on the butt of the weapon. Inside the car, the driver reached over and fumbled with something in the passenger seat.

The people who had gathered to voice their concerns to Jared now pressed close, eager to see what would happen. From the corner of his eye Jared saw one of the men wearing an Alabama shirt stumble as those behind him pressed forward. The crowd buzzed with questions and assumptions.

A large man wearing faded jeans and a blue t-shirt with some yellow logo across the chest got out of the car. His movements were off balance and awkward as he struggled to hold something. Above a thick, drooping mustache, two bloodshot eyes stared at Jared as he shut the door with the flick of a meaty arm. As soon as the door closed, his hand went back to supporting the thing he cradled to his chest – a large shape draped in a colorfully patterned quilt. Jared noticed a single red shoe, a child's sneaker, dangling from beneath one edge of the quilt.

Two others, a man and a woman, climbed out of the back seat of the car. They held each other as if to keep themselves from falling down, their faces flushed and streaked with tears. They staggered close behind the man carrying the quilt.

More questions and exclamations flew from the crowd as the man pushed his way toward the steps. He mounted the bottom one, and that's where his legs seemed to give out. Slipping to his knees, he stared up at Jared. "My boy," he managed, letting the quilt-wrapped thing slip down to the next stair.

Jared felt BB's hand on his shoulder, a caution against a possible threat, but Jared shrugged it off. The man stared at him, and Jared recognized the look of shock. "What's happened?" Jared asked.

At the question, the distant look vanished, and the man's face turned into a snarling mask. "My fucking son, you son of a bitch! He killed my boy! And where were you?"

"Our daughter, too! Our Alicia is dead!" The woman who had gotten out of the same car growled, "She's sitting against a tree with... half...half...." The words broke apart like eggshells on the pavement. The woman collapsed, crying. The other man - her husband, Jared guessed - clutched her against him while he stared daggers up the stairs at the sheriff.

Distantly, like it was background noise in a crowded mall, Jared heard the questions from the onlookers. He ignored them and reached for the quilt. Questions became screams, and Jared had to throw a hand out for balance as he felt the ground beneath him tilt. From beneath the blanket, the bleeding and broken remains of Russell Shance's head peered out at him.

CHAPTER 18

Morgan dreamt she floated above the clouds, higher than even birds dared fly. Freely she twisted and turned, doing aerial acrobatics thousands of feet over the patchwork of farms and homes divided by the small gray lines of roads.

As she soared, a series of soft knocks reverberated through the sky. Morgan turned away, her floating body racing higher and punching through a dark rain cloud. The knocks came again, and in the dream, she plummeted suddenly, her stomach lurching as gravity gripped her and ripped her to the earth. Morgan opened her eyes with a soft gasp, the sound muffled by the pillow.

The door opened, and her father's head poked in. "Oh, good, you're up. I was starting to wonder if you were going to sleep all day." Morgan rolled over, felt uncomfortable wetness on her cheek, and wiped it away with the sleeve of her sweatshirt. *Gross. Drooled on myself.*

"What if I did?" she grumbled.

Her father smiled. "I forgot how little of a morning person you are. Guess some things people never grow out of. I've got to take your mother to a hair appointment, so we'll be gone most of the day. We'll get lunch afterwards; maybe go to the botanical gardens if it's not too hot. We should be back late this afternoon. I'm going to cook steaks for dinner. Potatoes, broccoli, the works."

"Cool." There was a moment of quiet, and she could feel her father hesitating, waiting for something more.

Finally, he said, "Well, there's stuff in the fridge. You know where everything is. Love you, hon." Morgan nodded the sentiment back and rubbed her eyes. When she looked again, her father was gone, but the door remained open. She rolled her eyes. That was his M.O., to wake you up and then leave the door open so that any noise outside would keep you from going back to sleep. Subtle dad code for *'You've slept long enough, so get your ass up.'*

She remained in the comfortable tangle of sheets a bit longer, though, thinking about the day before. It had been so much better than she'd anticipated. Despite the news of the mill closing, her father had thrown them all in the family car, and they'd driven to Birmingham and gone to the new Galleria Mall. The mall had been larger than Morgan could have imagined, all gleaming floors and shining glass fronting the dozens upon dozens of stores. Even on a Friday, there'd been people everywhere. Afterwards, they'd eaten dinner at the Sizzler – something her mother had protested due to the cost, but which her father had waved off, repeating his insistence on celebrating Morgan's homecoming.

She'd not expected the reaction she'd gotten from her family. It was hard to believe that, despite their surprise at seeing her, no mention of her previous behavior had been made. *Of course*, she reasoned, *it'll come up at some point. They can't ignore it forever.* And when it did come up, would she be honest with them? Would she tell them the truth about her experiences? She knew what Ryan would say, and of course she'd agreed with his thoughts at the time, but now that she was here, wasn't it better to let everything be? Ignore the issue as long as it remained unspoken?

She pushed those questions aside. That was a bridge for another day.

Downstairs, she found the coffee pot still warm and poured a mug. She cobbled together a small breakfast and ate while she listened to the sounds of the house. It was quiet, naturally, but there'd always been a low undercurrent of humming within the quiet – a kind of comforting energy in the air of the home. When she'd been younger and experienced it, it had felt alien. Usually because, when she'd felt it, she'd been the only one in the house, due to having skipped school for the day. Now, it was one more thing among all of the soft creaks that made up the place which, while she'd never realized it before, had always been a safe haven for her.

She carried her coffee up to her room and sat on the edge of the bed, considering what lay ahead for her that day. She didn't think she could come up with a logical excuse to skip lunch with Jennifer, so that at least was going to happen. Maybe by the time they met up, Morgan could come up with an excuse about not seeing everyone later tonight. Something about needing family time. That felt good, she decided.

She picked up her hairbrush and began the task of fighting through knots and tangles. The plan began to flesh out in her mind. She'd suffer through lunch, maybe actually apologize to Jennifer and check one person off the long list of people she had to ask forgiveness from, but then she'd say that her parents had planned a family night at home. It only made sense, what with the mill and-

Something tapped on the window. Morgan cried out and spun, bringing the hairbrush up defensively. Scott's face peered inside. "You look stupid," he said, his voice muffled through the glass.

Morgan flipped him the finger and opened the window. "The fuck are you doing out there?" she demanded. "You scared the shit out of me."

"Relax!" Scott laughed. He jerked his head in the direction of outside. "Come on." Then, he was moving away, his feet scraping on the shingles. Morgan slipped shoes onto her bare feet and followed. She knew where he was going, the route along the second floor roofline being as familiar to her as the path from her bedroom down to the kitchen. They stopped in a small space between two dormers. It was a place they'd used throughout their childhood. Their secret hiding spot. Scott had nicknamed it Echo Base, further cementing his obsession with *The Empire Strikes Back* and all things *Star Wars*. Morgan simply thought of it as 'the spot.' Scott sat down cross-legged and picked up a coffee mug from where he'd left it on the shingles.

She settled in next to him, and they stared over the front yard and the street and houses beyond. Windows glowed with the brilliance of the morning sun, and Morgan tried to imagine what the people on the other sides of the curtains were doing at that moment. Were they all talking about the mill's closing? Were they all scared of what would come next? Or were they choosing to ignore the problem, sticking their heads in the proverbial sand?

"Since when do you drink coffee?" Morgan asked.

"I started a couple weeks after you moved out." He sipped his drink, then held the mug between his palms in his lap. "What was it like in the city?"

"It was cool," she answered. "It was fine."

"Which was it? Cool or fine?"

"There's a difference?"

"Of course."

Morgan turned her face to the sky, searching for clouds, birds, or an ICBM fired from a base in the woods outside of Moscow. Anything. "It was scary at first. I didn't know anyone, you know? But then I got a job. Met a couple people. It was alright."

"That doesn't sound exciting."

"Life in a bigger city isn't all that great. It's not much different than here – just more people. More stores. More traffic."

"You were kind of a bitch when you left, you know."

"I know. I'm sorry." The words felt plastic as they fell out of her mouth. She knew she meant them, but they didn't feel real. "Really. I was going through some stuff."

He nodded as if he understood. Finally, he said, "It's okay. I mean, Mom and Dad took it pretty hard for a while. You know how they are. We all knew you were going through some shit. I asked Mom once why she didn't make you talk about it, and she said you were an adult and you'd talk about it when you were ready. But?" He shrugged. "You left instead." He looked at her. "How bad could it have been for you to leave like that? I heard what you said to them that night."

Tears tickled their way down her cheeks. "I'm really sorry. I didn't mean to hurt you or them. I..." *Say it. You were raped in the mill by Geordie Dupont.* The words were right there, thick on her tongue, but she couldn't force them out. It wasn't fair to put that on Scott. At least not yet...not before she'd had a chance to talk to her parents about it. "That's why I came back. I thought running away from everything here would fix the problems, but it didn't. It only made things; only made *me* worse. I was a mess out there. It took me a while to figure it out and realize that I needed to come back and make amends. I'm going to tell you all about it, but I want to wait and talk to Mom and Dad first. Okay?"

Scott studied her, and she could see his own anger and frustration deep in his eyes. After a few seconds, it faded as he forced it down into whatever small box he pushed feelings. They sat in silence for a bit longer. "What do you think will happen now that the mill is closing?" he asked.

Morgan shook her head. "I have no idea. With that many people out of work, I don't know if the town can survive."

"I don't want to have to move," Scott said. His voice was small, almost a whine.

Morgan elbowed him. "What are you talking about? You're going to college soon. One more year of high school, and you're free. You'll move away then, right?" He gave a noncommittal shrug. "No," Morgan said, "you're going to college. You're not going to stay here in this dump of a town. You're going to get out and make something of yourself."

"There may not be a town to stay in," he said, his own face tilted upward, eyes closed against the sun. "If the mill really is closed."

"Still. You're going to go to school, get a good job, and start a whole new life. Then, I'll come and live with you and eat all your food and play all your computer games."

Scott laughed. "But you suck at computer games."

"So, I'll just lay on your couch and watch Donahue."

"As long as you pay for the beer."

Morgan leaned away, giving her brother an appraising look. "What do you know about beer?"

He rolled his eyes. "I'm almost a senior in high school. What do you think?"

A moment of quiet passed, Morgan looking at her brother in mild surprise. He was really growing up. She hated that she'd missed the last couple of years with him.

"What are you doing today?" Scott asked, bringing Morgan back to the moment.

"I'm having lunch with Jennifer at noon. I ran into her yesterday at the drugstore. She wants me to come to a party tonight."

"Jennifer Reynolds? Really?" Scott perked up. "She's such a fox. Can I come?"

"Gross," Morgan said. "You're way too young for her."

"I'm like four years younger. That's not that bad."

"She doesn't want a road pizza like you, okay? Besides," she said with a tone of mock indifference. "I haven't decided if I'm even going."

Scott sniffed. "Fine. Will there be any other girls at this party?"

"No. It's going to be me, Jennifer, Jason, Todd-"

"What about Chris?" Then, seeing something in her eyes, Scott began singing, "Ooooh, Chris, Oh my baby, Chris..."

Morgan groaned and got up. "I'm going to get dressed. Try not to be such a toad."

"I have plans of my own tonight anyway," Scott said.

"Locking yourself in your room and going through a quart of Vaseline?"

Scott gave her a deadpan look. "Gross. Doubly gross coming from my sister. No, spaz, I'm spending the night over at Kevin Appleton's. He rented *Nightmare on Elm Street* one and two, and a flick called "*I Spit On Your Grave.*" He grinned wide. "It's going to be awesome."

Morgan grimaced. "Sounds like a blast."

"Oh, it will be. He's got a Nintendo. We're gonna be up all night. Jolt and Twizzlers. May even prank call a few people."

"How are you a senior in high school? Shouldn't you guys be out trying to meet girls?"

"First of all, I asked to go to your party, and you said no. Second, what girls? In this town? Are you serious?" He looked at his watch. "I gotta go. I have a shift at Campbell's."

Morgan leaned back and put on a confused expression. "What the hell? I was around you all day yesterday – I'm just hearing that you have a job now?"

Scott shrugged. "It's just a little part-time job. I only catch a few hours each week. No biggie. Anyway, I won't be home before Kev's, so I'll see you tomorrow, okay?"

Morgan navigated her way back to her bedroom window. As she crouched to climb back in, Scott said, "Hey." She looked back. "It's good to have you back."

Morgan smiled and climbed into her room. She shut the window, locked it, and drew the curtains. As she gathered clothes and padded down the hall to shower, a bubble of happiness welled within her, bringing a tightness to her throat. Her eyes started to tear up, and she blinked, smiling as they rolled down her cheeks. Her brother was right.

It was good to be back.

CHAPTER 19

organ found a parking spot a block from the drugstore. She had an hour to kill before meeting Jennifer, so she decided to take a walk around the town square. The original feeling of unfamiliarity had started to pass and now things felt more in place, more comfortable. There were new things – Patty's Petals Flower Shop had a new sign, Mills Tobacco Products had a creepy wooden Indian statue next to the door, and the hardware store had new paint. But everything was in the same location, and mostly looked like she remembered it. A pickup truck passed with a throaty grumble and a belch of dark exhaust, and Morgan jogged across the street.

Her shoes whisked through the grass of the mall. Through the thin screen of trees at the end of the park, she caught a glimpse of the sign for Turtle Books. The logo sported a smiling turtle laying on its back, a book propped on its front legs. A few people strolled along the sidewalk in front of the shops, and Morgan watched them as she crossed the green. A battered pickup truck rumbled and coughed its way into an open slot along the curb. Morgan stumbled as her brain made the connection with what her eyes were seeing. She threw one hand out to grip the mouth of the cannon for support. Her chest heaved despite the barb of icy panic stabbing through her.

Across the street and near the end of the block, Geordie Dupont closed his truck door and ambled across the street, moving away from her. His hands were shoved into the pockets of his sagging jeans, causing his shoulders to angle sharply toward his ears. His gait hadn't changed, the movements of his legs the same sharp jerks as if a novice puppet master were working invisible strings overhead. She couldn't see his face - thank God for small favors - but knew that it would be fixed in his usual permanent scowl. Sunlight glinted off of his slicked-down hair, the foul-smelling pomade he always favored keeping it in place.

Morgan watched him as he vanished around the corner of Mills Tobacco. It took her several more seconds to regain command of her legs. Her entire body thrummed with the need to cross the mall and get back into her car. In that moment, she wanted nothing more than to crawl back into the dark, quiet solace of her bed. She took two faltering steps backward, and had started to turn when another thought came. It was something Ryan had said to her when he'd walked her to her car two nights ago.

"Take a long look at him. You'll see he's just a man. A pitiful, wasted excuse for a man, but a man. You've built him up as a monster - and he is, don't get me wrong, that son of a bitch has a heart blacker than Satan's asshole - but he's not twelve feet tall and able to knock down buildings. He's just a man. As soon as you can get that straight in your mind, you'll be able to do what you need to. You'll find the strength to look him in the eye and tell him how you feel."

Morgan stared at her car, the sunlight glistening on the chrome, and felt her head bob up and down in a nod. Ryan was right. She *had* to go look at him. She had to tear down the image she'd built in her mind.

Morgan crossed the short stretch of Washington Street until she stood at the corner of the block next to the tobacco store. She squeezed herself into the small gap between the wooden Indian chief and the brick corner of the building, and peered around.

Geordie wasn't on the sidewalk in front of the Mill Grill. Due to the glare on the front windows and the flyers taped to the glass (ads for the Fourth of July party, lost pet notices, and one large poster encouraging people to sign up for CPR classes to be held at the library), she could only see the outlines of people inside. Several sat at tables against the glass, and others stood in line for the takeout counter. She wondered if Geordie was inside standing in line, waiting to get to the counter and order a meatloaf sandwich to go. Scanning the rest of the street, she saw the lit neon sign of Martin's Liquors and felt a piece of the puzzle fall into place. Of course. It was a Saturday, and while a meatloaf sandwich might still be in Geordie Dupont's future, a bottle of cheap whiskey was a guarantee.

The bell over the door to the smoke shop chimed. Morgan ignored it, her attention solely on the sidewalk in front of the liquor store. When Geordie emerged, she would...what? Run to her car, speed back home, and crawl under the covers like a child scared by a noise down the hall? Or would she find courage and step into his path, to tell him how she felt and what she'd been through after his attack? What would that accomplish, really? Men like Geordie Dupont didn't care about the feelings of others, and certainly not those of a girl he'd forced himself on while shoving her face into the dirt-stained floor of a maintenance room. He would most certainly laugh at her...maybe even threaten to do it again, if given half a chance. No, a man like that wasn't 'only a man' no matter what Ryan said. A man like that was-

"A monster," she whispered.

"Who's a monster?"

Morgan gave a startled cry and lurched backward. The statue rocked as she hit it, and she spun and reached out to steady it. The thing was huge, easily over six feet tall and heavy as hell. The rough wood began sliding from her grasp. Another pair of hands joined hers, and together they stopped the statue from wobbling.

"Oh my god. Morgan?"

Morgan glanced up from the hideously chiseled face of the Indian chief and into the face of Chris Coffey. "Shit," she breathed out. "Hey."

Chris' expression shifted to one of confused amusement. "Hey? That's it?"

He took a small step forward, but Morgan held up a finger. "One second." She whirled back to the corner and peeked around. The door to Martin's Liquors was open, a man's thin arm holding it in place as the owner of the arm remained out of sight.

"What's going-" Chris began to ask again, but she threw up her index finger once more, silencing him. The man stepped out onto the sidewalk, adjusting a brown paper sack against his hip. Relief swarmed through her. It wasn't Geordie. Morgan let out a long breath and turned back to Chris. She leaned against the warm bricks. Chris looked around the corner. "Are you spying on someone?"

Morgan, her eyes closed as she relished the sudden absence of her fear, shook her head. "Long story." She looked back at Chris. "Hey."

"You said that already." He spread his arms and stepped close for a hug. At the movement, Morgan shuffled backward again, colliding with the wall. Her head tucked down and away. Chris checked his advance and moved back, his brow wrinkled in confusion at the abruptness of her reaction. For a long moment he seemed frozen, unsure of what to do or say. Finally, he drawled, "So...you're back in town?" The words held a note of coldness.

"Yeah. I got in yesterday morning."

Before he could reply, two women came from around the corner, to-go bags smelling of greasy meat and salt held by their sides. They barely acknowledged the two standing outside the tobacco shop. "...they were all chopped up," one said.

"I know. It had to be devil worshippers! You know, I heard that there's a place in the woods off of Briarwood where they meet. Sara said she's heard there's pentagrams..." The women continued past, their words melting into a gentle droning of unintelligible sounds.

Chris watched them go. "I guess you heard?"

"What?" Morgan asked. "The mill? Yeah, Dad came in yesterday morning all freaked out about it."

"No. The murders," Chris said. "How have you not heard about them?"

Morgan's face screwed up in confusion. "Is that what those women were talking about?" Chris gave her a knowing look. "I thought they were talking about a movie. What happened?"

Chris told her. "They found two families dead in their houses over on North Wind Drive." Morgan nodded. "My dad says they were completely destroyed. I don't know about the pentagram stuff, but they also found two bodies at the elementary school. A teacher and Eddie, the janitor. Brutal stuff."

"Jesus, that's horrible," she said.

Chris nodded. He blinked the moment away and asked, "How have you been? How's life outside of Elden Mills? What was it you were doing? Working for a bank or something? That's what your dad said I think."

If that was what her father had said, she wasn't going to contradict it. Not now. "Yeah. Executive assistant." Part of Morgan withered at the words as she heard herself say them. After the time she and Chris had spent together, the nights they'd shared, she couldn't even be honest with him.

"Must have been a heck of an opportunity," he said.

"What do you mean?"

Chris shifted on his feet. "Well, you left so suddenly, you know? I thought things were going pretty well with us, but then you...." He trailed off with a shrug. Morgan forced herself to look at him. Chris looked as good as he had two years ago. *Possibly better*, she thought. He'd always been trim, but seemed to have filled out a little more. His green, collared shirt with the alligator logo stretched across a muscular chest. He still wore his light brown hair parted down the middle and feathered back, and his green eyes still sparkled, like he was hearing punchlines in his head. The thin mustache was new, though.

"I'm sorry about that," she said, realizing how weak the words sounded.

"I just wish you'd said something," Chris said. "Did I do anything? I mean, you know, to make you want to leave?"

Before Morgan could answer, a siren whooped. The two watched as an Elden Mills Police cruiser's lights switched on. The car sped down the street past the drugstore and out of sight, tires squealing as it took a corner at high speed.

"Guess someone's having a doughnut sale," Chris joked half-heartedly.

Jennifer's voice called out as she walked up from the drug store. "There you are! Jeez, I thought I was getting stood up!" A flash of irritation passed across Chris' eyes. He deserved answers. They'd dated - well, not so much *dated* as had sex regularly - for a year or so before her encounter with Geordie had put a temporary hold on all of Morgan's thoughts of physical intimacy. She didn't know if what she'd been feeling for Chris at the time had been love, but she did know that if things had continued, her emotions would have grown into that. Chris had always been a good guy. She hated knowing that she'd hurt him. *You hurt everyone,* she thought. But then Jennifer was standing between them, her smile beaming as she rocked up and down on her toes.

"You wanna join us for lunch?" Jennifer asked Chris.

Chris glanced at Morgan and had just started to answer when a woman called his name. A short, thin, red-head wearing a red and white striped shirt over a white, knee-length skirt stood outside a store two doors down from the tobacco shop. She held a brown paper bag in one hand and fiddled with the thin leather strap of a purse that hung on her shoulder with her other hand. Her gaze shifted, and her face hardened when she saw Morgan. She gave Chris a tight-jawed look whose meaning was clear.

"Maybe next time," Chris said.

Jennifer giggled. "Maybe you can ask her to lend you your balls sometime. I hear she keeps them in a Cool-Whip container in the freezer."

Chris gave an anemic smile and shuffled toward the red-head. As he reached her, she threw another angry look at Morgan before pulling him down the sidewalk.

"I honestly don't know what the hell he's doing with Amanda," Jennifer said with a sad shake of her head. "She's a bitch to everyone." She cocked an eyebrow and gave a mischievous smile. "I hear she lets him come in through the back door." Morgan translated the phrase in her head and rolled her eyes. Jennifer laughed and slipped an arm around Morgan's to guide her toward the diner.

As they cleared the corner and Morgan's foot stepped down into the street, she glanced in the direction of the liquor store. It was an unconscious move, but when she saw the spidery form of Geordie Dupont stepping toward them, one fist clutching a bottle by the neck through his brown paper bag, her remaining foot planted on the sidewalk and she lurched awkwardly. Jennifer's arm slipped free, and she took two extra steps before realizing what had happened.

Geordie's attention was focused on his free hand, his thin fingers with weirdly thick knuckles shifting keys around. He'd moved to within only a few short steps of the women when he finally looked up. His jaw fell slack as he noticed Morgan standing half on the sidewalk, her face drained of color as she watched him, stuck like a rabbit staring between the brambles at a circling hawk. He recovered quickly, though, and his look of momentary surprise melted into a greasy smile.

"Well, lookie here," he said, almost singing the words. "I thought I saw you come into town yesterday. How you been?"

Morgan's throat closed so tightly that it felt as if all of the air had gone out of the world. Her vision began to dim at the edges as everything around her faded into nothingness, leaving only the short, gangly, dirty man in front of her. Her chest thrummed, her heart racing like a bird trapped in a cage. Her entire body vibrated as she stared at his leering face.

His lips turned down in a mock pout. "What, don't have anything to say to your old pal? I thought we were better friends than that." He shifted his eyes to Jennifer, who remained in the street, one arm reaching out toward Morgan's elbow as if she were in a movie that had been paused. "I seen you," he said to Jennifer. "You work over at the drugstore, don't you?" Looking back at Morgan, he said, "Maybe you could get us some drugs? We could all head back to my place and have a good time. Whadaya say, Morgan? Want to come back to my place? I'll be real good to you and your friend here." His eyes danced with mirth, and he slowly poked the tip of his tongue out, wetting his lower lip before he let the pink slug retract into his mouth.

The bird in Morgan's chest went into full panic mode, throwing itself against the cage bars. She had to get away. She had to get far, far away. Without even realizing she was moving, Morgan staggered to one side, her feet heavy as she hurried across the street. Dimly, she heard Jennifer calling her name, and as she pushed into the Mill Grill - not even aware that she had chosen this location, knowing only that it was a door and walls that she could put between herself and Geordie - she heard Geordie's soft chuckling.

"I'll see you soon, sweetheart!" he called as the diner door closed behind her.

CHAPTER 20

"Dude," Scott said when Kevin opened the front door, "you look like a bag of assholes."

Instead of responding, Kevin gave Scott the finger and went back into the house. Scott pushed the door open farther and slipped inside, sweeping it closed behind him. As Scott walked through the living room, he couldn't help but notice the smell of the home. Recently, he'd begun noticing that every one of his friends' homes had a slightly different smell. He found that interesting, as his own house had literally no smell unless his parents were cooking something. Kevin's house smelled like dryer sheets with a subtle, underlying sourness. It wasn't off-putting, and after he'd been in the space for a few minutes, he didn't notice it anymore.

The living room was wide, with a sofa, loveseat, and two recliners all positioned around a wooden coffee table. A massive wooden entertainment center with a nineteen-inch television and a multi-component stereo system dominated one wall. Pictures lined the shelves of the entertainment center – mostly school pictures of Kevin and his sister Misty, and family pictures of everyone. To the right of the entertainment center was a large stone fireplace with more pictures along the mantle. A single purple and red vase stood on the left edge of the mantle, and as he passed it, Scott felt a flush of shame.

Four years ago, he'd accidentally broken its partner while goofing off with Kevin one Saturday afternoon. Kevin's mother had waved it off, saying accidents happened and for him not to stress about it, but Scott had noticed the tight expression on her face as she bent to clean up the pieces. He'd spent the next month doing odd jobs until he'd earned twenty dollars to pay her for it. She'd accepted the money, but only after a brief argument.

Turning down the hallway that extended off the living room, Scott passed the kitchen. Expecting to see Kevin's mother, Scott slowed, but the space was empty. Immediately next to the kitchen doorway was an open stairwell leading down to not only the basement, but Kevin's room. The sounds of Def Leppard floated up the stairs, as Scott followed his friend down.

In the downstairs area, he ignored the closed door of the garage and the half-cracked door of the bathroom, proceeding instead to the third option, a door sporting a poster of Mr. T, his heavily ringed fist held up menacingly in front of his even more heavily necklaced chest. The door scraped across the thick carpet in Kevin's room, and the pounding rhythm of music almost punched Scott in the face.

Kevin's room was actually rather large compared to Scott's own bedroom, but his friend had so much crap in it that it felt tight and cramped. Clothes in questionable degrees of cleanliness littered the floor and furniture. A skateboard sat halfway across the floor, an empty can of Tab resting on its flat surface. A red guitar missing four strings leaned against a table, atop which sat a double cassette boombox. Posters covered the dark blue walls: Motley Crue, Def Leppard, and *Star Wars*, with magazine cutouts of various women in swimsuits spread out between the wall-hangings. But the centerpiece, the one mounted next to the small twin bed, was Scott's personal favorite...a large image of Paulina Porizkova wearing a very tight, and very revealing, black one-piece bathing suit. She gazed over one shoulder with what Scott liked to think of as predatory longing, the long waves of her hair cascading down her back. That look in her eyes was captivating, but the best part of the image was the uncovered swell of one breast that peered out from the edge of the swimsuit.

"Hello, my love," he said as he touched the poster reverently.

"Don't molest my wife," Kevin scolded as he kicked aside a stray shirt and sat on the floor amidst what looked like a very large life raft made of various pillows. He picked up a Nintendo controller and turned his attention to the twelve-inch television atop his dresser. The screen blinked to life, animated chimes barely audible over the music as Kevin manipulated Mario through a cartoon world.

Scott moved the skateboard and took a position next to his friend. He watched in silence for a few minutes, until Mario failed to make a leap to another cliff and went tumbling into the void off-screen. "You work today?" Kevin asked as he leaned over and grabbed a can of Jolt.

"Yeah," Scott said. "Just a few hours. Nothing big. Your sister here?"

Kevin gave Scott a menacing look. "She's at the grill. Why?"

Scott feigned innocence. "Just wondering. Didn't want her barging in here, ruining our hang-out, that's all."

"Liar."

Scott put his hand on Kevin's shoulder. "It's understandable that you have no idea how foxy your sister is. It'd be creepy if you did. But I also can't help it that, whenever she knows I'm here, she always finds an excuse to come down here."

"Does not," Kevin protested as he restarted his game.

"Remember two weeks ago when we were watching *Conan*? She kept coming down here? She was down here like five times over the course of that movie."

"Dude, that was because she was telling us to turn it down and to stop sword-fighting with those plastic tubes."

Scott raised an eyebrow. "Or was it? I mean, I didn't have a shirt on."

"Are you seriously suggesting that my sister couldn't get enough of your fucking baby bird chest?"

"I've been working out," Scott said, flexing. "Got some dumbbells in my room."

"The only workout you get is pulling your pud."

"Wouldn't you like to know?"

"What does that even mean?" The boys stared at each other and then broke into laughter. "You're so stupid," Kevin said as he worked the controller.

"Where're your parents?"

Kevin shrugged. "Dad went fishing with some guys from the mill. He got on with the crew that's helping downsize it, but won't start that till Monday. He said they've told them they'll be working long hours. Mom's at work."

"They okay? With the mill closing, I mean."

"I guess. They haven't said much to us about it. Of course, Misty's been at work a lot lately, too, so we haven't had family dinner in a few days." He hit a button on the controller, and Mario froze mid-jump. "What do you think about the murders? Pretty rad, huh? I heard they ate some of the bodies."

Scott rolled his eyes and gave the other boy a look of disbelief. "What? What murders? You been smoking crack again?"

"How the hell have you not heard? Some people over on North Wind Drive were killed in their houses. I heard there was satanic shit painted all over the walls. Black candles everywhere."

Scott waited for Kevin to start laughing, the prank to be revealed. "You're fucking with me."

"No, hand to God! The Weavers and the Butlers. Both families, completely obliterated. Randy Marshall said that they'd been dismembered and the body parts were nailed to the walls to form upside-down crosses."

Scott frowned. "That's sick."

"Fucking metal, is what it is," Kevin laughed. "Although, it's a shame about Stephanie Weaver. She was foxy."

"Do they know who did it?"

"Nope. Well, I mean, clearly it was devil worshippers, right?"

Scott wasn't sure how much of what came out of Randy Marshall's mouth could be trusted – the guy had been known to huff paint from time to time. It seemed no matter what happened, no matter how minor a crime, the immediate suspicion fell on 'devil worshippers.' Not that there were any known - or even suspected - satanists in Elden Mills. But, if you worshiped Satan, it was probably not something you went around advertising.

Kevin let out a long, deep belch. "I figured we can go over there later tonight. Ride out that way and see what we can see."

"Are you nuts? There's no way we'd get in there."

"Why not?"

"How dense are you? They're crime scenes. Hollister will have guys all over them."

"You think the Elden Police have that many guys? Please. They have to be able to patrol the rest of the town and look for the sickos who did it."

Scott breathed a nervous laugh. He was pretty sure that Kevin was joking now, but there was a chance the guy was serious. "I'm not going over there."

Kevin rolled his eyes. "You're just chicken shit. Afraid to see some blood and devil stuff."

He wasn't wrong, Scott admitted to himself. The thought of seeing images painted on a bedroom wall in dried blood soured his stomach. "I thought we were going to play games. Watch those flicks you rented. Besides, I wouldn't hate being here when Misty gets home. I'm sure she'll need a shower after all day standing in grease fumes. Maybe she'll need help scrubbing her back."

Pain exploded in his upper arm as Kevin punched him. Scott gasped and held a hand to the spot, then watched as his friend held up his fist, the middle knuckle raised higher than the others. "Next time, I'll frog your ass."

Scott laughed and pulled the controller out of Kevin's hands to start playing Mario.

After a few minutes, Kevin asked, "How's your dad doing with the mill? Dad says he wasn't kept on."

Scott shook his head. "I don't know. He hasn't said much, like yours. He was mad when he first came home with the news, but then he saw Morgan-"

Kevin flinched, almost choking on his drink. When he managed to swallow he said, "Wait. Your sister's in town?"

"Came in yesterday morning, early."

Kevin whistled. "You want to talk about a real fox. The whole town went to the dogs after she left. How's she doing? She like living in the city?"

"I don't know. She says it's great. Says she has a good job and all, or did, but..." he trailed off.

"You think she's lying?"

"Yeah. There's something off about her. I know she feels bad about leaving town the way she did. You remember. It was a huge fight with her and my parents. And I don't think she told any of her friends she was leaving. Just packed a couple of bags one afternoon. But now that she's back, she looks different."

"Oh shit, she didn't get, like, ugly or anything, did she?"

"Fuck off."

"Hey, we could trade sisters, if you know what I mean."

Scott laughed. "Yeah, you try to convince Misty of that and see how it works out for you. But no, she looks the same. Just...tired, you know?"

The boys fell into another easy silence.

Finally, Scott asked, "You ready for next year?"

"Fuck yes, I am. I'm going to print up a shit-ton of pool passes to sell to the freshmen. I'm going to rule that fucking school. Are you kidding?"

"Right. You. The movie nerd who has posters of half-naked girls in his bedroom and doesn't play sports is going to rule the school? I think Tyler Dunning has that position locked up."

"Fucking quarterback," Kevin grumbled. "Just because he's fucking Brittany."

"I'm pretty sure the football thing and the legion of friends he has play contributing roles. But I can think of something you do have that he doesn't."

"I swear if you say something about my sister—"

"No. Although her ta-ta's are so perfect...okay, okay!" He laughed and shifted away as Kevin raised his knuckle again. "No, I'm talking about the X-34." He raised his eyebrows in a *get my drift* expression.

Slowly, Kevin lowered his fist. "That thing is never going to be finished. We've been fucking around with it since seventh grade."

Scott conceded the point with a nod. Both boys had watched the original *Star Wars* at least five times in the theater and had worn out a VHS copy of the tape. One night during the seventh grade - they both claimed credit for being the originator of the idea - they'd decided to build their own working landspeeder. The project had consumed their free time from that moment on, for the next several years. Kevin's dad had graciously allotted them space in their detached garage, and the boys had set to work piecing together the vehicle using any scrap parts they could find. Truth be told, Scott had to admit, it looked like complete shit. The monstrosity resembled Luke's landspeeder only if you strained the limits of your imagination, and were rather gracious on top of that. But the hours spent slaving away on it in the poorly ventilated garage, the countless afternoons spent scouring the roads about town, and occasionally pooling enough money to pay for a car part from Simmons Pick and Pull, had all more than made up for it. Spending that time drawing concepts and building the speeder with Kevin had been the best of times.

An idea exploded in Scott's mind, so brilliant and intense that he dropped the controller and sat bolt upright with a gasp. Kevin coughed and sputtered on his drink. "The hell's wrong with you?" he demanded, his voice pinched as he fought to reopen his airway.

Scott grinned wide. "I just had the best idea."

Kevin raised his fist. "You're not hiding in Misty's closet again."

"No," Scott waved the comment off, "the videotape I recorded that time is still good." He continued despite Kevin's scowl. "The mill," he said. Kevin gave him a confused look. "Parts for the speeder. Think about it. The mill's closed. They're not reopening it, right? There's got to be all sorts of spare parts and things laying around up there. What are they going to do with it all? Most of it's probably scrap, right? So, they'd just toss it."

"You're suggesting we go up there and steal the parts?" Kevin asked.

"Why not? If it's going in the dumpster anyway, where's the harm? I'm not saying we disassemble a loom or something, but we could hit the supply room, the maintenance shed, or whatever, and snag a few things that would really help us get over the hump with the speeder." The truth was, they needed more than a few spare pieces of metal, but Scott dismissed that as irrelevant. "What do you say?"

Kevin chewed it over. Finally, he nodded. "I bet there's some pretty cool stuff up there that would come in handy." Scott held up his hand, and the boys high-fived. "But," Kevin said soberly, "we can't do it tonight."

"Why not?"

"Duh? We have a whole night planned already, or did you forget? Tonight's no good. Even if we wait until we're sure the coast is clear, I'm not going to be in the mood to hike my ass all the way across town to the mill at midnight or two in the morning. I plan on being deep into *Elm Street* and *I Spit on Your Grave* at that point. Plus, if we're there tonight, someone might see our flashlights. The better thing will be to do it tomorrow. The transition crew doesn't start till Monday, so the worst we'll have to deal with is one of the guards, and they'll probably never leave the guard's office. So if we're smart, nobody'll ever know we've even been there."

Scott's smile grew even wider. "And I plan on being deep into your sister by then." Kevin's fist shot out and collided with his shoulder again. The boys laughed, and Scott rubbed his throbbing arm.

"Tomorrow?" he asked.

Kevin chugged the last of his Jolt. "Tomorrow."

CHAPTER 21

"Nine-one-one."

"I think someone's trying to kill us." The voice was tight with fear, bordering on hysterics. "He's in our backyard. It's our neighbor, Henry Junkins."

Regina's fingers had long since gone numb from holding her pen, scribbling notes about the flood of calls that had been coming for the last few hours. She ignored the lock of hair that had found a way to escape her bobby pin and now hung at the corner of her left eye. She took in a quick, steadying breath. "Okay, calm down, I'll get someone over there as soon as possible. Where are you? What's the address?"

The voice raised a pitch. "Soon? We need someone now! He's walking around back there looking in windows. He-" The receiver was filled with muffled rustling. Through it, Regina could hear the girl shouting at someone. Gunshots cut her off, three of them, fast and loud even through the handset the girl must have been holding to her chest. Regina dropped the pen, flinching as each muffled boom came through the receiver. A sinking feeling passed through her, settling in her stomach like a sour lake.

The girl returned to the line. Her voice was tight, and shook in breathy gusts. "It's okay. Daddy shot him. You can't arrest him for that. It's self-defense, you know...." She continued to prattle on while

Regina noted the information and told the girl to stay where she was, and that an officer would be there in a few minutes. She disconnected the call and scanned her list of unit numbers and last-known locations. It was usually easy to mark those down, but now the page was a series of long columns of addresses. At the top of each column were the car numbers with the initials of the Elden Mills officer in them. She looked for the closest officer and pressed her fingers to her lips. The units were spread all over the town.

There was no way they could keep this up. Still, she picked one, called them, and told them to report to the location of the gunshots. That done, Regina tossed the pen onto the desk and pushed her chair back several inches. She lowered her head into her hands and closed her eyes, trying to focus on her breathing and not think about Lady, her eleven-year-old beagle, who sat at home waiting for a dinner which should have been served three hours ago. She would have to call one of her neighbors, probably Mrs. Sutton, to go feed the old dog. The thought of Lady being alone for so long bothered Regina, but there was no way she could stand to leave the station now. Not with the town where she'd lived her whole life falling apart. She'd told Sheriff Hollister earlier to have her relief, Allan Criswell get into the field. The sheriff had started to argue, but she'd made it very clear that she wasn't going to abandon her desk. If the guys were working overtime, she would be right here to support them.

The cacophony of multiple phone lines ringing assaulted her ears, filling the station with the shrill sounds of the town falling into chaos. The day had started well enough – that was until Roderick Shance had practically crashed his car into the building. She'd run outside along with everyone else, hearing the commotion and getting out there just in time to see Hollister pull back the blanket covering that poor child. Regina had only gotten a glimpse of the mess that had once been the boy's face. Then she'd shoved aside the officers nearest her, the large men staggering back from the ferocity of her movements, and she'd lost everything she'd eaten over the side rail of the stairs.

The panic that had gripped the crowd had spread like a disease through the town. Hollister had ordered those closest to disperse to their homes and told Regina - who had finally recovered - to call in reinforcements from the county. Moreover, he'd ordered her to issue a town-wide curfew of 7 p.m. All officers, regardless of duty status, had been called in and put on the streets. Shift schedules would be sorted out later.

She let out another long sigh and forced her hand to grab the red phone again. "Nine-one-one."

"Hey, I wanted to let you people know that I know what's going on around here. I know who killed the Weavers and the Butlers."

Regina fished briefly for the correct notebook and pulled it closer. "Go on," she said, even as she started to mark another tally number on the page.

"It was Todd Butler himself. Crazy son of a bitch lost it when the mill closed. Killed his family and then the Weavers."

"This isn't an emergency, sir."

"What?"

"You're calling the emergency line. You're holding up the line for true emergencies. If you have information about-"

The man began talking over her. "Fuck that. You people don't know what you're doing. Jerry Weaver conned Todd into a timeshare, and that's why he killed Jerry and his family. I know because my cousin 'Roo - we call him that on account that he-"

Regina hung up the phone, marked another tally next to "Time-share," and pushed the pad a few inches away. The tallies for time-share were being outnumbered by those indicating people who claimed Jerry Weaver had been having an affair with Todd's wife. Next to this notebook was another, across the top of which she'd scrawled "Satanists." There were over two dozen marks on that one, as the theory a gang of satanists had infiltrated the town and were killing families as part of a black mass. She used the word gang, but is that what they would be called, she wondered? A coven? A church? Despite having what she usually considered to be a cool head, Regina felt that theory to be the most likely. All of the talk shows had been filled with interviews and reports on the rise of satanism. It only made sense, despite the Sheriff's insistence that there was no evidence to support it. He'd not described the crime scenes in detail, but had gone so far as to tell her that there were no satanic images or symbols in either home.

She looked at the bank of flashing lights indicating calls waiting to be answered on the non-emergency lines. Every one a person calling to report a theory or blame a neighbor.

Regina felt her throat closing and hot tears filling her eyes as she thought of the look of pure anguish on the face of that father. His wild-eyed, frantic expression of horror, the not knowing what to do, not understanding what was happening or why it had happened to his only child. It hadn't been until a few hours later that word came about officers finding the body of Alicia Vaughan behind a tree on Geordie Dupont's property.

After that, the floodgates had opened. Most times, when a call came in on one of the four standard lines, Regina could use her discretion - backed up by years of experience working dispatch - to determine what actually needed officer involvement, and what was simply a person needing to be heard for a few minutes. But once a call came in on the red phone, there was no questioning the validity of it. If the red phone rang, you *had* to dispatch someone. Luckily, by the time it had started ringing non-stop, many of the county guys had arrived and were rolling on the streets, whether solo or partnered up with Elden Mills boys.

When the sun had begun to set, the sky turning a bruised purple, Regina had stopped answering the standard lines except in moments where she felt she had time to actually address the person. Priority went to the emergency line, and she was thankful that, for the most part, people kept their calls to that number limited to true emergencies.

"Nine-one-one," she answered again, snatching the handset up after only one ring.

"Um, I guess I need to report a body. There's a guy here all messed up."

"Where are you?" Regina noted the location and the caller's name. "Can you give me a description of the body?"

"Well, he ain't got a fucking head, if that's what you're wanting to know."

Regina winced. "No, sir, I mean what is he wearing? Do you know the victim?"

"Oh. Shit, I'm sorry. No, I don't know who he is, on account of the no-head thing." She told him not to touch the body, to remain where he was, and that an officer would be there soon. Looking at her notes again she picked a unit, called them, and told them to report to the headless man's location.

"Come on, Regina," Deke McIntyre responded, "we need a break. My partner here has to take a shit."

"Get to that location!" she snapped back.

After she signed off, Regina hurried to the wall between her office and the bullpen. A large map of the town and surrounding county hung there, easily seen by everyone in the station. She jabbed a red thumbtack into the large map and returned to her desk. Just as she sat down, the red phone began its shrill ringing.

"Nine-one-one."

"A man is walking down the alley carrying an ax over here on Clairmont. I'm pretty sure it's that no-good son of a bitch Frank Gallagher. I think he's going to kill someone!"

Regina glanced back at the map, at the red pins splashed across its tangled lines like blood drops from an opened vein.

They were everywhere.

Dear God, what is happening?

CHAPTER 22

"Get back inside, ma'am," Walter Clayton said, patting the air with his hand. *Ma'am?* he thought. *That's Mary Higgins. She's been to our house for dinner.* Mary stood on her small brick porch, a robe pulled around her thin frame, one hand clutching it together between her breasts. Her hair hung in wet clumps around a face that wore a stunned, scared expression.

Ignoring Walter's command, she pushed the screen door open a little wider. "He's in the backyard. I heard him on the porch as I was getting out of the shower." Her voice was tight with fear. "I didn't know what to do."

"Where's Brandon?" Walter asked. From the corner of his eye he saw the county officer he'd been paired with, a thick Black man named Nathan Bellamy, click on the high-powered beam of his flashlight. The beam lit a massive swath of the grassy driveway. Walter held his hand out to Bellamy, indicating for the man to stop and wait.

"He's at the Lantern with some of the guys. I told him about the curfew and that I didn't want to be alone, but..." She shrugged. "You know Brandon." Walter nodded that he did.

"Get back inside and lock the door. Let us take care of it." To his relief, she retreated into the house. His new partner was a few feet in front of the car, playing his light on the dark space that was the backyard. The light was broken up, engorged shadows thrown by the wire of the chain-link fence, but from where they stood, it was enough to see that nothing unusual lay beyond the gate.

"Let's go," Bellamy said in his '*I don't have time for this shit*' tone. Walter once more cursed Jared for not allowing him to partner up with Deke. But the sheriff had felt that having a local teamed up with a county boy was a better use of resources, so here he was.

Bellamy pushed open the gate, the thing squealing on its hinges, and stepped into the yard. Walter pulled his own flashlight and then his weapon before he followed. The Higgins' yard wasn't large, but did have a thicket of bamboo growing along the back. A rotting pile of firewood sat like a huge slug along the left wall of fencing. The porch was just a patio of paving stones, atop which sat old, faded chairs. Against the house, a small, rusted grill stood like a decrepit robot under a window.

The officers moved a few feet apart and followed their lights deeper into the yard. Walter branched to the left, crossed the patio, and tried to ignore Mary watching their progress from the window over the grill. Bellamy pressed along the right side of the fence, working his way slowly toward the bamboo.

Walter reached the corner of the house and peeked quickly around the edge. His light showed only the downspout and a patch of dirt before the fence angled back to connect to the bricks. He flashed his beam beyond the fence to the front, saw nothing, and then heard Bellamy call out.

"Police! Whoever you are, come out of there with your hands up!" The cold, demanding tone sent a wave of prickling fear through Walter.

Holy shit, did we find the guy? Walter spun, keeping his weapon and flashlight trained on the bamboo as he crossed the yard. He made sure to angle his approach and not get too close to the county officer.

"What'd you see?" he asked.

Bellamy stood with one foot in front of the other, bracing himself as he focused his sidearm on the tall stalks. "Movement there. Caught a flash of something white." As if his words had been some director's cue, leafy, whispering sounds of movement filtered out of the bamboo. Walter's prickling fear amped up, sending electric shockwaves throughout him. He tried to flex his fingers around the grip of his pistol, but couldn't. His knuckles ached from the tension, and all he could do was fight to hold the barrel steady. Beads of sweat rolled down his shoulder blades and tickled his back beneath his vest.

"I said come out. Now!" Bellamy ordered. *If that doesn't get him out,* Walter thought, *then nothing will.* Bellamy risked a look over at Walter. "Get ready." He took two quick steps toward the row of bamboo and stuck his flashlight between two trunks, angling it back and forth to see more deeply into the thicket.

Walter's mouth was a desert as he struggled to keep one eye on his partner and the other on the rest of the bamboo. More sounds of movement came now – great crashes – and in the brilliant white light of his flashlight, bamboo shifted as something pressed between stalks. A white face emerged only a couple of feet above the scrubby grass. Walter's stiff finger slid from the trigger guard to the curved metal of the trigger, his knuckle giving a soft but painful pop as he flexed it.

"Wait!" Bellamy barked as Walter felt the flesh of his finger pressing harder into the trigger. He pulled his finger away at the same time his brain made the connection to what his eyes were seeing. The dog looked at the two officers and opened its mouth, letting its long tongue loll to one side. It gave a few *"Aren't you proud of me?"* huffs and pushed the rest of the way out of the brush.

"For fuck's sake," Walter breathed, relaxing his arms. The dog padded clear, looking between him and Bellamy as if it were unsure which to approach. After a second, the dog seemed to shrug and jogged forward between the two men. It leapt the fence gracefully, and was gone. "I almost blasted that fucker."

The county trooper stared after the dog and then returned his attention to the bamboo. He raised his flashlight and moved along the row of green reeds, peering in at intervals. Walter returned his weapon to its holster and mopped his brow with his arm. Bellamy, satisfied that nothing else hid within the brush, holstered his own sidearm and stomped to the car.

"Hey, you alright?" Walter called as he hurried to catch up.

"I hate dogs," came the clipped reply.

Bellamy got into the cruiser while Walter approached the front door of the home. *Who hates dogs?*

Mary met him at the door. "What was it?"

"Dog. I didn't recognize it, but it's gone now."

"There wasn't anything else?" Mary looked toward the corner of the house. "You're sure?"

"I'm sure. All clear back there." He smiled reassuringly, trying to erase the visible tension on the woman's face. "Try to have a good night. Just keep everything locked up, and you'll be fine." He turned to go, but hesitated. "If you guys are free next weekend, maybe we can have you over. Throw some burgers on the grill. I know Christa would love to see you."

That seemed to defrost her some. "That sounds good. Thanks, Walt." He waved and waited while she shut and locked the front door.

Back in the cruiser, he started to ask why Bellamy hated dogs, but the man spoke first. "We gotta go. Dispatch just called about a shop owner claiming to have seen a man carrying an ax in the alley behind his store."

"What store?"

"Millside Grocers."

"That'd be Dennis Hatfield. No relation," he added and started the car.

"Relation?"

"To the Hatfields?" Walter asked. Bellamy gave him a blank stare. "Hatfields and McCoys? Please don't tell me you have no idea what I'm talking about." He dropped the gear shift into position and backed into the street.

"I do. Just didn't see the need for you to mention it."

Walter steered the car through an intersection. "Trying to lighten the mood a little." Bellamy gave a soft grunt and returned his attention to the streets around them.

Gonna be a long damned night, Walter thought.

The rest of the drive was quiet, the two men looking out the windows as their patrol car sped through the dark streets. The radio squawked with updates from various patrol cars around the town, interspersed with Regina's voice – *God, she sounds tired* - as she updated units with information from calls or asked for anyone available to attend the next. The whole night had been nuts from the jump. Walter was thankful he'd not been on shift that morning when the Shance boy's body had been delivered to the station house steps. But he, along with everyone else, had been called in immediately afterwards.

The first several hours of the day had been fine, at least from a patrol perspective. Hardly any calls had been related to the fear around the murders, and despite his having been assigned to ride with the piece of human granite that was Nathan Bellamy, Walter had found the day to be relatively easy.

But then the sun had set. It was well-known among law enforcement that, along with the setting sun, all sorts of weirdness came crawling from whatever hideaway they'd found, like bugs drawn out by the night. *At least it wasn't a full moon,* he'd told himself repeatedly. That *really* brought out the craziness. The calls had been mostly the same, people claiming to have seen a person - more usually, *persons* - in places they shouldn't be. Often, these claims were colored with descriptions of various weapons, or had the people dressed like monsters or wearing satanic clothing. Walter had absolutely no idea what constituted 'satanic clothing' other than that time he'd seen a teenager wearing a Slayer t-shirt in the mall in Birmingham. Of the five calls he and Bellamy had responded to up to this point, three had turned out to be either shadows or a neighbor patrolling their own yard. One had been the caller's own son playing a joke on his mother – and, knowing the mother, Walter was deeply grateful the boy hadn't been shot - before, finally, they'd had the call about the dog.

"How come you don't like dogs?" he asked.

Bellamy was silent for a long time, and after a while, Walter began to shrug it off as another one of the man's "asshole qualities." Then, quietly: "I got bit by one when I was a kid."

Walter winced. "Wow. How bad?"

"Bad." It was all he seemed willing to say on the matter, but Walter noticed the man running a hand unconsciously along his left leg.

Walter made a turn onto a tree-lined street full of houses. "I get that. But that doesn't mean that all dogs are bad. Hell, most of the ones I've ever known wouldn't bite for anything. They'd just-"

"Stop!" Bellamy yelled, throwing a hand toward the dash. Walter practically came out of his seat standing on the brake pedal, and the car screamed to a halt, the back end fishtailing. Walter swallowed a hard lump, staring out the windshield. A man who looked to be in his late fifties stood only a few feet in front of the car's grill, his own hands held out pleadingly. Through the windshield and the chatter of the radio, Walter could hear his voice, but couldn't make out the words. He opened his door while Bellamy yanked the microphone from its hook and called in their situation.

"Holy shit, man," Walter said as he got out and slammed his door. The moment of adrenaline-fueled panic was bleeding away and leaving anger in its wake. "I almost hit you! What the hell are you doing running out into the street like that? Are you nuts?"

The man, wearing jeans and a Dale Earnhardt shirt, took a wavering step toward him. Immediately, Bellamy's voice thundered from the other side of the car. "Stay where you are! Keep your hands where we can see them!"

The man twitched his terrified face toward the other officer and then back to Walter. "Please, you gotta help. It's my brother-in-law. He went after him."

"Went after who?" Walter asked. The man looked along an alley. Walter put a hand on the man's arm, gently turning him back. "Hey. Who did he go after?"

"I have no idea. We were in the kitchen, and Todd went out to check the grill. He comes back in saying that there's a man standing in the alley and looking over our fence into the yard. He went and grabbed my boy's baseball bat and went back out. I came out here in time to see him go out into the alley. He hasn't come back yet."

"How long ago was that?"

Earnhardt Shirt shook his head. "Couldn't have been more than five minutes. But the alley ain't that big. And with what happened earlier.... Could y'all go look?"

"We have another call," Bellamy started, but Walter spoke over him.

"Absolutely. Go back inside your house and wait. We'll check it out. What was Todd wearing?" The man gave a description, and Walter looked at his partner. "Come on. Dennis can wait a minute more."

"This is against regulations," Bellamy said.

"Then, fucking go on, man!" Walter snapped. He pointed down the dark path. "I'm going to look for this guy." Walter pulled his flashlight and weapon, and moved into the alley, not caring if Bellamy came or sat in the car and did the five finger shuffle on his prick. *Fucking county assholes don't give a shit about us anyway.*

He heard Bellamy calling in their status, and then the patrol car door slammed. His partner's footsteps came next, several yards behind him. Walter breathed out a quiet, relieved breath and refocused on the darkness ahead. The alley ran the length of the block. At the far end, he could see the icy glow of a streetlamp and Foxglen Road.

However, what the alley lacked in length, it more than made up for in offering places for someone to hide. The back fences of every house stood only a foot or so away from the pavement. Most were cluttered with trash cans or other detritus. Walter's light picked out an old commode laying on its side, a one-wheeled tricycle with its red and white paint long since gone to rust, and a stack of sodden cardboard boxes. On the other side of the fences, grew thick, old trees –

both pine and hardwood – with their branches extending out, giving the alley the feeling of a forested tunnel. Two of the houses contained large sheds near their back fence, both of them weathered and looked like a strong breeze could knock them down.

All perfect hiding spots.

Bellamy's light shifted as the man moved to the left side of the alley. Together, the officers pressed forward, sweeping the darkened yards and peering around piles of trash and thick bushes. With each passing step, Walter's tingling nervousness returned, buzzing its way through him.

"Stop." Bellamy's voice was barely a whisper, and Walter continued another two steps before he registered it. He froze. Bellamy's attention was straight ahead, his light pooling on a section of the alley that lay only about twenty feet in front of them. Walter shot him a questioning look. In response, Bellamy raised his eyebrows, nodding forward.

Walter strained, but couldn't see anything clearly in the darkness beyond the reach of the lights. "What?" he finally asked. Bellamy slowly raised his light until it spotlighted a dresser missing three of five drawers. The empty holes where the drawers belonged gaped like strange mouths belonging to some otherworldly horror. At the base of it lay several large and bulging black lawn bags. Another bag, this one white, lay on its side, a large rip in its plastic. Garbage spilled out into the alley, and Walter could see TV dinner trays with food stuck to their small aluminum wells, papers, several old coffee filters full of spent grounds, and a host of old foods that were black and green with mold. Flies buzzed everywhere, oblivious to the two officers as they feasted.

Walter began to ask 'what?' again, but the word shriveled in his throat. He saw *what* had stopped his partner, and a cold unease filled his guts. A man stood, half hidden, on the other side of the dresser. He faced away from the officers, but in the light from Bellamy's torch, Walter could see the patterning of acid wash jeans worn over dirty white sneakers and a section of a green and white shirt.

"Matches," he told Bellamy, who nodded without taking his eyes off the man. "Todd?" Walter called. The word came out as a throaty croak. He coughed and tried again. No response. Todd didn't even flinch at the sound of his name or the sudden presence of two other people in the alley.

Bellamy raised one hand and waved two fingers forward before drawing his weapon and training it on the figure. Walter understood and shifted forward, keeping a distance between himself and the unmoving man. He moved in line with Todd and glanced back at Bellamy, who gave another nod. Licking his lips, Walter took a step closer. He stood just outside arm's reach of Todd, who still hadn't given any indication that he'd heard his name being called. Walter's flashlight cast a wide sphere of light around the man, throwing shadows that crisscrossed a lot of the yard beyond him.

He stepped closer. "Todd? Elden Mills Police." No response. *Fuck. I'm going to have to touch him.* Walter reached out with his flashlight and prodded Todd's left shoulder. Todd moved then, in a gentle shift in response to being touched. His body swayed forward and then back. However, it didn't stop. When it swung back, it continued moving, Todd twisting and falling backward toward Walter, who gasped a curse and leaped back. The dead man landed with a wet, meaty thump at his feet.

Walter saw two things at once in that moment. The first was that Todd had no face. The entire front of his head was a confusion of blood, bone, and torn skin. Blood soaked the man's baseball tee.

The second thing was the pale white face on the other side of the fence. It stared at him from the edge of his flashlight's reach. But as Walter stared at it, the face receded into the darkness. It moved slowly, fading from view intentionally rather than turning and running in the way a guilty perpetrator would.

"What is it?" Bellamy demanded as he hurried to Walter's side.

Walter pointed. "There was someone standing in the yard. Wearing a mask." Bellamy stepped carefully but quickly over Todd's legs and leaned over the fence, shining his light through the yard. He gripped the top of the low chain-link fence and hoisted himself up and over before hurrying into the yard. Walter watched the man turn into a dark smudge against the brightness of his flashlight. A few moments later, he returned, shaking his head.

"Nobody there. I went all the way to the front of the house."

"He was there," Walter insisted. "He was right there."

CHAPTER 23

Morgan put her hair crimper onto the counter and tilted her head, looking at her handiwork from different angles. It wasn't the greatest job, but she didn't feel like taking another hour to get ready. Especially with the audience being only Jennifer and the gang. Still, her heart gave a single nervous pulse at the thought of seeing her friends. She forced herself to focus instead on finishing her makeup.

Why are you bothering? It's not like Chris cares. It's not like you're wanting to attract anyone.

That was true, she admitted, but standing under the lights of the upstairs bathroom, she found her face looking sallow with dark patches below both eyes. Some modicum of concealment was in order. When she finished, she stood back, adjusted her pink, blue, and yellow striped shirt, bloused it a little more over her pink shorts, and turned to leave.

Downstairs, the savory, meaty smell of dinner still hung in the air. She entered the living room, where both her parents sat on the couch. The wheelchair sat to the side of the couch like an outcast, and Morgan forced herself not to look at it. On the television, Sly Stallone wore sunglasses and chewed a match as he hunted a psychotic killer.

"Bit violent, considering what happened to those people, don't you think?" Morgan asked.

Her father shrugged. "It's either this or *The Golden Girls*, and I can't stand those women. Plus, your mom thinks Sly is sexy." Morgan's mom gave her husband a playful slap and smiled up at Morgan.

"You look nice. Where are you off to?"

Morgan glanced out the front window and then, not seeing her ride, sat down. "Jennifer's picking me up in a bit. Going to her house, I think. Some of the people from school are getting together."

"That'll be nice."

Her dad leaned forward slightly. "You mean you're not going to watch *Saturday Night Live*?" Morgan gave an apologetic smile and shook her head. "But it's our tradition!" he protested.

"Leave her alone. She hasn't seen her friends in a long time," her mom said. Then, to Morgan: "You'll be careful, won't you? I don't like you being out with...you know."

"We're just going to be at Jennifer's house. And there will be several of us. We'll be perfectly safe."

Her mom seemed to accept the answer, but kept her eyes on Morgan for a long moment before returning focus to the television. They watched Stallone be Stallone for a while. As the movie went to a commercial for fabric softener, Morgan glanced at her parents. The two sat close – not quite snuggling, but close enough that each could feel the other. An afghan covered her mother's thin legs, and the couple held hands atop the brown and gold fabric. Her heart swelled at the image, and she wondered if she'd ever be able to have what her parents had.

She needed to tell them what had happened to her. She needed to tell them how deeply sorry she was for how she'd acted, the things she'd said, and the way she'd blown out of the house like a storm. Nervous energy coursed through her, and as she opened her mouth to speak, she felt the tightening of her throat as the terrified part of her mind put up resistance.

Her mother looked over at her with a curious expression on her face. Morgan's heart slammed in her chest. She felt the words on her tongue, and the beginnings of an apology. But nothing would come. Her mother's face softened, her lips curved in a warm smile. She gave Morgan a gentle, almost imperceptible nod.

As headlights swept across the rocky facade of the fireplace, shadows stretched and light momentarily bathed her parents' faces. A car horn honked twice, breaking the spell that had gripped Morgan. She stood up, looping her purse over her shoulder. "That's Jennifer. I'll be back later. Don't wait up, please."

Her mom held out her arms, and Morgan leaned down to hug her. She felt her mother kiss her cheek, and she quickly returned the gesture before angling over and brushing her lips across the rough stubble on her father's cheek.

"Have fun," her mom said. "And please be careful."

"I will. Promise."

"Morg?" her dad said. Morgan paused at the door, one hand on the knob. "We're glad you're home." He smiled, and Morgan saw everything in that gesture: the understanding her parents had of the situation, the acknowledgment that she'd been through something and didn't want to talk about it yet, and the forgiveness for her behavior.

Morgan's chest ached, and her cheeks grew warm. Knowing tears were imminent, she nodded, not trusting herself to speak.

"We love you," her mother said, and blew a kiss.

Morgan mimed a kiss back, and then left.

CHAPTER 24

gnes Newman had lived her entire life in Elden Mills. She'd worked in the mill, as had her mother and father, and had even met her husband Gilbert in her first week of employment. After they'd had children, Agnes had left the mill to raise the kids and, once they'd been grown, started baking. To supplement Gil's paycheck, she sold her wares on Saturday mornings outside the steps of Town Hall; she didn't have a permit. The one time she'd been asked about it by Jared Hollister, when he'd first become sheriff, she'd told him that she'd sell whatever she damned well pleased wherever she damned well pleased, and he could take a flying piss up a rope if he didn't like it.

Agnes played a weekly game of hearts with seven other ladies, each rotating hostess duties for the game. Additionally, she volunteered at the library, reading to children and occasionally working the returns desk. She helped coordinate town events, and organize all of the community outreach programs that Brother Camden held at the Elden Mills First Baptist Church.

In other words, Agnes was plugged into the town of Elden Mills. As such, she was the person one went to if they wanted any of the best, most reliable gossip. During one marathon game of hearts, Agnes had regaled the group with the scandalous news regarding

Butch Simmons and his supposed affair with the wife of a certain mill supervisor. All but one of the women had tittered over the thought of anyone desperate enough to let the perpetually dirty and greasy-haired proprietor of the local junkyard touch them. Bernice Eaton had clucked her tongue disapprovingly. Agnes had proceeded with her news - and that's exactly what she considered it, not mere unsubstantiated rumors, but actual news - but taken notice that Bernice had adopted a posture of disapproval.

Later, as the party had been breaking up, the ladies all draping their jackets over their shoulders - it had been quite chilly that late September - Bernice had approached Agnes. She'd made it clear that she didn't feel such conversation was appropriate. Agnes had, without ceasing her sweeping of cookie crumbs from the tablecloth, told Bernice that if she truly felt that way, she was welcome to take her uppity, moth ridden cocktrap somewhere else to lose her money.

Even today, all these years later, Agnes got a good chuckle out of the look that'd been on Bernice's face before she'd stormed out. Good riddance to prissy cows.

Now, Agnes' reliability for town gossip was the reason she found herself sitting in her favorite recliner, talking on the phone to Irene Olsen while *Ohara* played silently on the television.

"I'm telling you," Irene said, a slightly musical lilt to her words. The woman was enjoying the conversation fully. "It's those damned devil worshippers. I hear they come to small towns like ours from larger cities – Birmingham, maybe even Cullman – and find people to sacrifice. They need human blood, you know."

Agnes made a scoffing sound deep in her throat. "If they needed human blood, don't you think they could have found someone better to sacrifice than Stephanie Weaver? It's well-known that girl was meeting boys after school for oral lessons. I'm sure I don't have to spell *that* out for you, do I?'

Again Irene's bubbly laughter. "You're so bad. But they didn't just kill Stephanie, did they? Got the whole family."

"My point. Everyone knows the Weavers weren't the best stock. Jerry was a fat slob who did nothing but drink when he wasn't working at the mill, and from what I heard, even that didn't stop him."

Irene tutted. "But that poor Shance child. It's a shame his father had to find him like that."

"But he didn't have to crash his car into the police station and present the boy's body like it was the centerpiece to Thanksgiving dinner, did he? No. He could have called Sheriff Hollister over and let him deal with things properly. Instead, he caused a scene and threw the whole damn town into a panic."

Irene was quiet for a moment. On the television, Pat Morita - Agnes had never minded him, for an Oriental - was questioning a suspect across an interview desk. Then, Irene was back in Agnes' ear. "You have to admit, it *is* pretty scary. All those people, killed so horribly. And the police have no idea who did it, do they? Not really."

"Of course, they don't. But Sheriff Hollister couldn't be trusted to find his asshole with both hands, a flashlight, and a guide dog. Still..." Agnes trailed off, her gaze moving from the television to the curtained window that overlooked the front yard. Through the sheer fabric, she saw the glow of a street lamp, but nothing more. "You're right. It's a frightening turn of events."

"And now there's the curfew! As if a curfew is going to stop someone from killing people."

"My point," Agnes said, her voice small as she stared at the window. Had there been movement out there? Something passing quickly across the glass, low to the bottom of the frame? She blinked the concern away and returned to the conversation. "A curfew wouldn't stop a five-year-old, much less someone intent on slashing people to pieces. I've seen people out all night. Nobody's paying attention to the curfew."

"Do you think it's someone who lives here?" Irene asked, her words pregnant with dread.

"Has to be," Agnes confirmed. "Who the hell would come to Elden Mills just to murder people?"

"Lands!" Irene exclaimed. "I can't imagine anyone here being that insane."

"Are you sure about that?" Agnes asked. "Clearly, you're over-looking Frank Gallagher or his little toadie, Geordie Dupont. Either of those two snakes have it in them. And with the mill closing and them both out of work? It's not hard to see how that would drive them to murder."

"Do you really think it's one of them? Oh, that sounds horrible to hear you say it. But I have to admit, it does hold a certain amount of plausibility. I, for one..." Irene continued to drone in her ear, but Agnes found her attention pulled to the window once more. This time, she was certain she'd seen movement. Something had absolutely passed across the frame.

Swallowing thickly, she said into the phone, "Irene, let me call you back."

Irene was instantly on guard. "Is everything alright?"

"Fine. Have to piss. I'll call you back when I'm done with all the paperwork." Agnes hung up the receiver without looking, all of her focus directed to the dark square of the window. She crossed to the window, stood against the curtains, and peered through the thin material. *What am I doing?* she chided herself. *Can't see a damned thing.* She tapped off the lamp that sat on a table nearby. Gil had bought the lamp and three others like it for the living room. Instead of relying on a switch or knob, some egghead had invented a method that only required a touch to the lamp's base to turn it on or off.

With the light doused, the glare on the window was eliminated, and Agnes peered through the curtain. The yard beyond it was as dark and still as the desert. She pulled the curtain aside, just a little, and studied the lawn. Everything seemed normal. No people were lurking behind the dogwood tree, no creeping miscreants were setting up a sacrificial altar next to the holly bushes, and no horned denizens from hades were salivating next to the azaleas.

Stepping back from the window, Agnes considered the front door. She could open it, step onto the porch, and make sure. Maybe what she'd seen had only been a shadow, a trick of the light from a car - she and Irene had both been talking about how many police cars were out and about tonight. It could easily have been a shadow from one of them, even from the next street over. "You're being ridiculous," she said to herself, deciding that the cop car theory was the correct one. "Jumping at shadows. And at your age, you're likely to give yourself a heart attack." And then where would Gil be? The old coot could barely make a bologna sandwich, let alone survive without her.

The phone began to ring, but Agnes let it go. That would be Irene, calling to make sure her friend wasn't spread out on a stone table, taking a satanic prick up the ole backdoor while an idiot in a cloaked robe prepared to cut her heart out. She waved an irritated hand at the phone as she passed it and went to the kitchen for a cup of tea.

She took the kettle to the sink and, before her hand could turn the knob to fill it, she heard the faint sound of a doorknob rattling. Her humming fear came back, in a great thrumming of chords that sent shockwaves through her. She stared at the back door. The door was solid wood with three small, frosted glass windows near the top. The decoration of the glass was so much that she couldn't see anything through it, but she didn't need to.

The gently rotating doorknob told her all she needed to know. Someone was standing on her back stoop, testing the knob. Agnes' mind screamed for her to get to the phone, to call someone, but her body was paralyzed. Who would she call? Gil? What good would that do? She'd call the bowling alley and get some lazy teenager working the counter who would then - if the layabout could even be bothered to focus and listen to her - have to go hunt Gil down. The alley would be packed tonight. And even if she did get him on the phone, it would take him, what, an hour or so to get home?

She risked a look at the clock. Unless he ran out of beer money, he wouldn't be home for another three hours. And even then, he'd be as drunk as a skunk. She could picture him, like previous times, trying to be quiet as he stumbled into the house and to bed, reeking of beer and cigar smoke. This was his one night a month to get out. Every time, he swore that he and the boys - he still called them 'the boys' even though most of them had a lot more time behind them than ahead - would make it an all-nighter. Rarely did he make it past eleven. So, no. Gil wasn't an option.

The cops, then. Agnes hated calling the police; she hated even the thought of it. In her experience, the small force that patrolled Elden Mills was inefficient at best, and trending toward incompetence. But the knob rattled again, this time a little more forcefully, and that decided it for her. With quick, short steps, she crossed the kitchen and plucked the phone from its wall-mounted cradle. The buttons weren't huge - she refused to get one of those phones - but they were big enough, and within seconds, she heard the connection as the operator picked up.

"Nine-one-one," a tired woman's voice said.

"Someone's trying to get into my house." Immediately, she gave the address.

"Mrs. Newman?" the dispatcher asked. The exhaustion had diminished now, the words becoming clearer and more focused.

"That's right."

"I'll send some of the guys out to you. They'll be there as soon as they can, but it may take them about another five to ten minutes. We're getting calls all over town, and the closest unit I have to you is out by the mill. Are your doors and windows locked?"

"Of course, they are!" Agnes snapped. "There's fucking satanic psychopaths roaming the town."

The dispatcher didn't respond to that, which a corner of Agnes' mind took as agreement. *Holy crippled Christ, Irene was right.* Instead, the woman told Agnes to double-check that everything was locked tight and to wait in a secured room – maybe the bathroom. Officers would be there as fast as they could. Agnes ended the call with a curse as the doorknob continued to rattle, only now with more force.

Agnes glared at the shifting knob and scowled. *They won't get me, the pricks.* She left the kitchen with a single thought cutting through the haze of fear that clouded her brain. Shuffling along the carpet that lined the hallway, she hurried to the back room where she and Gil had shared a bed for over fifty-five years. She opened the closet and, shoving Gil's suits aside, revealed a small shelf lined with neatly folded sweaters and a black metal case about the size of a shoebox. The case was heavy, but she managed to lower it to the floor. She looked at the clasp and small keyhole holding the lid closed, and for a heart-stopping moment thought she'd need the key, which would be on Gil's ring, buried deep in his hip pocket all the hell away and gone in Birmingham.

But the clasp flipped up easily, and she opened the case, revealing the silver .38 pistol nestled in black foam. Down the hall, she heard a thunderous bang on the back door, the sound a loud violation in the normal quiet of the home. Another followed, and Agnes snatched up the pistol. Oblivious of its weight. Gil had shown her how to use it, and she checked that it was loaded – except the chamber under the hammer.

"Revolvers don't have safeties," he'd said, *"so always keep that chamber empty."*

Back in the kitchen, Agnes positioned herself in front of the door. The knocks were coming hard and fast now, with the knob rattling like a pair of cymbals accompanying the bass drum beat. She started to call out, to say something, but decided not to. She was scared enough as is, and there was no point in letting the little shits hear it in her voice.

Agnes raised the gun and pointed it at the door. Her heartbeat thundered in her ears, the door rattling in its frame as the psychotic satanists on the other side fought to get through it, to get to her.

With a shaking hand, Agnes reached for the doorknob, thumbed the lock open, and twisted.

The back stoop was empty. Agnes stepped to the threshold and, holding onto the jamb, leaned forward to scan the yard. There was nothing. She gave either side of the door a quick glance and stepped back into the house, shut the door and threw the lock.

"What are you-"

The question gave Agnes' heart a kick. She screamed and spun, putting the door to her back as she raised the gun. A man stood in the kitchen, a huge black silhouette against the living room lights. He held the uneven bulk of a severed head in one hand. Before she was even finished with her turn from the door, Agnes raised the gun and fired.

As her finger squeezed the trigger, the intruder reached out with his free hand - *the one not holding a severed human head* - and flipped the light switch. The kitchen was instantly filled with bright light, just in time for Agnes to feel the bucking of the pistol and see the explosion of blood as the round punched into Gil's throat.

Her husband wavered on his feet, one arm still outstretched by the light switch, the other grasping his old bowling ball bag. He stared at her with eyes as wide as saucers with shock. Agnes' fingers lost their ability to function and let the pistol fall to the floor. Gil opened his mouth to say something, but the only thing that came out was a waterfall of blood. It cascaded over his chin and onto his checkered shirt. The hole in his neck was a tiny thing, but blood poured out of it like water from a busted pipe.

When the police finally made it to Agnes' house they found her, rocking gently back and forth on the floor next to the blood soaked body of her husband, mumbling to herself.

CHAPTER 25

Morgan closed the door to Jennifer's house and stood swaying gently on the stoop. Her head swam with the gauzy feeling brought on by half a dozen wine coolers and - thanks to Jason's unrelenting insistence - several shots of vodka. This was not going to feel good in the morning.

She reached forward and grasped the thin, twisted metal railing as she breathed in deeply, hoping the fresh air would quell the roiling in her stomach. The early summer night air seemed to intensify the pungent stench of cigarette smoke hanging on her clothes. The foul odor clung like a thick winter jacket, and she winced and fanned her hand in front of her face. Through the door behind her came a cacophony of laughter - Jennifer's being the loudest - and the steady drumbeat of the GoGo's. Heather had insisted on playing *Beauty and the Beat* repeatedly for most of the night, dancing on the couch and singing along into a wooden kitchen spoon that she'd used to smack anyone who asked her to play something else.

Even as Morgan stood there, she heard Todd complaining, begging Heather to let him put on anything else – Michael Jackson, Alabama, Kenny Rogers, anything. His pleas ended with a high-pitched, "Ow!" followed by a raucous burst of laughter from the others.

The door opened, and the music and laughter spilled onto the porch as Jennifer stepped out. "You didn't barf, did you?" she asked, pulling the door shut behind her and returning the din to a low thumping. Morgan shook her head. "Good," Jennifer said.

"I can't promise I won't though."

To be safe, Jennifer positioned herself on the other side of the porch and leaned against the railing. She lit a cigarette and blew the smoke upward. "You okay?"

"Yeah. Just...haven't had this much to drink in a while."

Jennifer laughed, tendrils of white smoke pouring through her lips. "Jason can be a dickhead when it comes to parties." She paused, her head cocked to one side. "You look different than when you came into the store yesterday. More relaxed. When I saw you standing there, I would have thought a mean look would practically kill you. But now..." she pointed a pink fingernail at Morgan. "You look happy."

"I am," Morgan admitted. The words brought a smile to her face. Admitting it out loud felt good. It felt as if a heavy, wet blanket had been draped on her shoulders for so long...and had now been removed. Of course, that could be the booze, but she chose to believe the source ran deeper than that. "I didn't know what to expect, coming here tonight. Coming home, for that matter."

Jennifer's face softened. "What are you talking about? What did you expect?"

For a second, Morgan felt the urge to blow it off, to say it was nothing, to change the subject. But the alcohol was doing its job and had sent her inhibitions packing for the night. "I left town without telling any of you I was going."

"I figured something was up," Jennifer admitted with a shrug. "You'd started acting all weird. I hardly ever saw you the last couple of weeks before you left."

"I didn't even tell Chris. And we were...you know."

"Porking. Yeah."

Morgan smiled sloppily. "Yeah. We'd been..." She laughed. "Anyway, I never mentioned it to him. Or Jason or Todd. Nobody. I barely told my own family. But I had to get out of here, you know? I couldn't stand the thought of spending the rest of my life in the mill, of being stuck here like...well, you know."

"Like the rest of us?" Jennifer finished, and sucked on her cigarette. "No, don't apologize, you're right. We all chose to stay. Of course, who the fuck knows how that's going to turn out now that the mill is closed." She paused while a police cruiser drove by. They could see the dark shapes of two people in the front seat, but the car never stopped. "Plus, apparently, now there are devil worshippers in town." She chuckled at the thought. "Fucking stupid." Jennifer inspected the cigarette, gave it a final suck, and flicked it into the grass. Blowing the smoke into the air, she said, "Now, how about you tell me why you really left? And why you really started acting the way you did right before."

The warm blanket of Morgan's buzz slipped off of her brain. "I don't know what..." she started, but Jennifer gave a dismissive snort.

"Don't start that shit. We're best friends. Or we were before you left. I hope we still are. I said I noticed you pulling away, acting all weird. Then, for you to just take off like that? Something happened to you." She lowered her voice. "What was it? You can tell me." She looked around dramatically. "I'm not going anywhere. No matter what it is." Jennifer pulled back, her eyes narrowing comically. "You didn't get pregnant, did you? Is that what it was? You left town to get an abortion?"

The dam of Morgan's mind resisted for only a heartbeat, but the need to unburden herself - riding a tsunami of booze - crashed through, and the words were out before she could stop them. "I was raped." Across the porch, Jennifer went still. Her eyes bore into Morgan with an unnerving intensity.

"What?"

Morgan dropped her gaze away from Jennifer. She picked at the polish on one of her fingers as she spoke. "At the mill. I was finishing my shift, putting some things away in the maintenance room. I-"

Jennifer pushed off of the railing. "Who?" she demanded. "Who the fuck was it? I want to know whose balls I'm cutting off tonight." An instant later, her eyes went wide. "No."

Morgan nodded, knowing that Jennifer had pieced it together. The relief of having it out there swirled through her, burning like acid. She had the sudden urge to retract it, to grab the words and cram them back inside her and undo their truth.

"Fucking Geordie Dupont?" Jennifer took a forceful step closer to the door. Her expression was pure hatred carved in granite. "I'm getting my knife. We're going to feed him his own cock."

Morgan touched Jennifer's arm, stopping her before she could pull the door open. "Don't. It's not worth it." The plea came out mealy and weak.

Jennifer's eyes blazed over her flushed cheeks. "Not worth it? Do you hear yourself? At least we have to report it to Hollister."

"I will. That's one of the reasons I came back." She let go of Jennifer's arm and exhaled a long breath. The urge to focus on her fingernails rose again, but she fought past it and concentrated on her friend. "That's why I left. Why I was such a dick to everyone right before. I couldn't handle things. I had no idea how to deal with it. I was so scared. Hurt. Angry. At everyone else *and* myself. I didn't tell anyone. You know how people react when they hear something like that. 'What was she wearing? Why did she put herself in that position? Maybe she was asking for it.'" She shook her head. "Leaving was easier than facing those things."

"I would have believed you!" Jennifer shot back. "If you'd told me then, Geordie Dupont would be auditioning for the Mormon Tabernacle Choir by now."

"I thought that by leaving I could start over, put it behind me, but I couldn't." She told Jennifer about Garrett and her own infidelity. "The other night, I seemed to wake up from a coma. I was in a dirty bed in an even dirtier trailer. The guy was in the shower and told me that he'd invited some friends over. At my request. I was going to let them do whatever they wanted. It..." she trailed off, her eyes focusing on that moment. "I think I was trying to regain some kind of control over things, but every time I fucked someone, no matter what I did to them or let them do to me, I felt worse. That sense of not being worth anything, of being the same level as dogshit, was still there. Sometimes, the feeling was worse. So, I left and went to a friend's house. I was ready to run, to head west. Seattle or someplace far away where I could start over again. But he told me that I needed to come back here and face what happened. To ask for forgiveness from you guys for how I treated you, and to confront Geordie. If I didn't do that, he said, I'd risk falling back into the same habits."

Jennifer grabbed Morgan and pulled her into a spine-crushing hug. Morgan returned the embrace, ignoring the tears that poured from her eyes. After several minutes, the two parted, and Jennifer reached up and smoothed Morgan's hair. "What do you need from me?"

The question broke something within Morgan that until that moment she'd not been fully aware existed. The care, the concern in those words ruptured the barrier that had built up inside Morgan over the last two years. It burst like an overfilled balloon and the sense of relief, the promise of peace and happiness that had been held back swarmed through her, threatening to knock her down.

"I just got it," Morgan answered as more tears streamed down her face. The two embraced again. Afterwards, Morgan said, "Don't tell the others yet. You're the first person I've told. I almost said something to my parents before you picked me up, but I couldn't. I will in the morning, though. But I don't want to tell them," she nodded toward the party. "I don't want to ruin the party. I'll talk to them tomorrow or one day next week."

"Consider it done. But seriously, my knife is in my nightstand. It's ready anytime." She gave Morgan a look. Her lips curled in a smile that hinted at a joke. But the hardness in her eyes told Morgan the truth. Jennifer would absolutely castrate someone if Morgan said so. All it would take would be a single word, and the blonde would happily maim Geordie. It scared Morgan a little, but made her love her friend even more.

"How do you keep from confusing it with your vibrator?" Morgan asked, and surprised herself by laughing at her own joke.

Jennifer's eyebrows rose in shock. "Maybe I don't," she said, and laughed. "Man, I'm happy you're back. It feels like you never left."

Morgan sighed and gave a sour expression. "I don't think Amanda likes that I'm back."

Jennifer threw a dirty look toward the door. "Fuck that bitch. I never liked her, and neither does Heather. She hasn't said anything to you tonight, has she? I'll break her nose if she did."

"No. They've kept away from me all night."

"If you want Chris back, I'm pretty sure it wouldn't be too hard. Amanda is pretty and probably good in the sack, but the bitch is as deep as a rain puddle. Come on, let's go back inside. I bet if one of us distracts Heather, we can finally get something else on the radio. If I have to hear 'We got the Beat' one more time, I'm going to *beat* my head against the refrigerator door." She gave Morgan's hand a light tug.

In the wake of the confession and the emotions of the night, Morgan was suddenly terribly exhausted. Her limbs felt heavy, as if filled with sand. She pulled her hand free of Jennifer's grasp and shook her head. "I can't drink any more tonight. I'm too far gone. I'm going to head home, take some Tylenol, and go to bed and sleep for three days."

Jennifer's head leaned back in surprise. "What? Girl, it's only—" She looked at her watch, "one in the morning. We got hours to go! I'm betting that Todd takes that Stephanie girl he brought to a bedroom soon. I'm thinking about taking bets on how long it'll take him. I personally don't think he'll get it out of his pants before it's over."

The image of Todd emerging from the bedroom shamefaced but trying to play it off as sexual prowess came to her and she gave a weary smile. It would be nice to put the emotions of the last few minutes behind her and bury them in more laughs and a few more drinks. But the thought of burrowing under the covers at home was stronger. "Y'all have fun," Morgan said, "but my bed is calling my name."

"You want me to give you a ride?" Jennifer asked, swaying ever so slightly.

Morgan took a step toward the stairs and looked up at the moon. "No, I'm good." *And you're wasted,* she thought, but didn't say. "It's not like I have to walk clear across town, and it'll help clear my head some. Maybe I won't be as hungover tomorrow."

Jennifer stuck out her lower lip in a pout, but hugged Morgan again. "Be careful. Don't let the satanists get you."

"I think I'll be okay. I heard they're only looking for virgins," Morgan quipped as she broke the hug.

Morgan trotted down the steps as Jennifer went back inside, calling out, "Okay, Heather, time for the GoGo's to fucking go! And don't even think about hitting me either, bitch!" Cheers and laughter welled up as the door shut.

Morgan walked slowly along the sidewalk, letting the cloudiness of her buzz help her drift. With each passing block, her smile widened even more as she thought back on the party. She'd genuinely missed her old friends. She hadn't realized how much she needed Jason and Todd's antics, Heather's energy, or Jennifer's silliness until she'd been in the middle of it all again. Even Chris' calm demeanor was comforting. He'd been drunk, too, slurring his words and occasionally spilling his drink as he danced with Amanda or threw down a winning hand of cards. But through it all, that old, trustworthy steadiness had been there. It was one of the things she'd found so attractive about him in the first place, which had led her to push beyond the friendly flirtations and finally kiss him.

Of course, it had taken her until after high school to reach that point. They'd known each other their entire lives, and been friends for most of that time, but it hadn't been until after graduation that she'd finally allowed herself to see him as someone more. God, his face after she'd finally kissed him. They'd been sitting on a park bench in Dunning Park after the Fourth of July party, empty beer cans stacked on the warped wood, with Jennifer and the others laid out on the grass watching the stars, and talking about the fireworks show they'd watched. The memory made her laugh. The sound of her laughter along the otherwise empty and silent street surprised her. She covered her mouth with one hand and giggled behind her palm as she looked around, embarrassed.

The street and sidewalks were empty.

Morgan reached her block and found herself humming "Our Lips are Sealed." She used her key on the front door, slipped inside, and leaned against the door as she reached behind her and thumbed the lock. Her head was a little more clear now, the walk having done its job of sobering her slightly. The house was dark and silent, save for the soft ticking of the wall clock in the kitchen. Morgan considered digging through the fridge for a late snack, something to help pad her stomach, but dismissed the idea, not wanting to risk the noise.

Instead, she went upstairs, one hand on the railing and climbing as quietly as she possibly could. She closed her bedroom door and toed off her shoes as she undressed in the dark. Her shorts and shirt landed in a pile in the far corner of the room next to the accordion doors of her closet, and from a drawer, she pulled out a pair of sweat shorts and an oversized t-shirt.

Morgan crawled into bed and pulled the blankets up to her chin. She lay still, basking in the lingering buzz, the familiar comfort of the mattress, and the smells of her parents' house. She was home. Her family and friends didn't hate her. She was making amends and getting closure. She was moving on, towards happiness.

Those thoughts followed her down into sleep.

CHAPTER 26

He stood in the shadows between houses, where the Things slept, and watched as a police car slid past. It moved slowly and quietly, like a shark creeping up on a seal basking in the sun on the water's surface. He could see the two Things inside looking. Looking for him.

Then, the car was gone and the street fell into silence once more. He remained where he was, the cool of the shadows surrounding him like a loving embrace. The street had been quiet for some time. There'd been no other cars, no other Things moving around. Even most of the houses were dark. That was okay, he knew, as it was only a matter of time before an opportunity came.

From his right came the soft taps of footsteps along the sidewalk. He waited – not shifting, not moving anything other than his eyes behind the mask as the Thing passed in front of him. It was a female Thing wearing pink shorts and a striped shirt. She moved somewhat unsteadily, her steps quick, the strides uneven as she passed along the sidewalk and out of sight to the left.

He moved then, walking slowly to the front edge of the house. There, he paused as the Thing crossed the street and angled across a yard. She climbed a short set of stairs and fumbled in a pocket for something before unlocking the door and stepping inside.

He followed, ready to hear the screaming.
Ready to see the blood as it erupted from corrupted flesh.

CHAPTER 27

Morgan peeled her eyes open and looked at the thin, red digital numbers on the clock. Just 2:23 in the morning. She glanced at the ceiling as she rolled over. It shifted back and forth as if it were caught in a time loop - *yep, still drunk* - and she squeezed her eyes shut again. She focused on slowing her breathing, trying to trick her body into falling back asleep, but the insistent pressure in her bladder had other plans for her. With a soft groan of irritation, she tossed back the sheet and swung her legs onto the floor. Sitting up, she gave another gasp as the room around her swam, tilting like a ship caught in a storm.

Weaving unsteadily, Morgan trailed her hand along the wall for balance as she passed along the dark hall. Twice, her fingers brushed the edges of pictures her mother had hung, the frames clattering as they fell back against the wall. Each time, she stopped, wincing at the loudness, her eyes going to the dark slit of her parents' partially opened bedroom door. She waited, expecting to hear her mother call out, to ask if she was okay, but the question never came. Exhaling relief, she entered the bathroom and, in the dark, fumbled her way to the toilet. When she finished, she felt her way to the door and stood, hands on the frame, as she waited for enough clarity to return to her bed without risking waking the entire neighborhood.

A quiet thump broke the stillness, and Morgan froze. What had she done this time? The sound came twice more, quickly. Morgan looked behind her, concerned something had fallen from a shelf. The bathroom was as tidy as it had always been. And out in the hall, pictures were in their usual places, the couple she'd bumped slightly crooked. So, what had that noise been?

"Wha-" the sound of her mother's voice, slurred with sleep, drifted from behind the door, but was quickly cut off by another of the sounds. Then another. And another.

As Morgan stood holding the doorway molding, a realization cut through the fog of sleep and drunkenness. The sounds were wet, meaty. A drunken, crooked smile split her face. Were her parents getting it on? How gross. Embarrassment flushed her cheeks.

She went back to her room, the sounds following her. After only a few steps, though, she paused again. No, this wasn't right. She'd *had* sex. Even drunk, she knew how sex sounded. There was usually heavy breathing, moans, the smacks of kissing. Turning back to the dark slit of her parents' room, she stared.

That wasn't sex. Something was wrong. And with that thought came an icepick of cold through her chest.

"Mom?" Only silence answered her. Even the wet sounds, those *wrong* sounds, had stopped. Slowly, Morgan approached the door, raised one hand, and touched her fingertips to its smooth surface. She hated going into her parents' room in the middle of the night. Even as a child, when she'd been awakened by a bad dream or scared by a movie, there had been this feeling of not belonging when she entered the bedroom while her parents slept. That same fear, the hesitation to disturb them, came over her in a powerful wave, and for a moment, she pulled her hand back. There was something about the quiet beyond the door that scared her. It felt like staring at a coiled snake, anticipating the flash of movement and the sting of the fangs piercing skin.

She couldn't hear her parents breathing. Usually, at the very least, she should have been able to hear the low, uneven buzz saw of her father's snores. But the bedroom was completely silent. Morgan took in a rattling breath and pushed the door open.

Silver moonlight from a window between her parents bed and the en suite bathroom fell on the carpet in a silver puddle, showing dark, uneven striped patterns in the carpet and on the walls. The rest of the room was a pitch black void. Slowly, still concerned about waking them despite the growing, gnawing fear working its way up her gut, Morgan approached the dark bed. With each step her eyes better adjusted to the gloom, and she found herself able to see the shapes of her parents beneath the covers; the light from the bare window reached that far, at least.

"Mom?" she whispered again. The lump that was her mother didn't answer. Morgan stared hard, trying to pick out her mother's face in the dim light, but the dark sheets blocked her view. Instead, she moved around toward her father's side. She stepped close to the mattress, her hand reaching out to give the man a gentle shake even as two things registered in her mind. The first was the patch of wetness beneath her bare foot, the carpet fibers sodden and shifting beneath her sole like worms. The second was that what she had origi-nally thought was a pattern on the sheets – a dancing kaleidoscope of dark colors and pure white – was wrong. That wasn't like her parents at all, to have psychedelic sheets. They were the white-sheets-only type of people.

With her heart a heavy lump at the base of her throat, Morgan forced herself to touch her father. The lumpy shape that was his shoulder beneath the sheet pushed in softly, giving way easily to her gentle touch. As she pressed, trying to understand why her father's shoulder should be so yielding, she felt the dampness of the sheet. Had he spilled something? She turned her hand over. In the muted light, her fingers looked like they were covered with oil. Before she could reconsider, Morgan grabbed the sheets and flung them back, revealing her parents on the mattress.

Morgan's world stopped turning for a long, heart-rending moment. Her parents' bodies lay in horribly misshapen angles, limbs twisted and broken so badly that she would later only be able to equate them to a pile of noodles. Blood covered everything. The mattress was nothing more than a black lake of it.

"Dad?" she whined. But her father's face wasn't there. Her father usually slept face down, his head to the side, but now his head - what remained of it - was nothing more than a pulverized, flattened mass of hair, shattered bone fragments, and blood. Beyond him, her mother's small form looked to be in even worse shape. Morgan couldn't make out a single feature of her mother's body. Shoulders were nothing more than deformed lumps; arms were buried beneath a heavy coat of blood with only the cold, white fragments of bone peering through. The face that had once looked at Morgan with unconditional love was now a perversion of itself. A lone eye, seemingly floating by itself amidst all the blood, stared out, seeing nothing.

Morgan staggered back until her father's tall dresser stopped her. She gave a strangled gasp as she connected with it, the hanging metal handles clacking like teeth snapping together. Her mouth opened to scream, but the sound came out as only a pitched whistle.

Movement on her mother's side of the bed forced her eyes from the mattress. Something shifted in the dark corner between the nightstand and her mother's low, long dresser with its trifold mirror and small bottles of perfume. Morgan stared and watched - *I have to be dreaming because there's no way I'm seeing this* - as a white mask appeared, the eyes nothing more than black pits above a ragged, slash of a mouth. Hair hung in long, swaying, blood-soaked clumps as the figure approached the edge of the bed.

The man stopped, and the mask tilted down as he observed his handiwork. The admiration lasted only a second before the face rotated back to focus on Morgan. Slowly, he raised a hand, and Morgan saw the weapon he held in one gloved fist. It was a hammer, but unlike any hammer she'd seen. The handle was long, but the head was massive. One end was long, slightly curved, and ended in a vicious point. The other end was wide and, instead of having the flat metal of other hammers, this one had a series of metal pyramids covering the surface. *It looks like a meat mallet,* she thought with a lurching sickness. Her nausea intensified as she saw that the metal spikes were smeared with blood. What made her knees start to buckle, though, were the small pieces of flesh and bone she could make out wedged between the spikes and dangling from their gore-smeared tips.

The air in the room expanded, filling the space between Morgan and the masked man. The pressure increasing until Morgan thought everything would explode. She stared at the man, and he watched her, his eyes invisible within the blackness of the eyeholes. Then, he was moving, sliding around the edge of the bed with lithe movements, his body graceful despite its size. Morgan stood paralyzed, her body unable to do anything that her brain was screaming at her to do. The man reached her – the hammer raised high, but starting its path down toward her head. Morgan snapped back to awareness and shifted to her right. She hunched low as she moved, legs propelling her to the doorway even as the hammer slammed into the dresser. The massive crack as the wood splintered sounded as loud as a gunshot, and the scream that had been building finally tore itself free from her chest.

Morgan raced toward the bedroom door, the wind behind her whistling as the man swung again. This time, a line of fire burned through her lower back as the pointed end of the hammer raked over her. For another heart-stopping second, it caught in her shirt and she felt the force of the fabric pulling tight against her chest. But then it came free with a horrible ripping, and Morgan went through the doorway and into the hall. Her feet carried her to the opening of the stairs, her hands out and groping as if she were blind.

Something slammed into her left shoulder. Dull, intense pain as hot as the sun radiated from where she'd been hit, and Morgan jerked forward, one leg catching the leading edge of the top stair. Then, she was falling, the stairs rushing up to meet her with unforgiving edges as she tumbled, rolling and sliding downward. She landed in a heap at the bottom, one leg resting atop the steps, facing the way she'd come, the rest of her in a breathlessly painful pile.

The masked man stood at the top of the stairs, hammer held by his side, watching her with eerie calm. Then, with terrifying slowness, he started down. The pointed end of the hammer trailed along the spindles of the railing, each impact being a dull, clock tick counting down until she was dead.

Get up. Get up. GET UP!

The man was halfway down the stairs, and Morgan blinked to clear the fog that had overtaken her mind. She rolled over, pulled her legs in and, gritting her teeth against the pain, stood. Morgan took her first shaky step. Her second step was better, the third even more so. By the fourth, she was able to push herself into a trot as she entered the living room. For a brief moment, she stood looking stupidly around. As she heard the thump of the man's feet coming off the last step, Morgan's mind flipped through her options like they were a slideshow of a family vacation.

Kitchen, basement, front door.

The kitchen had weapons and a door to the back deck. The basement was a bad idea.

The front door. That was the answer.

Get out, get away. Scream for neighbors. Get the cops over here.

The hammer made another awful hissing as the man swung at her in the same instant that she moved in the direction of the front door. She felt the wind of the attack rustle her hair. Her hands pulled on the front door, twisting the knob and yanking at it with soft, panicked grunts. But the door remained firmly closed.

"Shit!" she yelled, and threw herself to the right as the wall next to the door absorbed the impact of the hammer. Morgan careened off of her father's recliner, spun, and threw a hand out to keep herself from slamming into the couch. She stumbled into the kitchen, her eyes darting to the knife block on the counter, which may as well have been on the other side of town.

Her hands twisted the knob for the back door, and she almost fell backward onto her ass as it swung in and rebounded against the wall.

Bootsteps clocking on the linoleum galvanized her, and she slapped the push lever for the screen door. It opened, but in a flimsy, jerking motion. Morgan sprinted forward before it was even halfway ajar and felt one of her arms punch through the thin screen mesh. Her momentum carried her out onto the porch and spun her back to face the kitchen. She pulled her arm through the screen, the small wires scraping her skin. The masked man stood a foot away, practically filling the doorway, his bloody hammer coming up again.

Morgan stumbled across the deck. She grabbed a patio chair and flung it behind her, and then another. She reached out and grabbed the round, charcoal grill as she passed and pulled it over, the lid coming off and the grate clattering loudly. Holding onto both railings - she'd be damned if she fell down these stairs, as doing so would kill her as surely as that goddamned hammer - she thundered down to the lawn. The grass at the base of the steps was wet with dew, and rocks jabbed into her bare feet. Morgan grunted in pain, but raced around the side of the house to the front yard.

In the expanse of the yard, she skidded to another halt, her head whipping back and forth as she considered the best direction. All along the street, her neighbors' houses were dark, mute witnesses to her personal horror. Morgan risked a glance backward. The mask, a pale specter from a nightmare plane of existence, appeared around the corner. The evil eyes locked onto her.

The shadows around her elongated and began to shift. Morgan spun and saw headlights turning onto her block, the throaty grumble of a truck's engine cutting through the night.

CHAPTER 28

Garrett Ward stifled a yawn and pressed harder on the gas pedal. The Chevy truck surged forward along State Road 74 following the blazing spear points of its headlights. A sign flashed briefly in the glow of the lights, white lettering stating that Elden Mills was a short five miles away. He flexed his fingers on the steering wheel and focused on the road ahead.

After getting home only to find the flowers he'd bought still on the table and all of Morgan's things missing, his first impulse was to visit Ryan. Despite the hour, Ryan had answered the door with a look of sad resignation, with Morgan's letter held out by way of greeting.

Garrett,

I don't expect you to accept this as an excuse or even as justification as to how I've treated you. In October of 1984, I was raped by a man named Geordie Dupont. He and I both worked at the Avondale Fabric Works at the time, although I left immediately after.

After the attack, I stopped going to work. I didn't tell anyone because who would have believed me? He'd been at the mill for over ten years. Still is, I suppose. I was a high school fuck-up. I started fighting with my parents. I didn't know why. I just did. One day, I told them I was leaving.

That I didn't want to be stuck in that shithole town, another pathetic loser working in the mill, never actually doing anything with my life. I knew that would hurt them, and at the time, I didn't care. I was angry and confused. I packed up and hit the road. I didn't tell anyone where I was going.

I thought if I could get somewhere new I could start over, regain control of my life. I made a couple of friends, got a job. I thought I was healing. But the whole time, I was dead inside. Then I met you. For a little while, things were great. But I couldn't shake the fact that a part of me was missing. Something had been taken from me in that room at the mill, and I desperately wanted to get it back. I started cheating on you. I think maybe, to some degree, I felt like I didn't deserve how good you were to me. I felt like the only way I had value was by letting men use me however they wanted. I hated myself every time I did it.

Just know I never did it with the thought or intention of hurting you. It was never about you. But one time - the last time - I woke up and knew I couldn't do it anymore. I couldn't keep hurting you, even though you didn't know what I'd been doing.

I hope you get this letter. Ryan said he'd hold onto it. Maybe if you don't come looking, he'll find a way to get it to you. I need you to understand that I never wanted to hurt you. You were the only good thing in my life for a little while. I'm broken. Too broken for you to waste your time on. So, I'm going to go somewhere else and start over. Maybe I'll change my name. Who knows?

Thank you for everything you did for me. And I'm so, so, so sorry.

Morgan.

Garrett had read the letter standing in Ryan's doorway, each word cutting deeper and deeper into him. When he'd finished, Ryan had told him where she'd gone and why. To make amends with her family and to confront the man who'd assaulted her – before she tried to start her life over. Garrett absorbed that information and staggered, numb, back to his truck. Ryan called after him, but Garrett didn't hear. Instead, his mind was a symphony of memories of Morgan, and pain over her betrayal. He'd been nothing but kind to her, nothing but supportive and loving. And she'd thrown it all away for...what? Sex?

He'd driven back to the apartment he'd shared with her and walked slowly through every room, thinking of the moments he'd shared with her there; how happy they'd been. Her absence was massive, leaving the apartment feeling empty and hollow. He'd returned to the couch, dropped heavily onto it and reread the letter.

When he woke the next day, the light through the apartment's windows was the soft orange of late afternoon. The sting of her absence and the betrayal she'd confessed to in the letter was still present. He had spent the rest of the evening on the couch, staring at MTV and drinking. After every beer he picked up the letter and read it, his eyes searching the handwriting for some hidden message, something to help make it right.

By ten that night he had gone through all the beer he had and still come no closer to reconciling what Morgan had done. He had pawed at the phone next to the couch and punched in Ryan's number, only to learn that Ryan was working a double shift at the bowling alley. Garrett hung up the phone and sneered at the phrase, thinking about all the times Morgan had used the same excuse.

When he woke Saturday afternoon, Garrett found a message on his answering machine from Ryan. In it, Ryan apologized for what Garrett was going through, made a lame joke about Garrett's call waking up Greg, but then asked if Garrett would come by the bowling alley around seven that night. Ryan had a shift that started at eight, but felt that a conversation may go a long way towards helping Garrett.

They'd sat at the bar, in a corner next to a Ms. Pac-Man cabinet, and Ryan had explained to Garrett everything that Morgan had told him before she left. He talked about his experiences as an alcoholic and how he equated the steps towards recovery to what Morgan was dealing with. Despite his anger, Garrett had to admit that he honestly had no idea what sort of trauma an attack like what she'd endured entailed. He'd never been raped, and as far as he knew, didn't know anyone who had. Who was he to say what the correct response from a victim was?

When Ryan's shift began, the blonde man pulled Garrett into a quick hug, had asked him to please not hate Morgan, then went behind the bar and into the kitchen. Garrett drifted out to his truck. As he drove home, he thought back to all of the nights she'd been distant with him or seemed uninterested when he'd made even a modest romantic gesture. He thought about how sometimes she'd been timid and disassociated when they'd made love, and yet other times when she'd been almost feral, clawing at him and telling him to go harder, go farther, and do more.

Maybe all of that was the only way she could deal with what she'd been through. She'd even written that she felt undeserving and that the only way she could find a sense of value was by allowing others to abuse her. Was that a common theme among rape survivors? If that was the case, then nothing about her behavior was her fault. She'd said herself that she cared for him, and that she'd never meant to hurt him.

I'm too broken for you to waste your time on.

"The hell you are," he'd whispered.

If Morgan was going back to face what had happened to her, to make amends and confront the monster who'd attacked her, he'd be damned if he'd let her do it alone. He was at least going to let her know that he was there for her and that he'd do whatever was necessary to make sure she was safe. Who knew what kind of person this Dupont guy was? When Morgan finally confronted him, would he attack her again? What if she threatened to finally tell the police and he decided to kill her?

Just over five hours later, Garrett reached the River's Edge Inn. The bored, half asleep clerk had told him that she had no idea who Morgan Bell was, but did know that the town of Elden Mills was ten miles away and usually shut down pretty early every night. Garrett paid for a room with the plan of getting a couple hours sleep and driving into Elden Mills early the next morning.

The room had been smaller than he'd expected and smelled

disturbingly of disinfectant and stale cigarette smoke. The phone book in the room showed only two entries for Bell. Garrett tore the page out and stuffed it into his pocket.

A single twin bed jutted from the wood-paneled wall. Over the bed lay a blurry watercolor painting that, he supposed, was a rendering of a factory of some sort next to a river. He'd considered a shower, but one look at the dark stains in the tub changed his mind. He set the alarm clock and lay on top of the bedsheets and tried to sleep. But after only thirty minutes of his mind serving up thought after thought of Morgan, though, he decided he couldn't wait any longer.

To his great surprise, Elden Mills had a lot more life at two in the morning than he'd ever have imagined. Several times, he spied the flashing of emergency lights bouncing off of homes or trees as he crossed intersections. Residents stood either in the streets or on their lawns, hands clutching robes closed or jammed into jeans pockets as they watched the activity from a distance. Garrett never managed to see what exactly was going on, but found himself impressed by the sheer number of police cars present in a town this small.

Now Garrett yawned, squeezed his eyes tight, and tried to refocus by peering once more at the page from the phone book, comparing the printed address to the street signs he passed. He steered his truck past what appeared to be the town square and noticed a patrol car sitting at the next light. The two officers watched him pass and then pulled out behind him. Although he'd done nothing wrong – he hadn't been speeding and certainly hadn't had anything to drink – Garrett found himself watching them nervously in the rearview mirror.

He tried to distract himself by searching for the next street sign. The thin silver pole topped with the standard green and white sign appeared, rising from a thicket of bushes, and Garrett slowed for the turn. He wasn't sure if it would lead him to Morgan's street, but figured getting away from the cop car was more important.

The patrol car's red lights flashed, sending a drumbeat of panic through Garrett's chest. He'd already flipped his turn signal and begun to steer to the side of the road when the cop car sped around and past him. The passenger, a hulking man with a granite face, stared at him as they blew by. They turned one block farther up and were gone. Garrett let out a shaky breath and made his turn.

The new street was quiet, with dark stretches between the small cones of light thrown out by the street lamps. Some houses had porch lights on, others were completely shrouded in darkness. He stifled another yawn and resumed his scan for Bishop Street. After three blocks, he found it. Garrett smiled in triumph, only to remember that it was after two in the morning. What did he expect to do at this hour? Knocking on her door and waking her entire family wasn't the way to win her back.

But coffee and doughnuts would. *Yeah, that's the way to go,* he thought. *Find her house, then head back to the motel and get some sleep.* Returning in the daytime with food was the better plan. He was certain she'd be mad at him for tracking her down, but felt confident that once he explained how he felt about her, she would-

Something flashed in front of his truck, and Garrett slammed on the brakes. The Chevy's tires gave a short squawk of protest, and the nose of the car dipped, but it stopped. He stared, his heart thundering like a panicked jackrabbit, and saw someone hurrying along the fender, their hands working one over the other across his hood as if they were pulling themselves along until they reached his window. A hand slapped the glass, and then repeated the motion in rapid succession. Garrett cranked the handle. The instant the window was lowered a couple of inches, fingers hooked in, gripping the edge of it tightly.

"Oh Jesus, help me, please help me, you gotta help, he's right there..." The voice babbled, high-pitched and on the edge of hysteria.

Not on the edge. They've jumped off without a parachute.

"Morgan? Holy shit, are you alright?"

She seemed not to recognize him. "No! He's—" Her head twisted over one shoulder, her black hair whipping across the half-lowered window. Her eyes were wide with terror, her lips pulled back in a horrible grimace.

"What?" Garrett asked, searching the dark lawns behind her. "Who's-?"

The thunderous, hollow sound of something heavy hitting the metal of the truck drowned out his question. The steering wheel shook with hard reverberations that stung his palms. Garrett flinched, and Morgan screamed, leaping back from the window. Standing in the beam of his headlights was the huge, towering figure of a man dressed in all black, except for his face. The face was... *Sweet God in Heaven, what is that?* Garrett had never seen a face like this one, so pale and with such dark eyes, and that mouth...that crooked, jagged rip of a mouth. *That's a mask.* The man was wearing a mask and staring at him with a coldness that went directly to the marrow. One of the man's arms was extended toward the truck, and in it he clutched what looked like a hammer. The mallet end of the head rested in a deep depression in the hood.

"Son of a bitch," Garrett growled at the damage the masked freak had just done. He started to get out of the truck. At the same time, the passenger door opened, and Morgan, wearing a bloodied and torn, oversized t-shirt, climbed in and slammed her door.

"Fucking go!" she screamed at him. Garrett gave the mask only another quick glance before he decided he needed no more convincing. He hit the gas, the truck's engine snarling as the tires found traction and lurched forward. Garrett winced, waiting for the impact, but the man had stepped out of the way. There was a flash of movement to Garrett's left as the hammer spun in the man's hand, revealing a long, wicked-looking spike. The truck lurched again as another impact rocked it. The steering wheel shuddered. The tortured wildcat scream of metal being shredded filled the cabin, mixing with Morgan's shrieks, the noise of it all overpowering even the throaty roar of the Chevy.

Something jolted the truck once more, and then they were clear. Beside him, Morgan cried into her hands, emitting huge, racking sobs. Garrett held out a hand, making sure not to touch her. "Are you alright? Are you hurt?" Either she couldn't hear him or couldn't bring herself to answer. Instead, she slumped against the door and continued crying. As the truck sped down the street, Garrett looked into the rearview mirror.

In the dimming red glow of the tail lights, the pale mask stared after them from the middle of the street. Then, the night closed in, and it was gone.

CHAPTER 29

The man stood in the street and watched the truck speed away. Brake lights flared, followed by the distant sound of tires squealing as the Thing driving took a corner at high speed. He could hear the rumble of the engine for a few moments more, then that too faded away and he was left in the quiet. There was an uncomfortable feeling, a buzzing of irritation and anger that the Things had gotten away. That rarely happened, and for a long moment, the urge to follow them consumed him.

Then, to his right, a bedroom light came on, and he turned in that direction, sensing a new opportunity. But another came on in the house next to it, followed quickly by the twin porch lights. He stared at the house, deciding on a different course of action.

The man walked back toward the house he'd chased the Thing from after killing the ones who lay in their bed. He crossed the lawn and, at the same time, heard the door of one of the houses across the street open. A man's voice, thin and full of fear and false bravado, called out, "Who's there? Hey! You!" The masked man turned the corner and vanished into the dark between houses, the nagging irritation at losing the Things in the truck now no more than a smudge of a memory.

Three blocks later, he stood behind a tall bush at the corner of a house, waiting as a group of ten Things, chanting and laughing, and each carrying a weapon, passed along the street. Then, they were gone, their voices echoing off of the houses in gentle waves. The masked man continued on, seeking another opportunity.

CHAPTER 30

"How many so far?" Jared asked Regina as he studied the map between her desk and the bullpen. He was afraid of the answer, but he had to know. The past few hours had been some of the worst of his career, and the night was far from over. He desperately wanted to be back out there with his officers, and he had been for several hours. However, as Saturday afternoon had faded into night and the calls had grown more and more frequent, he'd been forced to return to his office to coordinate with county officials for more assistance. In between those conversations, he'd listened to the reports coming in and the chatter across units, a ball of ice forming in his bowels and growing larger and heavier with every discovered body.

It was bad enough that someone - or several someones, as the prevailing wisdom went - was killing people in their homes and businesses. That in itself was a nightmare. But the reports coming in from terrified citizens reporting neighbors, their spouses, and, in three cases, their own teenaged sons as the suspected culprits were somehow worse. A couple of these callers, Jared was certain, were simply miserable people finding an opportunity to twist the knife a little further into the belly of an old grudge. He could even understand a worried or scorned wife suspecting her husband who'd been more than a little distant or quick to temper. But people reporting their own children?

The possibility of having children was something he and Leigh had talked about off and on for the last few years, but it had never gone beyond that. Still, he knew kids got up to no good, and all the more so when they felt trapped in a small town like Elden Mills where there wasn't much to do. No movie theater, no bowling alley, and no skating rink. They had the Veil and video games, and that was about it. So, sure, you paired a bored teenager with little to no distractions and occasionally that factored out to some mischief. But even in those cases, they were usually talking about no more than some spray paint on a bridge or the side of a building, or maybe a house got rolled or a mailbox or two got smashed. Every once in a while, there were drugs involved, but mostly weed, which Jared tended to look the other way on. But for a parent to genuinely believe their child was capable of the level of violence he'd seen in the Butler or Weaver houses? He couldn't understand that.

What made all of the neighborly accusations even worse – the proverbial turd on top of a shit sundae, as his father used to say – were the acts of violence those same frightened citizens had enacted on their neighbors or loved ones. There'd been reports of intruders or sightings of the killer standing in a backyard; only, once officers reached the site, they found the caller screaming hysterically or near catatonic with shock as they stood over the body of a family member or friend who'd been mistaken for a threat.

Regina consulted her notebook, and Jared couldn't help but notice the pale, shell-shocked look on the woman's face. Once more, the urge to ask her to go home and get some rest rose within him, but he swallowed it back. She'd made it very clear after the last time that she wasn't leaving. "It's my town, too," she'd told him in a terse, clipped tone. "I'm going to stay right here and help the only way I can." He'd only half-jokingly reminded her that he could have one of the guys remove her and take her home. Regina had fixed him with a cold, hard stare and told him that if he went that route, he'd be down an officer due to severe testicular torsion, and that he himself would be seeing out of only one, non-blackened eye.

"So far, I've got seven bodies," Regina said. "At least three of them resulting from a mistaken ID." Her voice was thick and gravelly.

"The other four?"

The older lady's jaw flexed as she worked her teeth against one another. "They match the other murders. Two were found in their home – neighbors saw the body of one lying half out a window and called it in. The others have been found by our guys. An alley, a couple of back yards...."

Jared took in the pins and the names of streets, thinking about the people who lived in those houses. Other than the pins for the Butlers and Weavers, the deaths were spread out across the town. There was no immediately noticeable pattern, no clear trail. It was bad – there was no getting around it. How much worse it would get in the next few hours was anyone's guess.

His need to go check on Leigh was a powerful hum that reverberated throughout his entire body, a nest of spiders crawling in the corner of his brain and pulling his focus from other things. She'd called him a couple of hours ago and assured him that everything was locked up and she was sitting down to watch television with the .38 on the table next to the couch. He knew she was capable, and could handle the weapon if she needed to - they'd spent enough time plinking cans out in fields - but no amount of knowing her skills with a revolver would make him feel at ease about her being home alone. He wondered if he could convince her to come to the station.

Fuck it. He grabbed his hat off his desk and started back across the bullpen. He'd swing by, put eyes on her, and check all of the locks himself. As he passed the dispatch desk, Regina moved the microphone away from her mouth. "You going out?"

Jared put his hand on the handle of one of the glass doors. "Going to swing by the house, check on Leigh, and then I'll do a pass through town. I can't keep sitting here."

"You may need to wait on that check on Leigh," Regina said. "I got a call that there's a group of drunk guys armed with axes and shotguns walking down the middle of Evergreen. Brandon Higgins is with them."

Jared stared. "Are you serious?" When the dispatcher nodded, he tilted his head back. "Fuck me. And I guess all the other guys are tied up?" Another nod. "Shit in my shoe. Okay. I'll go talk to them. Do me a favor – call my wife and check in." He glanced at his watch. "You'll probably wake her up, but that's fine, do it anyway. Radio me after, okay?"

"Will do."

He found the group on Wesley Avenue, walking through the middle of the street like a platoon of idiots moving from one cathouse to another. Only, this platoon had quite a lot of weaponry. Jared parked his cruiser, called in his position, and got out, pulling his flashlight free. He didn't place a hand on the butt of his weapon, but kept that hand close to the holster. As his flashlight beam passed over the group, a few looked back at him.

"How's it going, Sheriff?" one called out, the man's voice thick with booze, but pitched high in a *welcome to the party* tone. The cluster of men stopped, everyone turning to see the approaching officer. A few of the men shifted as Brandon Higgins's large form pressed past them to stand in front of Jared. The man wore jeans and a dark t-shirt stretched tight over his large midsection. He didn't speak. Just watched Jared approach with dark frustration etched on his rough face.

"Looks like you guys decided to have a little party," Jared said. A few chuckles and good-natured insults floated back. "I appreciate you all taking the initiative to help keep folks safe, but I'm going to need all of you to call it a night and go home. Stay up if you like, keep your homes and families safe – that's perfectly fine. But leave the patrolling of the streets to me and my guys."

"Fat lot of good that's done so far," Brandon sneered. He patted a small hand-held walkie. "From what I'm hearing, all you're doing is running around like chickens with their heads cut off. You ain't got a clue who's doing this or where they are."

Jared looked around at the dark houses. "Seems you guys aren't doing much better. Now, I understand your frustration. I do. I know you're scared. That's-"

"We ain't scared!" spat one man, who then actually spat on the pavement. "We're just not going to sit around with our thumbs up our asses while some devil worshipers go around sacrificing people, trying to bring about the end of the world."

For fuck's sake. Jared groaned inwardly. *The end of the world?*

"Nobody's going to end the world," he told the man. Then, to Brandon, he said, "My men aren't running around. We're following up on several leads. Responding to emergency calls. It's bad enough that we're getting them from frightened people who think somebody's trying to break into their house when really it's their wife or husband who snuck down for a late-night snack. But if they look out and see a pack of people carrying blades and guns, things will get out of hand fast. Please. Please go home and let us handle things."

Brandon scowled and spat on the ground, his wad landing near where the first man's had. He wove through the group. "Come on," he commanded. The posse moved to follow him, a couple of the men throwing worried looks back at Jared. One of the men lingered – he was a slender guy with limp dark hair who carried an aluminum bat – pausing as if he wanted to say something. But one of the others called out to him, and he hurried to rejoin the group.

If I don't stop them, they're likely to kill someone, Jared thought. He trotted forward and began shoving his way roughly through the men. A couple responded with questions of whether or not Jared wanted an ax up his ass, but he had decided that if politeness wasn't going to work on them, then a show of force was warranted. He reached Brandon and grabbed the man by one thick arm, the spongy flesh dimpling beneath his fingers. Brandon glared down at the hand and roughly pulled away.

"I'm telling you now," Jared said, forcing iron into his voice. He pitched his voice higher. "I'm telling all of you! Go home. Right now. If you don't, I'll have units here and all of you will be placed under arrest."

Brandon laughed a wet, throaty sound. "Bullshit. You can't spare the men to come harass innocent civilians doing their civic duty to protect themselves, their families, and their property. Besides, you ain't got the cell space."

He was right, and Jared was glad for the darkness that hid the coloring in his cheeks. They only had the two small cells in the station, those usually reserved for drunks or guys who'd been fighting at the Lantern. The station house was more of a Mayberry-sized station than anything else. Plus, the way the calls had been coming in, he really couldn't spare the men to arrest a bunch of drunken rednecks who, as of yet, hadn't done anything.

Jared started to tell Brandon that county reinforcements were on the way and that they'd be more than happy to handcuff him and throw him in a county lockup on drunk-and-disorderly at the very least. But, as the first sounds came out of his mouth, the scrawny guy holding the bat shouted excitedly.

"Holy shit! I think that's him!" He pointed to the right, and Jared watched as a figure stumbled out of a house's side porch door. The man staggered forward, gripped the railing, and leaned over it. For a second, Jared thought the guy was going to be sick, but then he rebounded and ran down the stairs. Jared thumbed on his flashlight and darted to the edge of the group, who all stood stunned by what was happening. As the man reached the bottom of the stairs, the far edge of Jared's light caught him. Jared couldn't see the man's face, but did see blood smeared across his pale arms, and a shirt so soaked in blood that it clung to the man's back like a wetsuit.

"Stop! Elden Mills Police!" Jared yelled. At his command, the man flinched, but then he glanced over one shoulder and sprinted into the darkness.

The men standing in the road shouted a chorus of triumphant cheers and hurled insults after the man who was now just a dark smudge beyond the edge of the flashlight's reach. Then, they raced after him, their weapons raised in the air like the torches and pitch-forks carried by the villagers going after Frankenstein's monster. Jared watched them go, his body jostled as they flowed past him, shocked by the rapid turn of events.

Brandon was the last to leave, making a point to collide roughly with the sheriff. The mob leader's face wore a wide, shit-eating grin that exposed dirty, yellow teeth.

"You were saying?" Brandon cooed as he ran after the others.

Jared watched him trundle across the yard between the houses for only a moment before following. Not once in the moment of confusion and surprise did he even think to call it in.

CHAPTER 31

Saturday morning - hours before Sheriff Hollister went to find the drunken mob of vigilantes - James Turner woke with a jackhammer of a hangover. After forcing the headache and nausea back slightly with a breakfast of eggs and bacon, he settled onto the couch to watch several hours of television. His plan was that a mindless stream of programming would help him forget the face of Alex Vandermark and the abrupt end to Turner's thirty-seven years of service to the Avondale Fabric Works. However, as the morning dragged on, Turner found his eyes drifting to the corner of the living room where the light brown cardboard box sat. Folders and the sharp angles of picture frames peered out of the open top of the box which had PROPERTY OF AFW stamped on the side.

Thirty-seven years crammed into a single box. It was enough to make him want to start drinking again, but he had nothing left in the house. He'd finished the last of the old, dusty bottle of grape Mad Dog 20/20 around midnight. Yet his eyes shifted away from the flickering images on the TV more and more frequently, settling on the box for longer and longer.

By noon, he found himself standing in the aisles of Martin's Liquors, several bottles of whiskey clutched to his chest. Martin raised his eyebrows when Turner set them down on the counter, but being a good businessman - and obviously seeing something in Turner's dead-eyed expression - rang them up and double-bagged each one for protection.

He downed the first bottle while watching *Commando* on HBO. As the movie chugged on and Arnold's one-liners became more and more corny, Turner found his attention drifting back to the words Vandermark had said on the loading bay. Turner had always suspected that the reason he'd managed to stay on after Anna left him was related to Vandermark. And, to his own embarrassment, he was certain that his having reached the level of shift supervisor had absolutely been Vandermark's doing. As much as he hated to admit it, Turner knew he'd not been a model employee for most of his tenure at the mill.

They had known each other since tenth grade, when Vandermark's family had moved to town so that his father could take a managerial position in the mill. The boys had become fast friends, spending time together during every weekend that Turner wasn't with Anna, roaming the hills of the Veil or fishing in Mill Creek. They'd both started working at the mill at the same time, a month after graduating high school, and despite being assigned to different floors, they'd found a way to hang out as much as possible during the working days.

When Turner had been twenty-six, he'd proposed to his longtime sweetheart, Anna Waltrip. He'd known Anna since kindergarten, and been madly in love with her from the moment he'd seen her. When she'd said yes, Turner hadn't been able to feel the ground beneath his feet for a month. Then, three months before the wedding, Anna had called him. Her voice had been tight with stress, and in a rush, she'd called off the wedding, saying that she didn't feel right marrying him when she was in love with someone else. Turner had felt the ground beneath his feet then, in addition to the weight of the sky when the whole thing had crashed down on him with her final words, "It's Alex. I'm sorry, Jimmy, but I have to follow my heart."

Alex Vandermark had stolen the love of Turner's life, and now, almost thirty years later, the son of a bitch was stealing another. Only, this time, it wasn't just the love and companionship of a woman he was taking. It was money. It was security. It was the only thing Turner had left.

The prick had said that the decision was out of his hands, and that he had had no involvement in it whatsoever. But anyone with half a brain could see that the wormy shit was responsible. Well, maybe not directly responsible. It wasn't like the bastard had the power to decide to shut the mill down himself, but he would have been involved in the meetings. Maybe he'd even suggested it. Just tossed the idea out casually like it was a fish he'd caught that he wanted admired. And, naturally, the other monkeys in their suits at corporate had all fallen on it like the hungry jackals they were. *Close the mill? Sell off the equipment? Put a third of the town out of work and save a shitload of money in the process by not having to pay salaries or benefits? Yes, please, and can I have seconds on the fish eyeballs?*

"Pieces of shit," he mumbled, and opened a new bottle. They all deserved to be beaten, to have their smug, rich faces bashed in. What did they know about this town and the people in it? What did they care about what was going to happen to them with the mill closed? The decision was a death sentence to Elden Mills and the people within it. Turner had always considered himself a particularly communal person. He volunteered every time Brother Camden asked for help with food or clothing drives. He always signed up to help with events at the high school. He even led the tours of the mill the students took every year during their sophomore year. He wasn't the most important person in Elden Mills and had never wanted to be, but he loved the town and the people within it. And those assholes had taken that from him with the most casual ease.

They deserve to die. They're killing us, so it's only right that they suffer, too. But the problem was that Turner didn't know who *they* were or where *they* lived.

But he did know where Vandermark lived. The image of the smarmy plant manager on his knees, crying and begging, blossomed in his mind. It felt right. Hell, it felt good to imagine taking a knife – no, a meat cleaver – to the mill boss. Make each cut slow and deep, so the prick felt exactly what Turner and all of the others felt, or would feel with each passing week of no paycheck. *Offer a severance? I'll show you a severance when I cut your lying, fucking tongue out.* That's what they did to liars, wasn't it? And there was no mistaking it – Alex Vandermark was a liar. He'd lied when he'd said he'd had nothing to do with the closure decision. They most certainly would have involved him in those discussions.

He'd also lied when he'd said he wasn't losing his job. He most certainly was going to be offered a position somewhere else, or at least given such a large severance that he wouldn't have to worry for a long time.

And he'd lied when he'd said he hadn't intentionally stolen Anna away. That was the most damning lie of them all.

Yes, Vandermark was a liar and the root cause of all the woes that had plagued Turner's life for the last thirty years. Every time Turner felt like he was on solid ground, moving towards something resembling happiness, Vandermark pulled it away like he was Lucy moving the football just as Charlie Brown went to kick it. The poisonous black cloud that had been framing Turner's thoughts broke through and permeated his brain. Through the darkness, one simple thought blazed, and all of his focus coalesced around it.

Alex Vandermark needed to die for what he'd done.

That fire of thought turned into a full blaze when Irene Olsen called him, her voice tight with the excitement of gossip. Turner had helped Irene several times with small repairs around her house, and the two had worked the last four book drives for the high school together. Irene could be a bit of a bore, but if you wanted good gossip and couldn't get in touch with Agnes Newman, then Irene was your girl.

Irene told him about the murders, and did so with the fervor of a sideshow announcer teeing up the next strange wonder you were about to behold. The two families out on North Wind Drive, and the school teacher and janitor. Oh, and don't forget little Russell Shance and his babysitter. She said she thought an escaped lunatic was to blame, and that the cops had no idea what was going on. Turner agreed, since the theory about a pack of devil worshippers sounded as silly as blaming the murders on aliens.

She prattled on, but Turner had checked out of the conversation by then. If it was an escaped lunatic, the freak would keep killing people until he was caught, probably hiding naked in a closet somewhere, with shit smeared all over him, and laughing at the pink elephants that only he could see. But that also meant that any other deaths which happened before the crazy fucker was found could be blamed on him.

The fire within him blazed. Turner stood, wobbled a little, and caught himself then looked at his keys sitting on the coffee table. *No, he told himself. Don't drive. Someone'll see your car and remember it. Plus, there's a better than even chance you'll wreck going or coming from his house.*

But he did make it to Vandermark's house, only having to duck behind bushes a couple of times when police cars drove past. The officers inside scanning either side of the street for a blood-soaked man with an idiot's grin who wore state-issued underwear. Turner stood in front of Vandermark's house, a simple two-story with a side porch coming off the left side of the second floor. Small shrubs lined the first floor, partially obscuring dark windows. The yard sloped down to the right, to a cracked, oil-stained driveway. Through a window on the second floor, Turner could see the soft glow of a lamp and the strobing flicker of a television.

The asshole was watching television. Didn't have a care in the world, did he? Nope, everything was just perfect in ole Vandermark-land.

Turner crossed the yard and jammed his finger against the ochre-colored doorbell button. The chime inside dinged, while he stepped back and waited, his entire body humming with excitement. A few seconds later, he heard muffled thumps as Vandermark made his way down a set of stairs, and then the click of a lock. The door pulled inward, and Vandermark stood behind the crack wearing a pair of old jeans and an Atlanta Falcons t-shirt.

Vandermark blinked in confusion. "What's-" The question died with the meaty sound of Turner's knuckles connecting with the mill boss' nose, offering a lightning crack as the bone broke. Vandermark staggered backward, his hands flying to his face as blood streamed out. His heels hit the bottom stair and he toppled, sitting down awkwardly. Turner stepped inside and slammed the door behind him, twisting the deadbolt.

"You broke my nose!" Vandermark cried. The words came out thick and slurred. The plant manager stared at Turner with wide eyes from over his tented fingers.

"That's about to be the least of your worries, you piece of shit," Turner growled. He grabbed a fistful of the other man's hair and pulled as he climbed the stairs. Vandermark squealed in pain, and struggled to crab-walk backwards up the carpeted stairs. At the top, Turner turned to the left and into a living room with a puffy, but worn black leather couch and matching loveseat. Gold-framed pictures of lilies hung on the wall, and a large projection television sat in the corner to the left of the white stone fireplace. To the right of the hearth was the door that led to the side porch. Turner dragged his former boss to the middle of the room and let go of the man's hair. Vandermark twisted around to his knees and moved to stand, but fell flat as Turner delivered a vicious kick to his ribs.

As Vandermark lay on the carpet gasping for breath, Turner went into the kitchen and, after a quick search, found the largest knife he could. "You don't have a meat cleaver, do you?" he asked as he re-entered the living room.

"What?" Vandermark asked. He was on all fours, the carpet below his face spotted with blood from his ruined nose.

"Doesn't matter," Turner said. "This will do." He held the knife up and waved it back and forth. He smiled wide when he heard the throaty gurgle Vandermark gave as his eyes focused on the knife. Turner slashed out, raking the blade across the other man's arm. The scream that ripped out of Vandermark shocked Turner , and for a second, he pulled back, the knife held high and away. Blood from the deep cut streamed along Vandermark's arm. "Holy shit," Turner breathed out. "Holy shit." The last tendrils of his drunkenness evaporated at the sight of the blood.

"What do you want?" The question was almost a whine, and the pitiful tone cut through Turner's fear and shock.

"What do I want? What the fuck do you think? Did you think you could take away the last thirty-seven years of my life and not answer for it? Did you think you could steal everything in my life and not be called out?"

Vandermark's eyes searched the room as if he could find the answer on a table or the bookshelf tucked into the far corner. He returned his gaze to Turner and shook his head. "I can't do anything about your job. You have to understand, that was all out of my hands. I'm losing my job just like you."

The knife licked out again, opening the man's dark shirt. Vandermark screamed as a red, bloody mouth opened in the man's hairy chest. "You're not losing shit," Turner said. "What'd they do? Set you up with a new job somewhere else? Or did they pay you so much for fucking—" he kicked the kneeling man, who let out a howl, "us—" he kicked again, "over?" Turner had screamed the last word, and then he stabbed with the knife, feeling the thud of the impact; the brief resistance and then the give as the blade slid into the joint between Vandermark's chest and shoulder. The man grunted like he'd been punched in the gut and stared down at the knife. With a grunt of his own, Turner pulled out the blade. He blinked as droplets of blood splashed up across his cheeks.

"You..." Vandermark stammered. His face was pale. "You're insane. This won't...please...I didn't do..."

Turner plunged the knife into the man's throat. His mind was aware of the action, but it felt more like he was watching the events unfold on a small screen rather than it all happening right in front of him.

He twisted the blade. The handle slipped within his blood-soaked grasp as the knife hit something inside Vandermark's neck.

They always make it look so easy in the movies.

Vandermark stared at Turner – his mouth working, but only

producing wet gagging sounds. With effort, Turner ripped the knife free. The force of the movement caused him to lose his grip on it, and the knife flew across the room to land on the carpet behind him.

With the blade removed, blood sprayed out of Vandermark's neck, hitting Turner in the face. Instinctively, he put his back to the mess. Turner's hands shook, so he crossed his arms and pinned his hands against his sides. *You need to turn around and watch. You need to see him die.* He shook his head against the thoughts, squeezing his eyes shut. He pressed his hands against his ears to mute the gurgling, all those watery sounds of Vandermark struggling to breathe as his blood sluiced down his chest.

There was a quiet noise as the plant manager crumpled on his side. Slowly, the sounds of Vandermark fighting to stay alive went away, fading like footsteps disappearing down a long hallway. When Turner finally turned around, he saw the man he'd just killed laying on his side, one arm pinned under his body and the other draped across his chest. The carpet around the man was a sodden mess. Panic reached into Turner's chest and squeezed, needle-like pains spearing through him.

I have to go. I have to get out of here. Get out of town.

On numb legs, Turner hurried to the stairs. He stopped suddenly, one foot hanging over the top riser as a cold, terrifying thought flashed in his mind.

You have to do more.

Linda had told him that she'd heard the bodies found so far had been all cut up, like they'd been put through a wood chipper. The corpse before him, other than the large amount of blood, looked nothing like that. If Turner was going to pass this off as the work of the escaped lunatic, he had to....

"Oh Christ," he moaned, but there was nobody to offer a rebuttal. He had to do more. Turning back to the living room, he saw the knife where it had landed. Turner stepped carefully around the body of Vandermark and picked the knife up. The handle was tacky against his bloody skin, but he clutched it as if it were a lifeline.

Then, fighting to keep from throwing up, James Turner got to work.

Thirty minutes later, he collapsed backward, kicking his feet to get away from the mess, but his shoes only slipped on the blood-soaked carpet. Turner couldn't believe the thing in front of him had once been a man, and found himself transfixed by the piles of red. With great effort, he looked at himself. Every patch of skin on his arms was covered in gore, and his shirt clung to him as if he were a contestant in a wet t-shirt contest. That thought seemed to pop the bubble he'd put up around himself, and he felt his stomach give a great, heaving roll. He made it to the kitchen sink just in time.

Afterward, Turner leaned against the counter, closed his eyes, and took several deep breaths. When the dizziness passed, he returned to the living room and stared down. What remained of Alex Vandermark lay spread out on the carpet like a nightmarish art installation. A painful, buzzing terror swept over Turner, and he looked in the direction of the stairs. How would it look if he left through the front door? The porch lights would make him visible to anyone who happened to be out at that moment, including any police on patrol. The side door, then. It was dark on that side of the house. He ran and yanked it open, barely pausing to let the door clear the jamb before he stumbled outside.

He rebounded off the railing, caught his balance, and ran down the stairs. His feet hit the grass, and his brain screamed for him to stick to the woods behind the house, to not to go out into the street.

That's when he heard the shouts, and the ground around him started to glow with a faint white light.

"Stop! Elden Mills Police!"

But Turner didn't stop. *Couldn't* stop. He shambled, then caught his stride, and began running as hard as he could. Behind him, the shouts and jeers increased as the pack of men gave chase.

CHAPTER 32

The beam of Roderick Shance's powerful floating lantern bounced across the thick trees and brush as he crashed through the woods. Ahead, the man they chased moved like a frenetic shadow rabbit, darting around and between trees, and occasionally leaping over thick patches of undergrowth.

When Roderick had first approached Brandon Higgins and the rest of the men gathered in the parking lot of the Lantern Lounge, Roderick had said "I'm going" in a voice that had brooked no argument from anyone. All of them were drunk as skunks and sporting weapons that ranged from shotguns to axes and one aluminum baseball bat, with one idiot even holding an honest-to-God ninja sword. The men had simply nodded agreement, blinking stupidly in their inebriation as they'd stood in a loose cluster near the pay phone attached to the exterior wall of the bar.

Some of the men's resolve had wavered once Sheriff Hollister found them and tried to warn them off, but as far as Roderick was concerned, the presence of the lawman meant nothing. Roderick was going to find the evil son of a bitch who'd killed his son Russell, and there wasn't a force on earth that could stop him from doling out justice when he did.

Roderick's chest burned with exertion - he had to stop smoking,

Melanie had been hounding him for years to give it up - as he leapt over an old, rotting log. He screamed a threat at the fleeing man, his voice drowning out the thrashings of the rest of the search party as they struggled to keep up with him. Even Sheriff Hollister's cries - which had shifted pretty quickly from beseeching the men to stop and let law enforcement handle things to shouts for the suspect to stop - were but small pops amidst the roar of Roderick Shance's hate.

Despite the arbitrary path the man chose, Roderick saw that they seemed to be heading in a focused direction. *He keeps this up and we're going to end up on Messer Road.*

Roderick shouted his frustration again as the guy, a blur that flashed through a thin shaft of moonlight, darted to the left and around a particularly large pine tree. He didn't quite clear it, though. His shoulder scraped loudly, pine bark shearing off with a papery scratch. The man staggered from the impact, his arms pinwheeling as his legs took wide, leaping steps to keep from falling. Ahead of him, the trees thinned, a silvery strip of moonlit road just beyond them.

The killer burst out of the tree line, small saplings waving like enraged concert goers as he hurled past them and into the road. The man slowed, head whipping back and forth. A moment later, he sprinted to the right. Roderick's brain flashed the options the man would have as hiding spots. Messer was an old road that ended in a dead-end off to the left, but to the right, it ultimately reached Simmons' Pick and Pull. Another newer road connected to Messer several hundred yards down and was the primary avenue people took to reach Simmons'.

Roderick burst out of the trees and saw the man sprinting down the street, his destination clear. Forty yards away and across the street sat a single-story brick structure with graffiti-covered, boarded windows and a single door, also covered by a spray-painted sheet of plywood.

"He went into to the old pest control place," Roderick said, looking back at the closest man, the skinny fucker who'd first spotted the killer. The guy held an aluminum baseball bat and looked like he was about to shit his pants. The rest of the group arrived in a cacophony of snapping limbs and panting breath. Several of the guys bent over and placed their hands on their knees, heads lowered and backs heaving.

Aluminum Bat Guy was jolted aside as someone pushed past him. Brandon didn't even look at the smaller man as he took a few steps into the street, his heavy boots knocking on the pavement. "He go into Brown's?" Roderick nodded. "Let's go, then."

The posse jogged down the street, the few older or more out of shape men flagging behind, and stopped along the rough, uneven sidewalk that ran in front of the abandoned building. Not much larger than a small three bedroom house, the pest control office looked even smaller than Roderick remembered. He'd been inside only a couple of times when it was still open, before the owner, Steven Calderon killed himself fifteen years ago. *It hadn't been much to look at then*, he thought, *and it looked like a rotting corpse now*. Brandon scanned the group. "Steve, you, Jeff, and Huddie go around back. If I remember right, there's only a single door back there. Leads to a smoking area. Holler if he comes out that way."

The men gathered around the single entrance door. The spray-painted wood was warped and swollen from years of exposure, and it stood several inches open, blackness on the other side. From around the building, Steve called out, "The door's jammed shut! Or locked! He ain't getting out this way!"

"Stay there just in case!" Roderick shouted. He'd already reached for the partially open door to pull it fully ajar when Brandon grabbed his arm.

"Wait a minute, brother. You don't want to go in there just yet."

"I want that son of a bitch," Roderick growled.

"So do we. He's done enough to this town. We all want him. But consider what he's done to those people." Roderick tensed, ready to hit Brandon. He could see that the man wished he'd phrased that last point differently.

Sheriff Hollister stepped to the front and faced the group, his hands raised. "That's enough," he said. "Go back, and let me and my men handle this. We have him trapped, so let my officers go in and get him."

"Your officers couldn't catch a fucking cold!" Roderick snapped. "So, why don't you get out of here and let the grown-ups handle this?" He pointed to the door. "We found the guy, and we're going to deal with him."

One of the sheriff's hands drifted to the butt of his sidearm, the other reaching to his belt and pulling the radio free. "No," he said in a low, no-bullshit tone. "What you're going to do is step back into the street and do nothing else while we take him into custody. Nobody is going in there. We don't know what he may be armed with or what he's capable of now that he's trapped." He raised the radio to his mouth. But immediately, he reversed course, flinching back as the twin barrels of a shotgun pressed forward and stopped inches from his nose.

"No," Brandon Higgins said quietly. Roderick wondered where Brandon had gotten the shotgun. Then, he saw Doug Osborn on the other side of Brandon and remembered the older man had brought his twelve-gauge.

Hollister's hands raised slowly, the radio still held in one fist. "You don't want to do this," he said to Brandon, who didn't respond and only continued to glare at the sheriff.

To Aluminum Bat Guy, Roderick said, "Get his radio and gun."

The guy licked his lips, his eyes darting between Roderick and the sheriff like a hummingbird. "What?"

"I said, get his fucking radio and gun."

Doug stepped forward and snatched the radio out of Hollister's hand. He thumbed the snap off the holster and pulled the revolver out. It slid away with a leathery hiss. Doug handed both items to Roderick, who tucked the pistol into the waist of his jeans. He dropped the radio on the ground and slammed the heel of his thick, heavy boot into it. The radio crunched and snapped. Roderick gave it three more good stomps, grinding it into fragments.

Hollister watched with visible alarm. "Enough of this shit. You're all under arrest. Put your weapons down and-" He got no further, as

Brandon swiftly spun the shotgun around and slammed the butt of the weapon into the sheriff's head. Hollister stood there swaying for a few seconds before his eyes rolled back and he collapsed in a loose heap on the sidewalk.

"Holy shit," someone said.

As Brandon handed the shotgun back to Osborn, Roderick said, "Someone get him out of the way." Two men bent and carried the unconscious sheriff several feet down the sidewalk.

"What now?" Brandon asked.

Roderick pulled the sheriff's revolver from his belt and held it up. "We go get that son of a bitch." He pulled the door open, the wood grating angrily against the cement below. Without a glance backward, he plunged into the building, pistol held at the ready as he searched the darkness.

He stood in a small lobby with an old, broken desk to his left. More graffiti covered the walls. The floor was carpeted by dirt, dead leaves, and other trash. A single open doorway led to the deeper recesses of the office, and he moved that way as the others filed in behind him.

The doorway led to a hall off of which were several doorways, all missing their doors. A single metal door lay at the center of the far end of the hall. *That'd lead to the garage,* he thought. Roderick played his beam over the space. The first office was empty, save more trash and graffiti. The second and third offices were devoid of anything, as well.

In the fourth, he found what he was looking for. The room contained several old filing cabinets, many with missing drawers, like empty cavities in a mouth. As he stepped into the room, he heard breathing and jabbed his light toward a corner. There, huddled on the floor, knees to his chest, was the blood-soaked man. His face was a mask of red. The blood matted his hair flat to his scalp, and his face was buried against his thighs so that Roderick couldn't see his features.

"You find him?" Brandon asked from behind. The hallway was

filled with the scuffling of feet and wheezing breaths of the other men.

Roderick couldn't answer; his mouth seemed wired shut. His jaw clenched so tightly that the pressure sent sharp needles of pain through his teeth. He adjusted his grip on Hollister's pistol and approached the cowering man.

As Roderick raised his gun, a voice behind him muttered a curse. Brandon's harsh voice cut off anything else the man might have said. "Get the fuck out of here if you ain't got the guts. This is justice."

"No," the man said. "That's James Turner."

"The fuck, you say," Brandon said.

"Look at him. That's Turner, alright." Curses and mumbles of disbelief rippled through the group as men slowly backed away. Now that a name - and a name they all knew very well - had been assigned to the bloody man cowering in the corner, a deep sense of unease overtook them. Roderick stared down at the blood-soaked figure, aware of the eyes on him.

"Rod," Brandon started, but to Roderick, the voice was a faint, distant noise. His heartbeat in his ears was a raging thunderstorm, and with every lightning flash, his mind threw up images of Russell's broken and torn body.

The pistol's handle made a dull thump as it connected with the man's head. In the glow from the flashlights, blood welled out of Turner's scalp, black in the light. Turner gave a pained grunt and started to fall to his side, but Roderick knelt and grabbed him by the shirt. The material was sticky with blood, but he managed a good grasp. He considered the gun in his hand. It didn't feel adequate. It was too impersonal, considering what had been done to Russell. He let go of the shirt and Turner slumped back against the wall, one hand drifting up to the seeping wound in his scalp. Roderick stood and snatched the aluminum bat from the small man's hands, thrusting the pistol at him in exchange.

"You don't have to help," he growled to the group as he turned back to Turner. Roderick stood, chest heaving, and brought the bat down. It clacked against Turner's knee with a metallic sound, no different than if it had connected with a straight fastball on a Saturday afternoon. Turner screamed.

Roderick became vaguely aware, as his arms raised the bat again and again, that he was also screaming. He never noticed when Brandon and three others pulled the filing cabinets away and began battering the screeching man along with him. Their weapons slammed into Turner's flesh – they shattered bone, split skin, and sent blood spraying. Roderick bashed the bat against the side of the man's head and watched the eyeball bulge, blood welling around it and trickling down his already gore-covered face. A rifle butt slammed into Turner's jaw, and his screams turned to gurgles as blood and shattered teeth filled his mouth.

They continued to beat the man long after he'd stopped screaming, and well after he'd ceased moving. When they finished, Roderick couldn't feel the bat in his fingers any longer, and he let it slip free. The floor was a lake of blood that sucked at his boots as he stepped away from the ruined body. The panting of the other men was a distant soundtrack to the scene. "Let's go," he said.

"Dear God in Heaven," one of the men mumbled as the rest exited the old building and stood on the grass. On the curb, Sheriff Hollister lay on his back – one arm casually draped over his abdomen, his chest rising and falling slowly. If not for the blood running down from his scalp, Roderick would have thought the man had decided to take a quick nap.

"What now?" Doug Osborn asked. "Jesus, we beat James Turner to death."

Roderick looked at the older man calmly. "We killed the sick bastard who hurt my boy. That's all. I'm going home."

None of the other men spoke as they followed, stepping carefully around the unconscious form of the sheriff. They walked slowly as their minds grappled with what had happened. None of them noticed the pale face with black eyes that watched them, impassively, from the shadows of the trees next to the building.

The face shifted, leaning to one side ever so slightly as if it were curious about what it was seeing. Then, it straightened and faded into the shadows.

CHAPTER 33

Consciousness came to Jared in a tumbling confusion of sensations, but chief among them was pain. His head felt as if it had been slammed repeatedly with a brick, and tentative exploration sent a lance of agony through his skull. His fingers came away sticky with dried blood. There was more discomfort in his lower back, where the equipment on his belt dug into the muscles because of his position on the sidewalk. Tenderly, he pushed himself up to a sitting position, wincing at the aching wave that began in his back and rolled up to crash into his throbbing head.

The street around him was silent, the group of vigilantes having left. How long they'd been gone, he couldn't say. As he sat there, waiting for the pain to subside enough for him to stand, Jared remembered the man they'd cornered in the building. His training told him that there was no way to know if the man had been the one responsible for all the deaths, but considering he'd emerged from a house covered in blood and immediately ran, the odds leaned in that direction. The door to the structure stood open, and he couldn't remember if it had been that way before or not.

Jared pulled himself to his feet and staggered to the door, his steps wide, with one arm held out for balance as the ground tilted left and then right. He gripped the warped wood and put his head against his forearm, drawing in long, deep breaths. When the earth stopped its insane see-sawing, he entered the old pest control office. He pulled his flashlight from his belt - thank Christ they'd not taken that - and clicked it on. The powerful beam lit up the small room, and he passed it over a broken desk and across the floor covered in leaves and dirt.

A wide smear of blood on the edge of an open doorway that led to a pitch black hall caught Jared's attention as his light swept around the room. More blood, this time in the form of scuffed footprints, led him to a small filing cabinet filled room, and to the mangled remains of a body lying torn and broken in a large pool of blood. Bloody shoe prints tracked through the fluid and across the dirty floor.

"Sweet Jesus, they did it," he croaked. He hadn't thought the mob would really kill the man. Then again, he shouldn't have doubted them. They were all angry and scared, which were bad enough emotions on their own. But those feelings were made all the worse when alcohol was added to the mix, and pretty much every man there had been drinking since earlier in the night.

Not to mention Roderick Shance's anger over his son's death.

He had to call this in. His hand went to the place on his belt where his radio stayed, but found nothing but the belt's rough leather. *Where the hell?* Then, he remembered one of the men taking it and his.... A bolt of panic shot through him as he checked his holster.

Empty.

"Fuck me."

He exited the building and stood on the grass, taking in deep lungfuls of the clean air. With each breath, the fog in his mind cleared a bit more, the ground beneath him growing a bit more firm.

Without a radio, his only recourse was to get to a phone and call for help. Ahead, the road stretched into darkness - the few street-lights that were out here had a habit of getting broken, either by kids throwing rocks or shooting pellet guns, or by drunk adults shooting real ones - but he knew that the Pick and Pull was less than a quarter-mile down the road.

His shoes clicking softly against the hard surface of the blacktop, Jared made decent time despite the fact that he had to stop twice and wait for the throbbing in his head to subside. He made a mental promise to personally shove his nightstick up Roderick Shance's ass as soon as he could.

The faded metal sign for Simmons' Pick and Pull, its yellow and red paint peeling and its surface pockmarked with bullet holes, hung across the narrow road on a rusted chain that had been wrapped around two hardwood trees. Beyond the sign, the pavement ended, turning to a hard-packed and rutted dirt trail that wound between the ghostly corpses of cars, pickup trucks, and vans. A couple of sodium lights nailed to trees bathed the junkyard in an eerie blue glow. Jared passed under the gently swaying sign and moved toward a series of brighter lights farther ahead, which marked the small shed serving as Butch Simmons' office. Considering the hour, he doubted the old man was there, but it was possible. Sometimes, Butch liked to stay in his shack playing cards with himself and enjoying a bottle of gin rather than going home to his wife.

The rotting husks of cars stared at Jared with glassless eyes. They sat on either side of the path, slowly being overtaken by weeds. Raised or missing hoods exposed the dark, rusted entrails of engines. Jared tried not to look at them as he passed. The feeling of the vehicles being alive and waiting for him to get further from the exit was palpable.

He rounded a corner, and the dirt trail opened onto a wider patch of dirt. Cars ringed the space with additional paths running between them like spokes in a wheel. An old brick fire pit sat cold and ashen to the right. Rust-covered chairs - their padding ripped or missing - and three black plastic milk crates ringed the soot-stained bricks.

In the center of the space was the office, a one-room, gray-walled shed wearing a metallic skin of weathered and bent license plates and a couple of road signs. Faint light shone through a single dirty window to the right of the flimsy aluminum door. The space was lit by several exposed bulbs and two more of the sodium lights affixed to tall poles. As Jared crossed the clearing, he could hear music filtering through the shed door – Waylon Jennings crooning about Luckenbach, Texas.

He beat on the door several times with the side of his fist. "Butch! It's Sheriff Hollister. Open up." No answer came, not even a lowering of the music or the wooden sounds of the old man's feet on the plywood flooring. Jared twisted the loose bent knob and pulled the door open, immediately recoiling as a wave of flies borne on a current of warm air rushed out. The smell hit him as he waved his hand to clear the buzzing insects.

The inside of the office was cramped, with car parts stacked in every available corner. Headlights and rusted batteries perched on top of the dented metal filing cabinet, brake disks piled like dishes on the rough fabric of a chair's seat. The walls were covered with pages torn from *Playboy* and other, more risqué men's magazines, all held in place by crude strips of duct tape. The radio, a small silver transistor with a single antenna extended at a low angle, sat on top of a pile of papers on a desk filled with forms, more men's magazines, and an alternator.

Butch Simmons sat behind the desk in his usual chair, settled in front of a window that looked out onto a large section of the yard. His upper body rested on the desk, one arm hung loosely by his side and the other flung out across a corner of the desk. More flies buzzed and shifted on the bloody debris that had once been his head.

Automatically, Jared reached for his sidearm. When his palm slapped the empty holster, he grimaced. Instead, he pulled his nightstick. The rod of heavy, solid wood gave him some measure of reassurance, and he held it ready as he checked the tiny office. Finding nothing, he approached the desk and pushed some magazines away, revealing the heavy black phone. He moved the base so that he could dial without having to look at what had once been Butch Simmons. After what felt like an eternity of listening to the other extension ringing, Regina picked up. Jared quickly relayed the situation, and told her to call the volunteer fire group in addition to directing backup to his location. Regina's voice, which had been heavy and slow with exhaustion at first, brightened with urgency. Jared ended the call and let out a long breath as his eyes slid back over to Butch's body.

Jared froze. A man stood outside the shed, looking through the window behind the desk. He wore a white mask with black pits for eyes and a pitch black, jagged rip for a mouth. Long black hair hung down, framing the visage, and as Jared took this in, the mask shifted as the man directed his attention to Jared.

"Son of a bitch!" Jared gasped. As soon as the words left his lips, the masked man walked away, moving quickly toward one of the dirt paths ranging between cars. Through the dirty window, Jared could see the man carrying what looked like a large hammer with a huge spike on one side of the head. It hung by his side, held loosely in one fist. Jared stood still, stunned into paralysis for a couple of seconds before he blinked out of his stupor and shouted, "Hey!" He ran from the shed, the door slamming loudly against the building wall as he sprinted after the man. The masked man walked quickly but calmly along the dirt road and rounded a corner, vanishing behind a sky blue van with a shattered windshield.

Jared slowed as he reached the van, and paused long enough to peer quickly around the corner. The path ahead was empty, but it was also a short length, angling to the left at an old, red Chrysler. Jared stopped at that junction, his fingers flexing around the grip of the nightstick. He tried to envision the yard as a whole, to picture where the masked man could have gone. Butch owned five acres of land, most of which was woodland. The Pick and Pull wasn't massive, taking up only a single acre of the property. None of the cars here were stacked on top of each other, Butch didn't have the equipment for that. Some cars sat yards apart from their neighbors, with only thick grass, blackberry, or honeysuckle bushes between them. There were a few more of the sodium lights mounted to poles throughout the expanse, but those were few and far between. The one closest to where Jared crouched by the Chrysler was at least twenty yards away. Moths and other night insects flitted around it, the light it provided barely reaching his location.

That meant the masked man had the advantage of darkness.

Everything in Jared's mind screamed at him to retreat to the shed and wait for backup. That was the smart play. He had no sidearm or radio. If he got into trouble among the cars, he wouldn't be able to signal for help when the others arrived.

But if the masked man was able to reach the woods on the far side of the lot, he'd slip away, and any hope of tracking him down would be lost. Even if Jared could call in tracking dogs, it would be hours before they'd arrive and get started.

The analytical part of his mind, that of the trained cop, worked through the situation. There had been calls, reports throughout the evening of sightings of a man in a mask. That didn't make the person he had chased into the maze of cars the perpetrator, but it didn't rule him out. But if that were the case, who was the poor son of a bitch back in that building? Who had Brandon and Roderick and their stooges beaten into hamburger meat? There was no denying that whoever it had been had emerged covered in blood and run at the first sign of the others.

He hated to give any level of weight to unfounded rumors, but some of the chatter going around had been that there were multiple assailants, whether part of a gang or - God save him from even thinking it - satanists. So it was possible that both the dead man in the pest control building and the masked creep were responsible. Jared's stomach crawled at the unspoken possibility that there may still be others taking part in the bloody assault of Elden Mills. He would deal with that later. Right now he had a person of interest and he needed to apprehend them to learn more.

But still...the thought of that hammer chilled him. That was exactly the kind of weapon that Bill Parker had suggested was being used on the murder victims they'd found.

Jared stood and moved farther along the path, walking quickly while keeping his attention on every dark, weedy patch between cars. At each intersection, he paused, crouching and peering around the vehicles. After several minutes of careful pursuit, he stopped and scanned the lot. He'd not caught so much as a glimpse of the man after that first turn. Either the guy had reached the end of the lot and vanished into the woods, or he was waiting for Jared somewhere along the trail.

The first faint warbles of sirens reached Jared's ears, and relief blossomed in his chest. He gave the dark path ahead one more good look, willing the masked man to appear. But the lot was still and silent, and he let out a long breath of frustration as he went back to the shed and the approaching officers.

The hammer swung out from behind a tan, four-door coupe, its heavy face slamming into Jared's leg just below the knee. The blow drove the joint back in a hyperextension and shattered Jared's shin. The sheriff uttered a strangled gasp of shock and toppled to one side. He landed hard, his head barely missing the chrome bumper of a Ford pickup. Then, the pain was a white hot explosion that drove the breath from his chest. Jared writhed on the ground, his hands hovering over his broken leg and his mouth stretched wide in a silent scream.

Through the agony, he watched the dark form of the masked man rise from behind the car, an ink stain against the night. The pale face stared at him indifferently, even as the man reached out and placed one booted foot on Jared's injured lower leg. Huge splinters of burning torment stabbed into his guts. The scream came now, huge and raw.

The hammer swung again, this time coming up and over in a high, wood-splitting arc. All breath left Jared as his left hip exploded, and he twisted toward it, rolling protectively on instinct. No sooner had his body shifted than his right hip detonated in a brilliant burst of pain. Jared flopped to his back and lay there gasping. Overhead, the night sky and its stars watched with cosmic apathy. Then, even that was blotted out as the masked man stepped forward, straddling Jared's body.

Jared's hands flapped weakly at the man's legs, his fingers plucking ineffectively at the pants legs. Dimly, Jared was aware of his nightstick laying in the dirt inches away, but it may as well have been in the next county.

You have to get up, his brain screamed at him. *You have to get! UP!*

The hammer swung again.

Jared's cheek shattered. Blood filled his mouth, and he coughed it out, the hot wetness spilling across his face. Hard things came out with the gobs of blood, and he was faintly aware that they were his teeth. Jared continued to cough, needing to clear his mouth, but each convulsion sent mind-ripping waves of torment through him. The world began to dim, the edges of his vision growing fuzzy. Above him, the man's hand twitched, the head of that hammer rotating so that the large, curved spike faced down. Jared closed his eyes as he heard the horrible whisper of the spike cutting through air.

His body jerked, causing his hips to redouble their painsong. But now, a new pain joined in the chorus. Jared forced his eyes open and looked down to see his uniform shirt torn, exposing a huge, ragged tear across his belly. He stared, not understanding what he was seeing. From the hole in his stomach, wet purple and red lumps pushed out like grotesque worms. Had the man thrown worms on him? If that was the case, those were the largest worms he'd ever seen. Where did they get nightcrawlers that large around here?

A hard toe slid under Jared's shoulder, and he felt himself being pushed over, his face pressed into the blackness of the dirt.

This is it, he thought, and blinked hard to focus his mind. He conjured an image of Leigh, her perfect beauty smiling at him, her lips parting to tell him how much she lo-

Something slapped him hard in the back of the head, and Jared's mind filled with brilliant white light that flared and collapsed in on itself, pulling him into the blackness of oblivion.

CHAPTER 34

"What the fuck is going on?" Garrett asked as he steered the truck around another corner.

Morgan barely heard him. Her mind was a swirling confusion of images. The dark hall, her parents' door, the blood, the mass that had once been her mother's head.

The black eyes of the mask as they bored into her.

A hand touched her shoulder, and Morgan screamed, twisting away. Her body pressed hard against the solidity of the truck door, her face screwing up against the pain in her shoulder where the hammer had hit during her flight from her parents' bedroom. Through her tears, she saw Garrett, one hand held up and the other gripping the steering wheel as he alternated his attention between the road and her. "Are you okay? What the hell? Who was that?"

Morgan's brow bunched in confusion. What was Garrett doing here? How had she gotten here?

"Morgan?" Garrett asked, his voice thick with worry. Hearing her name popped the bubble of disorientation, and she remembered jumping into his truck after she'd run from her house. She lunged toward him, wrapping her arms tightly around him and burying her face against his chest. The truck swerved wildly for a moment before he regained control. He steered it to a stop against a curb and threw the gear into park. His body shifted as he turned toward her, his arms enveloping her.

Pain flared in her back as Garrett's hand pulled her close, and she gasped. "He cut me. His hammer – the spike." Morgan inhaled sharply as Garrett lifted her shirt, the fabric pulling away from the drying blood.

"Jesus," Garrett muttered. His voice was tight, his face a worried frown. "It looks pretty bad," he said. "I can't tell, there's a lot of blood. It's dry," he quickly added. "I'm not a doctor, but I don't think you need stitches. Are you hurt anywhere else?"

Morgan hurt all over – the fall down the stairs hadn't done her body any good – and she looked at her shoulder.

"I think he hit me there, too. But don't." She leaned back. "Don't pull the shirt off. It hurts too much. I can still move my arm." She gave it a little flap to demonstrate.

"Who the hell was that?" he asked.

She shook her head. "I don't know. He was in my house." Her face screwed up, tears welling again. "He killed my parents." The words came out a thin whine. Morgan pressed her lips together, fighting the emotions. After a moment, she was able to push them back. "Get me to the police station. I'll explain on the way." Garrett drove on, following her directions as Morgan recounted the night. She couldn't bring herself to tell him what she'd seen in her parents' room – only that she'd found them dead.

Through the glass doors of the station, she saw an older woman sitting behind a desk, a phone held to her ear. Her graying hair hung in thin clumps around her lined face. She sat hunched forward, leaning against the desk, and Morgan had the sense that it was the only thing keeping the woman off the floor. As they crossed the lobby, the woman hung up the phone and jotted something on a notepad. The phone began ringing again immediately, and she gave an exasperated grunt. She reached for the receiver, but her attention was diverted by Morgan and Garrett. Her face was sunken with exhaustion. Heavy, dark bags hung under her bloodshot eyes, and her lips curved in a weary frown.

"There's a curfew," she said, clearly trying to project some level of authority into her voice, but the words came out strained and thin. "You two need to get home."

"Someone broke into her house and killed her parents," Garrett said as he reached the desk. "He almost killed her, too."

The woman looked at Morgan. Her face was impassive for a beat, then her eyes widened as her brain seemed to register what she was seeing. "Dear Lord, girl, you're a mess! Do you need medical attention?" She started to get up, angling to come around the desk.

Morgan shook her head. The cut on her back hurt, but the feeling had dulled. "No. Not right now. Just some bruises and a scrape on my back." Morgan hoped the dispatcher didn't ask to see the cut. She gave the dispatcher her address.

"Did you recognize who did it?" the woman asked, returning to her chair. The phone next to her jangled its shrill ring. Her eyes flicked to it before returning to Morgan.

Again, Morgan shook her head. "He was wearing a mask."

"We're getting a lot of calls like that tonight," she said. "Among others. Whole town's gone insane. I'll send people over there. But it may take a little while." She pointed at the phone. "Every unit we have, plus backup from the county, is tied up with this...." Her hand gave a weak, circling wave and then dropped heavily to the desktop. Her jaw clenched and she swallowed. "I'm sorry about what happened. We're doing everything we can to find who's responsible. Can you stay here until Sheriff Hollister gets back? I'm sure he's going to want to hear what you have to say. It could help."

"Okay," Morgan said.

"We'll wait in my truck," Garrett told the dispatcher, who waved acknowledgement as she picked up the phone again. Garrett held his hand out, and Morgan grasped it and felt the smoothness of his skin, the reassurance in his touch. He led her back outside and into the truck. They sat in the quiet of the cab, Morgan watching the woman behind the desk without really seeing her. Garrett looked at the street. "So, this is where you grew up," he said, clearly trying to get her mind off of things.

"Why are you here?" she asked.

"I got your letter. I came to help. You shouldn't have to do that stuff alone. I wanted you to know that I forgive you, and that I'm...."

"You're what?"

He shook his head. "This isn't the time. We can talk about it tomorrow."

Seeing him, hearing his voice, brought a fresh round of grief tearing through her, and Morgan buried her face in her hands. After a moment, Garrett slid across the bench seat and held her. Morgan swiped her fingertips across her eyes, clearing the tears. "I'm sorry," she said. "I didn't want to hurt you."

Gently, he kissed her forehead. "It's okay. I forgive you," he said. "I love you, and I forgive you for everything."

"You can't!" she sobbed. "You can't forgive me."

"You don't get to decide that," he said as he hugged her again. This time, she sunk into him. They stayed that way for a long time, Morgan's tears coming, going, and returning. She didn't understand how he could forgive her after everything she'd done. She hadn't asked her parents for it, either, not formally, but had known from that first moment in the kitchen that they did.

"Oh shit," she said, sitting up as a new thought pushed its way to the front of her mind.

"What?" he asked, panic creeping into his voice as he looked at the street. "Did you hear something?"

"No. Jennifer. My friends."

"What about them?"

"They're having a party. I was there earlier. I don't live that far from Jennifer's house. If the guy is still out there, he may see them." She slapped his leg repeatedly. "Come on, we have to go. We have to warn them. I can't let anything happen to them, too."

"Shouldn't we wait for the sheriff? I'm sure he'll need to-"

"Drive the fucking truck!"

Garrett turned the ignition and backed out of the slot. As he accelerated down the street, Morgan beat a nervous rhythm on the dashboard, urging the truck to go faster.

CHAPTER 35

The man walked through the woods, keeping several yards off the sidewalk. He moved slowly, without concern or urgency. Around him, the forest was silent. Every living thing, from foxes to owls to ants, hid among the shadows as the figure of death passed.

Already, the thoughts of the Thing in the police uniform lying broken and leaking in the dirt were fading into the fog within his mind. All that mattered now was continuing forward, waiting for Chance to bring him more opportunities. More Things to destroy.

His path took him back toward the town, and after a few minutes, lights and the shapes of homes became visible through the trees. The man paused at the edge of the woods, watching and waiting. The street in front of him was empty, most of the homes along it dark, with the Things inside long since gone to bed. Behind the mask, his eyes shifted – looking at each home, considering them. One, a few houses down on the left, caught his attention. In its yard, along the path to the front door, were a series of small, plastic pinwheels. Most were still, most likely broken, but two spun lazily in the late night breeze.

Stepping out of the trees, the man approached the house. However, just before he reached the yard, something farther along caught his attention. A porch light burned, reflecting brightly off a glass storm door like a lighthouse beacon. Through the front window to the left of the porch, he saw shapes, dark smudges of Things moving in the room beyond the curtains. He drew closer and heard the muffled sounds of laughter mixed with soft thumps of music.

In his hand, the hammer vibrated with anticipation of blood. The man entered the yard and moved to the rear of the house, looking for a way in.

CHAPTER 36

"Here!" Morgan said, pointing.

Garrett pulled the truck to a stop. Morgan was out and running around the front of the truck before he could put the gear into park. She ran to the porch and pulled open the glass storm door, then shouldered the front door open. The storm door slammed behind her, its pneumatic hinges long past its prime. In the living room, Jennifer, Chris, and Amanda all stood with drinks in their hands, staring up at the intrusion with the slightly surprised grins of the heavily inebriated. Morgan hurried to the kitchen, scanned it and peered down the dim hall. There was no sign of Jason and Heather, or Todd and that girl he brought.

"You're back!" Jennifer said, raising her arms in triumph. Her red plastic cup tilted and liquid sloshed out, spilling along her hand and pattering on the carpet. She pouted. "Oh, shit." She licked the back of her hand and smiled.

"Where are the others?" Morgan asked. Again, the storm door slammed, and everyone jumped as Garrett came through the door. Jennifer cursed as more of her drink sloshed out.

"Who's that?" Chris asked. Despite the drunken look in his eyes, he watched Garrett with wary suspicion. Morgan went to the kitchen as Garrett introduced himself. The kitchen looked much the same as it had when she'd left hours ago, if littered with more empty bottles and cups. The stove held used and torn popcorn tins, and the room smelled faintly of burnt kernels. The door to the backyard stood open, and she glanced through the screen door into the yard. The glow of the porch lights showed a small ring of rocks encircling an unlit fire pit filled with old logs and tree trimmings. She pushed the heavy back door closed and returned to the living room.

"You didn't tell me your boyfriend was coming," Jennifer scolded her. She leaned close and, in a stage whisper, said, "He's cute. If you want to use my bedroom, go for it." Before Morgan could step away, Jennifer's hand caught her own. "Careful which door you open. Todd and Stephanie - you know he told us he picked her up at a gas station on the way here? - they're, um..." she giggled and made a circle with her thumb and forefinger, then pushed the index finger of her opposite hand in and out of it.

"We need to lock everything up," Morgan said.

Jennifer looked at Morgan, her eyes crinkled with confusion. "What do you mean, *lock up*?"

Morgan grabbed Jennifer and gave her a gentle shake. "Where. Are. Jason and Heather?"

"Dude, watch the drink!" Jennifer complained as she pulled free of Morgan's grasp. "Heather went home soon after you left. She got pissed I made her turn off the Go-Go's, the silly bitch. Jason's downstairs. Said he wanted to go find some kerosene or something for the fire pit. I told him it was way too late to make a damned fire, but you know Jason. Come to think of it, he's been down there a long time."

"What's going on?" Chris asked.

"She was attacked," Garrett said.

"What? Shit, are you okay?" Chris focused on Morgan, the dull look that had been in his eyes now gone.

Behind him, Amanda rolled her eyes. "Please," she moaned. "Attacked? I'm so sure!"

Morgan's vision dropped to a pinhole, her entirety focused on the petite woman. Her hands balled into fists as she took two fast steps toward Amanda, one fist coming up. Amanda flinched back, giving a mousy squeak as Morgan swung at her face. Before her fist connected, Chris stepped between the two women and blocked the punch. Morgan surged forward, leaning into Chris, who staggered back under the ferocity of her need to reach Amanda.

"My fucking parents died, you dumb cunt!" Morgan yelled. Tears flowed now, but she ignored them. "He killed my mom and dad!"

Garrett pulled her away from Chris and held her back as she cried. Everyone stood in stunned silence, with the party, the drinks, and the music all forgotten. Amanda took a step back and crossed her arms, her face set in a pout. "Doesn't mean you can try to hit me," she mumbled.

"Shut the fuck up!" Chris snapped at her. "What is wrong with you?"

"Please!" Amanda shot back. "If that actually happened - don't you come back over here, bitch, I swear I'll fuck you up," Amanda said, pointing at Morgan, who strained against Garrett's hold. "If that had happened, she'd be with the cops or at the hospital. Why'd she meet up with her boyfriend and then come back over here? Huh? Tell me that, Morgan. Did you think you could come back and tell your little story and get Chris to fuck you again?"

Chris stared, mouth open in shock. Morgan felt her strength ebbing and slumped in Garrett's arms. She focused on her breathing, letting Amanda's venom wash over her.

"Just because he was fucking you before you left doesn't mean you can come back into town and get him back, you know. He's moved on. He's-" The rifle crack of a slap cut off the rest of her sentence. Amanda's head rocked to one side. She stumbled back, hit the couch, and sat down hard. Jennifer stood over her, chest heaving, her hand raised for another blow.

"You shut your dirty fucking mouth," Jennifer seethed. Amanda glared up at her, her fingers resting against the red splotch on her cheek. "Say something else, I'll break your fucking nose," Jennifer warned her.

For a second, it looked like Amanda was going to say more. Instead, she stood up and stepped carefully around Jennifer. Grabbing Chris' hand, she said, "Let's go," and pulled him into the kitchen. The door's hinges squeaked as they went into the backyard.

Jennifer took a deep breath. The anger in her face melted away, replaced by pity. She pulled Morgan into a hug that Morgan returned, swallowing down another crying fit. She couldn't cry again. Not now. Instead, she held onto Jennifer, breathing in the smell of smoke and booze mingled with fruity shampoo.

Pulling back, Jennifer said, "What do you need? What can I do?"

Moving to the front door as she spoke, Morgan said, "We need to get everyone together and lock the house down." She closed the door and twisted the lock. "There's no telling where this guy is or where he's going, but if he's in the area, we don't want to be just sitting here with the doors open."

Jennifer frowned. "You really think he stuck around after that?" Instantly, her eyes widened. "Oh my god, do you think he's the one who killed those people on North Wind? I thought it was devil worshippers."

"I don't know. All I know is, he was wearing a mask and carrying a hammer. Whether he was alone or not, we need to lock this place down." She started toward the hall. "I'm going to go get Jason."

"What about those two?" Garrett asked as he followed Morgan. "The ones in the yard?"

For a split second, Morgan almost told him to leave them – that they could fend for themselves. And then... "Jen, will you get them?"

"I'll try," Jennifer answered as she went into the kitchen. "But I doubt that bitch will listen."

Morgan opened the door that led to the basement. The light that hung above the stairs was already lit, and a soft rustling drifted from the darkness beyond the bottom step. "Jason?" The wooden, hollow thunk of her steps on the risers filled the tight space. The air here was considerably cooler and carried a sweet, moldy stench. Morgan reached the bottom and squinted into the darkness.

A gray cinder block wall to the right extended toward the back of the basement for several feet. Dim light glowed at the end of it, suggesting an alcove or some other section of the space. Between the light in that space and the one above the stairs, the rest of the base-ment was thrown into total blackness. Threading carefully around stacked boxes and old furniture lining the wall, Morgan and Garrett approached the end of the wall and the source of light. The sounds of rustling increased as they drew closer, and Morgan tensed with each step. What if she was too late? What if the masked man was already there, standing over Jason's body, his bloody hammer in hand?

Don't be stupid. There's only one way into the basement, and we just came through it.

Morgan glanced back. The light from the stairs framed Garrett as a dark outline behind her. His head bobbed in a nod, and Morgan pressed forward, making the turn around the edge of the wall. The space on the other side was small, maybe four feet wide by six feet deep. A single naked bulb mounted to a beam in the ceiling and operated by a pull string was the only source of light. Shelves lined two walls, making the cramped space even tighter. Boxes and containers filled most of the shelves, along with coffee cans from which nails or other various hardware jutted. Jason stood near the rear wall, his back to them and his head bowed, focusing on some-thing in his hands.

"Hey," Morgan said, and Jason gave a shout as he jerked and spun around.

"Holy shit, you damned near gave me an aneurysm!" he gasped.

"I don't think that's how that works," Garrett said.

"I'm pretty sure it is. My cousin died that way." Jason looked from Morgan to Garrett. "Who are you?"

"My boyfriend," Morgan said. "We have to get upstairs. Come on."

"And leave all of this?" Jason asked, holding up what had consumed his attention. Morgan caught glimpses of exposed breasts and thick tufts of pubic hair among the pages of the magazine he held. "Jennifer's grandfather was a dirty old man!" Jason laughed. "He's got boxes of this shit. It's fantastic."

"That's good. We have to go. Come on – we're all getting together upstairs."

"But—"

"We're going to do shots. We need everyone together for that."

"Oh. Rad. Okay, let me grab a couple for the road, then." Jason plunged his hands into a bent and sagging cardboard box, retrieving a thick stack of colorful magazines. "He's got some I've never even heard of! What kind of magazine is Oui?" He pronounced it *Ooh-Wee*. Jason held one up, the white cover showing a pretty blonde wearing a denim jacket over white shorts and nothing else.

"That's French for yes," Garrett said. "It's pronounced 'we'."

Jason studied the cover and gave an appreciative frown. "Well, yes. Yes, I will." He tucked the stack under his arm and followed Morgan and Garrett upstairs.

Back in the living room, Jason sat on the couch and opened one of the magazines. "Are Todd and Stephanie still porking?"

Morgan didn't answer, instead she went to the back door, through which voices could be heard. Outside, Jennifer was at the edge of the cement patio arguing with Amanda. Chris was a couple feet behind his girlfriend, watching helplessly. Jennifer turned when Morgan stepped outside. She flapped her hand at the two. "The idiots don't believe us and want to start a fire."

Raising her voice slightly, Morgan said, "Amanda, you and I don't have to make up or anything. Jennifer won't hit you again, either, but we all need to be inside right now. It's the safest thing. We don't know where-"

"Where what? Your imaginary boogeyman is?" Amanda crossed her arms and scowled. "Please. I know you're making that up. You just want to get back with Chris."

"How does that even make sense?" Morgan yelled. "Yes, Chris and I fucked back in high school. For a little while after, too. But it wasn't like we were going to get married or anything. No offense, Chris."

"Yeah, sure," came the sad reply. "None taken."

"But you think whatever you want about me," Morgan continued. "Go right ahead. I don't care. I just want all of us inside." She scanned the yard. It was large, and most of it beyond the fire pit was shrouded in complete darkness. Morgan's skin crawled. If the masked man was here, he could be anywhere in the yard and they wouldn't see him until it was too late.

"What's all the commotion about?" Todd asked as he stepped outside. He wore jeans and held his shirt in one hand. Stephanie emerged behind him, her dyed blonde hair mussed horribly. "When did you get back?" he asked Morgan.

"And who's that?" Stephanie asked, pointing to Garrett.

"Todd, can you get a fire started?" Amanda asked.

Pulling on his shirt, Todd said, "Yeah, but I thought Jason was handling that. Where is that lazy fucker?"

Morgan thought she'd rip her hair out, the frustration was so intense. None of these people believed her, and thought they could just cruise the night away. She'd started to argue, to continue to press her case, when Garrett put a hand on her arm. He shook his head. "They're not going to listen."

"So, what? We let them build a bonfire and we sit out here where he could get any of us?"

"We'd all be together," he offered. "At least there may be safety in numbers."

Morgan gaped at him, unable to believe she was hearing him correctly. Meanwhile, Todd approached the pit and peered in. He said something to Chris, and the two crossed the yard to the dark corner of the house where a single, boxy air conditioning unit sat.

"What are they doing?" Morgan asked.

"Todd said something about getting more wood," Jennifer said. "There's a stack over there. It's old as shit, but should burn. Do you want to go inside? We can sit in there, lock the doors, and watch them through the kitchen window."

A thump and a grunt came from the corner where Todd and Chris were. Chris shouted, "Oh fuck!" and Morgan's heart froze in her chest. Immediately, Chris came stumbling out of the darkness, his face spattered with blood and his eyes the size of dinner plates. "He's..." The word died as the back of Chris' skull exploded in a spraying halo of blood and bone. Chris took three more faltering steps and flopped forward, sliding across the grass like a runner stealing third.

Amanda screamed and rushed toward her boyfriend, yelling his name while Morgan and the others stood transfixed, frozen by the suddenness of things. Amanda knelt by Chris' ruined head, her hands shaking as she reached down, unsure what to do or how to help. When the pale hideousness of the mask pushed out of the shadows, Amanda fell back on her ass and screamed. Her scream became a choking, wet gasping as a silver spike slammed into her neck, the gore-covered tip emerging from the other side. Amanda's hands flopped like dead fish in the grass, her legs spasming. The killer stepped close, his entire dark form towering over the small woman. With a powerful jerk of his arm, he ripped the spike free, tearing out the rest of Amanda's throat in a geyser of blood.

Morgan's knees buckled as cold terror pulsed through her. The man stood over Amanda's body for a moment more, looking at what he'd done. He then turned his horrible gaze to the people standing on the patio. Morgan felt the eyes lock onto her. She shivered as if worms and beetles scurried over her flesh.

The man seemed to stiffen, and a single thought tore through the screaming panic in Morgan's brain. *He recognizes me.*

Then, Garrett's arms were under her, lifting her. He shoved her toward Jennifer. "Get her inside!" He grabbed at Stephanie's shirt, snagging the sleeve and pulling the girl around. She turned slowly, as if in a trance. "Get inside!" he said, and gave her a rough shove that got the woman moving.

Jennifer pulled Morgan inside, then stepped away to allow Stephanie room to enter. Morgan watched helplessly as Garrett reached in, grabbed the knob of the heavy door and started to pull it closed. He looked at Jennifer. "Keep her safe. I'm going to draw him away."

"What?" Morgan coughed out. Surely, she hadn't heard what she thought she had. Garrett couldn't do anything out there! The man in the mask was too strong, too fast. "No!" she said as the fog in her mind cleared.

Garrett gave her a long, hard look. "I love you. I'll see you soon." Then, he pulled the door shut and stepped away. The thud of the door closing broke the last bricks of the dam in Morgan's mind, and she shot forward, her hand grasping for the knob.

Jennifer was there, though, pulling her arm back and wedging herself between Morgan and the door. Morgan heard the lock click home at the same time that Jennifer shouted for Stephanie to check the front door and call the cops. Morgan screamed Garrett's name. She pushed Jennifer aside, the blonde woman crashing against the counter with a painful gasp. Morgan's hands grabbed the knob and the lock, her fingers tensing to turn both as she stared through the glass of the door.

Garrett stood ten feet away at the edge of the patio, facing the masked man who watched him calmly from the yard. The mask angled left and then right, as if the man were searching for the people who'd been outside only seconds before. Not seeing them - *Doesn't he know we're inside?* - he returned his deadly focus to Garrett. Through the glass, Morgan heard her boyfriend say something, the words inaudible. The masked man didn't respond, giving no indication that he'd heard or understood. He simply stared at Garrett, the hammer held by his side.

Then, he stepped forward, closing the distance, and in that moment, Garrett sprinted away, angling to the right and the driveway. Morgan had just twisted open the lock and turned the doorknob when Jennifer's hand clamped down over hers, forcing the door to remain shut.

"No!" Jennifer shouted. "You go out there, you're dead. Let your guy do his thing."

Morgan bucked against her friend, struggling to break the grip, but Jennifer was stronger, her fingers like a vice and squeezing Morgan's hand painfully against the curve of the knob. "I have to help him!" Morgan protested, but no matter how hard she fought or how loudly she shouted, Jennifer's grasp was unrelenting.

Morgan caught a glimpse of the masked man turning the corner of the house. With a growl of frustration and fear, she pushed away from the door and raced to the front door. In the living room, Stephanie stood near the stereo, hands clutched between her breasts as she watched the commotion with a wide-eyed, panicked expression. She kept saying, "I called the cops. I called them." Morgan stumbled as Jennifer ran past her to block the front door. She held the knob with both hands, looking at Morgan defiantly as she shouted for Jason to guard the back door. Jason, magazines forgotten as soon as the screaming started, nodded dumbly and hurried away.

Morgan glared at her friend then pushed Stephanie aside and threw back the curtains. In the center of the lawn, where the paved walkway led to the street, Garrett stood. His head twisted left and right as if he were searching for the masked man or trying to decide where to run. Morgan slapped the window, pounding to get his attention as she screamed his name, telling him to run, to get out of there.

Movement drew her attention to the left, and Morgan's stomach dropped as the masked man appeared from around the side of the house. She screamed Garrett's name once more and was relieved when he broke into a run, angling to the right and the main street.

The masked man hurled the hammer. It tumbled through the air – a dark, blurry missile. Morgan couldn't hear the impact, but she saw Garrett go down. She screamed.

The light from the distant streetlamp was poor, but Morgan could see the dark shape of Garrett laying in the grass, moving slowly as he tried to climb to his feet. The man in the mask walked so calmly that he could have been on a casual stroll through a park on a warm summer afternoon. He picked up the hammer as Garrett pushed up to his knees.

Morgan was glad she couldn't hear the wet impact when the hammer hit the side of Garrett's head. He slammed back to the ground, his body shaking in huge jerks every time the hammer came back down.

Again.

Again.

Again.

Morgan had no air left in her lungs. Everything was empty, and she thought she would suffocate. Her mouth hung open in a silent scream, saliva spilling over her lips in a long string as she watched the shadow show of her boyfriend being slaughtered.

When the man was finished, he stood up stiffly and turned back to the house. His mask glowed with an eerie pall that burned into Morgan's brain like a branding iron. The mask took on a red, pulsing sheen, waves of color washing over it in a rhythmic rotation. He twisted his entire body and stared at something in the distance. Then, without a glance back toward her, he stepped away, moving into the dark shadows of the next yard. In the span of a heartbeat, he was gone.

Morgan stared at the shadow of Garrett's body as more of the lawn was bathed in the shifting red and blue lights. She continued staring even as patrol cars screeched to a halt, their occupants rushing out with weapons drawn. One officer knelt quickly beside Garrett, reached down with a hand then quickly stood. He said something to the others, but Morgan couldn't make it out. She didn't have to.

An officer hurried to the door and pounded on it. "Police! Open the door!" Jennifer unlocked the door and pulled it open.

Instantly, the house was filled with voices and the nasally static of radio chatter. Jennifer put her hands on Morgan's arms, the touch now gentle, loving. Jennifer's voice was in her ear. "We're safe."

Morgan heard none of it. Instead, she continued to stare at the dark, twisted shape which had been Garrett Ward.

SUNDAY, JUNE 7, 1987

CHAPTER 37

Scott woke to find himself alone in Kevin's bedroom. He crawled out of his blankets and stood, throwing his arms up and stretching. Sleeping over at Kevin's was usually fun, but the fact that he always ended up on the floor was a pain in the ass. A tugging at his pants drew his attention. The evidence of his fantastic dream about Heather Thomas was still pushing his sweatpants up in a tent. He gave himself a couple of minutes to let the erection subside, then thumped his way upstairs. In the hall, Scott shot a look to the door of Misty's room, hoping to catch a glimpse, but the door remained closed. However, further down the hall, the door to Kevin's parents' room was open a few inches. The lights in the room were on, and he could hear soft voices as they moved around. He found Kevin sitting at the kitchen table, eating cereal. A glass featuring the McDonald's character Mayor McCheese sat near his hand, half-filled with orange juice.

"If you're going to jerk off," Kevin said around a mouthful of Fruity Pebbles, "have the decency to go into the bathroom."

Scott retrieved a bowl and spoon, and poured himself some of the cereal. "I figured I'd go see if your sister was awake yet," he said, unable to hide the smile.

"Why? Did you want to borrow her magnifying glass and tweezers? I think there's some red food coloring in that drawer if you want to dye it so you can find it next time."

"Fuck you!" Scott laughed. He glanced around for a clock. "What time is it?"

"Ten after seven."

"What time do you want to get going?"

Kevin shrugged. "Earlier than later, I guess. Maybe we head over around eight? I figure people will be in church by then, so we won't risk too many seeing us heading there or back."

Settling into his seat, Scott said, "Your parents are up, by the way."

Kevin looked toward the hallway irritably. "Shit. Okay. We'll have to be slick about this, then. I thought we could get out of here before they woke up. Hurry up and eat."

Scott had finished and was tilting the bowl to get at the sugary sediment left behind when Kevin's mom came into the kitchen. Despite having worked the night before, Debora Appleton looked fresh-faced. Her short auburn hair was done, she had a full face of makeup, and she wore a black dress with gold flowers. Even though she was old - Scott guessed she was in her late thirties - he could see where Misty had gotten her good looks from.

Debora carried a stained white coffee mug which she put in the sink before she turned to face the boys. "Scott, hi. I forgot you were staying over last night." She gave him a thin smile. "Kevin, you need to finish up and go get dressed."

Kevin put his bowl down with a loud thump and looked at his mother. "What for?"

"We have to go to church today. Your father is getting his tie on now, so you need to hurry. I'm sorry, Scott, but you're going to have to go home."

"For chrissakes, Mom," Kevin protested, ignoring his mother's reproachful glare at the language. "We haven't gone to church in months. Why now? Scott and I had big plans for today."

"That may be so, but there were more people hurt last night. We need to get together and support our friends and neighbors. This is a time for community. Your plans for playing in the woods or whatever will have to wait. Besides, I don't want you off doing God knows what. They still don't know who did it, as far as I know." Kevin's continued protests fell on deaf ears as she disappeared back down the hall. Scott heard her knock on a door and tell Misty to hurry up, as they were leaving in ten minutes. A garbled reply was given, and Scott perked up at the prospect of seeing Misty Appleton, even if only for a moment or two before he had to leave.

Next to him, Kevin sulked, staring disgustedly at his mostly empty bowl. "Bullshit," he grumbled.

"Sorry, man."

Kevin dropped his spoon with a clatter. "What—" he looked toward the hall, then dropped his voice to a whisper, "fucking good does praying about shit do? Huh? It's not going to make those people come back. It's not going to make whoever did it walk into the police station and say, 'Here I am, arrest me.' It's bullshit."

Scott put his bowl in the sink. "Yeah, but what can you do? Look, I think I'm still going to go. Don't look at me like that. You said it yourself – this may be our only chance, right? Okay, so why lose it completely when I can still go? I won't be able to get as much stuff, sure, but I've been to the mill more than a few times. I know my way around. I'll scout it out, see what's good, and grab what I can. Then, maybe tonight, you and I can go back and get the rest of it."

Kevin thought it over, then nodded. "Yeah, alright." He stood to go get dressed. As Scott followed, Misty emerged from the hall. She seemed groggy from sleep, but had managed to pull her strawberry blonde hair up in a ponytail and put on a cornflower blue dress that showed her cleavage just enough to be tantalizing, but not so much that she'd get run out of church. Scott's chest fluttered as she rounded the corner, nearly colliding with him. She mumbled an apology and continued toward the coffee pot. Scott's eyes locked on her as she drifted across the kitchen. Then, Kevin grabbed him. "Come on, dingleberry."

Minutes later, Scott watched as Kevin's disgusted face stared out from the back seat of the Appleton family station wagon. Scott gave his friend a 'sorry' wave, which Kevin returned with his middle finger as they drove away.

When Scott reached Mill Road and crested it, he slowed to a crawl. Scanning the parking lot, he saw Harold Watkins' maroon Buick near the security gate. *Good*, he thought. Harold was an alright guy, but according to Scott's dad, he was about the laziest son of a bitch to ever shuffle across this planet. If Scott could make it across the parking lot to the rear of the mill without being spotted - not always a guarantee, but the odds were in his favor with Harold on duty - then he'd be free and clear. Cursing the bad luck that Kevin couldn't be there with him, he accelerated and, keeping his eyes on the windows of the guard's office, drove as quickly as he could across the open lot.

He reached the rear of the massive building, putting the main lot out of sight, and turned left onto a gravel and dirt path to pass through an open gate in the fence. After about twenty yards, he entered a shaded patch of land formed by the general U shape of the mill's footprint. He slowed his car to a stop next to the first of two large buildings that sat nestled in the dip. The cement structure next to him housed boilers for cooking the dye slurries. A massive brick smokestack rose out of the roof of the building, its mouth devoid of the usual dark plumes. Scott had no interest in the boilers, though, and proceeded to the second building that sat closer to the main factory.

The door to the structure was solid metal and had a flat handle that, to his surprise, turned easily. The room inside was stifling, and sweat immediately broke out on his brow as he made his way to the mechanic shop that dominated the right-hand side of the building. The shop was an open area with multiple tables and storage cabinets. Various pipes and gears were stacked in corners or laying on tables. Grinning fiendishly, Scott gathered several metal tubes and carried them to his car. He stuffed them in the trunk and returned for a second trip for more items.

After his third trip, he had to force himself to stop. He was already at risk of having taken too many things that would be noticed by the transition crew, and he still wanted to check the rest of the mill. He closed the trunk of his car and approached a small, nondescript door in the wall of the main building. The door pulled open with a loud scrape.

He paused in the thin strip of light that ran along the factory floor, reaching from the cracked door. Around him, the mill was silent. The quiet was so immense that it was unsettling. Never in his life had Scott been there when everything was shut down; in fact, he didn't think all this equipment had ever been shut off all at once.

Across the floor, large piles of cotton were stacked onto thick wooden pallets. Forklifts sat nearby, their forks set to various heights. Scott's shoes made soft crunching sounds as they passed over the dried husks of cotton seeds. The massive hulks of the seeding and cotton gin machines stood like alien tanks awaiting the order to fire. Several of the large pieces of equipment had some of their panels detached, exposing the chaos of internal parts. Others had had their huge rollers removed, each of the empty spaces resembling a hollow socket in a robotic jaw. Tools lay about on the floor, and nearby tables housed more implements. The tables made Scott think of some horrific operating room – something out of *Tales from the Darkside*, and he shivered.

Okay, man, focus. The factory floor continued into the distance. Beyond the receiving and cleaning area, and around a bend in the building's footprint, were the carding and spinning departments. It was around that bend, he remembered, that two more large storage rooms lay. However, he reminded himself, once there, he would have to exercise extreme caution, as he'd be closer to the security office and without the benefit of the massive processing machines' covering his movement. The only thing standing between him and Harold would be the spinning machines and drawing frames, where material was prepared for transport to the second floor.

Keeping to the wall, Scott turned the corner. He passed a wide, flat-topped table filled with bundles of white cloth, and reached the first storage room. The door's hinges creaked as it opened, sending Scott's heart into a burst of hammering. He stared along the rest of the building to the door and window to the security office. There were blinds over the window, the slats angled down to prevent anyone from seeing in or out. He waited, hand on the door, his body tensed to run at the slightest movement of the blinds or security door. When nothing happened, he slowly, carefully let out a shuddering breath and stepped into the supply room.

The room smelled musty, with a slight oily tint, and his hand flapped at the wall until he found the light switch. Fluorescent lighting flickered, shuddered, and then caught. A small path ran through the center of the room between floor-to-ceiling shelves that held everything from scrap cloth to cardboard tubing to spare parts for machines. He turned to the right and walked along the aisle, considering his options. His car could only hold so much, so he had to be selective. At the same time, he worried about missing something important.

Turning the corner, he perused the boxes and tubs, his fingers picking items up, turning them, and then discarding them. He'd shifted over to another shelf when something along the far end of the space caught his attention. Squinting in the gloom, he approached the thing. The light in the short end of the storage room wasn't as good; whoever had built it hadn't installed another fixture in the ceiling, relying on the smaller one at the junction behind him.

On the floor against the wall, mostly shrouded in darkness, was a pallet of blankets. The blankets weren't folded or stacked neatly, but rather laid out and wrinkled as if someone had lain on them. Around the blankets were empty cellophane wrappers from peanut butter crackers and a few small chip bags. Had one of the workers been sleeping here? That made no sense. Scott didn't know everyone who worked at the mill, but he couldn't think of a single one who would opt to sleep hidden in the back of a storage room.

His confusion slipped into concern when he noticed faint smudges on the back wall near the corner. He knelt and leaned close, cursing the lack of light and his own shadow that fell over the marks. Reaching out, Scott touched the painted cement wall, his fingers brushing over the rough surface and across what he'd seen. *Those are smears. Something wet was wiped here.* However, his fingers came away clean. Whatever it had been was dry, but even in the poor light, he knew with cold certainty what it was.

That's blood.

He stood up quickly, breath caught in his throat and eyes locked on the blemishes. Someone had bled here. But the blankets looked unstained. So, the person hadn't been bleeding from a cut on their body. Which meant....

"Oh shit," he whispered. "It wasn't their blood."

It was time to go. Fuck finding more supplies and fuck the land speeder. This wasn't right. He pushed the door open, the hinges screaming out their agony, and stepped quickly out to the inspection table.

As he came around the corner, he caught the flicker of movement to his right and reflexively flinched away. The entire mill exploded with thunder as something slammed into the machine only inches away from him. A yell of panic and surprise burst out of Scott, and he recoiled against the wall.

A huge man wearing a ghostly white mask stood at the edge of the machine, a heavy hammer in one hand. The weapon rested against one of the metal bars of the unit, its flat head in a depression in the metal. Scott saw the horrible curved spike on the other side of the hammer's head and could imagine it slamming into his chest, piercing his lungs and sending blood up his throat. That thought passed through his mind in the blink of an eye, and then the masked man was lifting the hammer and coming around the corner.

Scott scrambled to turn and sprinted forward just as the space where he'd been against the cement wall exploded in a shower of fragments. He raced for the exit even as he heard the hammer whistling through the air behind him. When he reached the metal access door, he gave the handle a hard twist.

It didn't budge.

Scott whimpered as he tried again, pulling with everything he had. But the door remained closed. He glanced back. The hammer cut through the air, toward Scott's head, and he leapt to the side as it smashed into the door, denting the metal and sending another thunderous boom throughout the factory.

Scott backpedaled even as the man reversed his swing, sending the spike toward Scott's chest. Scott's foot caught on something, and he went down. Pain blossomed in his lower back as he landed against the hard angles of another machine. The spike missed the top of his head by inches and tore into one of the rollers. The masked man tugged at it, but something had caught the spike and held it firm. As the man fought to free his weapon, Scott risked a quick glance at the black eyes and jagged mouth before crawling away, gritting his teeth against his screaming back.

After several yards, he stood and ran, moving deeper into the forest of the machines. He angled toward the near end of the factory, where a door led to the stairwell. If he could get to the second floor before his attacker, he could sprint to the opposite end of the building and take another set of stairs down. That would put him next to the security office, which was fine with him.

Behind him, the masked man had freed the hammer and was following, his pace steady and quick. Scott threw open the door and pounded up the dimly lit stairs two at a time. As he gained the top and grabbed the handle for the door, he heard the masked man enter the stairwell.

The second floor of the mill housed the Spinning, Twisting, and Quality Control departments. All of the equipment stood in long, silent rows. Most machines had streams of fabric running into or through them, their functions frozen mid-process. Despite the thudding of the masked man's boots on the stairs, Scott scanned the floor, thinking about his best option.

He darted forward between rows of twisting machines and ran for several yards before turning to the left. As he made the turn, the stairwell door slammed open. He flinched at the noise, then yelped in pain as his knee connected with the sharp edge of one of the pieces of equipment. Scott spun, staggered, and fell, catching himself at the last moment. He stayed on all fours, panting against the shock of the impact. The knee of his left pants leg flapped open, exposing scraped and bleeding skin. His knee pulsed painfully in time with his heart-beat, and he gritted his teeth against it, blinking away tears.

Carefully, he crouched and duck-walked, stopping a few yards away behind a new row of equipment. In the wake of the door opening, the floor filled with a deafening silence. Scott's hands shook as he held onto the metal side of the closest machine, forcing himself to peer over it.

The masked man's head and shoulders were visible a couple dozen feet away, the rest of his body obscured by a winding machine. The killer's head turned slowly, mechanically, as he searched for his prey. Before the horrible face angled in his direction, Scott slid back into his hiding place and glanced to his right. The machinery extended to the far wall, where another stairwell door sat. Large windows that stretched from floor to ceiling lined the primary wall, giving a full view of the parking lot and the woods beyond. On the shorter wall at the end of the floor the windows were smaller, mounted a few feet above the floor. One was open several inches, the glass angled out from the building.

Risking another glance over the machine covering his position, he saw that the masked man was closer, head swiveling left and right as he crossed the aisles.

Scott made up his mind.

His best option was to sprint to the other stairwell and hope he was faster than the masked man. He gathered himself, willing his shaking legs to bring him the speed he'd need, and hoping the cut to his knee wouldn't hinder him.

As he leaped from his crouch, he heard a man's voice cut through the thick quiet.

"Hey! You! What the hell are you doing?" As Scott's body gained momentum, he looked back, startled by the voice. Harold the security guard stood next to the stairwell door, his flashlight in one hand. Despite his fear and need to escape, Scott froze at the sound of the uniformed authority. His hands raised reflexively. Harold drew closer, his young face set in an authoritative scowl. "What the hell are you doing here?" he demanded.

Scott looked around. The masked man was gone. Scott searched the silent machines, desperate to catch a glimpse of the attacker. But there was nothing.

"There's someone here," he said. "He attacked me."

"Right. How many of you are there?" Harold angled his head up to project his voice. "Alright, you little shits, come on out! Jig's up!" To Scott, he said, "You're going to come with me. We're going to call the cops and let you explain to them why you thought it would be-"

The words cut off in a wet, choking sound. Harold's body jerked forward, the spike erupting through the shoulder of his uniform shirt. Blood soaked into the white fabric as Harold dropped the flashlight. It hit the floor and rolled away with a metallic clatter. Harold stared, dumbfounded, at the thing emerging from him. Harold gaped at Scott, his mouth opening and closing. Only wheezing gasps came out.

Scott's brain screamed at him to move, to run, to take advantage of the delay. The commands cut through his horrified paralysis, and he dashed for the door even as he heard the wet sound of the spike pulling free of Harold's body. He reached the door with his breath exploding from his mouth in tremulous bursts. The door swung out, revealing the dim throat of the stairwell. Scott fought the urge to look back and instead threw himself into the small space, leaping down the steps three at a time.

Harold's tortured screams followed him downward.

CHAPTER 38

By ten in the morning, Morgan's head was a maelstrom of thoughts. She'd spent most of the waning moments of the previous night sitting on the back of an ambulance, requisite blanket draped across her shoulders and a paper cup full of tepid, dusty-tasting water in hand. All around her, men and women in various uniforms had flitted, moving like strange phantasms that pulsed with blue and red light. She'd been checked out, the cut on her back administered to, and been given Tylenol for the pain in her shoulder after being told that it didn't seem to be broken.

She'd spoken to numerous police - she'd lost count at seven - most of whom wore the brown uniform of the county. They'd fired their questions at her with clipped, military precision, their faces showing only a hardened look of indifference. The Elden Mills police, Bill Adams and one other whose name she couldn't remember, had been softer in their delivery; each man kneeling in front of her as if about to pull a black velvet box from some hidden pocket. They'd touched her knee lightly, withdrawing the gesture with a mumbled apology when Morgan flinched.

Regardless of the uniform or the look in the cop's eyes, Morgan had told them all the same story, starting with her coming home from the party and ending with the cops bursting into Jennifer's house, weapons aiming at every corner. They nodded, jotted notes, and told her she'd been very brave. They all said that. That she'd been brave.

The sentiment struck her as odd, almost surreal.

She'd not been brave; she'd been terrified out of her mind. She'd run for her life after finding her parents' bodies. Then, at Jennifer's, all she'd done was try to get doors and windows locked. When Garrett had gone outside, her efforts to get to him hadn't been to help or to interfere, to take on the maniac herself, but rather to drag Garrett back inside. That hadn't been bravery. It had been selfishness. She'd acted simply because, in that moment, she hadn't wanted Garrett to die. She'd thought that if she lost him, she didn't know what she would do, or how she would go on.

More disturbingly, not one single officer or EMT had been able to locate Scott. She'd told them clearly that he'd spent the night at Kevin Appleton's. They'd absorbed the information, and each one had said they'd look into sending someone over there to get him. She could tell by the looks on their faces that this detail was of minor importance, and they were filing it away as such.

After several hours, though, the questions had dried up, and she sat in the living room with Jennifer, Jason, and Stephanie, watching through the front windows as men in dark coveralls loaded gurneys holding black plastic-shrouded forms into the ambulances. Forms that Morgan knew were people. People she'd known. People who, only hours ago, had been smiling, laughing, drinking, and enjoying their lives. One of whom had been the only man to truly love her, despite everything she'd been through and everything she'd become.

Once the bodies had been loaded, an EMT collected the blankets and tossed them into the back of an ambulance near one of the gurneys. Morgan and her friends watched the cruisers and ambulances drive away like relatives watching their kin leave a family gathering. After the last vehicle disappeared from sight, the group remained on the sofa, sitting close to one another in an attempt to draw some measure of comfort from the contact.

Morgan could sit for only a few minutes at a time before the buzzing in her brain forced her up, though. Each time the tension became too great, she went to the phone in the kitchen and dialed Kevin Appleton's house, listening while twirling the phone cord around one finger, then her hand, and then her arm as the connection on the other end rang and rang. Eventually, only the answering machine would pick up. She left messages the first three times, then hanging up as soon as the outgoing message began playing. After her fifth attempt, she went outside and, being careful not to cross the yellow tape which the police had strung up to section off where the bodies had been, lowered herself into one of the rough, wrought-iron chairs. She drew her legs up, wrapping her arms around her shins and resting her chin on her knees.

Her misery was a poisonous lead ball in her stomach. Garrett had been so good, and this was how his life had ended. With him screaming, being pounded into an oozing mass of bleeding meat. She squeezed her eyes shut, fighting to focus on Garrett's face as it had been, gentle and with a little scruff on the cheeks. The smile he'd always had when he looked at her; the soft care she could see reflected in his eyes.

And she'd been nothing but shit to him. He'd done everything right, had been patient with her, and hadn't asked about her past or why she whimpered and thrashed some nights in her sleep. Hadn't even questioned why sometimes she flinched when he reached out for her, and other times threw him on the nearest piece of furniture and had her way with him.

He hadn't deserved how she'd treated him.

But for him to follow her to Elden Mills.... He was dead because of her. That fact sat like a knife in her chest, sending spider legs of pain radiating out with every breath. Tears tickled her cheeks, but she refused to wipe them away. Garrett had accepted her, warts and all, and had died because of it. Her parents had accepted her back into their home, had all but said they'd forgiven her for the way she'd treated them, for saying the things she'd said, and all the fights, and ultimately for leaving abruptly that Saturday morning. Now their absence was a bottomless chasm in Morgan's soul. Being back in her parents' house and feeling their acceptance and love had given

Morgan the hope that she could finally heal. For the first time in years, Morgan had been able to see a path forward, a way out of the darkness. Surrounded by her parents' love, there'd been a chance to move on.

All of that was gone now.

With the swing of a hammer, another monster had come into Morgan's life and destroyed everything. He'd taken the chance for happiness from her and left her with nothing but a burning coal deep within her core. That coal glowed, pushing its heat farther into her body and filling her with hate. The fire fed on that hate and pulsed one thought in her mind. *Revenge.*

Dimly, Morgan noticed that her tears had dried up. The fire had burned them away, leaving her staring at the bloodstains on the cement – not seeing them; seeing the masked face instead.

Her fingers dug into her arms, fingernails pressing painful crescents into her flesh as she thought about the man in the mask.

"Morgan?" The voice cut through the dense haze of cold hatred, blowing it apart and bringing the world back into focus. Scott stood outside the door – his shirt dirty and torn, and his face dirty, save for streaks where his own tears had washed through the grime. His hair was a jumbled mess, and one of the knees of his jeans was torn and hanging loose like a flap of skin. A bloody knee peered through the porthole in the denim.

Morgan stood, her limbs uncoiling, and crossed to him. With every step, a new sense of relief filled her, pushing back the dark thoughts. Scott managed to croak, "Mom. Dad." Then, Morgan was hugging him, pulling her brother tightly against her. His hands gripped, pulled, repositioned, and gripped again in a desperate pattern as he held her tight. Morgan reached up and stroked her brother's hair, ignoring the warm wetness of his tears against her neck. She cried, softly and quietly, while Scott gave out heaving sobs. Between gasps, he tried to speak. "They're...gone." Morgan said nothing, only holding him more tightly. The fire within her gave another needful pulse.

Scott stepped back, sniffing and rubbing the heels of his hands across his red, watery eyes. His cheeks were flushed, and after a second, he puffed them as he exhaled in an attempt to gather himself. The glass door opened, and Jennifer leaned out, a sad smile on her face. "You guys want to come inside? It's less gruesome." Morgan gave her brother a gentle shove toward the door.

Inside, Jennifer handed Scott a blue and white can of Pepsi. She picked up a second from the counter next to the fridge and offered it to Morgan, who shook her head. Jennifer held it out, insisting with the gesture that it be taken and consumed.

Sipping the fizzing, sweet liquid, Morgan went back to the living room and sat on the loveseat. Scott fell heavily next to her. On the couch, Stepanie lay on her side, her head in Jason's lap. Her hands were tucked in a praying gesture beneath her cheek. Jason sat with his arms folded over his chest, staring at the television where MTV played soundlessly.

"What now?" Jennifer asked.

Nobody seemed to have an answer for several seconds. Morgan sipped her soda and thought about the coal fire that burned inside of her. She knew what she wanted to do, what she felt compelled to do, but had no idea where to start.

"I want to kill that fucker!" Jason spat in a voice as sharp as a spike. "I want to tear him to pieces for what he did to Todd and Chris."

Jennifer let out a long sigh. "That's what the cops are for. They're all over the place looking for him. You heard what they said. He's been doing this all over town. They have the county and the state here. Hell, they'll probably call in the National Guard next. They'll get him."

Jason snorted. "They couldn't catch a wet booger. They've been looking for his ass since Friday, and they still can't find him. The prick went all over town, and they're no closer to catching him."

"So, what's your big plan, huh?" Jennifer asked. "You think you're better than all those cops? What are you going to do? Get on your motorcycle and ride aimlessly? That's what they're already doing."

"It's better than sitting her on our asses," Jason fired back petulantly. On his lap, Stephanie scowled, and then she sat up.

"Do I have to remind you about the time you got lost trying to find that Tasty Burger?" Jennifer asked.

"What's your point?"

"My point is, you have no idea where to even start. This town is bigger than you think. There's all the houses, yards, parks, the Veil... everywhere that this guy could be. We have, what, a couple hundred cops running around also? They have a better chance than you."

Jason said nothing, only glared at her.

Jennifer continued, "And let's say you do find him. What then? You weren't out there!" She flung an arm in the direction of the kitchen and the yard beyond. "You didn't see the way he moved. You didn't see the huge fucking hammer he had. You didn't see...." Her lips trembled. She shook her head. "You didn't see," she finished softly.

Jason stayed quiet, and Morgan could see the war going on in his mind. It was etched on his face, in the small twitches at the corner of one eye and in the flaring of his nostrils. He wanted to do something, but he knew Jennifer was right. There was no possible way to know where to even start looking, much less any reasonable way to think that Jason alone could stop the man.

"We have to try," he said weakly as he slumped into the couch.

"Just leave it to the police," Jennifer answered.

"No," Morgan said. She drained the last of the Pepsi and put the can on the floor next to the loveseat. She looked coolly at Jason. "You're right. He needs to pay for what he did."

Jason's cheeks colored, and he stammered, "I didn't mean...I mean...I'm not trying to assume what you-" Morgan held up a hand and shook her head to stop the babble.

"That piece of shit took everything from me. Everything except Scott. And for a while last night, I thought even he was gone. I don't care how many police or army guys there are in town. I don't care if the fucking Marines parachute in with tanks. I'm tired of running. I'm tired of losing parts of myself." On the couch, Jason and Stephanie exchanged confused looks, but Morgan stared at Jennifer. After a moment, Jennifer gave a small, understanding nod.

"So," Jason said slowly, "where do we start?"

"I think I may know," Scott said from where he slouched deep among the cushions.

Morgan twisted toward him. "What do you mean?"

Scott's eyes were hard, and a new level of anger filled Morgan. Her brother shouldn't look like that. He was a gentle soul.

And then he began talking, relaying his trip to the mill that morning. Morgan and Jason exchanged a look when he described the pile of blankets. Jennifer gave a startled gasp when he told them about running and hiding from the masked man, and how Harold had distracted the killer, allowing Scott to escape.

"I went straight home and..." he said, but didn't finish. "Then, I remembered you were here."

Morgan nodded. Inside her, the coal fire pulsed and grew.

"Let's go," she said.

CHAPTER 39

Morgan got out of Jason's Jeep and stared at the mill. Beyond the chain-link fence, the dark brick of the factory rose out of the ground like a cancerous growth. Her eyes played over the windows, the thin grass that surrounded the structure like an algae-covered moat, and finally the small, shingled roof of the security guard's office. Nervous energy, mixed with black, cancerous hatred for the masked man rippled through her, touching her extremities and rebounding back. Her fingers tightened their hold around the handle of the knife she held, her knuckles turning white from the pressure. She shoved her free hand into the pocket of the jeans Jennifer had given her in order to subdue its shaking.

The others gathered, watching the building as if expecting it to grow arms and legs and come crashing toward them. *I really don't want to go in there,* Morgan thought as memories flashed through her mind – being pushed down onto the filthy floor, her pants being ripped down, and Geordie's hot, fishy breath on her skin as he grunted atop her.

"Security guard's here," Jason said, pointing to the maroon Buick. A beat later, he seemed to remember Scott's story. "Oh."

"You okay?" Jennifer asked, placing a hand on Morgan's shoulder.

Morgan forced herself to turn away. "Yeah." To Scott, she said, "I don't want you in there. Stay in the car, okay?"

He made a face. "Are you fucking kidding? Not happening."

Morgan could see the darkness in his eyes, and the determination etched on his face. She knew she could argue with him, wasting time by telling him how he was the only family she had left, and that she couldn't risk losing him. But it would all be just words. Scott could just as easily turn them back on her, and nothing he could say would convince her to sit on the sidelines. He'd lost just as much as she had. He had every right to go in there and kill the monster. Her mouth twitched in a weak smile.

"We doing this?" Jason asked.

"Yeah," Morgan said. "Let's hope we can get this done before Stephanie convinces the cops to come." The access gate was secured by several wraps of thick chain, a padlock holding it all in place. Morgan glared at it, then at the coiled barbed wire that ran across the top of the fence.

"We can get in around back," Scott said. "If we take the loading dock dirt road."

"Makes no sense to have this gate locked and that part open," Jason said.

"Maybe Harold meant to secure that one and just hadn't," Scott said. "But that's how I got in."

As they passed through the gate and Jason steered between the buildings, Morgan forced herself not to look at the building, but rather at the shallow line of trees separating the mill property from the wide ribbon of the river. As Jason turned to park between the main building and the smaller outbuildings, something in the trees glinted.

Before the Jeep had come to a complete stop, Morgan leaped out and jogged back around the corner of the building.

Beyond the trees, the Mill River flowed, small sparkles of sunlight reflecting in brief flashes. Something told her that wasn't what she'd seen. She narrowed her eyes against the glare and scanned the dense growth.

"What is it?" Scott asked.

"I thought I saw..." Morgan began, shaking her head. "Must have been the river." She'd started to turn back when she saw it. Off to the right, several feet in, was a dark shape. Although, from where she stood, the sun didn't hit it, the straight lines and the angled corners made the outline of the car unmistakable. Pointing, she asked, "Did you see that when you were here?"

"No," her brother answered. "But I was focused on stealing shit and not getting caught. Whose do you think it is?"

"Sure as hell doesn't belong to anyone who works here," Morgan answered, and crossed the open space to the trees. The car, a blue Ford, sat several feet in. Two thick trees flanked the rear doors so closely that no one could have opened them. The two front side windows were rolled down, and in the stagnant heat of the day, the smell of blood was staggering. Morgan's stomach rolled as she stepped into the stench. "Jesus," she whispered.

The front seats of the car were stained with dried blood. Lines of it covered the entire dashboard and streaked the windshield. Flies crawled across the seats and console, and buzzed happily all around the cabin. Morgan waved them away as she forced herself to lean close and look at the interior. Other than the blood and a single quarter stuck in the bloody film that covered the passenger seat, the car was empty.

"It's his," Scott said.

Morgan stepped back. Her brother was right. This had to be the masked man's car, although how anyone could have managed to sit in it for more than a few seconds in this condition - let alone however long it had taken him to drive from wherever he'd been - was beyond imagination. Understanding came to her as she stared at the car, ideas clicking into place. The man had done all of this before. Probably in some other distant small town. She'd never heard anything about it, not that she was an avid newspaper reader, but the idea felt right.

He'd done this before, leaving destruction and despair in his wake, and then somehow ended up in Elden Mills. Where he'd started all over. How had nobody stopped him, either in the town or along the way? Had he killed everyone? Or had he slipped away before those who'd survived were able to recover enough to put an end to the killing?

"He's not getting away this time," she said. She stepped to the closest tire and shoved her knife into the rubber. The tire emitted a hissing of air as she withdrew the blade. Quickly, she moved to the other front tire. As she bent to stab it, she heard more hissing as Scott attacked the rear tires.

Morgan stood and flipped her hair back from where it'd fallen across her face. The frame of the car sank as the tires bled their air, but it wasn't enough.

Her body hummed with fear and anger, the need to lash out overwhelming. A quick search found a tree limb that had fallen into the undergrowth. It was heavy, and she had to put her knife in her waistband to grab the wood with both hands.

As Scott watched, Morgan slammed the branch into the windshield over and over again. The glass cracked in a complex web of lines and then, as she continued to hit it, began to cave in. She smashed the headlights and beat huge dents into the hood and fenders. With two powerful swings, she obliterated one of the rear door windows. She continued bashing the car, trying to reduce it to nothing. Her breath came in fast spurts, grunts of effort and frustration accompanying each swing of the branch.

When she was done, she dropped the makeshift club and stood, her chest heaving with exertion. Her hands and shoulders burned from the impacts.

Scott met her eyes and gave a small smile. "Let's go find him now," he said.

Back at the factory, Morgan opened the same door Scott had used hours before. The air smelled of body odor and the powdery dust of cotton. Jason closed the door softly behind them, and the factory floor fell into gloom.

"You don't have to be that quiet," Scott said. "Harold is dead."

"But the asshole who killed him isn't," Jason answered. He held up the cleaver he'd brought. "Not yet."

"You said the place he's been sleeping in is a storage room on this floor?" Morgan asked her brother.

"Yeah. Down by Quality. That big one that's shaped like an L."

Morgan remembered the room. She'd worked on the third floor, and though it had been a few years, but she was pretty sure she knew the space.

Her nose wrinkled at the smell of the mill, the chemical stench with the underlying dustiness of the cotton. "I'd forgotten how bad it was in here," she said.

"This is so gross," Jennifer complained. "How does anyone work when it smells like this?"

"You get used to it," Morgan said. She pointed with her knife. "Let's go."

Morgan led the way through the equipment. Briefly, she considered telling the group to split up, to search the rows of machinery and behind the stacks of unprocessed cotton, but dismissed the idea. She wanted them all together when they found the area where the masked man had been sleeping. If he wasn't there, though, they'd have to split up. She hated the idea, but knew deep down that would be the only way for them to search the rest of the mill before Stephanie brought the cops.

They reached the storage room, and Morgan gave her friends a quick look before she pulled the door open and stepped inside, her knife held up and ready to be shoved into flesh. Scott pressed in behind her, then pushed around her. He walked to the junction and peered around the corner.

"He's not here."

Jason and Jennifer gave a chorus of relieved sighs. Morgan approached and inspected the pile of blankets, probing them and shifting empty wrappers with the tip of her knife.

"We have to search the rest of the mill," she said.

"Maybe we wait for the police?" Jennifer suggested. She held her knife in both hands, clutched against her chest. "Stephanie should be bringing them anytime now."

Morgan shook her head. "I'm not waiting or counting on them. There's no guarantee that Stephanie will be able to convince them, and I want to kill this asshole." Jennifer must have seen something in her eyes because the woman nodded.

Morgan walked across the factory and pulled open a door that revealed a stairwell. The shaft was bathed in a pallid light from dirty fixtures high on the wall.

On the second-floor landing, they paused by the door. Morgan said, "Scott and I will search the third floor. Jen, you and Jason take this one. Be careful, especially in the other storage rooms. If you see him, yell."

"Will you even be able to hear us?" Jason asked.

"Let's hope so," Morgan said. "It's dead silent in here, so maybe the sound will carry better."

She and Scott began the slow climb to the third floor. The heat in the narrow space was almost unbearable as they climbed. When she opened the door to the top floor, she gave a soft breath of relief. The third floor was still hot, but the expanse made the heat bearable.

Morgan looked at the space where she'd worked years ago. On the far end to her left was the Weaving area. Closer yet was another series of tables where inspection of fabrics was conducted. Directly across the floor lay several glass-walled offices, but she couldn't imagine the killer being in one of them. Further on were the large, boxy dye machines of the Finishing department. Finally, all the way to the right lay Packaging and Storage, where the finished fabric was readied to be taken down to the loading area for transport. Morgan had spent a lot of her time in that area, and knew that if the man was here, he most likely wouldn't be down there. There weren't a lot of hiding places in Packaging – only a few packing machines and storage racks, plus the freight elevator down to Shipping.

Flexing her fingers on the handle of her knife, Morgan glanced at Scott, who gave her a reassuring nod. With that, the siblings stepped

away from the relative safety of the doorway and into the depths of
the third floor.

CHAPTER 40

"Is he going to say anything?" Chuck whispered.

Frank shook his head. "Don't look like it." To his left, Geordie fidgeted in his seat like a child. Frank cut the man a stern look, and Geordie settled, but only for a moment before raising a hand and commencing to chew on his fingernails. Frank rolled his eyes and glanced around the nave. The usually full pews now held a pitiful headcount of ten, including himself, Linda, Chuck, Bill, and Geordie. The large space was eerily quiet, save for the occasional clearing of a throat or sniff.

Brother Camden stood at the pulpit, arms braced against the wooden structure, his head hanging. His hair, usually perfectly in place, hung in wispy clumps. He'd started the morning the way he always had before, by greeting the congregation with a smile, and inviting them into the first song while Grace Whittaker played the organ with her usual stoicism. Frank had clearly seen how much the man was bothered by the pitiful showing. It had been clear from the moment they'd entered that Camden had been expecting a full house, as the church had been decorated with the same care and intensity as every week before. Flowers were placed at the end of each row of pews, and candles were lit. Even the two elderly men,

Dan and Robert, were in their customary positions by the front doors handing out programs on light blue paper.

But once the first song and subsequent prayer had ended, it had become clear that the ten people were all that were coming. Brother Camden had launched into his prepared lesson, but immediately stumbled over his notes. He'd closed his notebook and removed his reading glasses, and addressed the congregation, speaking from the heart in a voice that oozed pain and concern. He had struggled to find words of comfort for those present, but after only a couple of minutes, lost the battle with his emotions and assumed the position he had now been in for at least five minutes.

At least he's stopped fucking crying, Frank thought. It was common knowledge that men who went into the church had weaker constitutions, and were much softer than those who did real work for a living, but Christ on a cracker, that didn't mean you had to cry over everything.

"Can we go?" Geordie asked around a mouthful of ring finger.

Frank glanced around the room again. "Yeah. Come on." He gestured to Linda, who slid to the end of the pew. The rest of them followed and walked single-file along the deep red carpet to the rear of the nave. Frank glanced back just before he passed through the door. Brother Camden hadn't moved, but his shoulders shook gently, indicating he'd started crying again. Frank shook his head in disgust.

Outside, Frank joined the others on the lawn near the marquee. Linda flapped her hands under her chin in a useless attempt to cool herself. Geordie unclipped his brown-striped tie and unfastened the top button of his short-sleeved shirt. "Fuck me running, it's hot," he complained.

"Well, that was pathetic," Chuck said. "Should we?" He gave his head a jerk, indicating the parking lot. Frank waited and watched as the family who'd come emerged from the church, the two children bouncing down the short steps and racing to the car. The father held his wife's hand and glanced at Frank and his group as they passed.

"Yeah," Geordie said. "Let's get out of here. Go burn that fucking place down." He jerked and breathed in a sharp gasp of pain as

Frank's fist connected hard with his shoulder. Rubbing it, he winced. "Jesus, man. What was that for?"

"Keep your voice down, idiot," Frank said.

Geordie watched the family climb into their car. "What? Them? They couldn't hear shit. Come on, what are we waiting for?"

Frank had no counterargument, but wasn't about to let Geordie or the others know that. Instead, he checked his watch, looked at the grass between all of them as if he were doing calculations, and then nodded. "Okay. Let's go. Two cars." To Chuck, he asked, "You got your cans?"

"Got three of them in the trunk. We gonna hit the Phillips?"

"Yeah. You do that. I'll meet you on Mill Road."

Thirty minutes later, Frank pulled his truck onto the weedy shoulder, the tires crunching on gravel and tall grass whispering as it brushed against the doors. Linda sat against the passenger door, Geordie wedged between them. The mill wasn't in view yet, but would be in a few moments. Frank kept his eyes on the side mirror, watching for Chuck to catch up. The trip through town had been slow due to the increase in both police and various news outlets. More than once, they'd had to turn around and detour several blocks due to the large news vans blocking entire streets.

"There he is," Geordie said as Chuck's car came creeping up alongside them. Chuck gave a quick thumb's-up, and Frank pulled ahead, leading them over the hill and down into the parking lot of the mill.

Frank turned behind the building and steered around the two cement buildings that housed the maintenance shed and boilers. "I saw Harold's truck out front," Linda pointed out. "But whose is that?"

Nestled in the shade between the buildings sat a gray Jeep. Frank watched it as he drove. He didn't recognize it, and a momentary flutter of nervousness rippled through his chest. Who else was here? Had Harold decided to take advantage of it being a Sunday and have a girl or one of his buddies come visit?

"Doesn't matter," Frank said.

"You think Harold has a girl in there?" Geordie asked with a chuckle. "Ole noodle dick gettin' him some?"

"Let's hope so," Frank said. The truck bounced over the small rail spur that allowed delivery of heavy cotton bales to both Storage and Receiving. He guided the vehicle to a stop against the raised platform of the loading dock, the battered and beaten black rubber pads only inches from his grill.

Frank climbed the concrete stairs, one hand trailing along the flecked paint of the iron railing as he approached a small metal door to the left of the large roll-up doors of the loading bays. The knob, loose in its moorings, rattled as it turned. The locking mechanism had been broken for years. It was just one of those things that nobody had ever bothered fixing. With the mill operating three shifts, there were always people around, so security hadn't been a concern.

Inside the shipping area the air was stifling, a thick woolen mass stagnating among the crates, tables, and forklifts that filled the massive space in organized confusion. Frank stepped into the dark, the only light coming in soft, lazy slants from windows positioned high on the outer wall, and he listened. The silence of the mill carried a sense of unease. He'd never heard the whole factory this quiet before - operations hadn't paused even when news of the *Challenger* explosion had hit - and it made his skin crawl. It was the same feeling as walking along a path in the woods and knowing a snake was coiled nearby, but being unable to see the threat.

Back on the dock, Geordie, Chuck, and Bill grunted and cursed as they wrestled the cans of gasoline up the short steps while Linda sucked on the last half inch of a cigarette and watched through partially squinted eyes. She crushed it out and jogged up the steps to hold the door for the men. Once they were all inside, Bill asked, "Where do we start?"

"You and Chuck carry two cans up to the second floor. Splash one of them good all around the spinners and any pallets of material you see up there. Use the second to run a trail down the stairs. Linda, you and Geordie take a couple and go to three, toward the offices. Get it all over the desks. Papers. Everything." He picked a single can up.

"I'm gonna go to Ginning," he said, nodding toward the large opening to the left. "I shouldn't need much. The cotton dust in there will go up pretty easily. I'll run a trail out the door over there and we'll meet back in the lot." He scanned their faces. There was an erratic eagerness on Geordie's, but the others' expressions displayed a quiet sense of concern. "You all good?" he asked.

"Yeah," Linda said, although her voice cracked. Bill and Chuck gave halting nods of assent, their nervousness obvious.

"Remember what these bastards are doing to us," Frank said. "They're destroying our lives. Taking our paychecks away. Taking food off your tables; out of your children's mouths. This town isn't going to survive this. This is how we punch back." He stayed where he was, watching as the group hefted their cans and split up, each pair melding with the darkness as they went to their assignments. Frank swiped a palm across his face, wiping away the sweat that covered his skin, and took his own can into the long rows of carding machines.

His footsteps echoed as he threaded his way through the equipment, the metal gas can thumping against his thigh as he walked. Beyond the carding machines stood the cleaners and blenders, where the ginned cotton had been freed of debris and blended to form a higher quality product. Frank unscrewed the cap on his can and splashed some of the gas across several of the machines, the liquid instantly soaking into the remnants of cotton inside the gears and rollers. More cotton scraps littered the floor - evidence that the third shift crew hadn't been allowed time to even clean their areas before being pulled off their lines. But these he left alone, knowing that gas would drip, or they would ignite as flaming pieces of cotton fell from the machinery.

Near the end of the building, he came to the ginning area, where the massive gins sat in a long row across the width of the building. To Frank, they'd always looked like colossal cigarette machines. He took his time pouring gas into the feeders of each one, then splashed more across the thick layers of cotton dust that coated the floor. He next, carefully, ran a trail fifteen feet to the access door. When he reached the door, his can was almost empty and he gauged that there'd be just enough to continue the trail out the door. Far enough to allow him to safely light it before hauling ass away. He set the can down to the right of the door and slowly walked to his left, taking a final look at the factory where he'd spent the last twenty-seven years.

As he approached the extreme edge of the carding machines, the scrape of a foot on the hard cement floor echoed through the factory. Frank stopped, one hand resting on the curved edge of a machine. His heart took up a jazz beat in his chest. He squinted into the darkness looking for Geordie or one of the others, and hoping it wasn't Harold deciding to take a lap after screwing whatever girl he had in the office. Frank would hate to have to hurt that boy, but he would if he had to.

The sound of a footstep came again – now farther to his right, deep within the rows. "Geordie?" No answer came back. "Chuck? Goddamnit, answer me." Only silence came from the darkness between the machines. "Pricks," he growled. "I'm going to slap the shit out of all of you."

Movement exploded out of the space between two machines to his left. A huge shape rushed toward him and, in less than the space of a heartbeat, a powerful hand gripped him by the throat. Frank was driven back, his feet struggling to keep him upright as he was propelled toward the rough wall. When he hit it, all of the air was driven from his lungs in a wheezing cough. His own hands flapped uselessly at the powerful arm that held him pinned even as his eyes adjusted to take in the fishbelly-pale mask with black eyes and an even blacker mouth.

His attacker watched him struggle for a while, and then he brought up his other arm. Frank watched helplessly as the hand holding a horrible hammer rose. The fingers shifted, turning the hammer around so that a nightmarish spike faced him. Alarm bells screamed in Frank's mind, and he redoubled his efforts to break the hold on his throat. His mouth opened and closed as he strained to catch a significant breath, but the vice-like grip would only allow the smallest trickle of air.

The spike moved closer, the masked man bringing it slowly toward Frank's left eye. Frank couldn't tear his focus from the thing. Closer and closer it came until it doubled, then tripled, and finally blurred in his vision. Frank squeezed his eyes closed and felt the pointed tip press against his eyelid.

He'll stop. He'll stop now. This is just to scare me. He'll stop.

The spike pierced the thin flap of skin. A horrendous flare of white light exploded in the blackness of Frank's vision, bringing insurmountable pain. Frank bucked, his legs and arms flailing wildly as the spike probed deeper into his eye socket. The pressure in his skull was beyond imagination. It felt like his entire head was being pumped full of hot air.

With a wet sucking noise, the spike pulled back, wrenching Frank's head as it retracted. Hot liquid spilled down his cheek. Frank desperately wanted to open his other eye, but found that he didn't have the strength even for that. His struggles against the arm that kept him pinned to the wall were slowing.

The spike touched his right eyelid. Frank's brain gave a whimpering thought. *No. Please.* Then, the pain and pressure erupted inside him again, this time bringing blackness crashing over him and shutting down everything.

CHAPTER 41

The man watched as the now eyeless Thing twitched and gasped. Blood poured from its eye sockets and down its face, filling the mouth as it opened and closed spasmodically. Hands and feet tapped a tattoo pattern on the floor, light and fluttering before falling still.

Turning from the cooling meat, the man froze, his eyes searching the factory floor and his ears tuned to even the slightest sound. Nothing moved.

Everything in his vision was a picture frozen in time.

But, somewhere within the expanse of the factory, other Things crept. He'd been aware of them as soon as they'd entered, and had allowed them to split up and gain the floors above.

He took one quiet step, then another. It was time to find them and hear their screams.

CHAPTER 42

Geordie Dupont was dying for a cigarette. The need had begun soon after they'd entered the mill, but had since grown from a scratching, buzzing itch at the base of his neck to a full-blown screaming bearcat in his mind. His fingers trembled as he sloshed more of the gas across a desk, the pale liquid running down the glass of a framed picture of a uniformed young girl kneeling, one hand resting on a basketball.

More than once, he caught his hand moving as if driven by its own mind, toward the bulge in his shirt pocket. Each time, he stopped himself, his fingers only caressing the creased cardboard flip-top of the hard pack. He could have a smoke after they were done. Maybe not even then, though. He couldn't be certain, but thought there was a good chance his clothes had taken in some backsplashes from the gasoline. The last thing he needed was to get home, sit on his couch, and spark up a stick only to turn into Geordie the Human Torch.

He shook off the urge to smoke and focused on the task at hand. His can was over half-empty by now and they'd just started on the last office. On the other side of the desk, her back to the windows that looked out over the packaging machines, Linda was busy dousing the fabric cushion of a chair.

"Don't use all of it on that fucking chair," Geordie told her. "We need enough to trail downstairs." Linda shot him an *I know what I'm doing* look and gave her can one more shake over the chair. Geordie winced as the fumes from the gas stung his nose and eyes. If they hadn't thought to leave the door open, they would both have passed out by now.

"I think we're good," Linda said, and gave a sharp cough as the fumes hit her. "Come on."

Geordie screwed the cap back onto his can as Linda gave another sharp, booming cough. "Chrissakes, woman, knock off that coughing," he said.

"That wasn't me," Linda answered. Her eyes were wide in surprise and fear. "Sounded like someone dropped something. It came from the other end of the floor, though. You think maybe Chuck or someone came up to check on us?"

Geordie craned his neck, but saw no movement outside the office. "Beats me. Lemme go look. Stay here. It may be Harold."

He left the office for the open, fresher air of the factory's third floor. Geordie hurried, weaving his way through the tables and machinery with his path taking him toward the center of the massive floor. Occasionally, he stopped and listened, eyes searching the silent rows of equipment that sat in the soft light from the windows. Dust motes drifted in the beams of sunlight, and Geordie crashed through them as he pushed deeper into the room. He was pretty sure that whoever was up here wasn't Frank or one of the other guys. He would have seen the man by now, or they would have called out.

Which meant it was Harold.

Geordie stopped by a loom and peered through its spindly arms, wondering what he'd tell the man. Or would he just grab something and hit the guard over the head? It wouldn't be any skin off of Geordie's back if the pissant died in the fire, as long as he wasn't around to identify any of them. Movement to the left, near the wall, pulled his attention and his breath caught.

Moving slowly, a knife held beside her thigh, Morgan Bell crept along the wall. A younger man - *that's her shithead brother* - followed close behind her, eyes scanning the massive space. Geordie watched Morgan, his eyes drinking her in. Her hair hung loose around her shoulders, and she walked with a liquid ease. As he dropped his focus down to her breasts and further down to her ass, Geordie remembered how she'd felt under him. Her smooth and slender body had writhed, pressing back against him as he'd pushed into her. Her hair had smelled so good. *Lemons.* He remembered that clearly. Her hair had smelled of lemons. And when he'd run his tongue over her skin....

Under his jeans, Geordie Dupont was fully at attention – painfully so. He had to experience her again.

The idea wasn't a conscious thought. It wasn't a want. It was a deep, primal need. He *had* to have her again.

Just gotta separate her from her brother.

At the same time, he remembered Linda. She'd have to be gotten rid of also. An idea came to him, and he slinked back through the rows of equipment to where Linda stood in the doorway of the office. The stench of gasoline was heavy even from several yards away, and his nose wrinkled as he approached. Linda looked at him expectantly.

"It's Harold," he said. Panic flooded Linda's face. Geordie handed her his can. "Take these, go down to two, and wait. I'll deal with him, and then we can finish the trail and meet up with Frank."

"What are you going to do?" she asked as she moved away from the door.

"Let me worry about that," he said, and gave her a shove. "Go on now. And be quiet." Linda gave him another uncertain look, but moved toward the stairwell. Geordie waited until he heard the soft click of the door as she eased it closed.

Smiling, he vanished between the rows of equipment, a plan already coming to mind.

CHAPTER 43

This is so stupid, Jennifer thought as she followed Jason through the immense floor. She should never have let Morgan split up the group. It was insane, sending them off like this to find a maniac who wore a mask and murdered people. What did Morgan think, that the woman who worked in the pharmacy and the guy who was apprenticing as an electrician were qualified to hunt down a psychopath? And not only that, but what, subdue him? Kill him? The serrated steak knife in her hand felt ridiculous. The only thing Jennifer had ever killed was an extra-large pizza and a two-liter of Coke. Maybe Jason had gone hunting when he'd been younger, but she was pretty sure he didn't spend his time carving up bad guys, either.

So stupid.

Not to mention how much noise they were making. Unlike downstairs, this floor was surprisingly clean, but despite their best efforts at walking quietly, their footsteps reverberated and squeaked.

She tried to stop worrying about the noise and instead focus on the search. They were halfway through one section filled with huge machines that stretched from wall to wall across the width of the floor. Each machine had hundreds of white spools mounted on it, with string running from the spool into the tangled mess of pipes and metal gears. Between the machines were stacks of thread on small spools and white plastic barrels that Jennifer assumed were used for trash, but could also have been something the machine operator had to wear via some kind of suspenders, for all she knew.

Jason slowed as he reached each new machine, creeping forward until he could peer around it and down the long aisle. Then, seeing nothing, he'd hurry to the next one and repeat the process. Jennifer had taken a position about three steps behind him because, at first, she'd kept running into him. Not only had it caused a distraction and more noise than she was comfortable with, but she was also terribly afraid that if it kept up, she may accidentally stab him in the back.

The almost endless rows of machines gave way to another impossibly long group of similar-looking ones. Jennifer was starting to wonder what the differences between them were and how the people who'd worked here could even keep things straight, but then Jason jerked to a halt. He held one hand out, palm down as if giving a traffic hand signal. Jennifer closed the distance between them. "What is it?" she whispered, glancing around. The cold feeling that someone was sneaking up behind them was a constant irritation in the back of her mind.

"Do you smell that?" Jason asked.

Jennifer gave the air a tentative sniff. There certainly was a smell there, but then, the entire mill stunk. How anyone had managed to work a full shift here, let alone do it day in and day out for years, was beyond her. Yet, this was different. Before, there'd been a greasy smell mixed with the thick smell of cotton. Now, there was something else…something sharp and acrid. "I swear, if you farted," she warned Jason, who shook his head.

"That's gasoline."

Another spike of fear raced through her. Had something leaked? Were these machines gasoline-powered and had a hose come loose, spilling gas everywhere? What would happen if someone turned on one of the machines? Would that ignite the gas? Or what about spontaneous combustion? She'd heard about that. One of the daytime talk shows had done a thing about it not too long ago. People bursting into flames out of nowhere. Surely, if a person could do that, then a room full of gas could, too, right? Maybe even more easily?

"Are you sure?" she asked.

Jason nodded as he looked around the edge of the nearest machine. "Positive. I-" He stiffened, and Jennifer almost screamed, but managed to clamp her lips down. "Hang on," he said. "I think I see something."

He stepped around the machine, moving down the long aisle. Jennifer slapped a hand out at him, trying to get him to stop. What if it was the killer, hiding and waiting for them? Jason crept down the row, his body in the middle of the two long machines and the meat cleaver held out by his side, ready to swing.

Jennifer felt naked standing there alone. All around her, the floor sat in silent repose, like a museum exhibit. *Or a tomb,* her mind offered. The sunlight that came in through the windows opposite her was muted, the glass dirty and filtering it so that only a muddied glow made it inside. As a result, most of the floor was held in deep pools of shadows. Jennifer's eyes bounced from those dark patches to the path they'd taken, and then back to Jason as he reached the midpoint of the aisle.

"Fuck this," she said to herself, and went after him, her feet scuffing on the floor as she hurried. Jason heard her coming and spun back to see her, cleaver coming up quickly. Jennifer skidded to a halt, both hands out defensively. "Wait!" she said, and immediately winced at the volume. Jason gave her a scolding wince and shook his head. Jennifer moved alongside him. "What did you see?" she demanded. Instead of answering, Jason pointed with the cleaver.

While the previous section of machines stretched in a continual line across the floor, this area sported two rows of machines with a central aisle between them, like pews in a church. She and Jason were currently moving perpendicular to that center path. What had caught his attention was in that space, just at the edge of one of the machines.

In the muddy light, it looked like a pool of black grease and Jennifer started to say so. It would make sense, regardless of how these machines were powered, that the gears would need grease to keep them from locking up. She didn't know much about engines, but she knew her daddy was always greasing things around the house or fussing about the oil that went into the cars. But as she stepped closer, she realized that what she was looking at wasn't black, but rather a deep red. "What kind of machine oil is red?" she asked softly.

Jason's jaw shifted. "That's not oil," he said. "Come on." He led her closer, and Jennifer saw that he was right. It wasn't oil at all. It was blood. The puddle was huge, running down the center path and branching out between machines for several rows. Reflections of the sunlit windows glistened on its surface.

She gripped Jason's arm. "What—" she started, but then she noticed the foot. It was three rows away on the left. Just the toe of a sneaker, but the way it lay told her that the person wearing it was dead. Jason took a long step to avoid the pool of blood. As he moved, his arm slipped out of Jennifer's hold. No longer connected to him, Jennifer's skin crawled with the sensation of being watched. She followed, having to make a slight leap to reach the clear patch of floor.

"Oh Jesus," Jason said as he reached the sneakered foot. Jennifer heard him, but was busy working to avoid the blood. When she finally caught up, she pulled up short, a sharp cry of disgust and horror slipping out of her throat. Instantly, she slapped her hand over her mouth and stared at the body. It was a man, or at least she assumed it had been based on the jeans and shirt. But that was where any chance of identification ended. The body inside the clothes was a mangled and shattered wreck. Parts of the denim of the jeans and the cotton of the shirt jutted up to a sharp point, suggesting bones that had punctured skin. The head was nothing more than a loose mess of dark hair, bone fragments, and something that looked like oatmeal all sitting in a huge pool of blood.

"There's another one," Jason said. His voice was thick, as if he were holding back the urge to vomit. Jennifer saw what had drawn his attention. Further along the row was another body. This one sat propped against a machine, the man's head slumped forward. The lower half of the man's face was a bloody cavern, and it took Jennifer a moment to understand that his jaw was missing.

"Do you recognize him?" she asked. Jason shook his head. "What do we do?"

Again, Jason shook his head. "I don't know."

"Let's leave, please." She gave his arm a tug. "Let's get Morgan and Scott, and get the hell out of here." The mention of leaving seemed to break through Jason's stupor.

"Yeah. I don't...I don't think we can deal with this."

Carefully, they began to step around the body of the jawless man. This time, the blood covered the floor so adequately that they were unable to avoid stepping in it. Their shoes squeaked as they passed over to a cleaner area.

"Chuck? Y'all down here?" a woman's voice broke the silence. She was pitching her voice low, but in the stillness of the floor, it was as if she'd spoken normally. "Bill? Where the fuck are you guys?" Jennifer's heart froze in her chest, and once more she clutched Jason's arm. They exchanged a glance.

"She may be able to help," he whispered, bending his face close to hers. "At least with three of us, we stand a better chance." Jennifer felt him start to pull away, but the terrified rabbit that her brain had become refused to allow her to break from where she stood. She clutched at him desperately even as he crept further away. Jason hunched forward and crept past the second body to the end of the aisle. Meanwhile, the woman's voice continued to call for - Jennifer assumed - the two dead men. Based on the volume, the woman was getting closer.

Jason looked back, gave what Jennifer assumed he thought was a reassuring nod, and stepped around the machine and into the path against the wall. As he straightened, the woman's voice morphed from a whisper to a quick shout of fear. A wet, meaty sound cut off the shout. Jennifer stared at Jason, who'd frozen in the act of stepping from behind his cover as more of the wet sounds filled the air. *That sounds like someone slapping a mop onto a soaked floor,* she thought grotesquely, and had to press her tongue to the roof of her mouth in an attempt to fight back her own gorge.

The sound of quick footsteps behind her ignited a scream that rocketed out of her lungs. A hand over her mouth stifled the noise. Jason pressed his lips close to her ear, his breath hot against her skin. "We have to go. Now." She nodded against his hand. "We'll go along that row against the wall, and get to the door for the stairs, but we have to go fast and quiet. Okay?" Slowly, he removed his hands and led her toward the wall.

They edged along the wall toward the door they'd come through. Jennifer's breath came in short gasps, and she held it every time they crossed an open area between rows of machines. Each time they stepped into the path, she expected to see a hammer flash out. They reached the door easily, though, and Jennifer sent up a prayer of thanks. She was especially grateful that they hadn't come across the body of the woman.

"Fuck." Jason gripped the handle of the door, but it wouldn't turn. His lips peeled back in a sneer as he fought against it.

"What's wrong?"

"It's fucking stuck! Locked. I don't know." He gave it a frustrated jerk, rattling it slightly in the frame. Jennifer scanned the floor, certain the noise would have drawn attention, but everything was silent. It made no sense that the door would be locked. They'd come through it only minutes ago.

The reality slithered across her mind. *The masked man did this. He locked or jammed the door somehow.* "Wait," she said, tapping Jason's shoulder for attention. "There." She pointed to the far end of the aisle, where another door sat in the wall, a white plastic sign with red lettering affixed to it. *Stairs.*

Eschewing quiet for speed, the two ran for the door. Jason's legs were longer, and he easily pulled ahead of Jennifer by several feet as they reached the end of the rows of machines. Beyond the last of the insectile-looking contraptions lay rows of tables, many covered in loose piles of fabric and tools. Jason was almost past the first table when it slammed forward. The leading corner hit him in the hip, and he spun, arms flailing as he connected with the wall in an explosion of breath. Jennifer skidded to a halt as he landed. She'd just reached to push the table aside when someone passed in front of her, blocking her view of Jason. The person bent, their wicked hammer rising and falling so fast that it was a blur. She heard Jason's cries of pain, and his sharp "No!"

Then, only the wet mop sounds came as the hammer continued to pummel him.

The hammer ceased its punishment, and the man stood, uncoiling from the floor like a serpent. The mask was spattered with blood. The black eyes locked on her. Jennifer couldn't make her legs move. The man's arm lashed out, and a burning pain seared across her stomach. She looked to see her shirt torn open, a thin bloody line across the smooth, pale skin. *He cut me,* she registered dully, and then she saw the wide table. *That got in his way, or I'd be dead.*

The masked man gripped the table and began to muscle it aside. The sound of its wheels squeaking as it rolled broke the spell in Jennifer's brain and she turned to run, her voice finally breaking through.

She screamed as she darted across the floor, the sounds of the man's footsteps ticking behind her.

CHAPTER 44

"What was that?" Scott asked.

Morgan turned, her brow furrowed. "What did you hear?"

"A scream, I think, but it's hard to tell. It was faint. Do you think...?"

Morgan chewed her lower lip and glanced around the massive floor. "Go. I'll stay and keep looking."

"We really shouldn't split up," Scott said. While the noise he'd heard had most certainly been a scream, meaning that Jennifer could be in trouble, the thought of leaving his sister alone felt wrong. Since finding her staring at a bloodstain on Jennifer's patio, he'd noticed a darkness in her – a subtle shift in her demeanor. Morgan had been through some bad things, he was certain, even though she'd not talked about it. But since that morning, there was something new...a determination that was scary. The laughing, happy girl who'd been his sister only a few years ago wasn't present in Morgan's eyes. She'd been replaced by someone.... All day, he'd been trying to find the right word, but all he could come up with was the image of a creature backed into a corner, terrified and ready to lash out at the world that had forced it there.

"I'll be fine," Morgan said.

Scott hesitated, unable to look away. She was the only family he had left, and a certainty gnawed at him – that, if he left her, he'd never see her again.

Morgan gave an exasperated sigh and rolled her eyes. "I'm fine, you stain. Quit wasting time and go make sure Jennifer is okay."

The door that Jason and Jennifer had entered was closed, and he gave it a shove only to find it locked. As he stepped back to consider his options, something near his foot caught his attention. A screwdriver had been wedged into the crack between the door and the jamb. He pulled it free and noticed something else – a small shape on the riser of the top step. A metal gas can sat against the wall. Frowning at the oddness of the can, Scott shoved the screwdriver into the waistband of his pants and pushed the door open, his knife up and ready.

At first glance, the floor appeared empty. The urge to call out to Jennifer and Jason rose in him, but he clamped his mouth against it. They were in here, and if she'd screamed, that meant the masked man was, as well. He jogged to the right, toward the inspection area. A single metal table stood out of place from the other orderly rows, canted at an angle.

On the other side of the table, a hand, fingers curled toward the palm like the legs of a dead spider, lay in a wide slick of blood. Connected to the hand - although barely - was a body. Scott's mind reeled for several seconds before it understood he was looking at Jason. He absorbed the destruction in flashes, like the strobes of a camera in a black room. With some effort, he managed to tear his gaze away and refocus.

Scott stepped away from the bloody ruin and slipped between the tables. He went deeper, moving quickly through the rows of machines and pausing only long enough to peer along each row as he traversed the center aisle. After another four rows, he came to another body sprawled on the ground. A quick glance told him it wasn't Jennifer. The clothing - what he could see through the blood - didn't match, so he pressed on. With every step, his skin began to crawl, buzzing with fear as the feeling of being watched intensified.

A thought came to him, sudden and fierce. What if the masked man had slipped by and was now upstairs? Scott could picture the maniac stalking Morgan the way a big cat would stalk a gazelle, moving silently through the grass and drawing ever closer, its claws ready to lash out and tear flesh. The image was so absolute that he started to turn back. He wanted to sprint back up the stairs and grab Morgan, to force her to leave with him. This wasn't something they could do. This was a job for the police. He knew Morgan was angry, but this was madness. The pain of losing their parents was a fresh, raw wound on both their hearts. Scott couldn't imagine what it would be like to lose Morgan also.

But if Jennifer was alive, he couldn't leave her. He couldn't live with the knowledge that he'd abandoned her to a horrible death.

"Fuck." Adjusting the grip on the knife, Scott entered the Spinning Department, a collection of dozens of spinning frames lined up like soldiers in groups of ten. Most held spools of thread, but several were empty. More than a few were clearly down for maintenance, their panels removed and inner workings exposed. Scott moved along these, peering beneath each machine. As he approached the wall that held windows overlooking the parking lot, a scraping sound brought him to a stop. His neck throbbed with his pulse as he slowly turned. The knife's handle was suddenly too loose in his hand, his sweaty palms and fingers unable to keep a firm grip.

The sound came again.

This time, it came with movement. Scott peered close and, between empty spool mounts of a nearby machine, saw blonde hair and a terrified eye. "Jennifer?"

A stuttering "Shhhh," drifted out of the twisted metal. "He's up here. He killed Jason and some other people."

"How the hell did you get in there?"

"There's an opening." She shifted and pointed. Through the bars and gears of the machine, he could see her dirty, streaked face. Her eyes were red and puffy from crying.

"Are you hurt?" he asked.

"My stomach and leg," she said. "He hit me with the hammer. I was running. He didn't hit me full-on. But..." her voice thickened as her tears came back, "it hurts so bad. I think it's broken." Scott ducked and peered into the machine. A rip in her shirt showed a nasty cut along her stomach. Dimly, a part of him marveled that he was looking at Jennifer Reynolds' stomach, but he easily pushed that thought aside. A quick scan of her legs showed no visible wound, the denim being intact. Scott risked a look around him and then bent back to the scared woman. "I don't see anything," he said. "Let's get you down to the car."

Jennifer's head shook. "I don't want to go out there. *He's* out there."

"It's okay. He's gone now. I've checked the whole floor." A small lie, but Scott figured that if it got her out, he would be forgiven. He held out a hand. "Let me get you somewhere safe."

Jennifer shifted, gave a soft grunt, and then whined, "I don't think I can get out. I'm caught on something." Scott studied the machine, trying to find a way to reach in and help. There were gaps through which his arm could pass, but from where he crouched, he couldn't see what had her trapped.

"Hang on," he said, and shifted to where she'd managed to enter. The space was narrow, less than a foot wide. Carefully, he maneuvered through it, thankful he was as thin as he was. Once inside the workings, he found almost no room to move, however. He knelt against Jennifer, her shoulder pressing into his chest. "Where are you caught?" he asked.

"I can't see. Something behind me." Scott snaked a hand along her back and found the offending part of the machine. Slowly, he worked his fingers in the material of her shirt until it came free.

"Got it," he said as he shifted back to face her. Jennifer's head turned, her nose only an inch from his. The freckles across her cheeks drew his eyes like stars in the night sky. Her breath was hot on his skin. Scott blinked hard to clear his mind. "I'm going to back out. Then, you can crawl out."

"I don't want to see the bodies," she said.

"No problem."

Scott leaned back, pushing one leg toward the small gap. As he began to shift his body, the machine around them shuddered violently. Scott's ears rang with the noise of the impact, and through the dulling of his senses, he heard Jennifer scream.

The pale, masked face stared at them through the metal bars for a moment and then leaned back as the man raised his hammer to slam against the machine once more. When the impact came, Scott was ready, and he lashed out with his knife. Due to the compactness of the machine, the blow was short and feeble, but he managed to hack at the man's exposed wrist. Blood welled and ran down his dirty, sweat-covered skin.

The masked man slammed the hammer against the machine in a maddened frenzy, each blow a deafening gunshot that pummeled Scott and Jennifer's ears. After several seconds, two of the small bars snapped off and fell with a tinny clatter to the floor. With the parts broken off, a slightly larger gap opened in their hiding place, and the masked man redoubled his efforts to break through. Scott continued to hack and slash whenever he could – missing more often than not, but still managing to cut into their attacker's arm. Blood splattered across the floor, and yet the man seemed oblivious to his wounds.

Scott thought his skull was going to split from the constant, furious assault. More pieces of the machine bent and snapped free, the gap growing wider. Eventually, the man was going to be able to reach them with the hammer. Jennifer shook and cried. Scott ignored her and focused on attacking the man with his kitchen knife. The hammer had just drawn back for another blow when a voice thundered across the floor.

"Hey, asshole!"

The masked man stopped at the shouted command, his head angling in confusion as he continued to stare at Scott and Jennifer through the mangled bars.

"Leave them alone, you son of a bitch." Halfway down the aisle, Morgan stood with her knife out to one side and a baleful look on her face.

"Morgan!" Scott called out. At the sound of his voice, the masked man began to turn back as if he'd forgotten his trapped quarry.

"Get her out of here!" Morgan said. "Come on, you mask-wearing fuck. You tried to kill me twice already. Think you can do it again? Come and get me, you piece of shit!"

The man hesitated, and Scott could imagine the debate raging in the nest of maggots that was his brain. But a decision came, and Scott watched in horror as the masked man stepped away from the machine.

Toward Morgan.

Scott shouted for his sister, but the only answer he got was the sound of the stairwell door slamming closed. Immediately, he wriggled his way free of the machine. As he backed out, he grabbed Jennifer's hand and gave her a pull.

"Can you get downstairs to the car on your own? I have to go help Morgan."

Jennifer climbed free of the machine and took a tentative step. She winced, but nodded when the leg held up. "I'm okay," she gasped. "I'll meet you guys at the car."

Scott gave her hand a squeeze and then dashed toward the stairs.

CHAPTER 45

Morgan pounded up the stairs, fear threatening to turn the muscles in her legs to water. Every step seemed to sap her energy. She pulled in air in short gulps, as if her chest were constricted with heavy bands of iron. It had been one thing to scream at the man, but once he'd set his focus on her and begun pursuit, terror had overwhelmed her. She reached the landing and shot a glance back down just in time to see the mask – its features framed by the long, swaying clumps of black hair – turn around the open doorway. It shifted upward, the powerful body following suit as the man began climbing.

Morgan raced for the far end of the third floor. She reached the first row of looms as the man in the mask passed through the door. Finding a machine that had a long stretch of colorful fabric still wound on the rollers, she lay flat and squeezed herself under the lowest roller.

Over the thundering in her ears and her own ragged, terrified breathing, she could hear the soft ticking of the man's footsteps as he searched. A hideous, metallic shriek blasted her ears. The sound stopped, then began again – short blasts of skull-splitting noise. *He's by the inspection tables, scraping that spike across their surface.* The understanding brought a sense of control to her, calming her fiery nerves. She flexed her fingers around the knife and took long, slow breaths as she watched through the small gap.

The screeching of metal stopped.

Morgan strained to hear the killer's footsteps, but got only silence. She tried to picture where he could be, maybe standing near the end of the long silver tables, hammer hanging by his side as he turned his head left and right, searching. He had to be standing there, she reasoned, as there was no way she wouldn't be hearing him move around.

A heavy black boot landed directly in front of her, the scuffed leather and rough tread less than a foot from her face. Morgan's arm tensed. She brought the blade up, wincing at the gentle sigh her sleeve made against the floor. The boots didn't move. Morgan ran her tongue over her dry lips and stared at the spot where she was going to shove the knife. Just as she started to move to stab, though, the machine over her reverberated with a deafening roar. Huge, thunderous explosions filled the room and she dropped the knife and slapped her hands over her ears. Things hit Morgan on the back, her butt, and her legs, and through the bedlam, she understood what was happening. Like he'd done with the spike on the table, the man was trying to break apart the machine under which she hid.

As suddenly as it had begun, the assault stopped and the man stepped away.

Morgan's head felt like a small ship that had just survived a tempest. She couldn't stay where she was any longer. If she didn't do something now, then eventually the man would return his focus to Scott and Jennifer. She wormed her way out of her hiding spot.

The man stood fifteen feet away with his back to her. The hammer was held at a slight angle from his body in one powerful hand as he studied the machines to either side of him. Morgan took a shaky, tentative step forward, then another, her eyes locked on the man's back, right where she would drive the knife.

A distant voice floated up from the doorway – a faint, frantic calling of her name. The man's head twitched in its direction. A bright flare of fear flashed through her chest as she saw his focus shift. Morgan knew - even as she heard Scott yell her name once more, this time louder and closer - what the masked man would do next.

Morgan's lips pulled back in a snarl as she raised the knife. She would not lose her brother to this monster. In four quick steps, she was on him, her knife swinging down. As the blade arced toward him, the masked man twisted, turning toward Morgan. The blade missed his back and instead carved into the meat on the outer edge of his left arm. Morgan lost her grip as the knife jolted with the impact, tearing open the dark sleeve and splitting the flesh beneath. The man made no sound, offering no indication that he'd been wounded. Instead, he drove the elbow of his bleeding arm out and slammed it into Morgan's cheek. Bright poppies of light exploded in her vision, and she staggered back.

The man followed, as Morgan leapt backward again and again as he swung the hammer, the heavy weapon slicing through the air with a deadly whistle.

Morgan pinwheeled as one attack came so close to her chin that she felt the wind from its passing caress her skin. The hammer slammed into a loom with a resounding, echoing clang followed by a series of clatters as the spike caught in the levers of the machine. The man's hand slipped from the handle, and the weapon fell, rattling to the floor. Morgan dove for it, her fingers reaching for the handle that protruded from between two vertical bars.

A powerful hand clamped down on her wrist, and pain flowed up her arm as the masked man wrenched the limb back and around, twisting it at an unnatural angle. Morgan screamed and kicked out even as the expressionless face watched her writhe and struggle. Her foot connected with the man's thigh. It felt as if she'd kicked a wall. The man twisted her arm again, and through the immense pain, Morgan felt herself sliding across the floor. Then, the man was on top of her, his bulk pressing down on her and her arm pinned to the floor as he brought his free hand up to her throat. Powerful fingers clamped down, and instantly, all of the air in the world was gone. Morgan's eyes bulged as she flailed, her mouth opening and closing in a desperate attempt to find any oxygen.

The black, depthless eyes watched her struggle. The jagged black mouth seemed to laugh at her helplessness.

"Morgan!"

Scott's voice split the air, but the masked man paid no attention to it. Through the haze of her air-starved world, Morgan saw her brother skid around the corner of a loom, his knife held out. She tried with everything she had to kick free, but already, her limbs were turning into dead weights.

Air seeped into her throat as the man shifted toward the sound of Scott's approach, the hand around her throat loosening its grip by the barest of margins. Morgan sucked in a breath, and the gauzy haze that had clouded her vision cleared. She looked past the man who knelt over her to Scott.

Her brother was still several feet away when he jerked violently. He took another drunken step before collapsing to the ground with a horrible crunch. Blood streamed out of his head and spread across the dirty floor.

Geordie Dupont stood over the limp and bleeding form of Scott, a metal stool held in both his hands. His sunken chest heaved as his eyes slid from Scott's body to Morgan, pinned beneath the masked man. Morgan's entire being shuddered in revulsion at the sight of the man who had raped her; the man who had invaded her and destroyed her sense of self, her sense of purpose. In that moment, the masked killer was forgotten and her entire world shrank to a pinprick of light – at the center of which stood Geordie Dupont.

Morgan croaked out, "Please." The word felt like a diseased slug on her tongue. That was all she managed before the masked man's hand reclaimed its punishing grasp around her neck. As the air was cut off again and the fuzziness returned to the edges of her eyes, Morgan watched Geordie continue to stare at her struggles, his eyes wide in fear. He set the stool down and hurried out of sight. Through ears that felt stuffed with cotton, Morgan heard the sound of the stairwell door closing behind him.

Inches above her, the expressionless mask continued to watch her die. The man shifted, repositioning himself. Keeping one hand around her neck, he reached for something with the other. A pinprick of pain stabbed her side, like a needle going into gums not quite dulled by anesthetic. The small dot blossomed into a heavy pressure along the edge of her ribcage. Forcing her eyes down, she saw the hammer, its spike buried vertically in her side.

Every movement she made, every weak jerk of her leg, sent a rolling wave of pain and nausea swelling through her. The feeling of the spike inside her was abominable.

Her revulsion at the penetration cut through the haze. Rage replaced it, burning and rabid. Morgan thrashed and kicked against the immovable form. Each time she connected with him, she felt a surge of hatred. The feeling of the cement floor beneath her and the body of the man atop her, holding her down, was more than she could bear. Hovering over her face, the mask transformed into Geordie's leering, gap-toothed grin, and back.

Not again.

Morgan brought a knee up, putting everything she had into the movement. The man stiffened. The grip around her throat loosened, and she sucked in air. She brought her arm around, her fingers hooked, and clawed at her attacker. Her nails raked across the side of his neck, digging red furrows into the skin. He shifted back, and Morgan pressed her momentum, bucking wildly. She slammed her arms against him, kneeing and kicking with every ounce of the fear and rage that consumed her.

The sensation of the spike pulling out of her side forced a grunt from her, and the masked man rolled away.

Ignoring the screaming pain in her ribs and the swelling of her throat, Morgan pushed herself across the floor. She pulled in breath through a throat that felt as if she'd swallowed glass. With effort, she staggered to her feet. She saw the bloody lines across the masked man's neck in the instant before the long black hair fell like curtains to hide them. The man hefted the hammer and took a menacing step forward.

Morgan ran, her legs slow and unsteady. She needed to get distance between them to give herself a chance to find something to defend herself with. At the same time, she wanted to draw him as far from Scott as possible.

If Scott is even still alive, she thought as she stumbled into a loom and rebounded away. Her side was a constant, fiery ache above the warm trickle of blood that ran down her ribs and soaked into her pants.

The swelling in her throat eased, and breathing became marginally easier as she wove through the looms and into the wide sea of inspection tables. She bounced off of one table, pushed past another, and used a third to propel herself toward the Packaging department at the far end of the floor. Behind her, like the ticking of a doomsday clock, came the slow and purposeful footsteps of the masked man. Metallic scraping filled the air once more as he dragged his hammer across the tables. The noise crashed into the walls, rebounding and slamming into her brain. Morgan screamed, the sound lost among the din of the hammer.

She passed the first of the packaging machines full of large rolls of clear wrap. Morgan blinked to clear her thoughts even as she stumbled left and right in an effort to get further from her pursuer. Her hands grasped blindly, hoping for anything to use as a weapon. The metal frames of the machines passed beneath her fingers, and then came the smooth rolls of wrapping and the layers of cotton material coiled around heavy cardboard tubing. Her right hand connected with something long and rough. The object was there one second and then clattering loudly to the floor.

Morgan knelt and grabbed it, realizing what it was even as she stood and spun.

The metal rod was heavy and solid – a tool that, when slid through a cardboard roll, could be used to carry the finished materials from the inspection tables to the packaging machines. Morgan grasped it in both hands like a spear and prayed for her strength to hold out a little longer.

With a growl that climbed into a scream, she stabbed it forward as the masked man stepped around the edge of a packaging machine, his hammer already swinging toward Morgan's head. Morgan's momentum closed the distance between them, and she shoved the end of the rod into the man's gut. It dimpled his clothes and then stabbed through, sliding into his body just above his hip. The blow knocked him back and to one side, dampening the force of his own attack. His arm hit Morgan high on the shoulder, the force of his swing knocking the hammer out of his hand.

Morgan let go of the rod and picked up the hammer. She swung, her attack clumsy as she tried to understand the weight of the weapon. Yet, the blow connected, and the masked man staggered backward.

He gripped the rod that extended from his abdomen and fought to pull it free even as Morgan swung the hammer again. She smashed it into his shoulder, pulled back, and slammed it into his other shoulder. With every hit, he stumbled back, the metal rod forgotten. Morgan attacked him mindlessly, battering his body with the hammer and not caring where she hit him as long as she connected. With every blow, her mind flashed images of Geordie groping her in the dark of the storage room, the bodies of her friends, the forgiving and loving smiles of her parents, and the men she'd let have their way with her body....

Garrett.

Morgan screamed, filling the air with her fury as she pummeled the killer with his own weapon. Everything had been taken from her. She'd been forced into darkness for so long, shoved unwillingly into a crevice of self-loathing and worthlessness. And right as she'd started to see the light, just as she'd begun to feel that a way out was possible, this monster, this...*thing*...had come and killed that. Had slammed the door on her, pushing her back down into that blackness.

The hammer smashed into the mask itself. A long, lightning bolt of a crack split the length of the visage. The man slumped back, his body broken and bleeding. He fell against the glass of one of the tall windows that overlooked the rear of the building. Beyond his shape, the robin's egg blue of the sky hung over a tapestry of greens, the forest beyond the mill stretched on for miles.

She stared at the killer who, despite the horrific damage he'd taken, struggled to push away from the window and come for her. The black eyes glared at her with a cold hatred.

"No more," she said, and twisted the hammer so that the spike faced forward. She swung, stepping into the movement like a batter shifting toward a straight fastball. The metal punched into his chest with a meaty thump. The force of the blow knocked the man back, and Morgan pulled the hammer free as he crashed through the glass. Sunlight caught the shards, throwing sparkles off like brilliant diamonds. The man's body seemed to float for a second, his arms and legs trailing out, the black hair floating around his mask like useless streamers.

Then, he fell, passing out of sight below the edge of the window. Seconds later came the crunch as he landed three floors below. Morgan stood staring at the open window for a long time, breathing slowly, her mind and body filled with a numb humming.

"No more," she said. But the words fell like old, dry bones in an empty room.

FRIDAY, JUNE 12, 1987

CHAPTER 46

Morgan buttoned her jeans and, careful of the tight skin around the stitches in her side, pulled the t-shirt gingerly over her head. The aches from the fight with the masked man were still there, but softer, muted versions of themselves.

She ran her fingers through her dark hair, brushing it behind her shoulders, and considered her shoes. The sneakers, their scuffed white leather sporting the splotchy red tint of blood despite intense scrubbing, lay where she'd kicked them off near the corner of the bed. Reaching out a toe, she snagged each shoe in turn and tugged them on.

Once the police had arrived and swarmed the mill, Morgan, Scott and Jennifer were transported to Saint Mark's. While a physician was applying Morgan's stitches, a county detective stood in the corner of the room, asking questions and jotting her answers in a small notebook. Morgan and the others had been released later that day. The doctors had been concerned about the blow Scott had taken to his head, but after a few tests determined it to be a concussion, advising him to rest for the next several days.

Morgan let out a long breath as she finished tying her shoe. In the tri-fold mirror atop the dresser, the face of a stranger looked out at her. The sallow skin and dark patches under her eyes gave her face the appearance of a living skeleton. Morgan found that she didn't mind. Despite the garishness, it was the face of a survivor.

Knuckles tapped lightly on the bedroom door a moment before it opened. Jennifer peered through the crack. Her normally teased blonde hair was now pulled back in a low ponytail. "You ready?" she asked without stepping into the room.

Morgan gave herself one last passing glance and stood. The wound in her side offered a faint belch of pain, and she paused, leaning one hand on the dresser with her other crawling up to press against the bandage beneath her shirt. "Yeah," she said, exhaling the discomfort. "Let me grab my bag."

"Don't," Jennifer said. She swung the door open and hurried to the foot of the bed, plucking the green gym bag up off the floor. As she reached for it, the sleeve of her blue and white baseball t-shirt pulled back to reveal her own, smaller bandage. Morgan knew there was another across her friend's stomach. Despite not being overly serious, the wound would still leave a scar. Jennifer straightened and looked around the room. "You got everything?"

"Not much to get."

"Okay. The car's packed. Need help?" Morgan waved her off.

In the living room, Scott sat on the couch, one leg stretched across the cushions, the other on the floor. He sat up as Morgan entered. He raised one eyebrow questioningly.

Morgan waved a hand. "I'm good." She looked around the room. "Where's your bag?"

"Jennifer loaded it already," he said. His tone was one of mild irritation. "She said I shouldn't be lifting anything. It was a concussion, not a spinal injury." He shifted his eyes to the blonde. "I'm fine."

"After what I had to go through in your room to get the bag packed," Jennifer said, "you really should be thanking me and apologizing for my mental suffering." To Morgan she said, "Do you have any idea how disgusting your brother is? His room is basically one giant, grody lab experiment. I don't even want to think about the things I was touching. Or the things he touches. Or who he thinks about when he does it."

"I'm right here," Scott protested.

"He is pretty gross," Morgan agreed and shared a chuckle with Jennifer.

"Can we just go now please?" Scott said. "I'd like to see the beach sometime this year."

"Take a pill," Jennifer said.

"We just have a couple of stops first," Morgan said as she followed Jennifer out. In the driveway, Jennifer's black Dodge Omni sat like a lump of coal. The handle of a suitcase and the crumpled canvass of a red gym bag peered over the headrests of the back seat. Morgan hesitated at the top of the stairs, the urge to look at the spot where Garrett had died a nagging pull in her mind. Scott's presence in the doorway behind her and his hand on her shoulder gave her the strength to resist.

While Jennifer loaded the bags, Morgan and Scott got into the car. "What stops?" Scott asked as Morgan held the passenger seat forward so he could access the back. "Other than to get mom and dad, I mean."

Morgan returned the seat to its original position and climbed in. "I need to stop at the lawyer's office and sign some paperwork for the house and the estate. I'll leave the information for where we're staying in case things get settled or he needs anything while we're gone."

"That's only one," Scott said. "You said you had a couple of stops." Morgan ignored the implied question.

"Okay," Jennifer said brightly as she settled behind the wheel. "Two weeks of mindless sand and surf, here we come."

The Omni's engine coughed to life and they pulled away from the house. Morgan turned and found the place where Garrett had lain, focusing on it until the yard was lost from sight. As they drove, she watched the trees and homes slide by with the interest of observing a family vacation slideshow. Despite their decision to get away for a while to clear their minds and heal, she knew that Elden Mills no longer held anything for her. It had, for one brief, shining moment, but all of that had died under the killing blow from that hammer. She'd instructed the lawyer to settle her parents' estate and get the house listed as soon as possible. She and Scott would stay with Jennifer until they decided on a better place. Seattle, maybe. Or Buttcrust, Arkansas, she mused.

Considering the healing and restorative powers of the beach and ocean, the choice of going there to recover had been a simple one. It also made sense to spread the ashes of their parents in the one place that held so many perfect memories of being together, being a family. With the large number of bodies, funeral homes from Cullman and Birmingham had offered services to aid the families affected by the killings. The day after she'd been treated in the hospital, Morgan had called and arranged the cremation at a place in Birmingham.

"Are you listening to me?" Jennifer asked. She waved one hand in front of Morgan's face and snapped her fingers.

"What?"

"You mean I've been talking to myself for the last several blocks?"

Morgan smiled. "You talk a lot. I'm sure you're used to talking to yourself." In the backseat, Scott laughed.

"Wow. Bitch much?" Jennifer asked in mock shock.

Morgan's smile widened. "Sorry," she said. "Please, continue."

"I was just saying that there seems to be even more cops than there were a few days ago." They passed Wesley Avenue, and Morgan saw that Jennifer was right. Along the road ahead, she counted no less than four cruisers. After two more blocks, she'd observed six more, all a mix of Elden Mills Sheriff's Office, county, and state.

"I guess that's what happens when a mask-wearing psycho carves up a small town," Scott said softly.

Jennifer leaned close and lowered her voice. "Speaking of. Why did you want me to bring...?" She gave her head a knowing incline toward the rear of the car.

"Something I need to do. After the lawyer."

The stop at the attorney's office took less than ten minutes. He presented Morgan with the appropriate paperwork, and nodded sympathetically when she told him where they were going and for how long. He gave his condolences, wished her luck and returned to his office.

Back in the car, she told Jennifer where to go. Minutes later, they turned onto Briarwood Circle. They passed the wooded expanse of the Veil and entered the row of old houses. "There." Morgan pointed, and Jennifer pulled to the curb.

"What are we doing here?" Scott asked. Morgan ignored the question. Instead, she and Jennifer looked at each other. Jennifer's expression of confusion morphed into shocked understanding, then acceptance. She nodded, and Morgan opened the door.

"Stay in the car," she told Scott. He started to protest, but she locked eyes with her brother and gave a firm shake of her head. "Stay. In. The. Car." Scott gave a frustrated scowl and shifted back in his seat. Satisfied he'd remain, Morgan went to the rear and lifted the hatch. She pulled the bags aside and reached for the hammer.

It was heavier than she remembered from when she'd held it in the mill, and the feeling of it in her palm made her skin crawl. It was smooth and slimy all at once, like touching a writhing snake. Morgan hefted it and closed the hatch, and then crossed the shaded, knobby grass of the yard.

The front door opened and swung in with a gentle squeak of hinges. Curtains were closed over every window against the mid-morning sun, coating the interior in darkness. The air was thick with the stench of cigarette smoke, body odor, and old food. A main hallway stretched out before her, and from the end of it came the sounds of a car chase.

Morgan moved down the hall, her footsteps lost under the roar of gunfire, squealing tires, and soundtrack. The hall ended in an open doorway, beyond which was a small living room. A heavy wooden console television showed the sweat-covered face of a broadly grinning Eric Estrada in full California Highway Patrol uniform.

The room was full of mismatched furniture, most of which was scratched or contained several rips in the fabric. Pictures of water-color landscapes hung on the wood-paneled walls, and small porcelain figurines - mostly of cats in various poses - adorned end tables and the mantle, and filled a rounded corner display case. The coffee table was littered with empty beer cans and an ashtray crammed full of crumpled white and yellow butts. Several of the filtered ends had fallen out and lay around the ashtray like drowning people desperate for a place on a raft.

A single person sat on the old, torn sofa. He sank into the tired and worn cushion so far that his knees were almost at head level. Morgan stepped into the room and around the end of the couch.

Geordie Dupont, a smoldering cigarette dangling from one corner of his mouth, slowly turned his eyes and then his head to her. His eyes swam drunkenly, and his eyebrows crinkled as he tried to make sense of what he was seeing. The cigarette bobbed as he asked, "The fuck you doing here?" He grinned. "You come for another round? I'll-"

Morgan swung the hammer. Geordie jerked, and blinked stupidly as a thick rivulet of blood streamed down his temple, angled across his cheek, and dripped from his jaw. He gasped, and the cigarette fell to the couch, where it bounced and rolled to the rear cushions. Geordie coughed, but then Morgan brought the hammer around and down again.

And again.

And again.

Afterward, Morgan's body burned with pain. Every joint and muscle screamed. The wound in her side buzzed with needle-like irritation, and she felt a small trickle of blood moving down her hip. Yet, through all of that, her mind was empty. Calm.

She watched the bloodied mess of Geordie Dupont slump farther onto its side even as the cushions of the couch began to smoke.

Her fingers released the handle of the hammer, and it fell with a leaden crunch to the carpet. Morgan entered the kitchen, ran her hands under a cold tap, and splashed the water across her face. She pulled paper towels from a flimsy plastic holder mounted beneath a counter and wiped her skin dry, then moved back into the hall and to the front door. From the living room, she heard the first pops and crackles of the flames beginning to eat at the couch.

When she sat back in the car, Jennifer looked her up and down. "All good?"

Morgan's eyes watched for flames through the front windows of the house, but didn't see any. *Too soon,* she thought. "Yeah," she said. "I'm good now."

Jennifer gave her leg a gentle pat. The Omni didn't protest as they pulled away and drove down the block. They turned at the corner, and Jennifer drove, heading for the town line.

CHAPTER 47

"Come on, you son of a bitch," Vernon growled through gritted teeth.

The bolt resisted a moment longer - *if it doesn't come loose this time, I'm going to burn this fucker to its hubcaps* – before it gave. The wrench shot forward, and pain bit into his knuckles as the skin scraped away. Vernon howled in anger and pain, and raised the wrench as if to strike the engine, but checked himself at the last moment. The Oldsmobile wasn't his; bashing it to pieces would only cause him more work. He'd been fighting with the damned thing for close to a week now and was ready to be rid of it.

Already wasted half the damned day on it, he thought bitterly as he stepped back, pressing the red shop rag to his bleeding knuckles. He let out a long breath. A warm wind blew in through the open bay door, and Vernon stepped out into the sunshine. Clouds hung thick in the wider azure, and he was thankful the weatherman had gotten the forecast right.

No rain meant he wouldn't be stuck in the stifling garage all day.

The approaching growl of an engine brought his attention to the road as a black Omni pulled into the station and stopped at the self-serve pump. A pretty blonde got out to fill the tank. Inside the car was another girl and what looked like a teenage boy in the back seat, but with the sun sending rippling shadows over the glass, it was hard to tell.

The pump bell dinged, and the blonde replaced the hose. She'd started toward the office to pay when Vernon called out. "Ain't nobody in there, hon. It's only me today." The girl stopped and appeared confused as to what to do. Vernon waved her on. "Just leave your money on the counter if it's exact."

A moment later, she returned to the car. Vernon heard her call out, "Keep the change!" He flapped the shop rag in a wave as the Omni pulled out and drifted out of sight, engine chugging it toward the highway.

The pain in his knuckles had faded by now, and his head was no longer fully in the 'burn down the Oldsmobile' lane, so he returned to his work. Now that that bastard bolt was loose, he could swap in the new part and test the ignition. Maybe even close up early.

On a red rolling toolbox, a battered silver FM radio, its antenna extended at an angle toward the parking lot of the Phillips 76, played the last strains of "Safety Dance." The music faded, and the DJ came in with an update on the killings in Elden Mills. Vernon let the report drone on in the background as he shoved his hands back into the grimy guts of the Olds.

The news about the deaths in that little town had been all over the airwaves, filling almost every break between blocks of music, and he was getting tired of hearing about it. Someone, identity unknown, had murdered...how many was it at this point? Twelve? Fifteen? It didn't matter. Too damned many, was the bottom line. Added to that was the hysteria that had swept through the residents and resulted in shootings, beatings, and stabbings, all from mistaken identities.

The old part came out, and Vernon swapped in the new one within minutes. He snagged the keys from a pegboard next to the office door. Behind the wheel of the Olds, he closed his eyes and whispered a quick prayer. The Oldsmobile coughed, coughed again, and then roared to life. Vernon's cries of triumph were lost over the revving of the engine. He shut it off and went into the office. A crumpled ten dollar bill lay on the scratched laminate surface next to the register. He had no idea if the girl had swiped anything – the rack of smokes was within easy reach, as were the lighters and a plastic jar of lollipops – but he figured it didn't matter right now. It was time to call that son of a bitch Collins to come get the piece of shit, but first....

He thumbed the button on a red and white cooler behind the counter and rolled the lid down. Four bottles of Michelob sat in a bed of ice beneath a foil-wrapped sandwich. He pulled one of the bottles free, snapped off the top, and took a long swig. Few things felt better than a beer after finishing work on a car. Especially a tougher-than-nails son-of-a-bitching car like that damned Olds. If he'd known better, he'd have thought -

The clatter of a tool dropping to the floor out in the garage shut off the thought and brought him around in his chair. Beyond the papers taped to the glass partition, the garage looked as empty of other people as it had been before.

He stood and slowly stepped to the doorway, scanning the quiet, cramped space. The walls on the other side of the Olds were covered in various tools hung on hooks, and the back wall of the shop held multiple toolboxes. From where he stood, he couldn't see what had fallen. Another gust of warm air pushed in through the open door, and his mind made the connection. He'd apparently left some wrench or ratchet on the edge of a table, and the wind - which was known to swirl around the interior of the garage – had unbalanced it.

Shaking his head in self-reproach, Vernon took another sip of his beer and walked to the rear of the car. Sure enough, on the ground lay a silver adjustable wrench. *Gotta get better about putting my shit away*, he told himself. He picked it up, placed it back in the drawer of the small toolbox that sat atop the table, and turned back to the office.

A man stood by the taillight of the Oldsmobile. Something was wrong with his face, and Vernon stopped short, the beer hovering just below his bottom lip. The man stood completely still, and it took Vernon a long second to process what he was seeing.

There wasn't anything wrong with the man's face. It was a mask.

"Jesus, man!" Vernon chuckled nervously. "You scared the shit out of me." The man gave no reply. A deep sense of unease filled Vernon, and he took a faltering step back. "This area's for employees only." The warning sounded lame, but it was all he could think to say.

Again, the masked man gave no indication that he'd heard or cared. He stared at Vernon from behind the mask. A long, jagged crack ran down the center of the facade, splitting the two deep black pits that were the eyes.

"Alright," Vernon said, mustering all the courage he had. "Enough of this shit." He pointed toward the open door. "Get out of my garage. Go on. Take your creepy fucking face and get out." The man didn't speak. Instead, he shifted his body, taking a small step forward. As he did, he raised one arm, and Vernon's mouth ran dry as he saw the wicked hammer with a long spike that the man clutched in a powerful fist. "Oh my dear God in Heaven," was the last thing Vernon said. After that, he had no time for anything else but screams.

MONDAY, JUNE 15, 1987

CHAPTER 48

The headlights of the Oldsmobile spotlighted the carcass of an armadillo near the faded yellow paint of the centerline. The lower half of the creature was a pulverized pink paste against the rough asphalt of the old county road. Then, the car was blowing past, tires not even registering a mild bump in the road as they ground it further into the pavement.

Outside the car, the landscape of open farmland was total blackness, the sun having long since tucked itself away behind the horizon. Only the road ahead mattered to the man driving. The road ahead and the next opportunity; the next calling of Chance.

He drove fast, but not recklessly. It wouldn't do to be pulled over. Although, if he was, it wouldn't be the first time he'd killed a Thing dressed as a police officer – only the first time he'd done it in Arkansas. The man rode with the driver's window down, his elbow propped on the door and the summer air whipping around his head. On the seat behind him lay his mask and the hammer. Occasionally, he would let his arm drift over the seats and gently place his fingers – though the red blisters he'd gotten from retrieving it from that burning house were very tender - on the hammer, as if to reassure himself it was still there.

His chest hurt, but it was a distant, mild irritation. This had happened before, and would again. It didn't matter. What mattered was following the pull of Chance. He drove in silence, eyes locked on the gently turning road ahead until something far in the distance caught his attention.

Despite the late hour and the lack of any other cars on the road, even for the last couple of hours, the Oldsmobile rolled to a gentle stop at the four-way intersection. A single flashing red light hung over the center of the road, and the man paused there, fingers of both hands gripping the wheel.

In the distance to the left, a soft glow filled the night sky over the black mass of trees. A small green sign a few yards away displayed the name of the town and a distance.

Bay 4mi.

To the right, another glowing smudge against the night, this one farther away.

Another sign: *Trumann 6mi.*

The man remained still, foot held lightly on the brake pedal, for several minutes. He reached to the open ashtray beneath the radio and plucked a dirty coin from the curved metal panel. Turning the quarter over, he studied its rough surface, noting the scratches across the presidential face. With a quick, smooth movement, the man thumbed the quarter into the air. It landed in his palm with a muted, fleshy thump. He glanced at the result, then at the corresponding sign.

The decision made, he casually turned the wheel, pressed the gas, and drove toward the next town.

Screams were yet to come, and he was anxious to hear them.

The End

Thank you for reading! If you enjoyed this book, please leave a short review. It doesn't have to be fancy. But, as I said at the front of this book, we authors live and die by reviews. They help me get more eyes on my work and I greatly appreciate every single one!

Find me on the web where you can email me, learn about new things coming soon and even get a free story for signing up for my newsletter! www.byjonathandaniel.com

ACKNOWLEDGMENTS

Thanks to every writer, director, actor and special effects artist on every slasher movie I've ever watched. It is your passion and story-telling that captured my imagination and helped bring this book to life.

I would like to extend my deepest personal thanks to the people who made this book possible. First, my wife, Kinley. Thank you for your constant support and encouragement, for your patience, for the brainstorming and for always pulling me out of a funk when the words aren't flowing and the characters aren't behaving. I love you.

Thanks to the Hellhound, Buster. Your constant insistence that I stop writing and play ball made this book take about 2 months longer than it should have, but also helped keep me sane-ish.

Thank you to Riley Quinn for the amazing cover art, and for being an all around great guy to work with.

Massive thanks to Jennifer Collins my editor for making the pile of words I threw together into something coherent and really remarkable. Also to Sabrina Daniel for a phenominal proofread.

If you find any errors in this book, they are my fault, not theirs.

And to all my friends and family for their encouragement and support.

Without any of you, this book would just be another file on my laptop. Your help means the world to me. Thank you.

ABOUT THE AUTHOR

Jonathan Daniel lives in Birmingham, Alabama with his wife and hyper Boston Terrier, Buster (the Hellhound). When not writing about nightmarish things, he enjoys cooking, reading, brewing beer and trying to watch every horror movie made in the 80's.

You can learn more about him and his other works as well as contact him at his website: www.byjonathandaniel.com

ALSO BY JONATHAN DANIEL

The Uninvited - An unrelenting creature horror novel

There's nowhere to run. Nowhere to hide. They're coming. And they're hungry.

Still struggling with the tragic death of his wife, Owen Decker is determined to battle the debilitating fear that continues to haunt him. Traveling to a tropical island to fully face the crippling terror he harbors appears to be his only option. However, Owen is unaware of the unforgiving evil awaiting him.

On the island, Owen awakes to a horror unlike any he's ever witnessed before. Survival seems impossible as the mutilated and the dead surround him. Teaming up with the only two other survivors of the massacre, the three search for an escape.

But something ravenous and incomprehensible refuses to let them off the island alive.

There's nowhere left to hide.

With time running out and the sinister beings close behind, will Owen's chance at a new beginning be the end he feared all along?

ALSO BY JONATHAN DANIEL

The Killing Tide

In the silence, doomsday whispers; in guilt, screams echo – who will survive the Killing Tide?

Colin Dowey can't forgive himself. Plagued with survivor's guilt for freezing up during a lethal workplace shooting, the bank teller pours his heavy heart into elaborate roleplaying games as the ultimate detective. But he lands one last chance to ease his conscience in real life when a deposit box's cryptic contents attract the attention of a psychotic assassin.

Desperate to stop the homicidal lunatic from gleefully torturing his loved ones, Colin takes the encoded info to the smartest pair of redneck preppers he knows. But when the wise-cracking brothers break the cypher, he's shocked to discover an obsessed billionaire with a gun aimed at the whole world's head.

Can he overcome his post-traumatic fears before his first live-action adventure triggers a deadly game over?

The Killing Tide is a fast-paced standalone thriller. If you like captivating protagonists, ethically driven villains, and hilarious sidekicks, then you'll love Jonathan Daniel's high-octane race for survival.